MURDER FOR CHRISTMAS
★ VOLUME II ★

EDITED BY THOMAS GODFREY

Illustrated by Gahan Wilson

THE MYSTERIOUS PRESS

New York • London • Tokyo

Grateful acknowledgment is made for permission to reprint the following:

'Mr. Big' by Woody Allen. Copyright © by Woody Allen. Reprinted by permission of Random House, Inc.

'Cambric Tea' by Marjorie Bowen. Copyright © by Gabrielle Margaret Vere Campbell Long. Reprinted by permission of Stella Jonckheere.

'Silent Night' by Baynard Kendrick. Copyright © by Baynard Kendrick. Reprinted by permission of Collier Associates and Mrs. Baynard Kendrick.

'The Stolen Christmas Box' by Lillian de la Torre. Copyright © 1945, 1973 by Lillian de la Torre. Reprinted by permission of Harold Ober Associates, Inc.

'Death on the Air' by Ngaio Marsh. Copyright © 1947 by The American Mercury, Inc., Renewed 1975 by Ngaio Marsh. Reprinted by permission of Harold Ober Associates, Inc.

'The Necklace of Pearls' from *Lord Peter* by Dorothy L. Sayers. Copyright © 1933 by Dorothy Leigh Sayers Fleming. Renewed by Lloyd's Bank Ltd., Executors. Reprinted by permission of Harper & Row, Publishers, Inc.

'Blind Man's Hood' from *The Department of Queer Complaints* by Carter Dickson. Copyright © 1940 by William Morrow and Company, Inc. Renewed 1968 by John Dickson Carr. By permission of William Morrow and Company.

'Christmas is for Cops' by Edward D. Hoch. Copyright © by Edward D. Hoch. Reprinted by permission of the author.

'Christmas Party' by Rex Stout. From *And Four to Go* by Rex Stout. Copyright © 1956, 1957 by Rex Stout. Reprinted by permission of Viking Penguin, Inc.

'Ring Out, Wild Bells' by D.B. Wyndham Lewis. Copyright © by D.B. Wyndham Lewis. Reprinted by permission A.D. Peters Ltd.

All cartoons copyright © by Gahan Wilson.

MYSTERIOUS PRESS EDITION

Mysterious Press books are published in association with Warner Books, Inc.
666 Fifth Avenue
New York, N.Y. 10103
A Warner Communications Company

Printed in the United States of America

Originally published in hardcover by The Mysterious Press.
First Mysterious Press Paperback Printing: December, 1988

10 9 8 7 6 5 4 3 2 1

To
Kathy
The Best Thing that ever
Happened to me

Contents

Thomas Godfrey *Introduction* ix

Ngaio Marsh *Death on the Air* 3

Woody Allen *Mr. Big* 36

Marjorie Bowen *Cambric Tea* 48

Anton Chekhov *A Terrible Night* 73

Edward D. Hoch *Christmas Is for Cops* 86

Mary Roberts Rinehart *The Butler's Christmas Eve* 104

Carter Dickson *Blind Man's Hood* 126

Baynard Kendrick *Silent Night* 148

Robert Louis Stevenson *Markheim* 175

Damon Runyon *Dancing Dan's Christmas* 198

Dorothy L. Sayers *The Necklace of Pearls* 212

O. Henry *A Chaparral Christmas Gift* 228

Lillian de la Torre *The Stolen Christmas Box* 237

Rex Stout *Christmas Party* 261

BOXING DAY BONUS

D.B. Wyndham Lewis *Ring Out, Wild Bells* 319

Introduction to Volume II Murder For Christmas

WHAT, back for more? Not satisfied by our first install-ment of yuletide mayhem? Craving more tales of mystery and suspense with a flavor of holly (berries) and (poison) ivy?

Then we will not disappoint. In your hand you hold the key to more year-end malfeasance from the great masters of mystery and suspense.

Here is your invitation to attend an unusual office Christmas party with Nero Wolfe, where the boss gets a most unusual pink slip. Or would you care to indulge in some festive parlour games with Lord Peter Wimsey and the house guests at Sir Septimus Shale's country house in Essex, for a little mystery under the mistletoe? Or perhaps your tastes run to a seasonal showdown amid the sagebrush and the cactus, with O. Henry.

Whatever your preference, you will certainly want to be part of a gentle Christmas Eve murder cooked up by Dame Ngaio Marsh, one of the *grand dames* of the art. And then puzzle over an eighteenth century "locked room" murder concocted by the Dean of the School of Locked Room Mys-tery—John Dickson Carr, under his pseudonym Carter Dickson. And then Santa Baby will get himself involved in an existential hard-boiled case to end all cases, as directed by the great Woody Allen. And then it's more fun-and-(fair) game at another country house setting with satirist D.B.

Wyndham Lewis, in what is surely the last word on the English Country House murder mystery.

There's an extra inducement, too. A real Christmas tingler from the pen of Anton Chekhov, not included in the original hardcover printing.

Go ahead. Treat yourself. You deserve it. A Christmas treat to savour along with all the great family traditions: the bloodstained Christmas stockings, the cranberry wine laced with strychnine (that made Uncle Hubert's last Christmas so memorable last year), the brightly colored lights with the little microphones hidden under the bulbs (so popular in Washington lately), and those Christmas cards with the personal greetings in newspaper block print (the one you sent the mayor last year paid for last season's festivities). This year, make it the most memorable Christmas of all. And God help us, every one!

Tom Godfrey

MURDER FOR CHRISTMAS
★ VOLUME II ★

New Zealand is traditionally regarded as a pastoral pair of islands tucked quietly away on the underside of the globe. When thought of at all, it conjures up visions of sheep and brightly colored birds, and more sheep and more brightly colored birds.

Once in a while a star blazes in the southern sky to remind us of this fragment of the British Commonwealth. Such celestial lights have been tennis star Evonne Goolagong Cawley, soprano Kiri Te Kanawa of the Metropolitan Opera, Covent Garden and royal weddings, and Ngaio Marsh, New Zealand's great lady of letters.

She first appeared in the literary firmament with her first book, A Man Lay Dead, in 1934. She continued to shine there uneclipsed for nearly five decades.

Although familiar with the English countryside and able to turn an English country house mystery with the best, she alone of the authors collected here grew up knowing Christmases that were not white but summery. Her achievement in capturing that cozy murder around a crackling fire is all the more remarkable.

In 'Death on the Air,' her series character Roderick Alleyn tackles a locked room case involving a wireless enthusiast. The term wireless may date the story, but the vigor and freshness of her writing keep it alive and ageless.

Death on the Air

by Ngaio Marsh

O N THE 25th of December at 7:30 a.m. Mr. Septimus Tonks was found dead beside his wireless set.

It was Emily Parks, an under-housemaid, who discovered him. She butted open the door and entered, carrying mop, duster, and carpet-sweeper. At that precise moment she was greatly startled by a voice that spoke out of the darkness.

"Good morning, everybody," said the voice in superbly inflected syllables, "and a Merry Christmas!"

Emily yelped, but not loudly, as she immediately realized what had happened. Mr. Tonks had omitted to turn off his wireless before going to bed. She drew back the curtains, revealing a kind of pale murk which was a London Christmas dawn, switched on the light, and saw Septimus.

He was seated in front of the radio. It was a small but expensive set, specially built for him. Septimus sat in an armchair, his back to Emily, his body tilted towards the radio.

His hands, the fingers curiously bunched, were on the ledge of the cabinet under the tuning and volume knobs. His chest rested against the shelf below and his head leaned on the front panel.

He looked rather as though he was listening intently to the interior secrets of the wireless. His head was bent so that

3

Emily could see his bald top with its trail of oiled hairs. He did not move.

"Beg pardon, sir," gasped Emily. She was again greatly startled. Mr. Tonks' enthusiasm for radio had never before induced him to tune in at seven-thirty in the morning.

"Special Christmas service," the cultured voice was saying. Mr. Tonks sat very still. Emily, in common with the other servants, was terrified of her master. She did not know whether to go or to stay. She gazed wildly at Septimus and realized that he wore a dinner-jacket. The room was now filled with the clamor of pealing bells.

Emily opened her mouth as wide as it would go and screamed and screamed and screamed. . . .

Chase, the butler, was the first to arrive. He was a pale, flabby man but authoritative. He said: "What's the meaning of this outrage?" and then saw Septimus. He went to the arm-chair, bent down, and looked into his master's face.

He did not lose his head, but said in a loud voice: "My Gawd!" And then to Emily: "Shut your face." By this vulgarism he betrayed his agitation. He seized Emily by the shoulders and thrust her towards the door, where they were met by Mr. Hislop, the secretary, in his dressing-gown. Mr. Hislop said: "Good heavens, Chase, what is the meaning—" and then his voice too was drowned in the clamor of bells and renewed screams.

Chase put his fat white hand over Emily's mouth.

"In the study if you please, sir. An accident. Go to your room, will you, and stop that noise or I'll give you something to make you." This to Emily, who bolted down the hall, where she was received by the rest of the staff who had congregated there.

Chase returned to the study with Mr. Hislop and locked the door. They both looked down at the body of Septimus Tonks. The secretary was the first to speak.

"But—but—he's dead," said little Mr. Hislop.

"I suppose there can't be any doubt," whispered Chase.

"Look at the face. Any doubt! My God!"

Mr. Hislop put out a delicate hand towards the bent head and then drew it back. Chase, less fastidious, touched one of the hard wrists, gripped, and then lifted it. The body at once tipped backwards as if it was made of wood. One of the hands knocked against the butler's face. He sprang back with an oath.

There lay Septimus, his knees and his hands in the air, his terrible face turned up to the light. Chase pointed to the right hand. Two fingers and the thumb were slightly blackened.

Ding, dong, dang, ding.

"For God's sake stop those bells," cried Mr. Hislop. Chase turned off the wall switch. Into the sudden silence came the sound of the door-handle being rattled and Guy Tonks' voice on the other side.

"Hislop! Mr. Hislop! Chase! What's the matter?"

"Just a moment, Mr. Guy." Chase looked at the secretary. "You go, sir."

So it was left to Mr. Hislop to break the news to the family. They listened to his stammering revelation in stupefied silence. It was not until Guy, the eldest of the three children, stood in the study that any practical suggestion was made.

"What has killed him?" asked Guy.

"It's extraordinary," burbled Hislop. "Extraordinary. He looks as if he'd been—"

"Galvanized," said Guy.

"We ought to send for a doctor," suggested Hislop timidly.

"Of course. Will you, Mr. Hislop? Dr. Meadows."

Hislop went to the telephone and Guy returned to his family. Dr. Meadows lived on the other side of the square and arrived in five minutes. He examined the body without moving it. He questioned Chase and Hislop. Chase was very voluble about the burns on the hand. He uttered the word "electrocution" over and over again.

"I had a cousin, sir, that was struck by lightning. As soon as I saw the hand—"

"Yes, yes," said Dr. Meadows. "So you said. I can see the burns for myself."

"Electrocution," repeated Chase. "There'll have to be an inquest."

Dr. Meadows snapped at him, summoned Emily, and then saw the rest of the family—Guy, Arthur, Phillipa, and their mother. They were clustered round a cold grate in the drawing-room. Phillipa was on her knees, trying to light the fire.

"What was it?" asked Arthur as soon as the doctor came in.

"Looks like electric shock. Guy, I'll have a word with you if you please. Phillipa, look after your mother, there's a good child. Coffee with a dash of brandy. Where are those damn maids? Come on, Guy."

Alone with Guy, he said they'd have to send for the police.

"The police!" Guy's dark face turned very pale. "Why? What's it got to do with them?"

"Nothing, as like as not, but they'll have to be notified. I can't give a certificate as things are. If it's electrocution, how did it happen?"

"But the police!" said Guy. "That's simply ghastly. Dr. Meadows, for God's sake couldn't you—?"

"No," said Dr. Meadows, "I couldn't. Sorry, Guy, but there it is."

"But can't we wait a moment? Look at him again. You haven't examined him properly."

"I don't want to move him, that's why. Pull yourself together, boy. Look here. I've got a pal in the C.I.D.— Alleyn. He's a gentleman and all that. He'll curse me like a fury, but he'll come if he's in London, and he'll make things easier for you. Go back to your mother. I'll ring Alleyn up."

That was how it came about that Chief Detective-Inspector Roderick Alleyn spent his Christmas Day in harness. As a matter of fact he was on duty, and as he pointed out to Dr. Meadows, would have had to turn out and visit his miserable

Tonkses in any case. When he did arrive it was with his usual air of remote courtesy. He was accompanied by a tall, thick-set officer—Inspector Fox—and by the divisional police-surgeon. Dr. Meadows took them into the study. Alleyn, in his turn, looked at the horror that had been Septimus.

"Was he like this when he was found?"

"No. I understand he was leaning forward with his hands on the ledge of the cabinet. He must have slumped forward and been propped up by the chair arms and the cabinet."

"Who moved him?"

"Chase, the butler. He said he only meant to raise the arm. *Rigor* is well established."

Alleyn put his hand behind the rigid neck and pushed. The body fell forward into its original position.

"There you are, Curtis," said Alleyn to the divisional surgeon. He turned to Fox. "Get the camera man, will you, Fox?"

The photographer took four shots and departed. Alleyn marked the position of the hands and feet with chalk, made a careful plan of the room and turned to the doctors.

"Is it electrocution, do you think?"

"Looks like it," said Curtis. "Have to be a p.m. of course."

"Of course. Still, look at the hands. Burns. Thumb and two fingers bunched together and exactly the distance between the two knobs apart. He'd been tuning his hurdy-gurdy."

"By gum," said Inspector Fox, speaking for the first time.

"D'you mean he got a lethal shock from his radio?" asked Dr. Meadows.

"I don't know. I merely conclude he had his hands on the knobs when he died."

"It was still going when the house-maid found him. Chase turned it off and got no shock."

"Yours, partner," said Alleyn, turning to Fox. Fox stooped down to the wall switch.

"Careful," said Alleyn.

"I've got rubber soles," said Fox, and switched it on. The radio hummed, gathered volume, and found itself.

"No-oel, No-o-el," it roared. Fox cut it off and pulled out the wall plug.

"I'd like to have a look inside this set," he said.

"So you shall, old boy, so you shall," rejoined Alleyn. "Before you begin, I think we'd better move the body. Will you see to that, Meadows? Fox, get Bailey, will you? He's out in the car."

Curtis, Hislop, and Meadows carried Septimus Tonks into a spare downstairs room. It was a difficult and horrible business with that contorted body. Dr. Meadows came back alone, mopping his brow, to find Detective-Sergeant Bailey, a fingerprint expert, at work on the wireless cabinet.

"What's all this?" asked Dr. Meadows. "Do you want to find out if he'd been fooling round with the innards?"

"He," said Alleyn, "or—somebody else."

"Umph!" Dr. Meadows looked at the Inspector. "You agree with me, it seems. Do you suspect—?"

"Suspect? I'm the least suspicious man alive. I'm merely being tidy. Well, Bailey?"

"I've got a good one off the chair arm. That'll be the deceased's, won't it, sir?"

"No doubt. We'll check up later. What about the wireless?"

Fox, wearing a glove, pulled off the knob of the volume control.

"Seems to be O.K.," said Bailey. "It's a sweet bit of work. Not too bad at all, sir." He turned his torch into the back of the radio, undid a couple of screws underneath the set, lifted out the works.

"What's the little hole for?" asked Alleyn.

"What's that, sir?" said Fox.

"There's a hole bored through the panel above the knob. About an eighth of an inch in diameter. The rim of the knob hides it. One might easily miss it. Move your torch, Bailey. Yes. There, do you see?"

Fox bent down and uttered a bass growl. A fine needle of light came through the front of the radio.

"That's peculiar, sir," said Bailey from the other side. "I don't get the idea at all."

Alleyn pulled out the tuning knob.

"There's another one there," he murmured. "Yes. Nice clean little holes. Newly bored. Unusual, I take it?"

"Unusual's the word, sir," said Fox.

"Run away, Meadows," said Alleyn.

"Why the devil?" asked Dr. Meadows indignantly. "What are you driving at? Why shouldn't I be here?"

"You ought to be with the sorrowing relatives. Where's your corpseside manner?"

"I've settled them. What are you up to?"

"Who's being suspicious now?" asked Alleyn mildly. "You may stay for a moment. Tell me about the Tonkses. Who are they? What are they? What sort of a man was Septimus?"

"If you must know, he was a damned unpleasant sort of a man."

"Tell me about him."

Dr. Meadows sat down and lit a cigarette.

"He was a self-made bloke," he said, "as hard as nails and—well, coarse rather than vulgar."

"Like Dr. Johnson perhaps?"

"Not in the least. Don't interrupt. I've known him for twenty-five years. His wife was a neighbor of ours in Dorset. Isabel Foreston. I brought the children into this vale of tears and, by jove, in many ways it's been one for them. It's an extraordinary household. For the last ten years Isabel's condition has been the sort that sends these psychojokers dizzy with rapture. I'm only an out-of-date G.P., and I'd just say she is in an advanced stage of hysterical neurosis. Frightened into fits of her husband."

"I can't understand these holes," grumbled Fox to Bailey.

"Go on, Meadows," said Alleyn.

"I tackled Sep about her eighteen months ago. Told him

the trouble was in her mind. He eyed me with a sort of grin on his face and said: 'I'm surprised to learn that my wife has enough mentality to—' But look here, Alleyn, I can't talk about my patients like this. What the devil am I thinking about."

"You know perfectly well it'll go no further unless—"

"Unless what?"

"Unless it has to. Do go on."

But Dr. Meadows hurriedly withdrew behind his professional rectitude. All he would say was that Mr. Tonks had suffered from high blood pressure and a weak heart, that Guy was in his father's city office, that Arthur had wanted to study art and had been told to read for law, and that Phillipa wanted to go on the stage and had been told to do nothing of the sort.

"Bullied his children," commented Alleyn.

"Find out for yourself. I'm off." Dr. Meadows got as far as the door and came back.

"Look here," he said, "I'll tell you one thing. There was a row here last night. I'd asked Hislop, who's a sensible little beggar, to let me know if anything happened to upset Mrs. Sep. Upset her badly, you know. To be indiscreet again, I said he'd better let me know if Sep cut up rough because Isabel and the young had had about as much of that as they could stand. He was drinking pretty heavily. Hislop rang me up at ten-twenty last night to say there'd been a hell of a row; Sep bullying Phips—Phillipa, you know; always call her Phips—in her room. He said Isabel—Mrs. Sep—had gone to bed. I'd had a big day and I didn't want to turn out. I told him to ring again in half an hour if things hadn't quieted down. I told him to keep out of Sep's way and stay in his own room, which is next to Phips' and see if she was all right when Sep cleared out. Hislop was involved. I won't tell you how. The servants were all out. I said that if I didn't hear from him in half an hour I'd ring again and if there was no answer I'd know they were all in bed and quiet. I did ring, got no answer, and went to bed myself. That's all. I'm off. Curtis knows where to find me. You'll want me for the inquest, I suppose. Goodbye."

When he had gone Alleyn embarked on a systematic prowl round the room. Fox and Bailey were still deeply engrossed with the wireless.

"I don't see how the gentleman could have got a bump-off from the instrument," grumbled Fox. "These control knobs are quite in order. Everything's as it should be. Look here, sir."

He turned on the wall switch and tuned in. There was a prolonged humming.

". . . concludes the program of Christmas carols," said the radio.

"A very nice tone," said Fox approvingly.

"Here's something, sir," announced Bailey suddenly.

"Found the sawdust, have you?" said Alleyn.

"Got it in one," said the startled Bailey.

Alleyn peered into the instrument, using the torch. He scooped up two tiny traces of sawdust from under the holes.

"'Vantage number one," said Alleyn. He bent down to the wall plug. "Hullo! A two-way adapter. Serves the radio and the radiator. Thought they were illegal. This is a rum business. Let's have another look at those knobs."

He had his look. They were the usual wireless fitments, bake-lite knobs fitting snugly to the steel shafts that projected from the front panel.

"As you say," he murmured, "quite in order. Wait a bit." He produced a pocket lens and squinted at one of the shafts. "Ye-es. Do they ever wrap blotting-paper round these objects, Fox?"

"Blotting-paper!" ejaculated Fox. "They do not."

Alleyn scraped at both the shafts with his penknife, holding an envelope underneath. He rose, groaning, and crossed to the desk. "A corner torn off the bottom bit of blotch," he said presently. "No prints on the wireless, I think you said, Bailey?"

"That's right," agreed Bailey morosely.

"There'll be none, or too many, on the blotter, but try, Bailey, try," said Alleyn. He wandered about the room, his eyes on the floor; got as far as the window and stopped.

"Fox!" he said. "A clue. A very palpable clue."

"What is it?" asked Fox.

"The odd wisp of blotting-paper, no less." Alleyn's gaze traveled up the side of the window curtain. "Can I believe my eyes?"

He got a chair, stood on the seat, and with his gloved hand pulled the buttons from the ends of the curtain rod.

"Look at this." He turned to the radio, detached the control knobs, and laid them beside the ones he had removed from the curtain rod.

Ten minutes later Inspector Fox knocked on the drawing-room door and was admitted by Guy Tonks. Phillipa had got the fire going and the family was gathered round it. They looked as though they had not moved or spoken to one another for a long time.

It was Phillipa who spoke first to Fox. "Do you want one of us?"

"If you please, miss," said Fox. "Inspector Alleyn would like to see Mr. Guy Tonks for a moment, if convenient."

"I'll come," said Guy, and led the way to the study. At the door he paused. "Is he—my father—still—?"

"No, no, sir," said Fox comfortably. "It's all ship-shape in there again."

With a lift of his chin Guy opened the door and went in, followed by Fox. Alleyn was alone, seated at the desk. He rose to his feet.

"You want to speak to me?" asked Guy.

"Yes, if I may. This has all been a great shock to you, of course. Won't you sit down?"

Guy sat in the chair farthest away from the radio.

"What killed my father? Was it a stroke?"

"The doctors are not quite certain. There will have to be a *post-mortem*."

"Good God! And an inquest?"

"I'm afraid so."

"Horrible!" said Guy violently. "What do you think was the matter? Why the devil do these quacks have to be so mysterious? What killed him?"

"They think an electric shock."

"How did it happen?"

"We don't know. It looks as if he got it from the wireless."

"Surely that's impossible. I thought they were foolproof."

"I believe they are, if left to themselves."

For a second undoubtedly Guy was startled. Then a look of relief came into his eyes. He seemed to relax all over.

"Of course," he said, "he was always monkeying about with it. What had he done?"

"Nothing."

"But you said—if it killed him he must have done something to it."

"If anyone interfered with the set it was put right afterwards."

Guy's lips parted but he did not speak. He had gone very white.

"So you see," said Alleyn, "your father could not have done anything."

"Then it was not the radio that killed him."

"That we hope will be determined by the *post-mortem*."

"I don't know anything about wireless," said Guy suddenly. "I don't understand. This doesn't seem to make sense. Nobody ever touched the thing except my father. He was most particular about it. Nobody went near the wireless."

"I see. He was an enthusiast?"

"Yes, it was his only enthusiasm except—except his business."

"One of my men is a bit of an expert," Alleyn said. "He says this is a remarkably good set. You are not an expert you say. Is there anyone in the house who is?"

"My young brother was interested at one time. He's given

it up. My father wouldn't allow another radio in the house."

"Perhaps he may be able to suggest something."

"But if the thing's all right now—"

"We've got to explore every possibility."

"You speak as if—as—if—"

"I speak as I am bound to speak before there has been an inquest," said Alleyn. "Had anyone a grudge against your father, Mr. Tonks?"

Up went Guy's chin again. He looked Alleyn squarely in the eyes.

"Almost everyone who knew him," said Guy.

"Is that an exaggeration?"

"No. You think he was murdered, don't you?"

Alleyn suddenly pointed to the desk beside him.

"Have you ever seen those before?" he asked abruptly. Guy stared at two black knobs that lay side by side on an ashtray.

"Those?" he said. "No. What are they?"

"I believe they are the agents of your father's death."

The study door opened and Arthur Tonks came in.

"Guy," he said, "what's happening? We can't stay cooped up together all day. I can't stand it. For God's sake what happened to him?"

"They think those things killed him," said Guy.

"Those?" For a split second Arthur's glance slewed to the curtainrods. Then, with a characteristic flicker of his eyelids, he looked away again.

"What do you mean?" he asked Alleyn.

"Will you try one of those knobs on the shaft of the volume control?"

"But," said Arthur, "they're metal."

"It's disconnected," said Alleyn.

Arthur picked one of the knobs from the tray, turned to the radio, and fitted the knob over one of the exposed shafts.

"It's too loose," he said quickly, "it would fall off."

"Not if it was packed—with blotting-paper, for instance."

"Where did you find these things?" demanded Arthur.

"I think you recognized them, didn't you? I saw you glance at the curtain-rod."

"Of course I recognized them. I did a portrait of Phillipa against those curtains when—he—was away last year. I've painted the damn things."

"Look here," interrupted Guy, "exactly what are you driving at, Mr. Alleyn? If you mean to suggest that my brother —"

"I!" cried Arthur. "What's it got to do with me? Why should you suppose—"

"I found traces of blotting-paper on the shafts and inside the metal knobs," said Alleyn. "It suggested a substitution of the metal knobs for the bakelite ones. It is remarkable, don't you think, that they should so closely resemble one another? If you examine them, of course, you find they are not identical. Still, the difference is scarcely perceptible."

Arthur did not answer this. He was still looking at the wireless.

"I've always wanted to have a look at this set," he said surprisingly.

"You are free to do so now," said Alleyn politely. "We have finished with it for the time being."

"Look here," said Arthur suddenly, "suppose metal knobs were substituted for bakelite ones, it couldn't kill him. He wouldn't get a shock at all. Both the controls are grounded."

"Have you noticed those very small holes drilled through the panel?" asked Alleyn. "Should they be there, do you think?"

Arthur peered at the little steel shafts. "By God, he's right, Guy," he said. "That's how it was done."

"Inspector Fox," said Alleyn, "tells me those holes could be used for conducting wires and that a lead could be taken from the—the transformer, is it?—to one of the knobs."

"And the other connected to earth," said Fox. "It's a job for an expert. He could get three hundred volts or so that way."

"That's not good enough," said Arthur quickly; "there

wouldn't be enough current to do any damage—only a few hundredths of an amp."

"I'm not an expert," said Alleyn, "but I'm sure you're right. Why were the holes drilled then? Do you imagine someone wanted to play a practical joke on your father?"

"A practical joke? On *him?*" Arthur gave an unpleasant screech of laughter. "Do you hear that, Guy?"

"Shut up," said Guy. "After all, he is dead."

"It seems almost too good to be true, doesn't it?"

"Don't be a bloody fool, Arthur. Pull yourself together. Can't you see what this means? They think he's been murdered."

"Murdered! They're wrong. None of us had the nerve for that, Mr. Inspector. Look at me. My hands are so shaky they told me I'd never be able to paint. That dates from when I was a kid and he shut me up in the cellars for a night. Look at me. Look at Guy. He's not so vulnerable, but he caved in like the rest of us. We were conditioned to surrender. Do you know—"

"Wait a moment," said Alleyn quietly. "Your brother is quite right, you know. You'd better think before you speak. This may be a case of homicide."

"Thank you, sir," said Guy quickly. "That's extraordinarily decent of you. Arthur's a bit above himself. It's a shock."

"The relief, you mean," said Arthur. "Don't be such an ass. I didn't kill him and they'll find it out soon enough. Nobody killed him. There must be some explanation."

"I suggest that you listen to me," said Alleyn. "I'm going to put several questions to both of you. You need not answer them, but it will be more sensible to do so. I understand no one but your father touched this radio. Did any of you ever come into this room while it was in use?"

"Not unless he wanted to vary the program with a little bullying," said Arthur.

Alleyn turned to Guy, who was glaring at his brother.

"I want to know exactly what happened in this house last night. As far as the doctors can tell us, your father died not less than three and not more than eight hours before he was found. We must try to fix the time as accurately as possible."

"I saw him at about a quarter to nine," began Guy slowly. "I was going out to a supper-party at the Savoy and had come downstairs. He was crossing the hall from the drawing-room to his room."

"Did you see him after a quarter to nine, Mr. Arthur?"

"No. I heard him, though. He was working in here with Hislop. Hislop had asked to go away for Christmas. Quite enough. My father discovered some urgent correspondence. Really, Guy, you know, he was pathological. I'm sure Dr. Meadows thinks so."

"When did you hear him?" asked Alleyn.

"Some time after Guy had gone. I was working on a drawing in my room upstairs. It's above his. I heard him bawling at little Hislop. It must have been before ten o'clock, because I went out to a studio party at ten. I heard him bawling as I crossed the hall."

"And when," said Alleyn, "did you both return?"

"I came home at about twenty past twelve," said Guy immediately. "I can fix the time because we had gone on to Chez Carlo, and they had a midnight stunt there. We left immediately afterwards. I came home in a taxi. The radio was on full blast."

"You heard no voices?"

"None. Just the wireless."

"And you, Mr. Arthur?"

"Lord knows when I got in. After one. The house was in darkness. Not a sound."

"You had your own key?"

"Yes," said Guy. "Each of us has one. They're always left on a hook in the lobby. When I came in I noticed Arthur's was gone."

"What about the others? How did you know it was his?"

"Mother hasn't got one and Phips lost hers weeks ago. Anyway, I knew they were staying in and that it must be Arthur who was out."

"Thank you," said Arthur ironically.

"You didn't look in the study when you came in," Alleyn asked him.

"Good Lord, no," said Arthur as if the suggestion was fantastic. "I say," he said suddenly, "I suppose he was sitting here—dead. That's a queer thought." He laughed nervously. "Just sitting here, behind the door in the dark."

"How do you know it was in the dark?"

"What d'you mean? Of course it was. There was no light under the door."

"I see. Now do you two mind joining your mother again? Perhaps your sister will be kind enough to come in here for a moment. Fox, ask her, will you?"

Fox returned to the drawing-room with Guy and Arthur and remained there, blandly unconscious of any embarrassment his presence might cause the Tonkses. Bailey was already there, ostensibly examining the electric points.

Phillipa went to the study at once. Her first remark was characteristic. "Can I be of any help?" asked Phillipa.

"It's extremely nice of you to put it like that," said Alleyn. "I don't want to worry you for long. I'm sure this discovery has been a shock to you."

"Probably," said Phillipa. Alleyn glanced quickly at her. "I mean," she explained, "that I suppose I must be shocked but I can't feel anything much. I just want to get it all over as soon as possible. And then think. Please tell me what has happened."

Alleyn told her they believed her father had been electrocuted and that the circumstances were unusual and puzzling. He said nothing to suggest that the police suspected murder.

"I don't think I'll be much help," said Phillipa, "but go ahead."

"I want to try to discover who was the last person to see your father or speak to him."

"I should think very likely I was," said Phillipa composedly. "I had a row with him before I went to bed."

"What about?"

"I don't see that it matters."

Alleyn considered this. When he spoke again it was with deliberation.

"Look here," he said, "I think there is very little doubt that your father was killed by an electric shock from his wireless set. As far as I know the circumstances are unique. Radios are normally incapable of giving a lethal shock to anyone. We have examined the cabinet and are inclined to think that its internal arrangements were disturbed last night. Very radically disturbed. Your father may have experimented with it. If anything happened to interrupt or upset him, it is possible that in the excitement of the moment he made some dangerous readjustment."

"You don't believe that, do you?" asked Phillipa calmly.

"Since you ask me," said Alleyn, "no."

"I see," said Phillipa; "you think he was murdered, but you're not sure." She had gone very white, but she spoke crisply. "Naturally you want to find out about my row."

"About everything that happened last evening," amended Alleyn.

"What happened was this," said Phillipa; "I came into the hall some time after ten. I'd heard Arthur go out and had looked at the clock at five past. I ran into my father's secretary, Richard Hislop. He turned aside, but not before I saw . . . not quickly enough. I blurted out: 'You're crying.' We looked at each other. I asked him why he stood it. None of the other secretaries could. He said he had to. He's a widower with two children. There have been doctor's bills and things. I needn't tell you about his . . . about his damnable servitude to my father nor about the refinements of cruelty he'd had to put up with. I think my father was mad, really mad, I mean. Richard gabbled it all out to me higgledy-piggledy in a sort of horrified whisper. He's been here two years, but I'd never realized until that moment that we . . . that . . ." A faint flush came into her cheeks. "He's such a funny little man. Not at all the sort I've always thought . . . not good-looking or exciting or anything."

She stopped, looking bewildered.

"Yes?" said Alleyn.

"Well, you see—I suddenly realized I was in love with him. He realized it too. He said: 'Of course, it's quite hopeless, you know. Us, I mean. Laughable, almost.' Then I put my arms round his neck and kissed him. It was very odd, but it seemed quite natural. The point is my father came out of his room into the hall and saw us."

"That was bad luck," said Alleyn.

"Yes, it was. My father really seemed delighted. He almost licked his lips. Richard's efficiency had irritated my father for a long time. It was difficult to find excuses for being beastly to him. Now, of course . . . He ordered Richard to the study and me to my room. He followed me upstairs. Richard tried to come too, but I asked him not to. My father . . . I needn't tell you what he said. He put the worst possible construction on what he'd seen. He was absolutely foul, screaming at me like a madman. He was insane. Perhaps it was D. Ts. He drank terribly, you know. I dare say it's silly of me to tell you all this."

"No," said Alleyn.

"I can't feel anything at all. Not even relief. The boys are frankly relieved. I can't feel afraid either." She stared meditatively at Alleyn. "Innocent people needn't feel afraid, need they?"

"It's an axiom of police investigation," said Alleyn and wondered if indeed she was innocent.

"It just *can't* be murder," said Phillipa. "We were all too much afraid to kill him. I believe he'd win even if you murdered him. He'd hit back somehow." She put her hands to her eyes. "I'm all muddled."

"I think you are more upset than you realize. I'll be as quick as I can. Your father made this scene in your room. You say he screamed. Did anyone hear him?"

"Yes. Mummy did. She came in."

"What happened?"

"I said: 'Go away, darling, it's all right.' I didn't want her to be involved. He nearly killed her with the things he did.

Sometimes he'd . . . we never knew what happened between them. It was all secret, like a door shutting quietly as you walk along a passage."

"Did she go away?"

"Not at once. He told her he'd found out that Richard and I were lovers. He said . . . it doesn't matter. I don't want to tell you. She was terrified. He was stabbing at her in some way I couldn't understand. Then, quite suddenly, he told her to go to her own room. She went at once and he followed her. He locked me in. That's the last I saw of him, but I heard him go downstairs later."

"Were you locked in all night?"

"No. Richard Hislop's room is next to mine. He came up and spoke through the wall to me. He wanted to unlock the door, but I said better not in case—he—came back. Then, much later, Guy came home. As he passed my door I tapped on it. The key was in the lock and he turned it."

"Did you tell him what had happened?"

"Just that there'd been a row. He only stayed a moment."

"Can you hear the radio from your room?"

She seemed surprised.

"The wireless? Why, yes. Faintly."

"Did you hear it after your father returned to the study?"

"I don't remember."

"Think. While you lay awake all that long time until your brother came home?"

"I'll try. When he came out and found Richard and me, it was not going. They had been working, you see. No, I can't remember hearing it at all unless—wait a moment. Yes. After he had gone back to the study from mother's room I remember there was a loud crash of static. Very loud. Then I think it was quiet for some time. I fancy I heard it again later. Oh, I've remembered something else. After the static my bedside radiator went out. I suppose there was something wrong with the electric supply. That would account for both, wouldn't it? The heater went on again about ten minutes later."

"And did the radio begin again then, do you think?"

"I don't know. I'm very vague about that. It started again sometime before I went to sleep."

"Thank you very much indeed. I won't bother you any longer now."

"All right," said Phillipa calmly, and went away.

Alleyn sent for Chase and questioned him about the rest of the staff and about the discovery of the body. Emily was summoned and dealt with. When she departed, awestruck but complacent, Alleyn turned to the butler.

"Chase," he said, "had your master any peculiar habits?"

"Yes, sir."

"In regard to the wireless?"

"I beg pardon, sir. I thought you meant generally speaking."

"Well, then, generally speaking."

"If I may say so, sir, he was a mass of them."

"How long have you been with him?"

"Two months, sir, and due to leave at the end of this week."

"Oh. Why are you leaving?"

Chase produced the classic remark of his kind.

"There are some things," he said, "that flesh and blood will not stand, sir. One of them's being spoke to like Mr. Tonks spoke to his staff."

"Ah. His peculiar habits, in fact?"

"It's my opinion, sir, he was mad. Stark, staring."

"With regard to the radio. Did he tinker with it?"

"I can't say I've ever noticed, sir. I believe he knew quite a lot about wireless."

"When he tuned the thing, had he any particular method? Any characteristic attitude or gesture?"

"I don't think so, sir. I never noticed, and yet I've often come into the room when he was at it. I can seem to see him now, sir."

"Yes, yes," said Alleyn swiftly. "That's what we want. A clear mental picture. How was it now? Like this?"

In a moment he was across the room and seated in

Septimus's chair. He swung round to the cabinet and raised his right hand to the tuning control.

"Like this?"

"No, sir," said Chase promptly, "that's not him at all. Both hands it should be."

"Ah." Up went Alleyn's left hand to the volume control. "More like this?"

"Yes, sir," said Chase slowly. "But there's something else and I can't recollect what it was. Something he was always doing. It's in the back of my head. You know, sir. Just on the edge of my memory, as you might say."

"I know."

"It's a kind—something—to do with irritation," said Chase slowly.

"Irritation? His?"

"No. It's no good, sir. I can't get it."

"Perhaps later. Now look here, Chase, what happened to all of you last night? All the servants, I mean."

"We were all out, sir. It being Christmas Eve. The mistress sent for me yesterday morning. She said we could take the evening off as soon as I had taken in Mr. Tonks's grog-tray at nine o'clock. So we went," ended Chase simply.

"When?"

"The rest of the staff got away about nine. I left at ten past, sir, and returned about eleven-twenty. The others were back then, and all in bed. I went straight to bed myself, sir."

"You came in by a back door, I suppose?"

"Yes, sir. We've been talking it over. None of us noticed anything unusual."

"Can you hear the wireless in your part of the house?"

"No, sir."

"Well," said Alleyn, looking up from his notes, "that'll do, thank you."

Before Chase reached the door Fox came in.

"Beg pardon, sir," said Fox, "I just want to take a look at the *Radio Times* on the desk."

He bent over the paper, wetted a gigantic thumb, and turned a page.

"That's it, sir," shouted Chase suddenly. "That's what I tried to think of. That's what he was always doing."

"But what?"

"Licking his fingers, sir. It was a habit," said Chase. "That's what he always did when he sat down to the radio. I heard Mr. Hislop tell the doctor it nearly drove him demented, the way the master couldn't touch a thing without first licking his fingers."

"Quite so," said Alleyn. "In about ten minutes, ask Mr. Hislop if he will be good enough to come in for a moment. That will be all, thank you, Chase."

"Well, sir," remarked Fox when Chase had gone, "if that's the case and what I think's right, it'd certainly make matters worse."

"Good heavens, Fox, what an elaborate remark. What does it mean?"

"If metal knobs were substituted for bakelite ones and fine wires brought through those holes to make contact, then he'd get a bigger bump if he tuned in with *damp* fingers."

"Yes. And he always used both hands. Fox!"

"Sir."

"Approach the Tonkses again. You haven't left them alone, of course?"

"Bailey's in there making out he's interested in the light switches. He's found the main switchboard under the stairs. There's signs of a blown fuse having been fixed recently. In a cupboard underneath there are odd lengths of flex and so on. Same brand as this on the wireless and the heater."

"Ah, yes. Could the cord from the adapter to the radiator be brought into play?"

"By gum," said Fox, "you're right! That's how it was done, Chief. The heavier flex was cut away from the radiator and shoved through. There was a fire, so he wouldn't want the radiator and wouldn't notice."

"It might have been done that way, certainly, but there's

little to prove it. Return to the bereaved Tonkses, my Fox, and ask prettily if any of them remember Septimus's peculiarities when tuning his wireless."

Fox met little Mr. Hislop at the door and left him alone with Alleyn. Phillipa had been right, reflected the Inspector, when she said Richard Hislop was not a noticeable man. He was nondescript. Grey eyes, drab hair; rather pale, rather short, rather insignificant; and yet last night there had flashed up between those two the realization of love. Romantic but rum, thought Alleyn.

"Do sit down," he said. "I want you, if you will, to tell me what happened between you and Mr. Tonks last evening."

"What happened?"

"Yes. You all dined at eight, I understand. Then you and Mr. Tonks came in here?"

"Yes."

"What did you do?"

"He dictated several letters."

"Anything unusual take place?"

"Oh, no."

"Why did you quarrel?"

"Quarrel!" The quiet voice jumped a tone. "We did not quarrel, Mr. Alleyn."

"Perhaps that was the wrong word. What upset you?"

"Phillipa has told you?"

"Yes. She was wise to do so. What was the matter, Mr. Hislop?"

"Apart from the . . . what she told you . . . Mr. Tonks was a difficult man to please. I often irritated him. I did so last night."

"In what way?"

"In almost every way. He shouted at me. I was startled and nervous, clumsy with papers, and making mistakes. I wasn't well. I blundered and then . . . I . . . I broke down. I have always irritated him. My very mannerisms—"

"Had he no irritating mannerisms, himself?"

"He! My God!"

"What were they?"

"I can't think of anything in particular. It doesn't matter does it?"

"Anything to do with the wireless, for instance?"

There was a short silence.

"No," said Hislop.

"Was the radio on in here last night, after dinner?"

"For a little while. Not after—after the incident in the hall. At least, I don't think so. I don't remember."

"What did you do after Miss Phillipa and her father had gone upstairs?"

"I followed and listened outside the door for a moment." He had gone very white and had backed away from the desk.

"And then?"

"I heard someone coming. I remembered Dr. Meadows had told me to ring him up if there was one of the scenes. I returned here and rang him up. He told me to go to my room and listen. If things got any worse I was to telephone again. Otherwise I was to stay in my room. It is next to hers."

"And you did this?" He nodded. "Could you hear what Mr. Tonks said to her?"

"A—a good deal of it."

"What did you hear?"

"He insulted her. Mrs. Tonks was there. I was just thinking of ringing Dr. Meadows up again when she and Mr. Tonks came out and went along the passage. I stayed in my room."

"You did not try to speak to Miss Phillipa?"

"We spoke through the wall. She asked me not to ring Dr. Meadows, but to stay in my room. In a little while, perhaps it was as much as twenty minutes—I really don't know—I heard him come back and go downstairs. I again spoke to Phillipa. She implored me not to do anything and said that she herself would speak to Dr. Meadows in the morning. So I waited a little longer and then went to bed."

"And to sleep?"

"My God, no!"

"Did you hear the wireless again?"

"Yes. At least I heard static."

"Are you an expert on wireless?"

"No. I know the ordinary things. Nothing much."

"How did you come to take this job, Mr. Hislop?"

"I answered an advertisement."

"You are sure you don't remember any particular mannerism of Mr. Tonks's in connection with the radio?"

"No."

"And you can tell me no more about your interview in the study that led to the scene in the hall?"

"No."

"Will you please ask Mrs. Tonks if she will be kind enough to speak to me for a moment?"

"Certainly," said Hislop, and went away.

Septimus's wife came in looking like death. Alleyn got her to sit down and asked her about her movements on the preceding evening. She said she was feeling unwell and dined in her room. She went to bed immediately afterwards. She heard Septimus yelling at Phillipa and went to Phillipa's room. Septimus accused Mr. Hislop and her daughter of "terrible things." She got as far as this and then broke down quietly. Alleyn was very gentle with her. After a little while he learned that Septimus had gone to her room with her and had continued to speak of "terrible things."

"What sort of things?" asked Alleyn.

"He was not responsible," said Isabel. "He did not know what he was saying. I think he had been drinking."

She thought he had remained with her for perhaps a quarter of an hour. Possibly longer. He left her abruptly and she heard him go along the passage, past Phillipa's door, and presumably downstairs. She had stayed awake for a long time. The wireless could not be heard from her room. Alleyn showed her the curtain knobs, but she seemed quite unable to take in their significance. He let her go, summoned Fox, and went over the whole case.

"What's your idea on the show?" he asked when he had finished.

"Well, sir," said Fox, in his stolid way, "on the face of it the young gentlemen have got alibis. We'll have to check them up, of course, and I don't see we can go much further until we have done so."

"For the moment," said Alleyn, "let us suppose Masters Guy and Arthur to be safely established behind cast-iron alibis. What then?"

"Then we've got the young lady, the old lady, the secretary, and the servants."

"Let us parade them. But first let us go over the wireless game. You'll have to watch me here. I gather that the only way in which the radio could be fixed to give Mr. Tonks his quietus is like this: Control knobs removed. Holes bored in front panel with fine drill. Metal knobs substituted and packed with blotting-paper to insulate them from metal shafts and make them stay put. Heavier flex from adapter to radiator cut and the ends of the wires pushed through the drilled holes to make contact with the new knobs. Thus we have a positive and negative pole. Mr. Tonks bridges the gap, gets a mighty wallop as the current passes through him to the earth. The switchboard fuse is blown almost immediately. All this is rigged by murderer while Sep was upstairs bullying wife and daughter. Sep revisited study some time after ten-twenty. Whole thing was made ready between ten, when Arthur went out, and the time Sep returned—say, about ten-forty-five. The murderer reappeared, connected radiator with flex, removed wires, changed back knobs, and left the thing tuned in. Now I take it that the burst of static described by Phillipa and Hislop would be caused by the short-circuit that killed our Septimus?"

"That's right."

"It also affected all the heaters in the house. *Vide* Miss Tonks's radiator."

"Yes. He put all that right again. It would be a simple enough matter for anyone who knew how. He'd just have to fix the fuse on the main switchboard. How long do you say it would take to—what's the horrible word?—to recondition the whole show?"

"M'm," said Fox deeply. "At a guess, sir, fifteen minutes. He'd have to be nippy."

"Yes," agreed Alleyn. "He or she."

"I don't see a female making a success of it," grunted Fox. "Look here, Chief, you know what I'm thinking. Why did Mr. Hislop lie about deceased's habit of licking his thumbs? You say Hislop told you he remembered nothing and Chase says he overheard him saying the trick nearly drove him dippy."

"Exactly," said Alleyn. He was silent for so long that Fox felt moved to utter a discreet cough.

"Eh?" said Alleyn. "Yes, Fox, yes. It'll have to be done." He consulted the telephone directory and dialed a number.

"May I speak to Dr. Meadows? Oh, it's you, is it? Do you remember Mr. Hislop telling you that Septimus Tonks's trick of wetting his fingers nearly drove Hislop demented. Are you there? You don't? Sure? All right. All right. Hislop rang up at ten-twenty, you said? And you telephoned him? At eleven. Sure of the times? I see. I'd be glad if you'd come round. Can you? Well, do if you can."

He hung up the receiver.

"Get Chase again, will you, Fox?"

Chase, recalled, was most insistent that Mr. Hislop had spoken about it to Dr. Meadows.

"It was when Mr. Hislop had flu, sir. I went up with the doctor. Mr. Hislop had a high temperature and was talking very excited. He kept on and on, saying the master had guessed his ways had driven him crazy and that the master kept on purposely to aggravate. He said if it went on much longer he'd . . . he didn't know what he was talking about, sir, really."

"What did he say he'd do?"

"Well, sir, he said he'd—he'd do something desperate to the master. But it was only his rambling, sir. I daresay he wouldn't remember anything about it."

"No," said Alleyn, "I daresay he wouldn't." When Chase

had gone he said to Fox: "Go and find out about those boys and their alibis. See if they can put you on to a quick means of checking up. Get Master Guy to corroborate Miss Phillipa's statement that she was locked in her room."

Fox had been gone for some time and Alleyn was still busy with his notes when the study door burst open and in came Dr. Meadows.

"Look here, my giddy sleuth-hound," he shouted, "what's all this about Hislop? Who says he disliked Sep's abominable habits?"

"Chase does. And don't bawl at me like that. I'm worried."

"So am I, blast you. What are you driving at? You can't imagine that . . . that poor little broken-down hack is capable of electrocuting anybody, let alone Sep?"

"I have no imagination," said Alleyn wearily.

"I wish to God I hadn't called you in. If the wireless killed Sep, it was because he'd monkeyed with it."

"And put it right after it had killed him?"

Dr. Meadows stared at Alleyn in silence.

"Now," said Alleyn, "you've got to give me a straight answer, Meadows. Did Hislop, while he was semi-delirious, say that this habit of Tonks's made him feel like murdering him?"

"I'd forgotten Chase was there," said Dr. Meadows.

"Yes, you'd forgotten that."

"But even if he did talk wildly, Alleyn, what of it? Damn it, you can't arrest a man on the strength of a remark made in delirium."

"I don't propose to do so. Another motive has come to light."

"You mean—Phips—last night?"

"Did he tell you about that?"

"She whispered something to me this morning. I'm very fond of Phips. My God, are you sure of your grounds?"

"Yes," said Alleyn. "I'm sorry. I think you'd better go, Meadows."

"Are you going to arrest him?"

"I have to do my job."

There was a long silence.

"Yes," said Dr. Meadows at last. "You have to do your job. Goodbye, Alleyn."

Fox returned to say that Guy and Arthur had never left their parties. He had got hold of two of their friends. Guy and Mrs. Tonks confirmed the story of the locked door.

"It's a process of elimination," said Fox. "It must be the secretary. He fixed the radio while deceased was upstairs. He must have dodged back to whisper through the door to Miss Tonks. I suppose he waited somewhere down here until he heard deceased blow himself to blazes and then put everything straight again, leaving the radio turned on."

Alleyn was silent.

"What do we do now, sir?" asked Fox.

"I want to see the hook inside the front-door where they hang their keys."

Fox, looking dazed, followed his superior to the little entrance hall.

"Yes, there they are," said Alleyn. He pointed to a hook with two latch-keys hanging from it. "You could scarcely miss them. Come on, Fox."

Back in the study they found Hislop with Bailey in attendance.

Hislop looked from one Yard man to another.

"I want to know if it's murder."

"We think so," said Alleyn.

"I want you to realize that Phillipa—Miss Tonks—was locked in her room all last night."

"Until her brother came home and unlocked the door," said Alleyn.

"That was too late. He was dead by then."

"How do you know when he died?"

"It must have been when there was that crash of static."

"Mr. Hislop," said Alleyn, "why would you not tell me how much that trick of licking his fingers exasperated you?"

"But—how do you know! I never told anyone."

"You told Dr. Meadows when you were ill."

"I don't remember." He stopped short. His lips trembled. Then, suddenly he began to speak.

"Very well. It's true. For two years he's tortured me. You see, he knew something about me. Two years ago when my wife was dying, I took money from the cash-box in that desk. I paid it back and thought he hadn't noticed. He knew all the time. From then on he had me where he wanted me. He used to sit there like a spider. I'd hand him a paper. He'd wet his thumbs with a clicking noise and a sort of complacent grimace. Click, click. Then he'd thumb the papers. He knew it drove me crazy. He'd look at me and then . . . click, click. And then he'd say something about the cash. He'd never quite accused me, just hinted. And I was impotent. You think I'm insane. I'm not. I could have murdered him. Often and often I've thought how I'd do it. Now you think I've done it. I haven't. There's the joke of it. I hadn't the pluck. And last night when Phillipa showed me she cared, it was like Heaven—unbelievable. For the first time since I've been here I *didn't* feel like killing him. And last night someone else *did!*"

He stood there trembling and vehement. Fox and Bailey, who had watched him with bewildered concern, turned to Alleyn. He was about to speak when Chase came in. "A note for you, sir," he said to Alleyn. "It came by hand."

Alleyn opened it and glanced at the first few words. He looked up.

"You may go, Mr. Hislop. Now I've got what I expected —what I fished for."

When Hislop had gone they read the letter.

> *Dear Alleyn,*
> *Don't arrest Hislop. I did it. Let him go at once if you've arrested him and don't tell Phips you ever suspected him. I was in love with Isabel before she met Sep. I've tried to get her to divorce him, but she wouldn't because of the kids. Damned nonsense, but there's no time to discuss it now. I've got to be quick. He suspected us. He*

reduced her to a nervous wreck. I was afraid she'd go under altogether. I thought it all out. Some weeks ago I took Phips's key from the hook inside the front door. I had the tools and the flex and wire all ready. I knew where the main switchboard was and the cupboard. I meant to wait until they all went away at the New Year, but last night when Hislop rang me I made up my mind at once. He said the boys and servants were out and Phips locked in her room. I told him to stay in his room and to ring me up in half an hour if things hadn't quieted down. He didn't ring up. I did. No answer, so I knew Sep wasn't in his study.

I came round, let myself in, and listened. All quiet upstairs but the lamp still on in the study, so I knew he would come down again. He'd said he wanted to get the midnight broadcast from somewhere.

I locked myself in and got to work. When Sep was away last year, Arthur did one of his modern monstrosities of painting in the study. He talked about the knobs making good pattern. I noticed then that they were very like the ones on the radio and later on I tried one and saw that it would fit if I packed it up a bit. Well, I did the job just as you worked it out, and it only took twelve minutes. Then I went into the drawing-room and waited.

He came down from Isabel's room and evidently went straight to the radio. I hadn't thought it would make such a row, and half expected someone would come down. No one came. I went back, switched off the wireless, mended the fuse in the main switchboard, using my torch. Then I put everything right in the study.

There was no particular hurry. No one would come in while he was there and I got the radio going as soon as possible to suggest he was at it. I knew I'd be called in when they found him. My idea was to tell them he had died of a stroke. I'd been warning Isabel it might happen at any time.

*As soon as I saw the burned hand I knew that cat
wouldn't jump. I'd have tried to get away with it if
Chase hadn't gone round bleating about electrocution and burned fingers. Hislop saw the hand. I
daren't do anything but report the case to the police, but I thought you'd never twig the knobs.
One up to you.*

*I might have bluffed through if you hadn't sus-
pected Hislop. Can't let you hang the blighter.
I'm enclosing a note to Isabel, who won't forgive
me, and an official one for you to use. You'll find
me in my bedroom upstairs. I'm using cyanide.
It's quick.*

*I'm sorry, Alleyn. I think you knew, didn't you?
I've bungled the whole game, but if you will be a
supersleuth . . . Good-bye.*

Henry Meadows

If the American cinema found a voice for the 1970's, it was that of Woody Allen, the writer-actor-director whose films came into their own during that fragmented decade. Neurotic, crowded, abused, but still surviving, Allen's self-absorbed characters trudged through these disappointing years in a fashion to which almost everyone could relate.

In his first collection of satirical writings, *Getting Even*, he included this send-up of the hard-boiled private eye, popularized by Dashiell Hammett and Raymond Chandler. Unlike many who have tried to parody this style, Allen gives strong evidence of knowing what he is sending up.

There is no Sam Spade or Philip Marlowe Christmas story. On the West Coast, Christmas looks pretty much like any other day, only with less traffic. So, in the absence of these quintessential private eyes, we have the tribulations of—hang on to your trenchcoats—Kaiser Lupowitz as he encounters 'Mr. Big.'

Mr. Big

by Woody Allen

I WAS SITTING in my office, cleaning the debris out of my thirty-eight and wondering where my next case was coming from. I like being a private eye, and even though once in a while I've had my gums massaged with an automobile jack, the sweet smell of greenbacks makes it all worth it. Not to mention the dames, which are a minor preoccupation of mine that I rank just ahead of breathing. That's why, when the door to my office swung open and a long-haired blonde named Heather Butkiss came striding in and told me she was a nudie model and needed my help, my salivary glands shifted into third. She wore a short skirt and a tight sweater and her figure described a set of parabolas that could cause cardiac arrest in a yak.

"What can I do for you, sugar?"

"I want you to find someone for me."

"Missing person? Have you tried the police?"

"Not exactly, Mr. Lupowitz."

"Call me Kaiser, sugar. All right, so what's the scam?"

"God."

"God?"

"That's right, God. The Creator, the Underlying Principle, the First Cause of Things, the All Encompassing. I want you to find Him for me."

I've had some fruit cakes up in the office before, but when they're built like she was, you listened.

"Why?"

"That's my business, Kaiser. You just find Him."

"I'm sorry, sugar. You got the wrong boy."

"But why?"

"Unless I know all the facts," I said, rising.

"O.K., O.K.," she said, biting her lower lip. She straightened the seam of her stocking, which was strictly for my benefit, but I wasn't buying any at the moment.

"Let's have it on the line, sugar."

"Well, the truth is—I'm not really a nudie model."

"No?"

"No. My name is not Heather Butkiss, either. It's Claire Rosensweig and I'm a student at Vassar. Philosophy major. History of Western Thought and all that. I have a paper due January. On Western religion. All the other kids in the course will hand in speculative papers. But I want to *know*. Professor Grebanier said if anyone finds out for sure, they're a cinch to pass the course. And my dad's promised me a Mercedes if I get straight A's."

I opened a deck of Luckies and a pack of gum and had one of each. Her story was beginning to interest me. Spoiled coed. High IQ and a body I wanted to know better.

"What does God look like?"

"I've never seen him."

"Well, how do you know He exists?"

"That's for you to find out."

"Oh, great. Then you don't know what he looks like? Or where to begin looking?"

"No. Not really. Although I suspect he's everywhere. In the air, in every flower, in you and I—and in this chair."

"Uh huh." So she was a pantheist. I made a mental note of it and said I'd give her case a try—for a hundred bucks a day, expenses, and a dinner date. She smiled and okayed the deal. We rode down in the elevator together. Outside it was getting dark. Maybe God did exist and maybe He didn't, but somewhere in that city there were sure a lot of guys who were going to try and keep me from finding out.

My first lead was Rabbi Itzhak Wiseman, a local cleric who owed me a favor for finding out who was rubbing pork on his hat. I knew something was wrong when I spoke to him because he was scared. Real scared.

"Of course there's a you-know-what, but I'm not even allowed to say His name or He'll strike me dead, which I could never understand why someone is so touchy about having his name said."

"You ever see Him?"

"Me? Are you kidding? I'm lucky I get to see my grandchildren."

"Then how do you know He exists?"

"How do I know? What kind of question is that? Could I get a suit like this for fourteen dollars if there was no one up there? Here, feel a gabardine—how can you doubt?"

"You got nothing more to go on?"

"Hey—what's the Old Testament? Chopped liver? How do you think Moses got the Israelites out of Egypt? With a smile and a tap dance? Believe me, you don't part the Red Sea with some gismo from Korvette's. It takes power."

"So he's tough, eh?"

"Yes. Very tough. You'd think with all that success he'd be a lot sweeter."

"How come you know so much?"

"Because we're the chosen people. He takes best care of us of all His children, which I'd also like to someday discuss with Him."

"What do you pay Him for being chosen?"

"Don't ask."

So that's how it was. The Jews were into God for a lot. It was the old protection racket. Take care of them in return for a price. And from the way Rabbi Wiseman was talking, He soaked them plenty. I got into a cab and made it over to Danny's Billiards on Tenth Avenue. The manager was a slimy little guy I didn't like.

"Chicago Phil here?"

"Who wants to know?"

I grabbed him by the lapels and took some skin at the same time.

"What, punk?"

"In the back," he said, with a change of attitude.

Chicago Phil. Forger, bank robber, strong-arm man, and avowed atheist.

"The guy never existed, Kaiser. This is the straight dope. It's a big hype. There's no Mr. Big. It's a syndicate. Mostly Sicilian. It's international. But there is no actual head. Except maybe the Pope."

"I want to meet the Pope."

"It can be arranged," he said, winking.

"Does the name Claire Rosensweig mean anything to you?"

"No."

"Heather Butkiss?"

"Oh, wait a minute. Sure. She's that peroxide job with the bazooms from Radcliffe."

"Radcliffe? She told me Vassar."

"Well, she's lying. She's a teacher at Radcliffe. She was mixed up with a philosopher for a while."

"Pantheist?"

"No. Empiricist, as I remember. Bad guy. Completely rejected Hegel or any dialectical methodology."

"One of those."

"Yeah. He used to be a drummer with a jazz trio. Then he got hooked on Logical Positivism. When that didn't work, he tried Pragmatism. Last I heard he stole a lot of money to take a course in Schopenhauer at Columbia. The mob would like to find him—or get their hands on his textbooks so they can resell them."

"Thanks, Phil."

"Take it from me, Kaiser. There's no one out there. It's a void. I couldn't pass all those bad checks or screw society the way I do if for one second I was able to recognize any authentic sense of Being. The universe is strictly phenomenological. Nothing's eternal. It's all meaningless."

"Who won the fifth at Aqueduct?"

"Santa Baby."

I had a beer at O'Rourke's and tried to add it all up, but it made no sense at all. Socrates was a suicide—or so they said. Christ was murdered. Nietzsche went nuts. If there was someone out there, He sure as hell didn't want anybody to know it. And why was Claire Rosensweig lying about Vassar? Could Descartes have been right? Was the universe dualistic? Or did Kant hit it on the head when he postulated the existence of God on moral grounds?

That night I had dinner with Claire. Ten minutes after the check came, we were in the sack and, brother, you can have your Western thought. She went through the kind of gymnastics that would have won first prize in the Tia Juana Olympics. After, she lay on the pillow next to me, her long blond hair sprawling. Our naked bodies still intertwined. I was smoking and staring at the ceiling.

"Claire, what if Kierkegaard's right?"

"You mean?"

"If you can never really *know*. Only have faith."

"That's absurd."

"Don't be so rational."

"Nobody's being rational, Kaiser." She lit a cigarette. "Just don't get ontological. Not now. I couldn't bear it if you were ontological with me."

She was upset. I leaned over and kissed her, and the phone rang. She got it.

"It's for you."

The voice on the other end was Sergeant Reed of Homicide.

"You still looking for God?"

"Yeah."

"An all-powerful Being? Great Oneness, Creator of the Universe? First Cause of All Things?"

"That's right."

"Somebody with that description just showed up at the morgue. You better get down here right away."

It was Him all right, and from the looks of Him it was a professional job.

"He was dead when they brought Him in."

"Where'd you find Him?"

"A warehouse on Delancey Street."

"Any clues?"

"It's the work of an existentialist. We're sure of that."

"How can you tell?"

"Haphazard way how it was done. Doesn't seem to be any system followed. Impulse."

"A crime of passion?"

"You got it. Which means you're a suspect, Kaiser."

"Why me?"

"Everybody down at headquarters knows how you feel about Jaspers."

"That doesn't make me a killer."

"Not yet, but you're a suspect."

Outside on the street I sucked air into my lungs and tried to clear my head. I took a cab over to Newark and got out and walked a block to Giordino's Italian Restaurant. There, at a back table, was His Holiness. It was the Pope, all right. Sitting with two guys I had seen in half a dozen police line-ups.

"Sit down," he said, looking up from his fettucine. He held out a ring. I gave him my toothiest smile, but didn't kiss it. It bothered him and I was glad. Point for me.

"Would you like some fettucine?"

"No thanks, Holiness. But you go ahead."

"Nothing? Not even a salad?"

"I just ate."

"Suit yourself, but they make a great Roquefort dressing here. Not like at the Vatican, where you can't get a decent meal."

"I'll come right to the point, Pontiff. I'm looking for God."

"You came to the right person."

"Then He does exist?" They all found this very amusing

and laughed. The hood next to me said, "Oh, that's funny. Bright boy wants to know if He exists."

I shifted my chair to get comfortable and brought the leg down on his little toe. "Sorry." But he was steaming.

"Sure He exists, Lupowitz, but I'm the only one that communicates with him. He speaks only through me."

"Why you, pal?"

"Because I got the red suit."

"This get-up?"

"Don't knock it. Every morning I rise, put on this red suit, and suddenly I'm a big cheese. It's all in the suit. I mean, face it, if I went around in slacks and a sports jacket, I couldn't get arrested religion-wise."

"Then it's a hype. There's no God."

"I don't know. But what's the difference? The money's good."

"You ever worry the laundry won't get your red suit back on time and you'll be like the rest of us?"

"I use the special one-day service. I figure it's worth the extra few cents to be safe."

"Name Claire Rosensweig mean anything to you?"

"Sure. She's in the science department at Bryn Mawr."

"Science, you say? Thanks."

"For what?"

"The answer, Pontiff." I grabbed a cab and shot over the George Washington Bridge. On the way I stopped at my office and did some fast checking. Driving to Claire's apartment, I put the pieces together, and for the first time they fit. When I got there she was in a diaphanous peignoir and something seemed to be troubling her.

"God is dead. The police were here. They're looking for you. They think an existentialist did it."

"No, sugar. It was you."

"What? Don't make jokes, Kaiser."

"It was you that did it."

"What are you saying?"

"You, baby. Not Heather Butkiss or Claire Rosensweig, but Doctor Ellen Shepherd."

"How did you know my name?"

"Professor of physics at Bryn Mawr. The youngest one ever to head a department there. At the midwinter Hop you get stuck on a jazz musician who's heavily into philosophy. He's married, but that doesn't stop you. A couple of nights in the hay and it feels like love. But it doesn't work out because something comes between you. God. Y'see, sugar, he believed, or wanted to, but you, with your pretty little scientific mind, had to have absolute certainty."

"No, Kaiser, I swear."

"So you pretend to study philosophy because that gives you a chance to eliminate certain obstacles. You get rid of Socrates easy enough, but Descartes takes over, so you use Spinoza to get rid of Descartes, but when Kant doesn't come through you have to get rid of him too."

"You don't know what you're saying."

"You made mincemeat out of Leibnitz, but that wasn't good enough for you because you knew if anybody believed Pascal you were dead, so he had to be gotten rid of too, but that's where you made your mistake because you trusted Martin Buber. Except, sugar, he was soft. He believed in God, so you had to get rid of God yourself."

"Kaiser, you're mad!"

"No, baby. You posed as a pantheist and that gave you access to Him—*if* He existed, which he did. He went with you to Shelby's party and when Jason wasn't looking, you killed Him."

"Who the hell are Shelby and Jason?"

"What's the difference? Life's absurd now anyway."

"Kaiser," she said, suddenly trembling. "You wouldn't turn me in?"

"Oh yes, baby. When the Supreme Being gets knocked off, *somebody's* got to take the rap."

"Oh, Kaiser, we could go away together. Just the two of us. We could forget about philosophy. Settle down and maybe get into semantics."

"Sorry, sugar. It's no dice."

She was all tears now as she started lowering the shoulder

straps of her peignoir and I was standing there suddenly with a naked Venus whose whole body seemed to be saying, Take me—I'm yours. A Venus whose right hand tousled my hair while her left hand had picked up a forty-five and was holding it behind my back. I let go with a slug from my thirty-eight before she could pull the trigger, and she dropped her gun and doubled over in disbelief.

"How could you, Kaiser?"

She was fading fast, but I managed to get it in, in time.

"The manifestation of the universe as a complex idea unto itself as opposed to being in or outside the true Being of itself is inherently a conceptual nothingness or Nothingness in relation to any abstract form of existing or to exist or having existed in perpetuity and not subject to laws of physicality or motion or ideas relating to nonmatter or the lack of objective Being or subjective otherness."

It was a subtle concept but I think she understood before she died.

What! Not a Christmas story, you say? I refer you to the winner of the fifth race at Aqueduct.

"Then Mrs. Cratchit entered, smiling proudly, with the pudding. Oh. a wonderful pudding! Shaped like a cannonball, blazing in half-a-quartern of ignited brandy bedight with Christmas holly stuck into the top, and stuffed full with plums and sweetmeats and sodium diacetate and monoglyceride and potassium bromate and aluminum phosphate and calcium phosphate monobasic and chloromine T and aluminum potassium sulfate and calcium propionate and sodium alginate and butylated hydroxyanisole and . . ."

Robin Hood's Epitaph

Hear undernead dis laith stean
Laiz Robert Earl of Huntington
Nea arcir ver az hie sa geude:
An piple kaud im Robin Heud.
Sic utlawz as hi an iz men,
Wil England never sigh agen.
  Obiit 24 kal. Decembris, 1247.

From a gravestone in
Kirklees Churchyard, Yorkshire.

Occasionally some killjoy turns up at Christmas to dampen everyone's joy. Take Sir Harry Strangeway. He keeps insisting that somebody is trying to poison him. He could ruin everyone's holiday if allowed to go on. Fortunately, Harry will not be around for long.

Marjorie Bowen, the lady behind this scenario, is a name known only to the most avid mystery reader. Yet, during her career, she wrote prolifically under a number of pseudonyms. As Joseph Shearing, she wrote a fascinating book called So Evil My Love which was turned into an atmospheric film starring Ray Milland and Ann Todd.

No less an authority than Joan Kahn, the venerable editor and anthologist, draws upon Bowen's stories for her own collections. She recalled that, when she began her celebrated years at Harper's, she dropped all its mystery writers save John Dickson Carr, Nicholas Blake (C. Day Lewis, then England's poet laureate), and Marjorie Bowen. A formidable recommendation, that.

Bowen has also written a second Christmas crime story, "The Prescription," which can be found in the excellent anthology Christmas Ghosts, edited by Gogo Lewis and Seon Manley.

Cambric Tea

by Marjorie Bowen

THE SITUATION WAS bizarre; the accurately trained mind of Bevis Holroyd was impressed foremost by this; that the opening of a door would turn it into tragedy.

"I am afraid I can't stay," he had said pleasantly, humouring a sick man; he was too young and had not been long enough completely successful to have a professional manner but a certain balanced tolerance just showed in his attitude to this prostrate creature.

"I've got a good many claims on my time," he added, "and I'm afraid it would be impossible. And it isn't the least necessary, you know. You're quite all right. I'll come back after Christmas if you really think it worth while."

The patient opened one eye; he was lying flat on his back in a deep, wide-fashioned bed hung with a thick dark, silk lined tapestry; the room was dark for there were thick curtains of the same material drawn half across the windows, rigidly excluding all save a moiety of the pallid winter light; to make his examination Dr. Holroyd had had to snap on the electric light that stood on the bedside table; he thought it a dreary unhealthy room, but had hardly found it worth while to say as much.

The patient opened one eye; the other lid remained fluttering feebly over an immobile orb.

He said in a voice both hoarse and feeble:

"But, doctor, I'm being poisoned."

Professional curiosity and interest masked by genial incredulity instantly quickened the doctor's attention.

"My dear sir," he smiled, "poisoned by this nasty bout of 'flu you mean, I suppose—"

"No," said the patient, faintly and wearily dropping both lids over his blank eyes, "by my wife."

"That's an ugly sort of fancy for you to get hold of," replied the doctor instantly. "Acute depression—we must see what we can do for you—"

The sick man opened both eyes now; he even slightly raised his head as he replied, not without dignity:

"I fetched you from London, Dr. Holroyd, that you might deal with my case impartially—from the local man there is no hope of that, he is entirely impressed by my wife."

Dr. Holroyd made a movement as if to protest but a trembling sign from the patient made him quickly subsist.

"Please let me speak. *She* will come in soon and I shall have no chance. I sent for you secretly, she knows nothing about that. I had heard you very well spoken of—as an authority on this sort of thing. You made a name over the Pluntre murder case as witness for the Crown."

"I don't specialize in murder," said Dr. Holroyd, but his keen handsome face was alight with interest. "And I don't care much for this kind of case—Sir Harry."

"But you've taken it on," murmured the sick man. "You couldn't abandon me now."

"I'll get you into a nursing home," said the doctor cheerfully, "and there you'll dispel all these ideas."

"And when the nursing home has cured me I'm to come back to my wife for her to begin again?"

Dr. Holroyd bent suddenly and sharply over the sombre bed. With his right hand he deftly turned on the electric lamp and tipped back the coral silk shade so that the bleached acid light fell full over the patient lying on his back on the big fat pillows.

"Look here," said the doctor, "what you say is pretty serious."

And the two men stared at each other, the patient examining his physician as acutely as his physician examined him.

Bevis Holroyd was still a young man with a look of peculiar energy and austere intelligence that heightened by contrast purely physical dark good looks that many men would have found sufficient passport to success; resolution, dignity and a certain masculine sweetness, serene and strong, different from feminine sweetness, marked his demeanour which was further softened by a quick humour and a sensitive judgment.

The patient, on the other hand, was a man of well past middle age, light, flabby and obese with a flaccid, fallen look about his large face which was blurred and dimmed by the colours of ill health, being one pasty livid hue that threw into unpleasant relief the grey speckled red of his scant hair.

Altogether an unpleasing man, but of a certain fame and importance that had induced the rising young doctor to come at once when hastily summoned to Strangeways Manor House; a man of a fine, renowned family, a man of repute as a scholar, an essayist who had once been a politician who was rather above politics; a man whom Dr. Holroyd only knew vaguely by reputation, but who seemed to him symbolical of all that was staid, respectable and stolid.

And this man blinked up at him and whimpered:

"My wife is poisoning me."

Dr. Holroyd sat back and snapped off the electric light.

"What make you think so?" he asked sharply.

"To tell you that," came the laboured voice of the sick man. "I should have to tell you my story."

"Well, if you want me to take this up—"

"I sent for you to do that, doctor."

"Well, how do you think you are being poisoned?"

"Arsenic, of course."

"Oh? And how administered?"

Again the patient looked up with one eye, seeming too fatigued to open the other.

"Cambric tea," he replied.

And Dr. Holroyd echoed:

"Cambric tea!" with a soft amazement and interest.

Cambric tea had been used as the medium for arsenic in the Pluntre case and the expression had become famous; it was Bevis Holroyd who had discovered the doses in the cambric tea and who had put his finger on this pale beverage as the means of murder.

"Very possibly," continued Sir Harry, "the Pluntre case made her think of it."

"For God's sake, don't," said Dr. Holroyd; for in that hideous affair the murderer had been a woman; and to see a woman on trial for her life, to see a woman sentenced to death, was not an experience he wished to repeat.

"Lady Strangeways," continued the sick man, "is much younger than I—I over persuaded her to marry me, she was at that time very much attracted by a man of her own age, but he was in a poor position and she was ambitious."

He paused, wiped his quivering lips on a silk handkerchief, and added faintly:

"Lately our marriage has been extremely unhappy. The man she preferred is now prosperous, successful and unmarried—she wishes to dispose of me that she may marry her first choice."

"Have you proof of any of this?"

"Yes. I know she buys arsenic. I know she reads books on poisons. I know she is eating her heart out for this other man."

"Forgive me, Sir Harry," replied the doctor, "but have you no near friend nor relation to whom you can confide your—suspicions?"

"No one," said the sick man impatiently. "I have lately come from the East and am out of touch with people. Besides I want a doctor, a doctor with skill in this sort of thing. I thought from the first of the Pluntre case and of you."

Bevis Holroyd sat back quietly; it was then that he thought of the situation as bizarre; the queerness of the whole thing was vividly before him, like a twisted figure on a gem—a carving at once writhing and immobile.

"Perhaps," continued Sir Harry wearily, "you are married, doctor?"

"No." Dr. Holroyd slightly smiled; his story was something like the sick man's story but taken from another angle; when he was very poor and unknown he had loved a girl who had preferred a wealthy man; she had gone out to India, ten years ago, and he had never seen her since; he remembered this, with sharp distinctness, and in the same breath he remembered that he still loved this girl; it was, after all, a common-place story.

Then his mind swung to the severe professional aspect of the case; he had thought that his patient, an unhealthy type of man, was struggling with a bad attack of influenza and the resultant depression and weakness, but then he had never thought, of course, of poison, nor looked nor tested for poison.

The man might be lunatic, he might be deceived, he might be speaking the truth; the fact that he was a mean, unpleasant beast ought not to weigh in the matter; Dr. Holroyd had some enjoyable Christmas holidays in prospect and now he was beginning to feel that he ought to give these up to stay and investigate this case; for he could readily see that it was one in which the local doctor would be quite useless.

"You must have a nurse," he said, rising.

But the sick man shook his head.

"I don't wish to expose my wife more than need be," he grumbled. "Can't you manage the affair yourself?"

As this was the first hint of decent feeling he had shown, Bevis Holroyd forgave him his brusque rudeness.

"Well, I'll stay the night anyhow," he conceded.

And then the situation changed, with the opening of a door, from the bizarre to the tragic.

This door opened in the far end of the room and admitted a bloom of bluish winter light from some uncurtained, high windowed corridor; the chill impression was as if invisible snow had entered the shaded, dun, close apartment.

And against this background appeared a woman in a smoke coloured dress with some long lace about the shoulders and a high comb; she held a little tray carrying jugs and a glass of crystal in which the cold light splintered.

Dr. Holroyd stood in his usual attitude of attentive courtesy, and then, as the patient, feebly twisting his gross head from the fat pillow, said:

"My wife—doctor—" he recognized in Lady Strangeways the girl to whom he had once been engaged in marriage, the woman he still loved.

"This is Doctor Holroyd," added Sir Harry. "Is that cambric tea you have there?"

She inclined her head to the stranger by her husband's bed as if she had never seen him before, and he, taking his cue, and for many other reasons, was silent.

"Yes, this is your cambric tea," she said to her husband. "You like it just now, don't you? How do you find Sir Harry, Dr. Holroyd?"

There were two jugs on the tray; one of crystal half full of cold milk, and one of white porcelain full of hot water; Lady Strangeways proceeded to mix these fluids in equal proportions and gave the resultant drink to her husband, helping him first to sit up in bed.

"I think that Sir Harry has a nasty turn of influenza," answered the doctor mechanically. "He wants me to stay. I've promised till the morning, anyhow."

"That will be a pleasure and a relief," said Lady Strangeways gravely. "My husband has been ill some time and seems so much worse than he need—for influenza."

The patient, feebly sipping his cambric tea, grinned queerly at the doctor.

"So much worse—you see, doctor!" he muttered.

"It is good of you to stay," continued Lady Strangeways equally. "I will see about your room, you must be as comfortable as possible."

She left as she had come, a shadow-coloured figure retreating to a chill light.

The sick man held up his glass as if he gave a toast.

"You see! Cambric tea!"

And Bevis Holroyd was thinking: does she not want to know me? Does he know what we once were to each other? How comes she to be married to this man—her husband's name was Custiss—and the horror of the situation shook the calm that was his both from character and training; he went to the window and looked out on the bleached park; light, slow snow was falling, a dreary dance over the frozen grass and before the grey corpses that paled, one behind the other, to the distance shrouded in colourless mist.

The thin voice of Harry Strangeways recalled him to the bed.

"Would you like to take a look at this, doctor?" He held out the half drunk glass of milk and water.

"I've no means of making a test here," said Dr. Holroyd, troubled. "I brought a few things, nothing like that."

"You are not so far from Harley Street," said Sir Harry. "My car can fetch everything you want by this afternoon— or perhaps you would like to go yourself?"

"Yes," replied Bevis Holroyd sternly. "I would rather go myself."

His trained mind had been rapidly covering the main aspects of his problem and he had instantly seen that it was better for Lady Strangeways to have this case in his hands. He was sure there was some hideous, fantastic hallucination on the part of Sir Harry, but it was better for Lady Strangeways to leave the matter in the hands of one who was friendly towards her. He rapidly found and washed a medicine bottle from among the sick room paraphernalia and poured it full of the cambric tea, casting away the remainder.

"Why did you drink any?" he asked sharply.

"I don't want her to think that I guess," whispered Sir Harry. "Do you know, doctor, I have a lot of her love letters —written by—"

Dr. Holroyd cut him short.

"I couldn't listen to this sort of thing behind Lady Strangeways's back," he said quickly. "That is between you and her. My job is to get you well. I'll try and do that."

And he considered, with a faint disgust, how repulsive this man looked sitting up with pendant jowl and drooping cheeks and discoloured, pouchy eyes sunk in pads of unhealthy flesh and above the spiky crown of Judas-coloured hair.

Perhaps a woman, chained to this man, living with him, blocked and thwarted by him, might be wrought upon to—

Dr. Holroyd shuddered inwardly and refused to continue his reflection.

As he was leaving the gaunt sombre house about which there was something definitely black and unfriendly, a shrine in which the sacred flames had flickered out so long ago that the lamps were blank and cold, he met Lady Strangeways.

She was in the wide entrance hall standing by the wood fire that but faintly dispersed the gloom of the winter morning and left untouched the shadows in the rafters of the open roof.

Now he would not, whether she wished or no, deny her; he stopped before her, blocking out her poor remnant of light.

"Mollie," he said gently, "I don't quite understand—you married a man named Custiss in India."

"Yes. Harry had to take this name when he inherited this place. We've been home three years from the East, but lived so quietly here that I don't suppose anyone has heard of us."

She stood between him and the firelight, a shadow among the shadows; she was much changed; in her thinness and pallor, in her restless eyes and nervous mouth he could read signs of discontent, even of unhappiness.

"I never heard of you," said Dr. Holroyd truthfully. "I didn't want to. I liked to keep my dreams."

Her hair was yet the lovely cedar wood hue, silver, soft and gracious; her figure had those fluid lines of grace that he believed he had never seen equalled.

"Tell me," she added abruptly, "what is the matter with my husband? He has been ailing like this for a year or so."

With a horrid lurch of his heart that was usually so steady, Dr. Holroyd remembered the bottle of milk and water in his pocket.

"Why do you give him that cambric tea?" he counter questioned.

"He will have it—he insists that I make it for him—"

"Mollie," said Dr. Holroyd quickly, "you decided against me, ten years ago, but that is no reason why we should not be friends now—tell me, frankly, are you happy with this man?"

"You have seen him," she replied slowly. "He seemed different ten years ago. I honestly was attracted by his scholarship and his learning as well as—other things."

Bevis Holroyd needed to ask no more; she was wretched, imprisoned in a mistake as a fly in amber; and those love letters? Was there another man?

As he stood silent, with a dark reflective look on her weary brooding face, she spoke again:

"You are staying?"

"Oh yes," he said, he was staying, there was nothing else for him to do.

"It is Christmas week," she reminded him wistfully. "It will be very dull, perhaps painful, for you."

"I think I ought to stay."

Sir Harry's car was announced; Bevis Holroyd, gliding over frozen roads to London, was absorbed with this sudden problem that, like a mountain out of a plain, had suddenly risen to confront him out of his level life.

The sight of Mollie (he could not think of her by that sick man's name) had roused in him tender memories and poignant emotions and the position in which he found her and his own juxtaposition to her and her husband had the same devastating effect on him as a mine sprung beneath the feet of an unwary traveller.

London was deep in the whirl of a snow storm and the light that penetrated over the grey roof tops to the ugly slip of a laboratory at the back of his consulting rooms was chill and forbidding.

Bevis Holroyd put the bottle of milk on a marble slab and sat back in the easy chair watching that dreary chase of snow flakes across the dingy London pane.

He was thinking of past springs, of violets long dead, of roses long since dust, of hours that had slipped away like lengths of golden silk rolled up, of the long ago when he had loved Mollie and Mollie had seemed to love him; then he thought of that man in the big bed who had said:

"My wife is poisoning me."

Late that afternoon Dr. Holroyd, with his suit case and a professional bag, returned to Strangeways Manor House in Sir Harry's car; the bottle of cambric tea had gone to a friend, a noted analyst; somehow Doctor Holroyd had not felt able to do this task himself; he was very fortunate, he felt, in securing this old solitary and his promise to do the work before Christmas.

As he arrived at Strangeways Manor House which stood isolated and well away from a public high road where a lonely spur of the weald of Kent drove into the Sussex marshes, it was in a blizzard of snow that effaced the landscape and gave the murky outlines of the house an air of unreality, and Bevis Holroyd experienced that sensation he had so often heard of and read about, but which so far his cool mind had dismissed as a fiction.

He did really feel as if he was in an evil dream; as the snow changed the values of the scene, altering distances and shapes, so this meeting with Mollie, under these circumstances, had suddenly changed the life of Bevis Holroyd.

He had so resolutely and so definitely put this woman out

of his life and mind, deliberately refusing to make enquiries about her, letting all knowledge of her cease with the letter in which she had written from India and announced her marriage.

And now, after ten years, she had crossed his path in this ghastly manner, as a woman her husband accused of attempted murder.

The sick man's words of a former lover disturbed him profoundly; was it himself who was referred to? Yet the love letters must be from another man for he had not corresponded with Mollie since her marriage, not for ten years.

He had never felt any bitterness towards Mollie for her desertion of a poor, struggling doctor, and he had always believed in the integral nobility of her character under the timidity of conventionality; but the fact remained that she had played him false—what if that *had* been "the little rift within the lute" that had now indeed silenced the music!

With a sense of bitter depression he entered the gloomy old house; how different was this from the pleasant ordinary Christmas he had been rather looking forward to, the jolly homely atmosphere of good fare, dancing, and friends!

When he had telephoned to these friends excusing himself his regret had been genuine and the cordial "bad luck!" had had a poignant echo in his own heart; bad luck indeed, bad luck—

She was waiting for him in the hall that a pale young man was decorating with boughs of prickly stiff holly that stuck stiffly behind the dark heavy pictures.

He was introduced as the secretary and said gloomily:

"Sir Harry wished everything to go on as usual, though I am afraid he is very ill indeed."

Yes, the patient had been seized by another violent attack of illness during Dr. Holroyd's absence; the young man went at once upstairs and found Sir Harry in a deep sleep and a rather nervous local doctor in attendance.

An exhaustive discussion of the case with this doctor

threw no light on anything, and Dr. Holroyd, leaving in charge an extremely sensible looking housekeeper who was Sir Harry's preferred nurse, returned, worried and irritated, to the hall where Lady Strangeways now sat alone before the big fire.

She offered him a belated but fresh cup of tea.

"Why did you come?" she asked as if she roused herself from deep reverie.

"Why? Because your husband sent for me."

"He says you offered to come; he has told everyone in the house that."

"But I never heard of the man before to-day."

"You had heard of me. He seems to think that you came here to help me."

"He cannot be saying that," returned Dr. Holroyd sternly, and he wondered desperately if Mollie was lying, if she had invented this to drive him out of the house.

"Do you want me here?" he demanded.

"I don't know," she replied dully and confirmed his suspicions; probably there was another man and she wished him out of the way; but he could not go, out of pity towards her he could not go.

"Does he know we once knew each other?" he asked.

"No," she replied faintly, "therefore it seems such a curious chance that he should have sent for you, of all men!"

"It would have been more curious," he responded grimly, "if I had heard that you were here with a sick husband and had thrust myself in to doctor him! Strangeways must be crazy to spread such a tale and if he doesn't know we are old friends it becomes nonsense!"

"I often think that Harry is crazy," said Lady Strangeways wearily; she took a rose silk lined work basket, full of pretty trifles, on her knee, and began winding a skein of rose coloured silk; she looked so frail, so sad, so lifeless that the heart of Bevis Holroyd was torn with bitter pity.

"Now I am here I want to help you," he said earnestly. "I am staying for that, to help you—"

She looked up at him with a wistful appeal in her fair face.

"I'm worried," she said simply. "I've lost some letters I valued very much—I think they have been stolen."

Dr. Holroyd drew back; the love letters; the letters the husband had found, that were causing all his ugly suspicions.

"My poor Mollie!" he exclaimed impulsively. "What sort of a coil have you got yourself into!"

As if this note of pity was unendurable, she rose impulsively, scattering the contents of her work basket, dropping the skein of silk, and hastened away down the dark hall.

Bevis Holroyd stooped mechanically to pick up the hurled objects and saw among them a small white packet, folded, but opened at one end; this packet seemed to have fallen out of a needle case of gold silk.

Bevis Holroyd had pounced on it and thrust it in his pocket just as the pale secretary returned with his thin arms most incongruously full of mistletoe.

"This will be a dreary Christmas for you, Dr. Holroyd," he said with the air of one who forces himself to make conversation. "No doubt you had some pleasant plans in view —we are all so pleased that Lady Strangeways had a friend to come and look after Sir Harry during the holidays."

"Who told you I was a friend?" asked Dr. Holroyd brusquely. "I certainly knew Lady Strangeways before she was married—"

The pale young man cut in crisply:

"Oh, Lady Strangeways told me so herself."

Bevis Holroyd was bewildered; why did she tell the secretary what she did not tell her husband?—both the indiscretion and the reserve seemed equally foolish.

Languidly hanging up his sprays and bunches of mistletoe the pallid young man, whose name was Garth Deane, continued his aimless remarks.

"This is really not a very cheerful house, Dr. Holroyd— I'm interested in Sir Harry's oriental work or I should not remain. Such a very unhappy marriage! I often think," he added regardless of Bevis Holroyd's darkling glance, "that it would be very unpleasant indeed for Lady Strangeways if anything happened to Sir Harry."

"Whatever do you mean, sir?" asked the doctor angrily.

The secretary was not at all discomposed.

"Well, one lives in the house, one has nothing much to do—and one notices."

Perhaps, thought the young man in anguish, the sick husband had been talking to this creature, perhaps the creature *had* really noticed something.

"I'll go up to my patient," said Bevis Holroyd briefly, not daring to anger one who might be an important witness in this mystery that was at present so unfathomable.

Mr. Deane gave a sickly grin over the lovely pale leaves and berries he was holding.

"I'm afraid he is very bad, doctor."

As Bevis Holroyd left the room he passed Lady Strangeways; she looked blurred, like a pastel drawing that has been shaken; the fingers she kept locked on her bosom; she had flung a silver fur over her shoulders that accentuated her ethereal look of blonde, pearl and amber hues.

"I've come back for my work basket," she said. "Will you go up to my husband? He is ill again—"

"Have you been giving him anything?" asked Dr. Holroyd as quietly as he could.

"Only some cambric tea, he insisted on that."

"Don't give him anything—leave him alone. He is in my charge now, do you understand?"

She gazed up at him with frightened eyes that had been newly washed by tears.

"Why are you so unkind to me?" she quivered.

She looked so ready to fall that he could not resist the temptation to put his hand protectingly on her arm, so that, as she stood in the low doorway leading to the stairs, he appeared to be supporting her drooping weight.

"Have I not said that I am here to help you, Mollie?"

The secretary slipped out from the shadows behind them, his arms still full of winter evergreens.

"There is too much foliage," he smiled, and the smile told that he had seen and heard.

Bevis Holroyd went angrily upstairs; he felt as if an invisible net was being dragged closely round him, something which, from being a cobweb, would become a cable; this air of mystery, of horror in the big house, this sly secretary, these watchful-looking servants, the nervous village doctor ready to credit anything, the lovely agitated woman who was the woman he had long so romantically loved, and the sinister sick man with his diabolic accusations, a man Bevis Holroyd had, from the first moment, hated—all these people in these dark surroundings affected the young man with a miasma of apprehension, gloom and dread.

After a few hours of it he was nearer to losing his nerve than he had ever been; that must be because of Mollie, poor darling Mollie caught into all this nightmare.

And outside the bells were ringing across the snow, practising for Christmas Day; the sound of them was to Bevis Holroyd what the sounds of the real world are when breaking into a sleeper's thick dreams.

The patient sat up in bed, fondling the glass of odious cambric tea.

"Why do you take the stuff?" demanded the doctor angrily.

"She won't let me off, she thrusts it on me," whispered Sir Harry.

Bevis Holroyd noticed, not for the first time since he had come into the fell atmosphere of this dark house that enclosed the piteous figure of the woman he loved, that husband and wife were telling different tales; on one side lay a burden of careful lying.

"Did she—" continued the sick man, "speak to you of her lost letters?"

The young doctor looked at him sternly.

"Why should Lady Strangeways make a confidante of

me?" he asked. "Do you know that she was a friend of mine ten years ago before she married you?"

"Was she? How curious! But you met like strangers."

"The light in this room is very dim—"

"Well, never mind about that, whether you knew her or not—" Sir Harry gasped out in a sudden snarl. "The woman is a murderess, and you'll have to bear witness to it—I've got her letters, here under my pillow, and Garth Deane is watching her—"

"Ah, a spy! I'll have no part in this, Sir Harry. You'll call another doctor—"

"No, it's your case, you'll make the best of it—My God, I'm dying, I think—"

He fell back in such a convulsion of pain that Bevis Holroyd forgot everything in administering to him. The rest of that day and all that night the young doctor was shut up with his patient, assisted by the secretary and the house-keeper.

And when, in the pallid light of Christmas Eve morning, he went downstairs to find Lady Strangeways, he knew that the sick man was suffering from arsenic poison, that the packet taken from Mollie's work box was arsenic, and it was only an added horror when he was called to the telephone to learn that a stiff dose of the poison had been found in the specimen of cambric tea.

He believed that he could save the husband and thereby the wife also, but he did not think he could close the sick man's mouth; the deadly hatred of Sir Harry was leading up to an accusation of attempted murder; of that he was sure, and there was the man Deane to back him up.

He sent for Mollie, who had not been near her husband all night, and when she came, pale, distracted, huddled in her white fur, he said grimly:

"Look here, Mollie, I promised that I'd help you and I mean to, though it isn't going to be as easy as I thought, but you have got to be frank with me."

"But I have nothing to conceal—"

"The name of the other man—"

"The other man?"

"The man who wrote those letters your husband has under his pillow."

"Oh, Harry has them!" she cried in pain. "That man Deane stole them then! Bevis, they are your letters of the olden days that I have always cherished."

"*My* letters!"

"Yes, do you think that there has ever been anyone else?"

"But he says—Mollie, there is a trap or trick here, some one is lying furiously. Your husband is being poisoned."

"Poisoned?"

"By arsenic given in that cambric tea. And he knows it. And he accuses you."

She stared at him in blank incredulity, then she slipped forward in her chair and clutched the big arm.

"Oh, God," she muttered in panic terror. "He always swore that he'd be revenged on me—because he knew that I never cared for him—"

But Bevis Holroyd recoiled; he did not dare listen, he did not dare believe.

"I've warned you," he said, "for the sake of the old days, Mollie—"

A light step behind them and they were aware of the secretary creeping out of the embrowning shadows.

"A cold Christmas," he said, rubbing his hands together. "A really cold, seasonable Christmas. We are almost snowed in—and Sir Harry would like to see you, Dr. Holroyd."

"I have only just left him—"

Bevis Holroyd looked at the despairing figure of the woman, crouching in her chair; he was distracted, overwrought, near to losing his nerve.

"He wants particularly to see you," cringed the secretary.

Mollie looked back at Bevis Holroyd, her lips moved twice in vain before she could say: "Go to him."

The doctor went slowly upstairs and the secretary followed.

Sir Harry was now flat on his back, staring at the dark tapestry curtains of his bed.

"I'm dying," he announced as the doctor bent over him.

"Nonsense. I am not going to allow you to die."

"You won't be able to help yourself. I've brought you here to see me die."

"What do you mean?"

"I've a surprise for you too, a Christmas present. These letters now, these love letters of my wife's—what name do you think is on them?"

"Your mind is giving way, Sir Harry."

"Not at all—come nearer, Deane—the name is Bevis Holroyd."

"Then they are letters ten years old. Letters written before your wife met you."

The sick man grinned with infinite malice.

"Maybe. But there are no dates on them and the envelopes are all destroyed. And I, as a dying man, shall swear to their recent date—I, as a foully murdered man."

"You are wandering in your mind," said Bevis Holroyd quietly. "I refuse to listen to you any further."

"You shall listen to me. I brought you here to listen to me. I've got you. Here's my will, Deane's got that, in which I denounced you both, there are your letters, every one thinks that *she* put you in charge of the case, every one knows that you know all about arsenic in cambric tea through the Pluntre case, and every one will know that I died of arsenic poisoning."

The doctor allowed him to talk himself out; indeed it would have been difficult to check the ferocity of his malicious energy.

The plot was ingenious, the invention of a slightly insane, jealous recluse who hated his wife and hated the man she had never ceased to love; Bevis Holroyd could see the nets very skilfully drawn round him; but the main issue of the mystery remained untouched; who *was* administering the arsenic?

The young man glanced across the sombre bed to the dark figure of the secretary.

"What is your place in all this farrago, Mr. Deane?" he asked sternly.

"I'm Sir Harry's friend," answered the other stubbornly, "and I'll bring witness any time against Lady Strangeways. I've tried to circumvent her—"

"Stop," cried the doctor. "You think that Lady Strangeways is poisoning her husband and that I am her accomplice?"

The sick man, who had been looking with bitter malice from one to another, whispered hoarsely:

"That is what you think, isn't it, Deane?"

"I'll say what I think at the proper time," said the secretary obstinately.

"No doubt you are being well paid for your share in this."

"I've remembered his services in my will," smiled Sir Harry grimly. "You can adjust your differences then, Dr. Holroyd, when I'm dead, *poisoned, murdered*. It will be a pretty story, a nice scandal, you and she in the house together, the letters, the cambric tea!"

An expression of ferocity dominated him, then he made an effort to dominate this and to speak in his usual suave stilted manner.

"You must admit that we shall all have a very Happy Christmas, doctor."

Bevis Holroyd was looking at the secretary, who stood at the other side of the bed, cringing, yet somehow in the attitude of a man ready to pounce; Dr. Holroyd wondered if this was the murderer.

"Why," he asked quietly to gain time, "did you hatch this plan to ruin a man you have never seen before?"

"I always hated you," replied the sick man faintly. "Mollie never forgot you, you see, and she never allowed *me* to forget that she never forgot you. And then I found those letters she had cherished."

"You are a very wicked man," said the doctor dryly, "but

it will all come to nothing, for I am not going to allow you to die."

"You won't be able to help yourself," replied the patient. "I'm dying, I tell you. I shall die on Christmas Day."

He turned his head towards the secretary and added:

"Send my wife up to me."

"No," interrupted Dr. Holroyd strongly. "She shall not come near you again."

Sir Harry Strangeways ignored this.

"Send her up," he repeated.

"I will bring her, sir."

The secretary left, with a movement suggestive of flight, and Bevis Holroyd stood rigid, waiting, thinking, looking at the ugly man who now had closed his eyes and lay as if insensible. He was certainly very ill, dying perhaps, and he certainly had been poisoned by arsenic given in cambric tea, and, as certainly, a terrible scandal and a terrible danger would threaten with his death; the letters were *not* dated, the marriage was notoriously unhappy, and he, Bevis Holroyd, was associated in every one's mind with a murder case in which this form of poison, given in this manner, had been used.

Drops of moisture stood out on the doctor's forehead; sure that if he could clear himself it would be very difficult for Mollie to do so; how could even he himself in his soul swear to her innocence!

Of course he must get the woman out of the house at once, he must have another doctor from town, nurses—but could this be done in time; if the patient died on his hands would he not be only bringing witnesses to his own discomfiture? And the right people, his own friends, were difficult to get hold of now, at Christmas time.

He longed to go in search of Mollie—she must at least be got away, but how, without a scandal, without a suspicion?

He longed to have the matter out with this odious secretary, but he dared not leave his patient.

Lady Strangeways returned with Garth Deane and seated

herself, mute, shadowy, with eyes full of panic, on the other
side of the sombre bed.

"Is he going to live?" she presently whispered as she
watched Bevis Holroyd ministering to her unconscious husband.

"We must see that he does," he answered grimly.

All through that Christmas Eve and the bitter night to the
stark dawn when the church bells broke ghastly on their wan
senses did they tend the sick man who only came to his
senses to grin at them in malice.

Once Bevis Holroyd asked the pallid woman:

"What was that white packet you had in your work box?"

And she replied:

"I never had such a packet."

And he:

"I must believe you."

But he did not send for the other doctors and nurses, he
did not dare.

The Christmas bells seemed to rouse the sick man from
his deadly swoon.

"You can't save me," he said with indescribable malice.
"I shall die and put you both in the dock—"

Mollie Strangeways sank down beside the bed and began
to cry, and Garth Deane, who by his master's express desire
had been in and out of the room all night, stopped and
looked at her with a peculiar expression. Sir Harry looked at
her also.

"Don't cry," he gasped, "this is Christmas Day. We ought
all to be happy—bring me my cambric tea—do you hear?"

She rose mechanically and left the room to take in the tray
with the fresh milk and water that the housekeeper had
placed softly on the table outside the door; for all through
the nightmare vigil, the sick man's cry had been for "cambric tea."

As he sat up in bed feebly sipping the vapid and odious
drink the tortured woman's nerves slipped her control.

"I can't endure those bells, I wish they would stop those
bells!" she cried and ran out of the room.

Bevis Holroyd instantly followed her; and now as suddenly as it had sprung on him, the fell little drama disappeared, fled like a poison cloud out of the compass of his life.

Mollie was leaning against the closed window, her sick head resting against the mullions; through the casement showed, surprisingly, sunlight on the pure snow and blue sky behind the withered trees.

"Listen, Mollie," said the young man resolutely. "I'm sure he'll live if you are careful—you mustn't lose heart—"

The sick room door opened and the secretary slipped out.

He nervously approached the two in the window place.

"I can't stand this any longer," he said through dry lips. "I didn't know he meant to go so far, he is doing it himself, you know; he's got the stuff hidden in his bed, he puts it into the cambric tea, he's willing to die to spite you two, but I can't stand it any longer."

"You've been abetting this!" cried the doctor.

"Not abetting," smiled the secretary wanly. "Just standing by. I found out by chance—and then he forced me to be silent—I had his will, you know, and I've destroyed it."

With this the strange creature glided downstairs.

The doctor sprang at once to Sir Harry's room; the sick man was sitting up in the sombre bed and with a last effort was scattering a grain of powder into the glass of cambric tea.

With a look of baffled horror he saw Bevis Holroyd but the drink had already slipped down his throat; he fell back and hid his face, baulked at the last of his diabolic revenge.

When Bevis Holroyd left the dead man's chamber he found Mollie still leaning in the window; she was free, the sun was shining, it was Christmas Day.

Ceremony upon Candlemas Eve

Down with the rosemary, and so
Down with the bays and mistletoe;
Down with the holly, ivy, all
Wherewith ye dressed the Christmas Hall:
That so the superstitious find
No one least branch there left behind:
For look, how many leaves there be
Neglected, there (maids, trust to me)
So many Goblins you shall see.

The Ceremonies for
Candlemas Day

Kindle the Christmas brand, and then
*   Till Sunset let it burn;*
Which quench'd, then lay it up again
*   Till Christmas next return.*
Part must be kept wherewith to teend
*   The Christmas log next year,*
And where 'tis safely kept, the fiend
*   Can do no mischief there.*

Upon Candlemas Day

End now the white loaf and the pie,
And let all sports with Christmas die.

Robert Herrick

"Look, Daddy—the first robin!"

For those of you seeking an antidote to yet another recitation of "A Visit from St. Nicholas," here is a rather different Christmas Eve tale from the pen of the creator of Uncle Vanya *and* The Cherry Orchard. *No visions of sugarplums here. No stockings hung by the chimney with care, either. Just pure humbug, Russian style, with a touch of Poe lurking about. A most unusual Christmas story, one not included in the first edition of the book.*

A Terrible Night

by Anton Chekhov

IVAN PETROVITCH REQUIEMOV became pallid, put out the lamp and began in an agitated voice:

"Not a glimmer of light pierced the thick darkness that hung over the earth on Christmas Eve, 1883. I was returning home from the house of a friend, who is now dead, where we had all remained late holding a spiritistic séance. For some reason the small bystreets, through which I had to go, were dark, and I had to make my way by groping. I was living at the time in Moscow, near the church of the Assumption on the Tombsta, in a house belonging to the government official Cadaverov, one of the most obscure parts of the Arbat. My thoughts as I walked home were sad and depressing.

"'Your life is drawing to an end.... Repent....'

"These were the words Spinoza, whose spirit we had been able to call up, had addressed to me at the séance. I had asked for them again, and the saucer had not only repeated them, but had added 'to-night.' I am no believer in spiritism, but the thoughts of death, makes me gloomy. Ladies and gentlemen, death is unavoidable, is a daily occurrence, but nevertheless to man's nature it is a subject abhorrent. Now, when I was surrounded by cold, impenetrable darkness, when before my eyes I could only see torrents of raindrops, when the wind howled plaintively above my head, and there was not a single living soul anywhere near me, nor was a human sound to be heard, my soul became filled with an undefined, unaccountable dread. I, a man free from prejudices, hastened along fearing to look back, or to the side. It seemed to me if I looked back I would inevitably see death like a spectre behind me."

Requiemov breathed heavily, he gulped down a glass of water, and continued:

"This undefined dread, you will understand, did not leave me even when having mounted to the fourth story of Cadaverov's house I opened the door and entered my room. It was dark in my modest dwelling. The wind moaned in the stove as if begging to be let into the warmth, and knocked at the door of the ventilator.

"'If Spinoza is to be believed,' I said to myself, smiling, 'I am to die tonight amid this lamentation. It certainly is eerie!'

"I lit a match. . . . A furious gust of wind passed over the roof of the house. The gentle wailing changed into wrathful roars. Somewhere below a half-detached shutter clattered and the door of my ventilator squeaked plaintively for help. . . .

"'It's bad for the houseless on a night like this,' I thought.

"But it was no time to give oneself up to such reflections. When the sulphur on the match I had lighted gave out a blue flame, and I cast my eyes round the room, I saw an unexpected and terrible sight. . . . What a pity the gust of wind had not reached my match! Then, perhaps I would have seen nothing and my hair would not have stood on end. I shrieked, I made a step towards the door, and filled with horror, despair and amazement I closed my eyes.

"There was a coffin in the middle of the room.

"The blue light burnt but a short time; still I had been able to discern the outlines of the coffin. . . . I saw the pink glimmer and sparkle of the brocade, I saw the gold galloon cross on the lid. There are things, ladies and gentlemen, that stamp themselves on your memory, though you have seen them only for an instant. So it was with this coffin. I only saw it for a second, but I can remember it in all its smallest details. It was a coffin for a person of middle height, and judging by its pink colour it was for a young girl. The rich brocade, the feet, the bronze handles—all denoted that the corpse was rich.

"I rushed headlong out of my room and without reasoning, without thinking, only feeling an inexpressible dread, I tore down the stairs. The corridors and the staircase were dark, my legs got entangled in the skirts of my long fur coat, and it was a marvel that I did not fall down and break my neck. When I found myself in the street I leaned against a wet lamp-post and began to get calm. My heart palpitated, my breathing was heavy..."

One of the listeners turned up the lamp and moved closer to the narrator, who continued:

"I would not have been surprised if I had found my room on fire, if a robber or a mad dog had been there.... I would not have been surprised if the ceiling had fallen down, if the floor had collapsed, if the walls had fallen in.... All that is natural and comprehensible. But how could a coffin have got into my room? Where did it come from? An expensive, a woman's coffin, evidently made for some young aristocrat —how could it have found its way into the wretched room of a small government official? Was it empty, or did it contain a corpse?... Who was she, this rich girl who had died so inopportunely, and was now paying me this strange and terrible visit? A painful secret!

"'If this is no miracle it must be a crime,' shot through my head.

"I was lost in conjectures. During my absence the door had been locked and the place where I hid the key was known only to my most intimate friends. My friends could not have placed the coffin there!... It might also be supposed that the coffin had been brought to me by the undertakers owing to some error. They might have mistaken the house or gone to the wrong story or the wrong door, and had carried the coffin into the wrong flat. But who does not know that our coffin-makers will never leave a room until they have been paid for their work, or at least have received a good tip?

"'The spirits have foretold my death,' I thought. 'Can it be they who have taken the trouble to provide me with a coffin in due time?'

"Ladies and gentlemen, I do not believe nor have I ever believed in spiritism, but such a coincidence might even plunge a philosopher into a mystical frame of mind.

"'All this is stupid, and I am as cowardly as a school-boy,' I decided at last. 'It was only an optical illusion—nothing more! While walking home my frame of mind had been so gloomy that it is not surprising that my unstrung nerves made me see a coffin. . . . Of course, it was only an optical illusion! What else could it be?'

"The rain beat in my face, and the wind tore fiercely at my coat and cap. . . . I was cold and wet through and through. I had to go somewhere—but where? To return to my own room would expose me to the risk of again seeing the coffin, and it would be beyond my strength to bear that sight. Without a single living soul near me, not hearing a single human sound, left alone face to face with that coffin in which perhaps a corpse was lying, I might lose my senses. On the other hand, to remain in the street under the torrents of rain and in the cold was impossible.

"I decided to go and pass the night at my friend Restov's room, who, as you all know, afterwards shot himself. At the time he was living in furnished rooms in the house belonging to the merchant Skullov, situated in the Dead Lane."

Requiemov wiped away the cold sweat that had appeared on his pale face, and, heaving a deep sigh, continued:

"I did not find my friend in. I knocked at his door, and at last being convinced that he was out, I felt about on the transom for the key, opened the door and went in. I threw my wet fur-coat on the floor, groped about in the darkness for the sofa and sat down to rest. It was dark. . . . The wind hummed sadly in the window ventilator. The cricket was singing its monotonous song in the stove. The bells in the Kremlin were ringing for the Christmas matins. I hastened to strike a match. But the light did not relieve me of my gloomy mood; on the contrary, a terrible, an inexpressible horror mastered me once more. I shrieked, staggered and rushed out of the room almost beside myself.

"In my friend's room, as in my own, I also saw a coffin!

"My friend's coffin was nearly twice the size of mine, and the brown material with which it was covered gave it an especially gloomy appearance. How had it got there? It could only be an optical illusion—how was it possible to doubt it. . . . There could not be coffins in every room! My nerves were evidently diseased. . . . I had hallucinations. Wherever I might go now I would always see before me the terrible dwelling of the dead. Consequently I was mad, I was infected with something like 'coffin-mania' and the cause of my mental derangement was not far to seek: it was only necessary to remember the spiritistic séance and Spinoza's words. . . .

"'I am going mad!' I thought in terror, seizing my head in my hands. 'My God! My God! What am I to do?'

"My head was ready to burst, my legs failed me. . . . The rain poured down as if out of buckets, the wind pierced me through and through, and I had neither a fur-coat nor a cap I could not go back to fetch them from the room . . . that was beyond my strength. . . . Dread clasped me firmly in its cold embrace. My hair stood on end, cold perspiration streamed down my face, although I believed that it was only hallucinations.

"What was I to do?" Requiemov continued. "I was out of my mind, and I risked catching a severe cold. Fortunately, I remembered that my good friend Godsacreov, who had but lately received his doctor's degree, was living not far from the Dead Lane. He had also been with us at the spiritistic séance. I hastened to him. . . . At that time he had not yet married the rich merchant's daughter, and was living in the fifth story of the house belonging to the State Councillor Graveyardin.

"At Godsacreov's my nerves were destined to be subjected to further torture. As I was mounting to the fifth story I heard a terrible noise. Somebody was running about upstairs, stamping heavily with his feet and slamming doors.

"'Help!' I heard somebody cry in a voice that pierced the very soul. 'Help! Porter!'

"A moment later a dark figure in a fur-coat and a crushed silk hat rushed down the stairs towards me.

"'Godsacreov,' I cried, recognizing my friend. 'Is it you? What is the matter?'

"When Godsacreov reached the landing on which I was standing he stopped and seized me convulsively by the hand. He was pale, he breathed heavily and trembled. His eyes wandered restlessly around, his chest heaved. . . .

"'Is that you, Requiemov?' he asked in a hoarse voice. 'Is it really you? You are pale, like one risen from the grave. . . . But no, are you not a hallucination? My God. . . . You look terrible! . . .'

"'But what's the matter with you? You look like a ghost!'

"'Och! wait, my dear fellow, let me recover my breath. . . . I am glad to have met you, if it really is you and not an optical illusion. That damned spiritistic séance. . . . It has so upset my nerves that, would you believe it, just now, when I came home, I saw in my room . . . a coffin!'

"I could not believe my own ears, and asked him to repeat what he had said.

"'A coffin, a real coffin!' the doctor repeated, sitting down on the steps quite exhausted. 'I am no coward, but the devil himself would be frightened if, after a spiritistic séance, he ran up against a coffin.'

"Stammering and confusedly I told the doctor about the coffins I had seen. . . .

"For a minute we looked at each other with staring eyes, and open-mouthed with astonishment. Then to convince ourselves that we were not dreaming we began pinching each other.

"'We both feel pain,' the doctor said, 'so at the present moment we are not asleep, and we are not dreaming of each other. Therefore, my coffin and both your coffins were not optical illusions, but something that exists. What are we to do now, old man?'

"We stood for a whole hour on the cold staircase, lost in guesses and conjectures; we got terribly cold and at last decided to conquer our cowardly fear, arouse the man-servant on duty and go with him to the doctor's room. So we went. We entered the room, lit a candle and we really saw a coffin covered with white silver brocade with gold fringe and tassels. The man-servant piously crossed himself.

"'Now we can find out,' the doctor said, still trembling in every limb, 'if the coffin is empty or if it is . . . inhabited!'

"After long and quite comprehensible hesitation the doctor bent over the coffin and, pressing his lips together from fright and expectation, he tore off the lid of the coffin.

"We looked into the coffin and . . .

"The coffin was empty. . . .

"There was no corpse in it, but instead we found the following letter:

> "'DEAR GODSACREOV,
>
> "'You know that my father-in-law's business has got into a terrible mess. He is over head and ears in debt. Tomorrow or the day after there will be an execution in his house, and this would entirely ruin his family and mind, and would ruin our honour too, which is more precious than anything else for me. At a family council we held yesterday we decided to hide everything valuable or of worth. As the whole of my father-in-law's property consists of coffins (he is, as you doubtless know, the best undertaker in town), we decided to hide away all the best coffins. I entreat you, as a friend, to save our property and our honour! Hoping that you will help us to save our goods, I send you, dear old fellow, one coffin, with the request that you will hide it in your rooms, and keep it till called for. Without the assistance of our friends and acquaintances we are

ruined. I hope that you will not refuse me this
assistance, all the more as the coffin will not remain with you for more than a week. To everyone
whom I consider as our sincere friend I have sent
a coffin, trusting in their magnanimity and nobility.

" 'Your affectionate,
" 'IVAN JAWIN.'

"For three months after that I had to undergo a cure for
my shattered nerves, while our friend, the undertaker's son-
in-law, saved both his honour and his property, and is now
the owner of an undertaker's business; he arranges funeral
processions, sells monuments and gravestones. His business, however, is not getting on very well, and every evening when I come home I always expect to find next to my
bed a white marble monument or a catafalque."

"God rest ye merry gentlemen, Let nothing you dismay...."

TEN FILMS ABOUT CRIME
AND CHRISTMAS

Christmas Holiday (1944) in which socio-path Gene Kelly terrorizes his wife Deanna Durbin with the help of his mother Gale Sondergaard. No dancing, just guns and psychopathology.

The Lemon Drop Kid (1951) in which con artist Bob Hope sets up a phoney old folks home for Jane Darwell and her friends in order to swindle some mobsters out of $10,000 in old racing debts.

Lady in the Lake (1946) in which Robert Montgomery (Philip Marlowe) is seen only in reflections as he solves a case of disappearance and murder in this adaptation of Raymond Chandler's classic, reset at Christmastime.

The Thin Man (1933) in which William Powell (Nick Charles) shoots the ornaments off his Christmas tree while he and Myrna Loy (Nora) contemplate the fate of a missing inventor.

Larceny Inc. (1942) from S. J. Perelman's play "The Night Before Christmas" in which

Edward G. Robinson's attempts to go straight are thwarted by Anthony Quinn.

I'll Be Seeing You (1944) in which furloughed convict Ginger Rogers becomes romantically involved with emotionally disturbed GI Joseph Cotten at Christmastime.

Remember the Night (1940) in which shoplifter Barbara Stanwyck gets invited home for Christmas by assistant-D.A. Fred MacMurray.

Three Godfathers (1947) in which John Wayne as one of three outlaws on the run at Christmastime acquires a baby on the way to New Jerusalem, Arizona.

The Mystery of Edwin Drood (1935) in which Claude Rains is suspected of a Christmas Eve murder in an adaptation and completion of Charles Dickens's unfinished novel.

Black Christmas (1974) in which Margot Kidder and Olivia Hussey are stalked by an unseen killer in a sorority house as detective John Saxon tries to discover why.

There have been many prolific authors in the mystery genre, but few have been so completely identified with the short story as Edward D. Hoch. In a time when writers were turning short story ideas into novels for greater financial gain, Hoch has found equal success telling his stories in the form to which they are best suited.

Though he has written four novels, his reputation unquestionably rests on the hundreds of short stories that have come from his pen. He has created four series characters; Nick Velvet, the raffish, Rafflish thief; Simon Ark, the 2000-year-old detective; "Rand," a British cryptographer and spy, and Captain Leopold, the protagonist of "Christmas Is For Cops."

Leopold is representative of the detective as he has survived the socio-economic upheaval of the last twenty years. The police, and the police procedural, became an instrument for voicing social concern while adhering to the basic outlines of the traditional mystery story. It had begun in the late 1940's with the works of Lawrence Treat and Hillary Waugh, and continues to flourish today in the works of Lawrence Sanders, Ed McBain and many others. About a decade ago it reached the zenith of its popularity, both in television (Kojak) and films (The French Connection).

Hoch's own durability comes from his mastery of this form and many others, and the straight-forward, unaffected way he addresses his reader. No gimmicks, no posturing, just good honest story-telling.

Christmas Is for Cops

by Edward D. Hoch

"GOING TO THE Christmas party, Captain?" Fletcher asked from the doorway. Captain Leopold glanced up from his eternally cluttered desk. Fletcher was now a lieutenant in the newly reorganized Violent Crimes Division, and they did not work together as closely as they once had. "I'll be there," Leopold said. "In fact, I've been invited to speak."

This news brought a grin to Fletcher's face. "Nobody speaks at the Christmas party, Captain. They just drink."

"Well, this year you're going to hear a speech, and I'm going to give it."

"Lots of luck."

"Is your wife helping with the decorations again this year?"

"I suppose she'll be around," Fletcher chuckled. "She doesn't trust me at any Christmas party without her."

The annual Detective Bureau party was, by tradition, a stag affair. But in recent years Carol Fletcher and some of the other wives had come down to Eagles Hall in the afternoon to trim the tree and hang the holly. Somehow these members of the unofficial Decorations Committee usually managed to stay on for the evening's festivities.

The party was the following evening, and Captain Leopold was looking forward to it. But he had one unpleasant task to perform first. That afternoon, feeling he could delay it no longer, he summoned Sergeant Tommy Gibson to his office and closed the door.

Gibson was a tough cop of the old school, a bleak and burly man who'd campaigned actively for the lieutenancy which had finally been given to Fletcher. Leopold had never liked Gibson, but until now he'd managed to overlook the petty graft with which Gibson's name was occasionally linked.

"What seems to be the trouble, Captain?" Gibson asked, taking a seat. "You look unhappy."

"I am unhappy, Gibson. Damned unhappy! While you were working the assault and robbery detail I had no direct command over your activities. But now that I'm in charge of a combined Violent Crimes Division, I feel I should take a greater interest in them." He reached across his desk to pick up a folder. "I have a report here from the District Attorney's office. The report mentions you, Gibson, and makes some very grave charges."

"What kind of charges?" the sergeant's tongue forked out to lick his dry lips.

"That you've been accepting regular payments from a man named Freese."

Gibson went pale. "I don't know what you're talking about."

"Carl Freese, the man who runs the numbers racket in every factory in this city. You know who he is, and you know what he's done. Men who've opposed him, or tried to report his operations to the police, have been beaten and nearly killed. I have a report here of a foreman at Lecko Industries. When some of his men started losing a whole week's pay in the numbers and other gambling controlled by Freese, he went to his supervisor and reported it. That night on the way home his car was forced off the road and he was badly beaten, so badly that he spent three weeks in the hospital. You should be familiar with that case, Gibson, because you investigated it just last summer."

"I guess I remember it."

"Remember your report, too? You wrote it off as a routine robbery attempt, despite the fact that no money was taken from the victim. The victim reported it to the District Attorney's office, and they've been investigating the whole matter of gambling in local industrial plants. I have their report here."

"I investigate a lot of cases, Captain. I try to do the best job I can."

"Nuts!" Leopold was on his feet, angry now. There was nothing that angered him more than a crooked cop. "Look, Gibson, the D.A.'s office has all of Freese's records. They show payments of $100 a week to you. What in hell were you doing for $100 a week, unless you were covering up for them when they beat some poor guy senseless?"

"Those records are wrong," Gibson said. "I didn't get any hundred bucks a week."

"Then how much did you get?"

Leopold towered over him in the chair, and Gibson's burly frame seemed to shrivel. "I think I want a lawyer," he mumbled.

"I'm suspending you from the force without pay, effective at once. Thank God you don't have a wife and family to suffer through this."

Tommy Gibson sat silently for a moment, staring at the floor. Then at last he looked up, seeking Leopold's eyes. "Give me a chance, Captain. I wasn't in this alone."

"What's that supposed to mean?"

"I didn't get the whole hundred by myself. I had to split it with one of the other men—and he's the one who introduced me to Freese in the first place."

"There's someone else involved in this? One of the detectives?"

"Yes."

"Give me his name."

"Not yet." Gibson hesitated. "Because you wouldn't believe it. Let me give you evidence."

"What sort of evidence?"

"He and Freese came to me at my apartment and told me the type of protection they needed. That was the night we agreed on the amount of money to be paid each week. I wasn't taking any chances, Captain, so I dug out an old recording machine I'd bought after the war, and rigged up a hidden microphone behind my sofa. I got down every word they said."

"When was this?" Leopold asked.

"More than a year ago, and I've kept the recording of the conversation ever since. What's it worth to me if I bring it in?"

"I'm not in a position to make deals, Gibson."

"Would the D.A. make one?"

"I could talk to him," Leopold replied cautiously. "Let's hear what you've got first."

Gibson nodded. "I'll take the reel off my machine and bring it in to you tomorrow."

"If you're kidding me, Gibson, or stalling—"

"I'm not, Captain! I swear! I just don't want to take the whole rap myself."

"I'll give you twenty-four hours. Then the suspension goes into effect regardless."

"Thank you, Captain."

"Get the hell out of here now."

"Thank you, Captain," he said again. "And Merry Christmas."

On the day of the Christmas party, activities around the Detective Bureau slacked off very little. It was always pretty much business as usual until around four o'clock, when some of the men started drifting out, exchanging friendly seasonal comments. The party would really commence around five, when the men on the day shift arrived at Eagles Hall, and it continued until well past midnight, enabling the evening men to join in after their tours of duty.

Then there would be a buffet supper, and lots of beer, and even some group singing around the big Christmas tree. Without the family attachments of Fletcher and the other men, Leopold tended to look forward to the party. In many years it was the main event of his otherwise lonely holiday season.

By four o'clock he had heard nothing from Sergeant Tommy Gibson. With growing irritation he called Fletcher into his office. "Gibson's under your command now, isn't he, Fletcher?"

"That's right, Captain."

"What's he working on today?"

Fletcher's face flushed unexpectedly. "Well, Captain, it seems—"

"Where is he?"

"Things were a bit slower than usual, so I told him he could go over to Eagles Hall and help put up the tree for the party."

"*What!*"

Fletcher shifted his feet uneasily. "I know, Captain. But usually I help Carol and the other wives get it up. Now that I'm a lieutenant I didn't feel I could take the time off, so I sent Gibson in my place."

Leopold sighed and stood up. "All right, Fletcher. Let's get over there right away."

"Why? What's up?"

"I'll tell you on the way."

Eagles Hall was a large reasonably modern building that was rented out for wedding receptions and private parties by a local fraternal group. The Detective Bureau, through its Benevolent Association, had held a Christmas party there for the past five seasons, and its central location had helped make it a popular choice. It was close enough to attract some of the uniformed force as well as the detective squad. All were invited, and most came at some time during the long evening.

Now, before five o'clock, a handful of plainclothesmen from various divisions had already arrived. Leopold waved to Sergeant Riker of the Vice Squad, who was helping Carol Fletcher light her cigarette with a balky lighter. Then he stopped to exchange a few words with Lieutenant Williams, a bony young man who headed up the Narcotics Squad. Williams had made his reputation during a single year on the force, masquerading as a hippie musician to penetrate a group selling drugs to high school students. Leopold liked him, liked his honesty and friendliness.

"I hear you're giving a little speech tonight," Williams said, pouring him a glass of beer.

"Herb Clarke roped me into it," Leopold answered with a chuckle. "I'd better do it early, before you guys get too beered up to listen." He glanced around the big hall, taking in the twenty-foot Christmas tree with its lights and tinsel. Three guy wires held it firmly in place next to an old upright piano. "See Tommy Gibson around?"

Williams stood on tiptoe to see over the heads of some newly arrived uniformed men. "I think he's helping Carol finish up the decorations."

"Thanks." Leopold took his beer and drifted over to the far end of the room. Carol had put down her cigarette long enough to tug at one of the wires holding the tree in place. Leopold helped her tighten it and then stepped back. She was a charming, intelligent woman, and this was not the first time he'd envied Fletcher. As wife and mother she'd given him a fine home life.

"I'm surprised to see you here so early, Captain."

He helped her secure another of the wires and said, "I'm always on time to help charming wives with Christmas trees."

"And thank you for Sergeant Gibson too! He was a great help with the tree."

"I'll bet. Where is he now?"

"He took the hammer and things into the kitchen. I think he's pouring beer now." She produced another cigarette and searched her purse. Finally she asked, "Do you have a light?"

He lit it for her. "You smoke too much."

"Nervous energy. Do you like our tree?"

"Fine. Just like Christmas."

"Do you know, somewhere in Chesterton there's mention of a tree that devours birds nesting in its branches, and when spring comes the tree grows feathers instead of leaves!"

"You read too much, Carol."

She smiled up at him. "The nights are lonely being a detective's wife." The smile was just a bit forced. She didn't always approve of her husband's work.

He left her by the tree and went in search of Gibson. The burly sergeant was in the kitchen, filling pitchers of beer. He looked up, surprised, as Leopold entered. "Hello, Captain."

"I thought we had an appointment for today."

"I didn't forget. Fletcher wanted me over here."

"Where's the evidence you mentioned?"

"What?"

Leopold was growing impatient. "Come on, damn it!"

Tommy Gibson glanced out at the growing crowd. "I've got it, but I had to hide it. He's here."

"Who? The man who's in this with you?"

"Yes. I'm afraid Freese might have tipped him off about the D.A.'s investigation."

Leopold had never seen this side of Gibson—a lonely, trapped man who was actually afraid. Or else was an awfully good actor. "I've given you your twenty-four hours, Gibson. Either produce this recording you've got or—"

"Captain!" a voice interrupted. "We're ready for your speech."

Leopold turned to see Sergeant Turner of Missing Persons.

standing in the doorway. "I'll be right there, Jim." Turner seemed to linger just a bit too long before he turned and walked away. Leopold looked back at Gibson. "That him?"

"I can't talk now, Captain."

"Where'd you hide it?"

"Over by the tree. It's safe."

"Stick around till after my talk. Then we'll get to the bottom of this thing."

Leopold left him pouring another pitcher of beer and walked out through the crowd. With the end of the afternoon shifts the place had filled rapidly. There were perhaps sixty members of the force present already, about evenly divided between detectives and uniformed patrolmen. Several shook his hand or patted him on the back as he made his way to the dais next to the tree.

Herb Clarke, president of the Detective Bureau Benevolent Association, was already on the platform, holding up his hands for silence. He shook Leopold's hand and then turned to his audience. "Gather around now, men. The beer'll still be there in five minutes. You all know we're not much for speeches at these Christmas parties, but I thought it might be well this year to hear a few words from a man we all know and admire. Leopold has been in the Detective Bureau for as long as most of us can remember—" The laughter caused him to add quickly, "Though of course he's still a young man. But this year, in addition to his duties as Captain of Homicide, he's taken on a whole new set of responsibilities. He's now head of the entire Violent Crimes Division of the Bureau, a position that places him in more direct contact with us all. I'm going to ask him to say just a few words, and then we'll have some caroling around the piano."

Leopold stepped over to the microphone, adjusting it upward from the position Herb Clarke had used. Then he looked out at the sea of familiar faces. Carol Fletcher and the other wives hovered in the rear, out of the way, while their husbands and the others crowded around. Fletcher himself stood with Sergeant Riker, an old friend, and Leopold noticed that Lieutenant Williams had moved over near Tommy Gibson. He couldn't see Jim Turner at the moment.

"Men, I'm going to make this worth listening to for all that. You hear a lot at this time of the year about Christmas being the season for kids, but I want to add something to that. Christmas is for kids, sure—but Christmas is for cops, too. Know what I mean by that? I'll tell you. Christmas is perhaps the one time of the year when the cop on the beat, or the detective on assignment, has a chance to undo some of the ill will generated during the other eleven months. This has been a bad year for cops around the country—most years are bad ones, it seems. We take a hell of a lot of abuse, some deserved, but most of it not. And this is the season to maybe right some of those wrongs. Don't be afraid to get out on a corner with the Salvation Army to ring a few bells, or help some lady through a puddle of slush. Most of all, don't be afraid to smile and talk to young people."

He paused and glanced down at Tommy Gibson. "There have always been some bad cops, and I guess there always will be. That just means the rest of us have to work a lot harder. Maybe we can just pretend the whole year is Christmas, and go about righting those wrongs. Anyway, I've talked so long already I've grown a bit thirsty. Let's get back to the beer and the singing, and make it good and loud!"

Leopold jumped off the platform and shook more hands. He'd meant to speak longer, to give them something a bit meatier to chew on, but far at the back of the crowd some of the younger cops were already growing restless. And, after all, they'd come here to enjoy themselves, not to listen to a lecture. He couldn't really blame them.

Herb Clarke was gathering everyone around the piano for songs, but Leopold noticed that Tommy Gibson had suddenly disappeared. The Captain threaded his way through the crowd, searching the familiar faces for the man he wanted. "Great talk, Captain," Fletcher said, coming up by his side.

"Did he tell you any more?"

"Only that he had to hide the tape near the Christmas tree. He said the other guy was here."

"Who do you make it, Captain?"

Leopold bit his lower lip. "I make it that Tommy Gibson is one smart cookie. I think he's playing for time, maybe waiting for Freese to get him off the hook somehow."

"You don't think there's another crooked cop in the Detective Bureau?"

"I don't know, Fletcher. I guess I don't want to think so."

The door to the Men's Room sprang open with a suddenness that surprised them both. Sergeant Riker, his usually placid face full of alarm, stood motioning to them. Leopold quickly covered the ground to his side. "What is it, Riker?"

"In there! My God, Captain—in there! It's Gibson!"

"What?"

"Tommy Gibson. He's been stabbed. I think he's dead."

Leopold pushed past him, into the tiled Men's Room with its scrubbed look and disinfectant odor. Tommy Gibson was there, all right, crumpled between two of the wash basins, his eyes glazed and open. A long pair of scissors protruded from his chest.

"Lock all the outside doors, Fletcher," Leopold barked. "Don't let anyone leave."

"Is he dead, Captain?"

"As dead as he'll ever be. What a mess!"

"You think one of our men did it?"

"Who else? Call in and report it, and get the squad on duty over here. Everyone else is a suspect." He stood up from examining the body and turned to Riker. "Now tell me everything you know, Sergeant."

Riker was a Vice Squad detective, a middle-aged man

with a placid disposition and a friendly manner. There were those who said he could even make a street-walker like him while he was arresting her. Just now he looked sick and pale. "I walked in and there he was, Captain. My God! I couldn't believe my eyes at first. I thought he was faking, playing some sort of a trick."

"Notice anyone leaving before you went in?"

"No, nobody."

"But he's only been dead a few minutes. That makes you a suspect, Sergeant."

Riker's pale complexion seemed to shade into green at Leopold's words. "You can't think I killed him! He was a friend of mine! Why in hell would I kill Tommy Gibson?"

"We'll see," Leopold said, motioning him out of the Men's Room. The other detectives and officers were clustered around, trying to see. There was a low somber hum of conversation. "All right, everyone!" the Captain ordered. "Keep down at the other end of the room, away from the tree! That's right, move away from it."

"Captain!" It was little Herb Clarke, pushing his way through. "Captain, what's happened?"

"Someone killed Tommy Gibson."

"Tommy!"

"One of us. That's why nobody leaves here."

"You can't be serious, Captain. Murder at the police Christmas party—the newspapers will crucify us."

"Probably," Leopold pushed past him. "Nobody enters the Men's Room," he bellowed. "Fletcher, Williams—come with me." They were the only two lieutenants present, and he had to trust them. Fletcher he'd trust with his life. He only hoped he could rely on Williams too.

"I can't believe it," the bony young Narcotics lieutenant said. "Why would anyone kill Tommy?"

Leopold cleared his throat. "I'll tell you why, though you may not want to believe it. Gibson was implicated in the District Attorney's investigation of Carl Freese's gambling empire. He had a tape recording of a conversation between Freese, himself, and another detective, apparently concerning bribery. The other detective had a dandy motive for killing him."

"Did he say who it was?" Williams asked.

"No. Only that it was someone who got here fairly early today. Who was here before Fletcher and I arrived?"

Williams creased his brow in thought. "Riker was here, and Jim Turner. And a few uniformed men."

"No, just detectives."

"Well, I guess Riker and Turner were the only ones. And Herb Clarke, of course. He was here all day with the ladies, arranging for the food and the beer."

"Those three," Leopold mused. "And you, of course."

Lieutenant Williams grinned. "Yeah, and me."

Leopold turned toward the big Christmas tree. "Gibson told me he hid the tape recording near the tree. Start looking, and don't miss anything. It might even be in the branches."

The investigating officers were arriving now, and Leopold turned his attention to them. There was something decidedly bizarre in the entire situation, a fact which was emphasized as the doctor and morgue attendants and police photographers exchanged muted greetings with the milling party guests. One of the young investigating detectives who'd known Tommy Gibson turned pale at the sight of the body and had to go outside.

When the photographers had finished, one of the morgue men started to lift the body. He paused and called to Leopold. "Captain, here's something. A cigarette lighter on the floor under him."

Leopold bent close to examine it without disturbing possible prints. "Initials. C.F."

Lieutenant Williams had come in behind him, standing at the door of the Men's Room. "Carl Freese?" he suggested.

Leopold used a handkerchief to pick it up carefully by the corners. "Are we supposed to believe that Freese entered this place in the midst of sixty cops and killed Gibson without anybody seeing him?"

"There's a window in the wall over there."

Leopold walked to the frosted pane and examined it. "Locked from the inside. Gibson might have been stabbed from outside, but he couldn't have locked the window and gotten across this room without leaving a trail of blood."

Fletcher had come in while they were talking. "No dice on that, Captain. My wife just identified the scissors as a pair she was using earlier with the decorations. It's an inside job, all right."

Leopold showed the lighter. "C.F. Could be Carl Freese."

Fletcher frowned and licked his lips. "Yeah." He turned away.

"Nothing," Williams reported.

"Nothing *in* the tree? It could be a fairly small reel."

"Nothing."

Leopold sighed and motioned Fletcher and Williams to one side. He didn't want the others to hear. "Look, I think Gibson was probably lying, too. But he's dead, and that very fact indicates he might have been telling the truth. I have to figure all the angles. Now that you two have searched the tree I want you to go into the kitchen, close the door, and search each other. Carefully."

"But—" Williams began. "All right, Captain."

"Then line everybody up and do a search of them. You know what you're looking for—a reel of recording tape."

"What about the wives, Captain?"

"Get a matron down for them. I'm sorry to have to do it, but if that tape is here we have to find it."

He walked to the center of the hall and stood looking at the tree. Lights and tinsel, holiday wreaths and sprigs of mistletoe. All the trappings. He tried to imagine Tommy Gibson helping to decorate the place, helping with the tree. Where would he have hidden the tape?

Herb Clarke came over and said, "They're searching everybody."

"Yes. I'm sorry to spoil the party this way, but I guess it was spoiled for Gibson already."

"Captain, do you have to go on with this? Isn't one dishonest man in the Bureau enough?"

"One is too many, Herb. But the man we're looking for is more than a dishonest cop now. He's a murderer."

Fletcher came over to them. "We've searched all the detectives, Captain. They're clean. We're working on the uniformed men now."

Leopold grunted unhappily. He was sure they'd find nothing. "Suppose," he said slowly. "Suppose Gibson unreeled the tape. Suppose he strung it on the tree like tinsel."

"You see any brown tinsel hanging anywhere, Captain? See any tinsel of any color long enough to be a taped message?"

"No, I don't," Leopold said.

Two of the sergeants, Riker and Turner, came over to join them. "Could he have done it to himself?" Turner asked. "The word is you were going to link him with the Freese investigation."

"Stabbing yourself in the chest with a pair of scissors isn't exactly common as a suicide method," Leopold pointed out. "Besides, it would be out of character for a man like Gibson."

One of the investigating officers came over with the lighter. "Only smudges on it, Captain. Nothing we could identify."

"Thanks." Leopold took it, turning it over between his fingers.

C.F. Carl Freese.

He flicked the lever a couple of times but it didn't light. Finally, on the fourth try, a flame appeared. "All right," he said quietly. Now he knew.

"Captain—" Fletcher began.

"Damn it, Fletcher, it's your wife's lighter and you know it! C.F. Not Carl Freese but Carol Fletcher!"

"Captain, I—" Fletcher stopped.

Leopold felt suddenly very tired. The colored lights of the tree seemed to blur, and he wished he was far away, in a land where all cops were honest and everyone died of old age.

Sergeant Riker moved in. "Captain, are you trying to say that Fletcher's *wife* stabbed Tommy Gibson?"

"Of course not, Riker. That would have been quite a trick for her to follow him into the Men's Room unnoticed. Besides, I had to give her a match at one point this evening, because she didn't have this lighter."

"Then who?"

"When I first arrived, you were helping Carol Fletcher with a balky lighter. Yes, you, Riker! You dropped it into your pocket, unthinking, and that's why she didn't have it later. It fell out while you were struggling with Gibson. While you were killing him, Riker."

Riker muttered a single obscenity and his hand went for the service revolver on his belt. Leopold had expected it. He moved in fast and threw two quick punches, one to the stomach and one to the jaw. Riker went down and it was over.

Carol Fletcher heard what had happened and she came over to Leopold. "Thanks for recovering my lighter," she said. "I hope you didn't suspect me."

He shook his head, eyeing Fletcher. "Of course not. But I sure as hell wish your husband had told me it was yours."

"I had to find out what it was doing there," Fletcher mumbled. "God, it's not every day your wife's lighter, that you gave her two Christmases ago, turns up as a clue in a murder."

Leopold handed it back to her. "Maybe this'll teach you to stop smoking."

"You knew it was Riker anyway?"

"I was pretty sure. With sixty men drinking beer all around here, no murderer could take a chance of walking out of that Men's Room unseen. His best bet was to pretend finding the body, which is just what he did. Besides that, of the four detectives on the scene early, Riker's Vice Squad position was the most logical for Freese's bribery."

"Was there a tape recording?" Fletcher asked.

Leopold was staring at the Christmas tree. "I think Gibson was telling the truth on that one. Except that *he* never called it a tape. I did that. I jumped to a conclusion. He simply told me it was an old machine, purchased after the war. In those early days tape recorders weren't the only kind. For a while wire recorders were almost as popular."

"Wire!"

Leopold nodded and started toward the Christmas tree. "We know that Gibson helped you put up the tree, Carol. I'm betting that one of those wires holding it in place is none other than the recorded conversation of Carl Freese, Tommy Gibson, and Sergeant Riker."

"Kill!"

Still regarded as the Queen of American mystery writers over thirty years after her death, Mary Roberts Rinehart is better known by reputation than first-hand acquaintance. She turned to her craft as a sideline after nursing school, to support her physician husband and three small sons during a period of economic hardship. Her works were successful from the start and began a career that extended over half a century.

Among the best of her output are the novels The Man in Lower Ten, The Red Lamp, and The Yellow Room; the short stories "Alibi for Isabel" and "The Lipstick"; and The Circular Staircase, which was later adapted into the much revived play, The Bat, a success on Broadway, in its movie version (with Agnes Moorehead and Vincent Price), and on television (with Helen Hayes and Jason Robards).

Mrs. Rinehart is best remembered as the founder of the Had-I-But-Known school of mystery writing, which critics often also regard as the None-Too-Bright-Damsel-in-Distress school of suspense. This does her memory a disservice. She was at her finest a skilled manipulator of plots, perhaps the closest thing to an Agatha Christie that this country produced.

If you know Mary Roberts Rinehart only by reputation, I think you are in for a pleasant surprise. This is an excellent story from one of America's greatest mystery writers.

The Butler's
Christmas Eve

by Mary Roberts Rinehart

WILLIAM STOOD IN the rain waiting for the bus. In the
fading daylight he looked rather like a freshly washed
eighty-year-old and beardless Santa Claus, and underneath
his raincoat he clutched a parcel which contained a much-
worn nightshirt, an extra pair of socks, a fresh shirt and a
brand-new celluloid collar. It also contained a pint flask of
the best Scotch whisky.

Not that William drank, or at least not to speak of. The
whisky was a gift, and in more than one way it was definitely contraband. It was whisky which had caused his trouble.

The Christmas Eve crowd around him was wet but amiable.

"Look, mama, what have you done with the suitcase?"

"What do you think you're sitting on? A bird cage?"

The crowd laughed. The rain poured down. The excited
children were restless. They darted about, were lost and
found again. Women scolded.

"You stand right here, Johnny. Keep under this umbrella.
That's your new suit."

When the bus came along one of them knocked William's
package into the gutter, and he found himself shaking with

anxiety. But the bottle was all right. He could feel it, still intact. The Old Man would have it, all right, Miss Sally or no Miss Sally; the Old Man, left sitting in a wheelchair with one side of his big body dead and nothing warm in his stomach to comfort him. Just a year ago tonight on Christmas Eve William had slipped him a small drink to help him sleep, and Miss Sally had caught him at it.

She had not said anything. She had kissed her grandfather good-night and walked out of the room. But the next morning she had come into the pantry where William was fixing the Old Man's breakfast tray and dismissed him, after fifty years.

"I'm sorry, William. But you know he is forbidden liquor."

William put down the Old Man's heated egg cup and looked at her.

"It was only because it was Christmas Eve, Miss Sally. He was kind of low, with Mr. Tony gone and everything."

She went white at that, but her voice was even.

"I am trying to be fair," she said. "But even without this —You have worked a long time, and grandfather is too heavy for you to handle. I need a younger man, now that—"

She did not finish. She did not say that her young husband had enlisted in the Navy after Pearl Harbor, and that she had fought tooth and nail against it. Or that she suspected both her grandfather and William of supporting him.

William gazed at her incredulously.

"I've handled him, one way and another, for fifty years, Miss Sally."

"I know all that. But I've talked to the doctor. He agrees with me."

He stood very still. She couldn't do this to him, this girl he had raised, and her father before her. She couldn't send him out at his age to make a life for himself, after living a vicarious one in this house for half a century. But he saw helplessly that she could and that she meant to.

"When am I to go?" he asked.

"It would be kinder not to see him again, wouldn't it?"

"You can't manage alone, Miss Sally," he said stubbornly. But she merely made a little gesture with her hands.

"I'm sorry, William. I've already arranged for someone else."

He took the breakfast tray to the Old Man's door and gave it to the nurse. Then he went upstairs to his room and standing inside looked around him. This had been his room for most of his life. On the dresser was the faded snapshot of the Old Man as a Major in the Rough Riders during the Spanish War. There was a picture of Miss Sally's father, his only son, who had not come home from France in 1918. There was a very new one of Mr. Tony, young and good-looking and slightly defiant, taken in his new Navy uniform. And of course there were pictures of Miss Sally herself, ranging from her baby days to the one of her, smiling and lovely, in her wedding dress.

William had helped to rear her. Standing there he remembered the day when she was born. The Major—he was Major Bennett then, not the Old Man—had sent for him when he heard the baby's mother was dead.

"Well," he said heavily, "it looks as though we've got a child to raise. A girl at that! Think we can do it?"

"We've done harder things, sir," said William.

"All right," said the Major. "But get this, William, I want no spoiled brat around the place. If I find you spoiling her, by the Lord Harry I'll fire you."

"I won't spoil her," William had said sturdily. "But she'll probably be as stubborn as a mule."

"Now why the hell do you say that?" the Major had roared.

But William had only smiled.

So she had grown up. She was lovable, but she was wild as a March wind and as stubborn as the Bennetts had always been. Then—it seemed almost no time to William—she met Mr. Tony, and one day she was walking down a church aisle on her grandfather's arm, looking beautiful and sedate, and when she walked out again she was a married woman.

The old house had been gay after that. It was filled with youth and laughter. Then one day Miss Sally had gone to the hospital to have her baby, and her grandfather, gray of face, had waited for the news. William had tried to comfort him.

"I understand it's a perfectly normal process, sir," he said. "They are born every day. Millions of them."

"Get your smug face out of here," roared the Major. "You and your millions! What the hell do I care about them. It's my girl who's in trouble."

He was all right then. He was even all right when the message came that it was over, and Miss Sally and Mr. Tony had a ten-minute-old son. But going out of the hospital he had staggered and fallen, and he had never walked again. That was when the household began to call him the Old Man. Behind his back, of course.

It was tragic, because Miss Sally had had no trouble at all. She wakened at the hospital to learn that she had borne a man-child, asked if he had the proper number of fingers and toes, stated flatly that she had no intention of raising him for purposes of war, and then asked for a cigarette.

That had been two years ago, and she had come home on Christmas Eve. Mr. Tony had a little tree for the baby in the Old Man's bedroom, with Miss Sally's battered wax angel on the top, and the Old Man lay in his bed and looked at it.

"I suppose this kind of thing will save us, in the end," he said to William. "Damn it, man, people will go on having babies, and the babies will have Christmas trees, long after Hitler is dead and rotted."

The baby of course had not noticed the tree, and there was nothing to indicate that a year later William would be about to be dismissed, or that Mr. Tony, feverishly shaking a rattle before his sleeping offspring, would be in his country's uniform and somewhere on the high seas.

It was a bad year, in a way. It had told on Miss Sally, William thought. Her grandfather had taken his stroke badly. He would lie for hours, willing that stubborn will of his to move an arm, a leg, even a finger, on the stricken side.

Nothing happened, of course, and at last he had accepted it, wheelchair and all. William had helped to care for him, turning his big body when the nurse changed the sheets, bathing him when he roared that he would be eternally damned if he would allow any woman to wash him. And during the long hours of the night it had been William who sat with him while he could not sleep.

Yet Miss Sally had taken it bravely.

"He cared for me all my life," she said. "Now I can care for him. William and I."

She had done it, too. William had to grant her that. She had turned a wing of the ground floor over to him, with a porch where he could sit and look out at the sea. She gave him time and devotion. Until Pearl Harbor, that is, and the night when Mr. Tony had slipped into the Old Man's room while William was playing chess with him, and put his problem up to them.

"You know Sally," he said. "I can't even talk to her about this war. But she's safe here, and the boy too. And—well, somebody's got to fight."

The Old Man had looked down at that swollen helpless hand of his, lying in his lap.

"I see," he said. "You want to go, of course?"

"It isn't a question of wanting, is it?"

"It is, damn it," said the Old Man fiercely. "I wanted to go to Cuba. Her father couldn't get to France fast enough. I wouldn't give a tinker's curse for the fellow who doesn't want to go. But"—his voice softened—"it will hurt Sally like hell, son. She's had enough of war."

It had hurt her. She had fought it tooth and nail. But Tony had enlisted in the Navy almost at once, and he had gone a few days before Christmas. She did not cry when she saw him off, but she had the bleak look in her face which had never since entirely left it.

"I hope you enjoy it," she said.

"I don't expect to enjoy it, darling."

She was smiling, a strange stiff smile.

"Then why are you going?" she asked. "There are plenty

of men who don't have to leave a wife to look after a baby and a helpless old man. Two old men," she said, and looked at William, standing by with the bags.

She was still not crying when after he had gone she had walked to the Old Man's room. William was there. She stood in the doorway looking at them.

"I hope you're both satisfied," she said, her voice frozen. "You can sit here, safe and sound, and beat the drums all you like. But I warn you, don't beat them where I can hear them. I won't have it."

Her grandfather eyed her.

"I raised you," he said. "William and I raised you. I guess we went wrong somewhere. You're spoiled after all. And I'll beat the drums all I damn please. So will William."

Only William knew that she had not gone to bed at all that night. Some time toward morning he had seen her down on the beach in the cold, staring out at the sea.

He had trimmed the boy's tree for him that Christmas Eve. And when it was finished, with the same ancient wax angel on the top, the Old Man had suddenly asked for a drink.

"To hell with the doctors," he said. "I'll drink to Tony if it's the last thing I ever do."

As it happened, it was practically the last thing William had to do for him. For of course he had just got the liquor down when Miss Sally walked in.

She dismissed William the next morning. He had gone upstairs and packed, leaving his livery but taking the photographs with him in his battered old suitcase. When he came down the stairs Miss Sally was waiting for him. He thought she had been crying, but the bleak look was in her face again.

"I'm sorry it has to be like this, William," she said stiffly. "I have your check here, and of course if you ever need any help—"

"I've saved my money," he told her stiffly. "I can manage. If it's all right I'd like to see the baby before I go."

She nodded, and he left her and went outside. The baby

toddled to him, and William picked him up and held him close.

"You be a good boy," he said. "Be a good boy and eat your cereal every day."

"Dood boy," said the child.

William stood for a minute, looking out at the winter ocean where perhaps even now Mr. Tony might be. Then he put the child down.

"Look after him, Miss Jones," he told the nurse huskily. "He's about all his great-grandfather has left."

He found he was shaking when he got into the station wagon. Paul, the chauffeur, had to lift his suitcase. Evidently he knew. He looked concerned.

"This'll be hard as hell on the Old Man," he said. "What happened, anyhow?"

"Miss Sally's upset," said William evenly. "Mr. Tony going, and all that. She has no reason to like war."

"Who does?" said Paul glumly. "What do you bet they'll get me next?"

As they left a taxi was turning in at the gate. There was a tall swarthy man inside, and William disliked him instantly. Paul grunted.

"If that's the new fellow the Old Man will have him on his backside in a week," he said.

But so far as William knew the man was still there, and now he himself was on his way back, after a year, on some mysterious business he did not understand.

The bus rattled and roared along. The crowd was still amiable. It called Merry Christmas to each other, and strangers talked across the aisle. It was as though for this one night in the year one common bond united them. William, clutching his parcel, felt some of its warmth infecting him.

He had been very lonely. He had taken a room in the city, but most of the people he knew had died or moved away. He took out a card to the public library, and read a good bit. And when the weather was good he sat in the park at the edge of the river, watching the ships on their way up to the Sound to join their convoys. They traveled one after the other, great grayish black monsters, like elephants in a circus holding each others' tails. Sometimes they were battleships, sometimes freighters, laden to their Plimsoll marks, their decks covered with tanks and huge crates. So close were they that once on the bridge of a destroyer he thought he saw Mr. Tony. He stood up and waved his old hat, and the young officer saluted. But it was not Tony.

When the sinkings began he watched the newspapers, his heart beating fast. Then one day he saw Tony's picture. His ship had helped to rescue a crew at sea, and Tony was smiling. He looked tired and older, however. William had cut it out and sent it to the Old Man. But the only acknowledgment had been a post card. It had been duly censored for the United States Mail, and so all it said was: "Come back, you blankety blank fool."

However, if the Old Man had his pride, so did William. He had not gone back.

Then, just a week before, he had received a telegram. It too had evidently been censored, this time for the benefit of the telegraph company. So it read: DRAT YOUR STIFF-NECKED PRIDE. COME AND SEE ME. LETTER FOLLOWS.

As the bus rattled along he got out the letter. The crowd had settled down by that time. One by one the tired children had dropped off to sleep, and even the adults looked weary, as though having worked themselves into a fine pitch of excitement they had now relapsed into patient waiting. He got out his spectacles and re-read the letter.

It was a very odd sort of letter, written as it was in the Old Man's cramped hand. It was almost as though he had expected someone else to read it. If there was anything wrong it did not say so. In fact, it alluded only to a Christmas surprise for the baby. Nevertheless the directions were puzzling. William was to arrive quietly and after dark. He was to leave his taxi at the gate, walk in, and rap on the Old Man's bedroom window. It added that the writer would get rid of the nurse if he had to drown her in the bathtub, and it closed with what sounded like an appeal. "Don't be a damn fool. I need you."

He was still thinking about it when the bus reached its destination. The rain had continued, and the crowd got out to an opening of umbrellas and another search for missing parcels. William was stiff from the long ride, and the town surprised him. It was almost completely blacked out and his taxi, when he found one, had some sort of black material over all but a narrow strip on its headlights.

"Good thing too," said the driver companionably. "We're right on the coast. Too many ships getting sunk these days. One sunk off here only a week ago. If you ask me them Germans has fellows at work right in this place. Where'd you say to go?"

"The Bennett place. Out on the beach."

The driver grinned.

"Used to drive the Major now and then," he said. "Kind of a violent talker, ain't he?"

"He's had quite of bit of trouble," said William.

"Well, his granddaughter's a fine girl," said the driver. "Know where she is tonight? Trimming a tree out at the camp. I seen her there myself."

"She always was a fine girl," said William sturdily.

The driver protested when he got out at the gate.

"Better let me take you in. It's raining cats and dogs."

But William shook his head.

"I want to surprise them. I know the way."

The cab drove off to an exchange of Christmas greetings, and William started for the house. There were no lights showing as he trudged along the driveway, but he could hear ahead of him the steady boom of the waves as the Atlantic rolled in, the soft hiss of the water as it rolled up the beach. Just so for fifty years had he heard it. Only now it meant something new and different. It meant danger, men in ships watching against death; Mr. Tony perhaps somewhere out there in the dark, and the Old Man knowing it and listening, as he was listening.

He was relieved when he saw the garage doors open and no cars inside. He made his way cautiously around the house to the Old Man's wing, and stood listening under the bedroom window. There was no sound inside, however, and he wondered what to do. If he was asleep—Suddenly he sneezed, and he almost jumped out of his skin when a familiar voice spoke, almost at his ear.

"Come in, damn it," said the voice irritably. "What the hell are you waiting for? Want to catch your death of pneumonia?"

Suddenly William felt warm and comfortable again. This was what he had needed, to be sworn at and shouted at, to see the Old Man again, to hear him roar, or to be near him in contented silence. He crawled through the window, smiling happily.

"Nothing wrong with your voice, anyhow," he said. "Well, here I am, sir."

"And about time," said the Old Man. "Turn up the light and let me look at you. Shut the window and draw those curtains. Hah! You're flabby!"

"I've gained a little weight." William admitted.

"A little! Got a tummy like a bowl of jelly."

These amenities over they grinned at each other, and the Old Man held out his good hand.

"God," he said, "I'm glad to see you. We're going straight to the devil here. Well, a Merry Christmas to you anyhow."

"The same to you, sir."

They shook hands, and William surveyed the Old Man, sitting bolt upright in his wheelchair. He looked as truculent as ever, but some of the life had gone out of his face.

"So you ran out on me!" he said. "Why the devil didn't you turn Sally over your knee and spank her? I've seen you do it."

"I'm not as strong as I used to be," said William apologetically. The Old Man chuckled.

"She's a Bennett," he said. "Always was, always will be. But she's learning. Maybe it's the hard way, but she's learning." He eyed William. "Take off that coat, man," he said.

"You're dripping all over the place. What's that package? Anything in it but your nightshirt?"

"I've got a pint of Scotch," William admitted.

"Then what are we waiting for?" shouted the Old Man. "Sally's out. The nurse is out. Jarvis is out—that's the butler, if he is a butler and if that's his name. And the rest have gone to bed. Let's have it. It's Christmas Eve, man!"

"They oughtn't to leave you like that," William said reprovingly.

"Each of them thinks somebody else is looking after me." The Old Man chuckled. "Get some glasses. I guess you know your way. And take a look around when you get there."

William went back to the familiar rear of the house. His feet were wet and a small trickle of water had escaped his celluloid collar and gone down his back; but he walked almost jauntily. Until he saw his pantry, that is.

He did not like what he saw. The place even smelled unclean, and the silver was only half polished, the glasses he held to the light were smeared, and the floor felt sticky under his feet.

Resentfully he washed two glasses, dried them on a not too clean dish towel, and went back. The Old Man watched him from under his heavy eyebrows.

"Well, what do you think of it?" he inquired. "Is the fellow a butler?"

"He's not a good one, sir."

But the Old Man said nothing more. He took his glass and waited until William had poured his own drink. Then he lifted the glass.

"To Tony," he said. "A safe Christmas to him, and to all the other men with the guts to fight this war."

It was like a prayer. It probably was a prayer, and William echoed it.

"To Mr. Tony," he said, "and all the rest."

Then at last the Old Man explained his letter. He didn't trust the man Jarvis. Never had. Too smooth. Sally, of

course, did not suspect him, although he was damned inefficient. Anyhow what could she do, with every able-bodied
man in service or making armament?

"But there's something queer about him," he said. "And
you may not know it, but we had a ship torpedoed out here
last week. Some of the men landed on the beach. Some
never landed anywhere, poor devils."

"I heard about it," said William. "What do you want me
to do?"

"How the hell do I know?" said the Old Man. "Look
around. See if there's anything suspicious. And if there
isn't, get rid of him anyhow. I don't like him."

A thin flush rose to William's wrinkled face.

"You mean I'm to stay?" he inquired.

"Why the devil do you suppose I brought you back?"
shouted the Old Man. "Don't stand there staring. Get busy.
We haven't got all night."

William's strictly amateur activities, however, yielded
him nothing. His old room—now belonging to Jarvis—surprised him by its neatness, but unless that in itself was suspicious, there was nothing more. No flashlight for signaling,
no code book, which William would certainly not have recognized anyhow, not even a radio.

"Tidy, is it?" said the Old Man when he reported back.
"Well, I suppose that's that. I'd hoped to hand the F. B. I. a
Christmas gift, but—All right, no spy. I've got another job
for you, one you'll like better." He leaned back in his chair
and eyed William quizzically. "Sally's not having a tree this
year for the boy. I don't blame her. For months she's worked
her fool head off. Army, Navy, and what have you. She's
tired. Maybe she's breaking her heart. Sometimes I think she
is. But by the Lord Harry he's having a tree just the same."

William looked at his watch.

"It's pretty late to buy one," he said. "But of course I can
try."

The Old Man grinned, showing a perfect set of his own
teeth, only slightly yellowed.

"Think I'm getting old, don't you?" he scoffed. "Always did think you were smarter than I was, didn't you? Well, I'm not in my dotage yet. The tree's on the porch. Had it delivered tonight. Unless," he added unkindly, "you're too feeble to drag it in!"

William also grinned, showing a perfect set of teeth, certainly not his own, except by purchase.

"I suppose you wouldn't care to take a bet on it, sir?" he said happily.

Ten minutes later the tree was in place in a corner of the Old Man's sitting room. William was perspiring but triumphant. The Old Man himself was exhilarated with one small drink and an enormous pride. Indeed, both were eminently cheerful until, without warning, they heard the sound of a car outside.

It was Sally, and before she had put up her car and got back to the house, William was hidden in the darkened sitting room, and her grandfather was sedately reading in his chair beside a lamp. From where he stood William could see her plainly. She had changed, he thought. She looked older. But she looked gentler, too, as though at last she had learned some of the lessons of life. Her eyes were no longer bleak, but they were sunken in her head. Nevertheless William felt a thrill of pride. She was their girl, his and the Old Man's, and now she was a woman. A lovely woman, too. Even William, no connoisseur, could see that.

"Good gracious, why aren't you in bed?" she said, slipping off her fur coat. "And where's the nurse?"

"It's Christmas Eve, my dear. I sent her off for a while. She'll be back."

But Sally was not listening. Even William could see that. She sat down on the edge of a chair and twisted her fingers in her lap.

"There wasn't any mail, was there?"

"I'm afraid not. Of course we don't know where he is. It may be difficult for him to send any."

Suddenly she burst out.

"Why don't you say it?" she demanded. "You always say what you think. I sent Tony off wrong. I can't forgive myself for that. I was wrong about William, too. You miss him, don't you?"

"Miss him?" said the Old Man, deliberately raising his voice. "Why would I miss the old rascal? Always pottering around and doing nothing! I get along fine without him."

"I think you're lying to make me feel better," she said, and got up. "I was wrong about him, and tonight I realized I'd been wrong about the baby's tree. When I saw the men around the one we'd fixed for them—I've made a mess of everything, haven't I?"

"Most of us do, my dear," said her grandfather. "But we learn. We learn."

She went out then, closing the door quietly behind her. When William went into the bedroom he found the Old Man staring somberly at the fire.

"Damn war anyhow," he said violently. "Damn the blasted lunatics who wished it on the earth. All I need now is for some idiots to come around and sing 'Peace on earth, good will to men!'"

As though it might have been a signal, from beyond the window suddenly came a chorus of young voices, and William gingerly raised the shade. Outside, holding umbrellas in one hand and clutching their blowing cassocks around them with the other, the choir boys from the nearby church were singing, their small scrubbed faces earnest and intent. They sang about peace, and the King of peace who had been born to save the world, and the Old Man listened. When they had gone he grinned sheepishly.

"Well, maybe they're right at that," he said. "Sooner or later peace has to come. How about a small drink to the idea, anyhow?"

They drank it together and in silence, and once more they were back where they had been a year ago. No longer master and man, but two friends of long standing, content merely to be together.

"So you've been doing fine without me, sir?" said William, putting down his glass.

"Hell, did you hear that?" said the Old Man innocently.

They chuckled as at some ancient joke.

It was after eleven when William in his socks made his way to the attic where the trimmings for the tree were stored. Sally was still awake. He could hear her stirring in her room. For a moment he stood outside and listened, and it seemed no time at all since he had done the same thing when she was a child, and had been punished and sent to bed. He would stand at her door and tap, and she would open it and throw herself sobbing into his arms.

"I've been a bad girl, William."

He would hold her and pat her thin little back.

"Now, now," he would say. "Take it easy, Sally. Maybe William can fix it for you."

But of course there was nothing he could fix now. He felt rather chilly as he climbed the attic stairs.

To his relief the attic was orderly. He turned on the light and moving cautiously went to the corner where the Christmas tree trimmings, neatly boxed and covered, had always stood. They were still there. He lifted them, one by one, and placed them behind him. Then he stiffened and stood staring.

Neatly installed behind where they had been was a small radio transmitter.

He knew it at once for what it was, and a slow flush of fury suffused his face as he knelt down to examine it.

"The spy!" he muttered thickly, "the dirty devil of a spy!"

So this was how it was done. This was how ships were being sunk at sea; the convoys assembling, the ships passing along the horizon, and men like Jarvis watching, ready to unleash the waiting submarine wolves upon them.

He was trying to tear it out with his bare hands when he heard a voice behind him.

"Stay where you are, or I'll shoot."

But it was not Jarvis. It was Sally, white and terrified, in a dressing gown over her nightdress and clutching a revolver in her hand. William got up slowly and turned, and she gasped and dropped the gun.

"Why, William!" she said. "What are you doing here?"

He stood still, concealing the transmitter behind his stocky body.

"Your grandfather sent for me," he said, with dignity. "He was planning a little surprise for you and the boy, in the morning."

She looked at him, at his dependable old face, at the familiar celluloid collar gleaming in the light, at his independent sturdy figure, and suddenly her chin quivered.

"Oh, William," she said. "I've been such a dreadful person."

All at once she was in his arms, crying bitterly.

"Everything's so awful," she sobbed. "I'm so frightened, William. I can't help it."

And once more he was holding her and saying:

"It will be all right, Sally girl. Don't you worry. It will be all right."

She quieted, and at last he got her back to her room. He found that he was shaking, but he went methodically to work. He did what he could to put the transmitter out of business. Then he piled up the boxes of trimmings and carried them down the stairs. There was still no sign of Jarvis, and the Old Man was dozing in his chair. William hesitated. Then he shut himself in the sitting room and cautiously called the chief of the local police.

"This is William," he said. "The butler at Major Bennett's. I—"

"So you're back, you old buzzard, are you?" said the chief. "Well, Merry Christmas and welcome home."

But he sobered when William told him what he had discovered. He promised to round up some men, and not—at William's request—to come as if they were going to a fire.

"We'll get him all right," he said. "We'll get all these dirty polecats sooner or later. All right. No siren. We'll ring the doorbell."

William felt steadier after that. He was in the basement

getting a ladder for trimming the tree when he heard Jarvis come back. But he went directly up the back stairs to his room, and William, listening below, felt that he would not visit the attic that night.

He was singularly calm now. The Old Man was sound asleep by that time, and snoring as violently as he did everything else. William placed the ladder and hung the wax angel on the top of the tree. Then he stood precariously and surveyed it.

"Well, we're back," he said. "We're kind of old and battered, but we're still here, thank God."

Which in its way was a prayer too, like the Old Man's earlier in the evening.

He got down, his legs rather stiff, and going into the other room touched the sleeper lightly on the shoulder. He jerked awake.

"What the hell did you do that for?" he roared. "Can't a man take a nap without your infernal interfering?"

"The tree's ready to trim," said William quietly.

Fifteen minutes later the nurse came back. The bedroom was empty, and in the sitting room before a half-trimmed tree the Old Man was holding a small—a very small—drink in his hand. He waved his glass at her outraged face.

"Merry Christmas," he said, a slight—a very slight—thickness in his voice. "And get me that telegram that came for Sally today."

She looked disapprovingly at William, a William on whom the full impact of the situation—plus a very small drink—had suddenly descended like the impact of a pile-driver. Her austere face softened.

"You look tired," she said. "You'd better sit down."

"Tired? Him?" scoffed the Old Man. "You don't know him. And where the hell's that telegram?"

She brought it, and he put on his spectacles to read it.

"Sally doesn't know about it," he explained. "Held it out on her. Do her good." Then he read it aloud. "Home for breakfast tomorrow. Well. Love. Merry Christmas. Tony."

He folded it and looked around, beaming.

"How's that for a surprise?" he demanded. "Merry Christmas! Hell, it will be a real Christmas for everybody."

William stood still. He wanted to say something, but his voice stuck in his throat. Then he stiffened. Back in the pantry the doorbell was ringing.

"Now exactly at what hour of the evening of December the twenty-fourth did Professor Pohlman query you as to the best method of killing Miss Burkhardt?"

"Straight ahead, Bernie, dear."

From *The Spectator* Letter Bag of Friday, December 28, 1711

Mr. Spectator

I am a Footman in a great Family, and am in Love with the Housemaid. We were all at Hot Cockles last Night in the Hall these Holidays; when I lay down and was blinded, she pulled off her Shoe, and hit me with the Heel such a Rap, as almost broke my Head to Pieces. Pray, sir, was this Love or Spite?

Richard Steele

Any discussion of impossible crimes must get around to John Dickson Carr. Whether under his own name or his pseudonym Carter Dickson, he literally wrote the book on the subject of locked-room crimes. He liked concocting puzzles and presenting them to his readers as a literary challenge. The characters in his stories were usually second-rate. Motive didn't count for much either. What mattered was how the crime had been done.

Though born in Uniontown, Pennsylvania, Carr became a through-and-through Anglophile, spending the major portion of his professional career in Britain. He became head of London's famous Detection Club, an elite group of writers that numbered Dorothy L. Sayers, Agatha Christie and G. K. Chesterton among its members. In his last years, Carr was also a book critic and wrote a column for Ellery Queen's Mystery magazine.

Besides a fondness for things English, Carr also had a penchant for costume melodrama and historical settings. Both are in evidence in "Blind Man's Hood," which appeared in his famous collection The Department of Queer Complaints (1940).

Carr would later cite G. K. Chesterton as one of the great inspirations of his writing, but this story indicates a debt to Dickens as well.

Blind Man's Hood

by Carter Dickson

ALTHOUGH ONE SNOWFLAKE had already sifted past the lights, the great doors of the house stood open. It seemed less a snowflake than a shadow; for a bitter wind whipped after it, and the doors creaked. Inside, Rodney and Muriel Hunter could see a dingy narrow hall paved in dull red tiles, with a Jacobean staircase at the rear. (At that time, of course, there was no dead woman lying inside.)

To find such a place in the loneliest part of the Weald of Kent—a seventeenth-century country house whose floors had grown humped and its beams scrubbed by the years—was what they had expected. Even to find electricity was not surprising. But Rodney Hunter thought he had seldom seen so many lights in one house, and Muriel had been wondering about it ever since their car turned the bend in the road. "Clearlawns" lived up to its name. It stood in the midst of a slope of flat grass, now wiry white with frost, and there was no tree or shrub within twenty yards of it. Those lights contrasted with a certain inhospitable and damp air about the house, as though the owner were compelled to keep them burning.

"But why is the front door *open?*" insisted Muriel.

126

In the drive-way, the engine of their car coughed and died. The house was now a secret blackness of gables, emitting light at every chink, and silhouetting the stalks of the wistaria vines which climbed it. On either side of the front door were little-paned windows whose curtains had not been drawn. Towards their left they could see into a low dining-room, with table and sideboard set for a cold supper; towards their right was a darkish library moving with the reflections of a bright fire.

The sight of the fire warmed Rodney Hunter, but it made him feel guilty. They were very late. At five o'clock, without fail, he had promised Jack Bannister, they would be at "Clearlawns" to inaugurate the Christmas party.

Engine-trouble in leaving London was one thing; idling at a country pub along the way, drinking hot ale and listening to the wireless sing carols until a sort of Dickensian jollity stole into you, was something else. But both he and Muriel were young; they were very fond of each other, and of things in general; and they had worked themselves into a glow of Christmas, which—as they stood before the creaking doors of "Clearlawns"—grew oddly cool.

There was no real reason, Rodney thought, to feel disquiet. He hoisted their luggage, including a big box of presents for Jack and Molly's children, out of the rear of the car. That his footsteps should sound loud on the gravel was only natural. He put his head into the doorway and whistled. Then he began to bang the knocker. Its sound seemed to seek out every corner of the house and then come back like a questing dog; but there was no response.

"I'll tell you something else," he said. "There's nobody in the house."

Muriel ran up the three steps to stand beside him. She had drawn her fur coat close around her, and her face was bright with cold.

"But that's impossible!" she said. "I mean, even if they're out, the servants—! Molly told me she keeps a cook and two maids. Are you sure we've got the right place?"

"Yes. The name's on the gate, and there's no other house within a mile."

With the same impulse they craned their necks to look through the windows of the dining-room on the left. Cold fowl on the sideboard, a great bowl of chestnuts; and, now they could see it, another good fire, before which stood a chair with a piece of knitting put aside on it. Rodney tried the knocker again, vigorously, but the sound was all wrong. It was as though they were even more lonely in that core of light, with the east wind rushing across the Weald, and the door creaking again.

"I suppose we'd better go in," said Rodney. He added, with a lack of Christmas spirit: "Here, this is a devil of a trick! What do you think has happened? I'll swear that fire has been made up in the last fifteen minutes."

He stepped into the hall and set down the bags. As he was turning to close the door, Muriel put her hand on his arm.

"I say, Rod. Do you think you'd better close it?"

"Why not?"

"I—I don't know."

"The place is getting chilly enough as it is," he pointed out, unwilling to admit that the same thought had occurred to him. He closed both doors and shot their bar into place; and, at the same moment, a girl came out of the door to the library on the right.

She was such a pleasant-faced girl that they both felt a sense of relief. Why she had not answered the knocking had ceased to be a question; she filled a void. She was pretty, not more than twenty-one or two, and had an air of primness which made Rodney Hunter vaguely associate her with a governess or a secretary, though Jack Bannister had never mentioned any such person. She was plump, but with a curiously narrow waist; and she wore brown. Her brown hair was neatly parted, and her brown eyes—long eyes, which might have given a hint of secrecy or curious smiles if they had not been so placid—looked concerned. In one hand she carried what looked like a small white bag of linen or cotton.

And she spoke with a dignity which did not match her years.

"I am most terribly sorry," she told them. "I *thought* I heard someone, but I was so busy that I could not be sure. Will you forgive me?"

She smiled. Hunter's private view was that his knocking had been loud enough to wake the dead; but he murmured conventional things. As though conscious of some faint incongruity about the white bag in her hand, she held it up.

"For Blind Man's Bluff," she explained. "They do cheat so, I'm afraid, and not only the children. If one uses an ordinary handkerchief tied round the eyes, they always manage to get a corner loose. But if you take this, and you put it fully over a person's head, and you tie it round the neck"—a sudden gruesome image occurred to Rodney Hunter—"then it works so much better, don't you think?" Her eyes seemed to turn inward, and to grow absent. "But I must not keep you talking here. You are—"

"My name is Hunter. This is my wife. I'm afraid we've arrived late, but I understood Mr. Bannister was expecting—"

"He did not tell you?" asked the girl in brown.

"Tell me what?"

"Everyone here, including the servants, is always out of the house at this hour on this particular date. It is the custom; I believe it has been the custom for more than sixty years. There is some sort of special church service."

Rodney Hunter's imagination had been devising all sorts of fantastic explanations: the first of them being that this demure lady had murdered the members of the household, and was engaged in disposing of the bodies. What put this nonsensical notion into his head he could not tell, unless it was his own profession of detective-story writing. But he felt relieved to hear a commonplace explanation. Then the woman spoke again.

"Of course, it is a pretext, really. The rector, that dear man, invented it all those years to save embarrassment. What happened here had nothing to do with the murder, since the dates were so different; and I suppose most people have forgotten now why the tenants *do* prefer to stay away during seven and eight o'clock on Christmas Eve. I doubt if Mrs. Bannister even knows the real reason, though I should imagine Mr. Bannister must know it. But what happens here cannot be very pleasant, and it wouldn't do to have the children see it—would it?"

Muriel spoke with such directness that her husband knew she was afraid. "Who are you?" Muriel said. "And what on earth are you talking about?"

"I am quite sane, really," their hostess assured them, with a smile that was half-cheery and half-coy. "I daresay it must be all very confusing to you, poor dear. But I am forgetting my duties. Please come and sit down before the fire, and let me offer you something to drink."

She took them into the library on the right, going ahead with a walk that was like a bounce, and looking over her shoulder out of those long eyes. The library was a long, low room with beams. The windows towards the road were un-curtained; but those in the side-wall, where a faded red-brick fireplace stood, were bay windows with draperies closed across them. As their hostess put them before the fire, Hunter could have sworn he saw one of the draperies move.

"You need not worry about it," she assured him, follow-ing his glance towards the bay. "Even if you looked in there, you might not see anything now. I believe some gentleman did try it once, a long time ago. He stayed in the house for a wager. But when he pulled the curtain back, he did not see anything in the bay—at least, anything quite. He felt some hair, and it moved. That is why they have so many lights nowadays."

Muriel had sat down on a sofa, and was lighting a ciga-rette: to the rather prim disapproval of their hostess, Hunter thought.

"May we have a hot drink?" Muriel asked crisply. "And then, if you don't mind, we might walk over and meet the Bannisters coming from church."

"Oh, please don't do that!" cried the other. She had been standing by the fireplace, her hands folded and turned outwards. Now she ran across to sit down beside Muriel; and the swiftness of her movement, no less than the touch of her hand on Muriel's arm, made the latter draw back.

Hunter was now completely convinced that their hostess was out of her head. Why she held such fascination for him, though, he could not understand. In her eagerness to keep them there, the girl had come upon a new idea. On a table behind the sofa, book-ends held a row of modern novels. Conspicuously displayed—probably due to Molly Bannister's tact—were two of Rodney Hunter's detective stories. The girl put a finger on them.

"May I ask if you wrote these?"

He admitted it.

"Then," she said with sudden composure, "it would probably interest you to hear about the murder. It was a most perplexing business, you know; the police could make nothing of it, and no-one ever has been able to solve it." An arresting eye fixed on his. "It happened out in the hall there. A poor woman was killed where there was no-one to kill her, and no-one could have done it. But she was murdered."

Hunter started to get up from his chair; then he changed his mind, and sat down again. "Go on," he said.

"You must forgive me if I am a little uncertain about dates," she urged. "I think it was in the early eighteen-seventies, and I am sure it was in early February—because of the snow. It was a bad winter then; the farmers' livestock all died. My people have been bred up in this district for years, and I know that. The house here was much as it is now, except that there was none of this lighting (only paraffin lamps, poor girl!); and you were obliged to pump up what water you wanted; and people read the newspaper quite through, and discussed it for days.

"The people were a little different to look at, too. I am sure I do not understand why we think beards are so strange nowadays; they seem to think that men who had beards never had any emotions. But even young men wore them then, and looked handsome enough. There was a newly-married couple living in this house at the time: at least, they had been married only the summer before. They were named Edward and Jane Waycross, and it was considered a good match everywhere.

"Edward Waycross did not have a beard, but he had bushy side-whiskers which he kept curled. He was not a handsome man, either, being somewhat dry and hard-favoured; but he was a religious man, and a good man, and an excellent man of business, they say; a manufacturer of agricultural implements at Hawkhurst. He had determined that Jane Anders (as she was) would make him a good wife, and I dare say she did. The girl had several suitors. Although Mr. Waycross was the best match, I know it surprised people a little when she accepted him, because she was thought to have been fond of another man—a more striking man, whom many of the young girls were after. This was Jeremy Wilkes: who came of a very good family, but was considered wicked. He was no younger than Mr. Waycross, but he had a great black beard, and wore white waistcoats with gold chains, and drove a gig. Of course, there had been gossip, but that was because Jane Anders was considered pretty."

Their hostess had been sitting back against the sofa, quietly folding the little white bag with one hand, and speaking in a prim voice. Now she did something which turned her hearers cold.

You have probably seen the same thing done many times. She had been touching her cheek lightly with the fingers of the other hand. In doing so, she touched the flesh at the corner under her lower eyelid, and accidentally drew down the corner of that eyelid—which should have exposed the red part of the inner lid at the corner of the eye. It was not red. It was of a sickly pale colour.

"In the course of his business dealings," she went on, "Mr. Waycross had often to go to London, and usually he was obliged to remain overnight. But Jane Waycross was not afraid to remain alone in the house. She had a good servant, a staunch old woman, and a good dog. Even so, Mr. Waycross commended her for her courage."

The girl smiled. "On the night I wish to tell you of, in February, Mr. Waycross was absent. Unfortunately, too, the old servant was absent; she had been called away as a midwife to attend her cousin, and Jane Waycross had allowed her to go. This was known in the village, since all such affairs are well known, and some uneasiness was felt—this house being isolated, as you know. But she was not afraid.

"It was a very cold night, with a heavy fall of snow which had stopped about nine o'clock. You must know, beyond doubt, that poor Jane Waycross was alive after it had stopped snowing. It must have been nearly half-past nine when a Mr. Moody—a very good and sober man who lived in Hawkhurst—was driving home along the road past this house. As you know, it stands in the middle of a great bare stretch of lawn; and you can see the house clearly from the road. Mr. Moody saw poor Jane at the window of one of the upstairs bedrooms, with a candle in her hand, closing the shutters. But he was not the only witness who saw her alive.

"On that same evening, Mr. Wilkes (the handsome gentleman I spoke to you of a moment ago) had been at a tavern in the village of Five Ashes with Dr. Sutton, the local doctor, and a racing gentleman named Pawley. At about half-past eleven they started to drive home in Mr. Wilkes's gig to Cross-in-Hand. I am afraid they had all been drinking, but they were all in their sober senses. The landlord of the tavern remembered the time because he had stood in the doorway to watch the gig, which had fine yellow wheels, go spanking away as though there were no snow; and Mr. Wilkes in one of the new round hats with a curly brim.

"There was a bright moon. 'And no danger,' Dr. Sutton always said afterwards; 'shadows of trees and fences as clear

as though a silhouette-cutter had made 'em for sixpence.'
But when they were passing this house Mr. Wilkes pulled up
sharp. There was a bright light in the window of one of the
downstairs rooms—this room, in fact. They sat out there
looking round the hood of the gig, and wondering.

"Mr. Wilkes spoke: 'I don't like this,' he said. 'You know,
gentlemen, that Waycross is still in London; and the lady in
question is in the habit of retiring early. I am going up there
to find out if anything is wrong.'

"With that he jumped out of the gig, his black beard jutting out and his breath smoking. He said: 'And if it is a
burglar, then by Something, gentlemen'—I will not repeat
the word he used—'by Something, gentlemen, I'll settle
him.' He walked through the gate and up to the house—they
could follow every step he made—and looked into the windows of this room here. Presently he returned looking relieved (they could see him by the light of the gig lamps), but
wiping the moisture off his forehead.

"'It is all right,' he said to them; 'Waycross has come
home. But, by Something, gentlemen, he is growing thinner
these days, or it is shadows.'

"Then he told them what he had seen. If you look through
the front windows—there—you can look sideways and see
out through the doorway into the main hall. He said he had
seen Mrs. Waycross standing in the hall with her back to the
staircase, wearing a blue dressing-wrap over her nightgown,
and her hair down round her shoulders. Standing in front of
her, with his back to Mr. Wilkes, was a tallish, thin man like
Mr. Waycross, with a long greatcoat and a tall hat like Mr.
Waycross's. *She* was carrying either a candle or a lamp; and
he remembered how the tall hat seemed to wag back and
forth, as though the man were talking to her or putting out
his hands towards her. For he said he could not see the
woman's face.

"Of course, it was not Mr. Waycross; but how were they
to know that?

"At about seven o'clock next morning, Mrs. Randall, the

old servant, returned. (A fine boy had been born to her cousin the night before.) Mrs. Randall came home through the white dawn and the white snow, and found the house all locked up. She could get no answer to her knocking. Being a woman of great resolution, she eventually broke a window and got in. But, when she saw what was in the front hall, she went out screaming for help.

"Poor Jane was past help. I know I should not speak of these things; but I must. She was lying on her face in the hall. From the waist down her body was much charred and—unclothed, you know, because fire had burnt away most of the nightgown and the dressing-wrap. The tiles of the hall were soaked with blood and paraffin oil, the oil having come from a broken lamp with a thick blue-silk shade which was lying a little distance away. Near it was a china candlestick with a candle. This fire had also charred a part of the panelling of the wall, and a part of the staircase. Fortunately, the floor is of brick tiles, and there had not been much paraffin left in the lamp, or the house would have been set afire.

"But she had not died from burns alone. Her throat had been cut with a deep slash from some very sharp blade. But she had been alive for a while to feel both things, for she had crawled forward on her hands while she was burning. It was a cruel death, a horrible death for a soft person like that."

There was a pause. The expression on the face of the narrator, the plump girl in the brown dress, altered slightly. So did the expression of her eyes. She was sitting beside Muriel; and moved a little closer.

"Of course, the police came. I do not understand such things, I am afraid, but they found that the house had not been robbed. They also noticed the odd thing I have mentioned, that there was both a lamp *and* a candle in a candlestick near her. The lamp came from Mr. and Mrs. Waycross's bedroom upstairs, and so did the candlestick; there were no other lamps or candles downstairs except the lamps waiting to be filled next morning in the back kitchen.

But the police thought she would not have come downstairs carrying both the lamp *and* the candle as well.

"She must have brought the lamp, because that was broken. When the murderer took hold of her, they thought, she had dropped the lamp, and it went out; the paraffin spilled, but did not catch fire. Then this man in the tall hat, to finish his work after he had cut her throat, went upstairs, and got a candle, and set fire to the spilled oil. I am stupid at these things; but even I should have guessed that this must mean someone familiar with the house. Also, if she came downstairs, it must have been to let someone in at the front door; and that could not have been a burglar.

"You may be sure all the gossips were like police from the start, even when the police hem'd and haw'd, because they knew Mrs. Waycross must have opened the door to a man who was not her husband. And immediately they found an indication of this, in the mess that the fire and blood had made in the hall. Some distance away from poor Jane's body there was a medicine-bottle, such as chemists use. I think it had been broken in two pieces; and on one intact piece they found sticking some fragments of a letter that had not been quite burned. It was in a man's handwriting, not her husband's, and they made out enough of it to understand. It was full of—expressions of love, you know, and it made an appointment to meet her there on that night."

Rodney Hunter, as the girl paused, felt impelled to ask a question.

"Did they know whose handwriting it was?"

"It was Jeremy Wilkes's," replied the other simply. "Though they never proved that, never more than slightly suspected it, and the circumstances did not bear it out. In fact, a knife stained with blood was actually found in Mr. Wilkes's possession. But the police never brought it to anything, poor souls. For, you see, not Mr. Wilkes—or anyone else in the world—could possibly have done the murder."

*   *   *

"I don't understand that," said Hunter, rather sharply.

"Forgive me if I am stupid about telling things," urged their hostess in a tone of apology. She seemed to be listening to the chimney growl under a cold sky, and listening with hard, placid eyes. "But even the village gossips could tell that. When Mrs. Randall came here to the house on that morning, both the front and the back doors were locked and securely bolted on the inside. All the windows were locked on the inside. If you will look at the fastenings in this dear place, you will know what that means.

"But, bless you, that was the least of it! I told you about the snow. The snowfall had stopped at nine o'clock in the evening, hours and hours before Mrs. Waycross was murdered. When the police came, there were only two separate sets of footprints in the great unmarked half-acre of snow round the house. One set belonged to Mr. Wilkes, who had come up and looked in through the window the night before. The other belonged to Mrs. Randall. The police could follow and explain both sets of tracks; but there were no other tracks at all, and no-one was hiding in the house. ·

"Of course, it was absurd to suspect Mr. Wilkes. It was not only that he told a perfectly straight story about the man in the tall hat; but both Dr. Sutton and Mr. Pawley, who drove back with him from Five Ashes, were there to swear he could not have done it. You understand, he came no closer to the house than the windows of this room. They could watch every step he made in the moonlight, and they did. Afterwards he drove home with Dr. Sutton and slept there; or, I should say, they continued their terrible drinking until daylight. It is true that they found in his possession a knife with blood on it, but he explained that he had used the knife to gut a rabbit.

"It was the same with poor Mrs. Randall, who had been up all night about her midwife's duties, though naturally it was even more absurd to think of *her*. But there were no other footprints at all, either coming to or going from the house, in all that stretch of snow; and all the ways in or out were locked on the inside."

It was Muriel who spoke then, in a voice that tried to be crisp, but wavered in spite of her. "Are you telling us that all this is true?" she demanded.

"I am teasing you a little, my dear," said the other. "But really and truly, it all did happen. Perhaps I will show you in a moment."

"I suppose it was really the husband who did it?" asked Muriel in a bored tone.

"Poor Mr. Waycross!" said their hostess tenderly. "He spent that night in a temperance hotel near Charing Cross Station, as he always did, and, of course, he never left it. When he learned about his wife's duplicity"—again Hunter thought she was going to pull down a corner of her eyelid— "it nearly drove him out of his mind, poor fellow. I think he gave up agricultural machinery and took to preaching, but I am not sure. I know he left the district soon afterwards, and before he left he insisted on burning the mattress of their bed. It was a dreadful scandal."

"But in that case," insisted Hunter, "who did kill her? And, if there were no footprints and all the doors were locked, how did the murderer come or go? Finally, if all this happened in February, what does it have to do with people being out of the house on Christmas Eve?"

"Ah, that is the real story. That is what I meant to tell you."

She grew very subdued.

"It must have been very interesting to watch the people alter and grow older, or find queer paths, in the years afterwards. For, of course, nothing did happen as yet. The police presently gave it all up; for decency's sake it was allowed to rest. There was a new pump built in the market square; and the news of the Prince of Wales's going to India in '75 to talk about; and presently a new family came to live at 'Clearlawns,' and began to raise their children. The trees and the rains in summer were just the same, you know. It must have been seven or eight years before anything happened, for Jane Waycross was very patient.

"Several of the people had died in the meantime. Mrs. Randall had, in a fit of qunsy; and so had Dr. Sutton, but that was a great mercy, because he fell by the way when he was going to perform an amputation with too much of the drink in him. But Mr. Pawley had prospered—and, above all, so had Mr. Wilkes. He had become an even finer figure of a man, they tell me, as he drew near middle age. When he married he gave up all his loose habits. Yes, he married; it was the Tinsley heiress, Miss Linshaw, whom he had been courting at the time of the murder; and I have heard that poor Jane Waycross, even after *she* was married to Mr. Waycross, used to bite her pillow at night, because she was so horribly jealous of Miss Linshaw.

"Mr. Wilkes had always been tall, and now he was finely stout. He always wore frock-coats. Though he had lost most of his hair, his beard was full and curly; he had twinkling black eyes, and twinkling ruddy cheeks, and a bluff voice. All the children ran to him. They say he broke as many feminine hearts as before. At any wholesome entertainment he was always the first to lead the cotillion or applaud the fiddler, and I do not know what hostesses would have done without him.

"On Christmas Eve, then—remember, I am not sure of the date—the Fentons gave a Christmas party. The Fentons were the very nice family who had taken this house afterwards, you know. There was to be no dancing, but all the old games. Naturally, Mr. Wilkes was the first of all to be invited, and the first to accept; for everything was all smoothed away by time, like the wrinkles in last year's counterpane; and what's past *is* past, or so they say. They had decorated the house with holly and mistletoe, and guests began to arrive as early as two in the afternoon.

"I had all this from Mrs. Fenton's aunt (one of the Warwickshire Abbotts), who was actually staying here at the time. In spite of such a festal season, the preparations had not been going at all well that day, though such preparations usually did. Miss Abbott complained that there was a nasty earthy smell in the house. It was a dark and raw day, and the chimneys did not seem to draw as well as they should. What is more, Mrs. Fenton cut her finger when she was carving the cold fowl, because she said one of the children had been hiding behind the window-curtains in here, and peeping out at her; she was very angry. But Mr. Fenton, who was going about the house in his carpet slippers before the arrival of the guests, called her 'Mother' and said that it was Christmas.

"It is certainly true that they forgot all about this when the fun of the games began. Such squealings you never heard! —or so I am told. Foremost of all at Bobbing for Apples or Nuts in May was Mr. Jeremy Wilkes. He stood, gravely paternal, in the midst of everything, with his ugly wife beside him, and stroked his beard. He saluted each of the ladies on the cheek under the mistletoe; there was also some scampering to salute him; and, though he *did* remain for longer than was necessary behind the window-curtains with the younger Miss Twigelow, his wife only smiled. There was only one unpleasant incident, soon forgotten. Towards dusk a great gusty wind began to come up, with the chimneys smoking worse than usual. It being nearly dark, Mr. Fenton said it was time to fetch in the Snapdragon Bowl, and watch it flame. You know the game? It is a great bowl of lighted spirit, and you must thrust in your hand and pluck out a raisin from the bottom without scorching your fingers. Mr. Fenton carried it in on a tray in the half-darkness; it was flickering with that bluish flame you have seen on Christmas puddings. Miss Abbott said that once, in carrying it, he started and turned round. She said that for a second she thought there was a face looking over his shoulder, and it wasn't a nice face.

"Later in the evening, when the children were sleepy and there was tissue-paper scattered all over the house, the grown-ups began their games in earnest. Someone suggested Blind Man's Buff. They were mostly using the hall and this room here, as having more space than the dining-room. Various members of the party were blindfolded with men's handkerchiefs; but there was a dreadful amount of cheating. Mr. Fenton grew quite annoyed about it, because the ladies almost always caught Mr. Wilkes when they could; Mr. Wilkes was laughing and perspiring heartily, and his great cravat with the silver pin had almost come loose.

"To make it certain nobody could cheat, Mr. Fenton got a little white linen bag—like this one. It was the pillow-cover off the baby's cot, really; and he said nobody could look through that if it were tied over the head.

"I should explain that they had been having some trouble with the lamp in this room. Mr. Fenton said: 'Confound it, Mother, what is wrong with that lamp? Turn up the wick, will you?' It was really quite a good lamp from Spence and Minstead's, and should not have burned so dull as it did. In the confusion, while Mrs. Fenton was trying to make the light better, and he was looking over her shoulder at her, Mr. Fenton had been rather absently fastening the bag on the head of the last person caught. He has said since that he did not notice who it was. No-one else noticed, either, the light being so dim and there being such a large number of people. It seemed to be a girl in a broad bluish kind of dress, standing over near the door.

"Perhaps you know how people act when they have just been blindfolded in this game. First they usually stand very still, as though they were smelling or sensing in which direction to go. Sometimes they make a sudden jump, or sometimes they begin to shuffle gently forward. Everyone noticed what an air of *purpose* there seemed to be about this person whose face was covered; she went forward very slowly, and seemed to crouch down a bit.

"It began to move towards Mr. Wilkes in very short but quick little jerks, the white bag bobbing on its face. At this time Mr. Wilkes was sitting at the end of the table, laughing, with his face pink above the beard, and a glass of our Kentish cider in his hand. I want you to imagine this room as being very dim, and much more cluttered, what with all the tassels they had on the furniture then; and the high-piled hair of the ladies, too. The hooded person got to the edge of the table. It began to edge along towards Mr. Wilkes's chair; and then it jumped.

"Mr. Wilkes got up and skipped (yes, skipped) out of its way, laughing. It waited quietly, after which it went, in the same slow way, towards him again. It nearly got him again, by the edge of the potted plant. All this time it did not say anything, you understand, although everyone was applauding it and crying encouraging advice. It kept its head down. Miss Abbott says she began to notice an unpleasant faint smell of burnt cloth or something worse, which turned her half-ill. By the time the hooded person came stooping clear across the room, as certainly as though it could see him, Mr. Wilkes was not laughing any longer.

"In the corner by one bookcase, he said out loud: 'I'm tired of this silly, rotten game; go away, do you hear?' Nobody there had ever heard him speak like that, in such a loud, wild way, but they laughed and thought it must be the Kentish cider. 'Go away!' cried Mr. Wilkes again, and began to strike at it with his fist. All this time, Miss Abbott says, she had observed his face gradually changing. He dodged again, very pleasant and nimble for such a big man, but with the perspiration running down his face. Back across the room he went again, with it following him; and he cried out something that most naturally shocked them all inexpressibly.

"He screamed out: 'For God's sake, Fenton, take it off me!'

"And for the last time the thing jumped.

"They were over near the curtains of that bay window, which were drawn as they are now. Miss Twigelow, who was nearest, says that Mr. Wilkes could not have seen anything, because the white bag was still drawn over the woman's head. The only thing she noticed was that at the lower part of the bag, where the face must have been, there was a curious kind of discoloration, a stain of some sort which had not been there before: something seemed to be seeping through. Mr. Wilkes fell back between the curtains, with the hooded person after him, and screamed again. There was a kind of thrashing noise in or behind the curtains; then they fell straight again, and everything grew quiet.

"Now, our Kentish cider is very strong, and for a moment Mr. Fenton did not know what to think. He tried to laugh at it, but the laugh did not sound well. Then he went over to the curtains, calling out gruffly to them to come out of there and not play the fool. But, after he had looked inside the curtains, he turned round very sharply and asked the rector to get the ladies out of the room. This was done, but Miss Abbott often said that she had one quick peep inside. Though the bay windows were locked on the inside, Mr. Wilkes was now alone on the window seat. She could see his beard sticking up, and the blood. He was dead, of course. But, since he had murdered Jane Waycross, I sincerely think he deserved to die."

For several seconds, the two listeners did not move. She had all too successfully conjured up this room in the late 'seventies, whose stuffiness still seemed to pervade it now.

"But look here!" protested Hunter, when he could fight down an inclination to get out of the room quickly. "You say he killed her after all? And yet you told us he had an absolute alibi. You said he never went closer to the house than the windows . . ."

"No more he did, my dear," said the other.

"He was courting the Linshaw heiress at the time," she resumed; "and Miss Linshaw was a very proper young lady who would have been horrified if she had heard about him and Jane Waycross. She would have broken off the match, naturally. But poor Jane Waycross meant her to hear. She was much in love with Mr. Wilkes, and she was going to tell the whole matter publicly: Mr. Wilkes had been trying to persuade her not to do so."

"But—"

"Oh, don't you see what happened?" cried the other in a pettish tone. "It is so dreadfully simple. I am not clever at these things, but I should have seen it in a moment: even if I did not already know. I told you everything so that you should be able to guess.

"When Mr. Wilkes and Dr. Sutton and Mr. Pawley drove past here in the gig that night, they saw a bright light burning in the windows of this room. I told you that. But the police never wondered, as anyone should, what caused that light. Jane Waycross never came into this room, as you know; she was out in the hall, carrying either a lamp or a candle. But that lamp in the thick blue-silk shade, held out there in the hall, would not have caused a bright light to shine through this room and illuminate it. Neither would a tiny candle; it is absurd. And I told you there were no other lamps in the house except some empty ones waiting to be filled in the back kitchen. There is only one thing they could have seen. They saw the great blaze of the paraffin oil round Jane Waycross's body.

"Didn't I tell you it was dreadfully simple? Poor Jane was upstairs waiting for her lover. From the upstairs window she saw Mr. Wilkes's gig drive along the road in the moonlight, and she did not know there were other men in it; she thought he was alone. She came downstairs—

"It is an awful thing that the police did not think more about that broken medicine-bottle lying in the hall, the large bottle that was broken in just two long pieces. She must have had a use for it; and, of course, she had. You knew that the oil in the lamp was almost exhausted, although there was a great blaze round the body. When poor Jane came downstairs, she was carrying the unlighted lamp in one hand; in the other hand she was carrying a lighted candle, and an old medicine-bottle containing paraffin oil. When she got downstairs, she meant to fill the lamp from the medicine-bottle, and then light it with the candle.

"But she was too eager to get downstairs, I am afraid. When she was more than half-way down, hurrying, that long nightgown tripped her. She pitched forward down the stairs on her face. The medicine-bottle broke on the tiles under her, and poured a lake of paraffin round her body. Of course, the lighted candle set the paraffin blazing when it fell; but that was not all. One intact side of that broken bottle, long and sharp and cleaner than any blade, cut into her throat when she fell on the smashed bottle. She was not quite stunned by the fall. When she felt herself burning, and the blood almost as hot, she tried to save herself. She tried to crawl forward on her hands, forward into the hall, away from the blood and oil and fire.

"That was what Mr. Wilkes really saw when he looked in through the window.

"You see, he had been unable to get rid of the two fuddled friends, who insisted on clinging to him and drinking with him. He had been obliged to drive them home. If he could not go to 'Clearlawns' now, he wondered how at least he could leave a message; and the light in the window gave him an excuse.

"He saw pretty Jane propped up on her hands in the hall, looking out at him beseechingly while the blue flame ran up and turned yellow. You might have thought he would have pitied, for she loved him very much. Her wound was not really a deep wound. If he had broken into the house at that moment, he might have saved her life. But he preferred to let her die; because now she would make no public scandal and spoil his chances with the rich Miss Linshaw. That was why he returned to his friends and told a lie about a murderer in a tall hat. It is why, in heaven's truth, he murdered her himself. But when he returned to his friends, I do not wonder that they saw him mopping his forehead. You know now how Jane Waycross came back for him, presently."

There was another heavy silence.

The girl got to her feet, with a sort of bouncing motion which was as suggestive as it was vaguely familiar. It was as though she were about to run. She stood there, a trifle crouched in her prim brown dress, so oddly narrow at the waist after an old-fashioned pattern; and in the play of light on her face Rodney Hunter fancied that its prettiness was only a shell.

"The same thing happened afterwards, on some Christmas Eves," she explained. "They played Blind Man's Buff over again. That is why people who live here do not care to risk it nowadays. It happens at a quarter-past-seven—"

Hunter stared at the curtains. "But it was a quarter-past-seven when we got here!" he said. "It must now be—"

"Oh, yes," said the girl, and her eyes brimmed over. "You see, I told you you had nothing to fear; it was all over then. But that is not why I thank you. I begged you to stay, and you did. You have listened to me, as no-one else would. And now I have told it at last, and now I think both of us can sleep."

Not a fold stirred or altered in the dark curtains that closed the window bay; yet, as though a blurred lens had come into focus, they now seemed innocent and devoid of harm. You could have put a Christmas-tree there. Rodney Hunter, with Muriel following his gaze, walked across and threw back the curtains. He saw a quiet window-seat covered with chintz, and the rising moon beyond the window. When he turned round, the girl in the old-fashioned dress was not there. But the front doors were open again, for he could feel a current of air blowing through the house.

With his arm round Muriel, who was white-faced, he went out into the hall. They did not look long at the scorched and beaded stains at the foot of the panelling, for even the scars of fire seemed gentle now. Instead, they stood in the doorway looking out, while the house threw its great blaze of light across the frosty Weald. It was a welcoming light. Over the rise of a hill, black dots trudging in the frost showed that Jack Bannister's party was returning; and they could hear the sound of voices carrying far. They heard one of the party carelessly singing a Christmas carol for glory and joy, and the laughter of children coming home.

Time has not been kind to Baynard Kendrick. A founding father of the Mystery Writers of America, its first President and a Grand Master, his work was once widely read. Now few of his books or stories remain in print, and his name has been forgotten by all but the most serious mystery reader.

His series hero, Captain Duncan Maclain, a blind detective, came to the screen three times, twice with actor Edward Arnold (also a screen Nero Wolfe) in the role. In addition, there are twelve novels, three novelets and two short stories about the fascinating detective whose finest hour occurs in "Silent Night."

Remarkable for its strong sense of mood, this tale is notable for its force of characterization. Maclain's blindness is no literary eccentricity, but a genuine affliction that is integral to the personality of the detective and the development of the plot.

A reacquaintance with the work of Baynard Kendrick may be something of a revelation to the contemporary reader. Not only will it make his present neglect seem unjustified, but downright incomprehensible.

Silent Night

by Baynard Kendrick

ON FRIDAY, DEC. 20th, a week to the day since six-year-old Ronnie Connatser had been kidnapped from Miss Murray's School, Arnold Cameron, Special Agent in Charge of the New York F.B.I., telephoned early in the morning to make an appointment with Capt. Duncan Maclain. It was arranged for 10:00 A.M. in Maclain's penthouse office twenty-six stories above 72nd Street and Riverside Drive. Cameron arrived promptly, bringing with him Special Agent Hank Weeks and Alan Connatser, Ronnie's father. The men were silent, grim.

Capt. Maclain, an ex-Intelligence Officer blinded in World War I, had carried on the work of a Private Investigator with the aid of his partner, Spud Savage, for nearly forty years. To him being a Licensed P.I. was a dedicated profession. He hoped by developing his remaining four senses, hearing, feeling, taste, and smell to the highest point of proficiency to prove to the world before he died that a blind man with sufficient intelligence could be just as good, if not a little bit better, than millions of people who had eyes with which to see.

Waiting for Cameron, the Captain had a gratified feeling that maybe after all these years he had at last succeeded.

Duncan Maclain was no superman. He had certain peculiar talents that had proved most useful through the years to various law-enforcement agencies, among them the New York Police Department, and on several occasions the F.B.I.

He had known Arnold Cameron for a long time, and worked with him before Cameron became S.A.C. of the New York office. The Captain was the first to admit that neither he, nor any private operator, no matter where he worked, could get to first base without the co-operation of the local police or the F.B.I.

Cameron hadn't said what this case was about, except that it concerned the kidnapping of Connatser's six-year-old son. The Captain had heard about Alan Connatser, President and Treasurer of Connatser Products, Inc., the big plant that sprawled over acres on the edge of Long Island City. It was one of those industrial mushrooms that had grown in importance since World War II, mainly through Connatser's personality and engineering genius. The company did a lot of top security defense work, but the F.B.I. was quite capable of handling any violations of security on their own. Kidnapping, too, for that matter.

Why go on guessing? Speculation was always fruitless and a waste of time. He'd know the details soon enough. Whatever they were he hoped he could help. It was flattering that Arnold Cameron had dealt him in.

At 9:55 Rena, the Captain's secretary showed the three men in. Maclain shook hands around. Cameron's grip was friendly as usual. Special Agent Hank Weeks was properly official, neither cold nor warm, with an element of doubt in it as though he didn't intend to commit himself even on the say-so of the S.A.C. unless he was shown. Maclain suppressed a grin. He was skeptical himself about people who claimed they saw everything—even when they had 20-20 vision.

Alan Connatser wrung the Captain's hand with a grip that was full of despairing appeal. "Mr. Cameron thinks that you can help us, Captain Maclain. My son's been gone for a week now—more like a lifetime to Evelyn, my wife, and me. She has collapsed and is under a doctor's care. It isn't a question of money—I can pay a million and not be hurt. It's the life of my boy—our only child and we can never have another."

A very strong man, Alan Connatser, the Captain judged. Six foot, slow spoken, powerful as flexible steel, and younger than one would imagine. From his voice—not yet forty. And right now he was on the verge of flying into little pieces.

Maclain released himself wordlessly from the clinging grip and went to the bar set in the paneled wall near the diamond-paned doors to the terrace. He sloshed a liberal portion of cognac into a bell goblet and took it to the red leather divan where Connatser had slumped down.

"Slug it!" His face was grave with deep concern. "Your hand is as cold as a frozen fish. It won't help your boy if you crack up now and have a chill."

"Thanks. I guess you're right." Connatser downed the burning brandy in a gulp. "I'm afraid we're saddling you with a hopeless task."

"The world considers blindness hopeless. I haven't found it so." The Captain walked to his broad flat-top desk and sat down. "You say your son has been missing for a week?"

"He was kidnapped last Friday, Dec. 13th at ten past three," Arnold Cameron said. "He'd been to a Christmas party at his school. Miss Murray's at 66th Street and Fifth Avenue. The Connatsers live in a duplex at 82nd and Fifth —sixteen blocks away. Miss Murray saw Ronnie get into his father's Chrysler Imperial in front of the school at three-ten. The car was driven by a substitute chauffeur, who called himself Jules Rosine.

"Rosine stuck up Leon Gerard, who has driven for the family for years, in Gerard's apartment on East 82nd Street —right across the street from the garage where the Chrysler is kept. That was about eleven the night before. Rosine wore a stocking mask. He forced Leon to telephone at gun-point. Leon talked to Mrs. Murchison, the Connatser's housekeeper, said he was ill, and would send a reliable man to take his place the next day. Nobody thought it suspicious since it had happened a few times before. Leon is getting along in years and his health isn't too good."

Cameron paused. The Captain said, "If you fellows believe his story then I do, too."

"We don't believe anything until we've convinced ourselves that it's true," Cameron went on. "Weeks released Leon in his apartment after the kidnapping was reported to us on the evening of the thirteenth. The poor old guy was trussed up like a turkey with adhesive. Anyhow, nothing has been seen of Ronnie, or this Jules Rosine since ten past three in the afternoon a week ago."

A hopeless task, Connatser had said! The Captain ran a hand through his dark graying hair. The details of Charles A. Lindbergh, Jr., Bobby Greenlease, Jr., and the tiny month-old Peter Weinberger, all coolly murdered by their kidnappers, were much too vivid in his mind not to realize that Connatser's fears were far from being groundless.

He kept his repellent thoughts to himself and tried to speak reassuringly: "I've known Arnold Cameron for many years, Mr. Connatser. Neither he nor the F.B.I. consider this hopeless or he wouldn't have brought you here to talk with me." His dark sightless eyes, so perfect that many people thought he could see, turned from Connatser to fix themselves on the S.A.C. "You must have some very good reason for thinking Ronnie is still alive, Arnold."

"We happen, in this case, to know he was alive on Tuesday or Wednesday, and probably yesterday."

"What proof?"

"The sound of his voice, Captain, plus an answer to a couple of questions asked by Ronnie's mother—answers that only Ronnie would know."

"Then you must have made contact by phone." The Captain's expressive eyebrows went up a fraction.

"No. They're the ones who have been in touch," Cameron said. "One-way touch, by Audograph records. Three of them. You've told me often that you live in a world of sound. I also know that you're the best man living on identification of voices. Furthermore, you work with an Audograph all the time and are familiar with its sounds and foibles. Isn't that true?"

Maclain nodded. "I have one right here in my desk drawer." He referred to a compact efficient dictating machine used in thousands of business offices. Not more than nine inches square and five inches high, it records dictation on a flexible blue disc, and the dictation can be played back through its built in loud-speaker, or through plugged-in headphones at the flip of a lever.

"Here's the first of the three. The first word from Ronnie's captors, for that matter, from Friday to Monday. Let the family suffer. Die a thousand deaths. It softens them up. I could—"

He broke off abruptly, leaned forward and put a brown manila envelope on the Captain's blotter. It was a standard mailing envelope for the feather light discs. Seven inches square. Printed on the front was: GRAY AUDOGRAM FOR—a space for the address—and below that the words PLEASE DO NOT FOLD. The envelopes, like the discs, could be obtained from any Audograph dealer in cities throughout the country.

For an instant the Captain stared at the envelope as though by sheer intentness, he might develop some superhuman power to penetrate its secret.

"That was mailed to Mrs. Connatser at her home," Cameron explained. "Air mail. It's postmarked: Miami, Florida, Dec. 15th. That was last Sunday."

Maclain touched it gingerly with his forefinger. "I know what a working over you must have given these things. I was wondering about handwriting, or typing, on the address."

"Not this bird, Captain! He hasn't forgotten that we went through two million specimens of handwriting before we nailed LaMarca as kidnapper of the Weinberger baby.

There's not even typewriting. No return address, of course. Mrs. Connatser's name and address has been stamped on with one of those kid's rubber stamps that has separate removable rubber letters. You can buy them in any store or Five-and-ten."

The Captain took his Audograph machine from the deep bottom left-hand desk drawer. He put it on the desk, then brought up a hand microphone which he plugged into a six-slotted receptacle on the left-hand side of the machine. A switch in the handle of the mike controlled the playing of the record, turning it on when pressed in. For continuous playing, a flick of the thumb could lock the switch.

He took the record from the envelope, felt for the grooved side with his finger-nail, and turning it upward put the record on the machine. Unlike a regular phonograph record, the Audograph recorded from the center to the edge.

The Captain slid it into place, turned on the machine, and pushed a lever over to LISTEN. A red indicator light glowed. When recording, the light showed green. He locked the switch on the hand mike and laid the mike gently on the blotter beside the machine.

Out of nowhere the boyish treble of Ronnie Connatser's voice began to speak. Maclain reached out and turned the volume higher, as though that might help to bring the six-year-old closer to his home.

"Mommy, Mommy, can you hear me? The man says to tell you that I'm all right and that if I talk in here you can hear me. He says that Daddy can hear me, too, and that if you do what the man says he'll bring me home. Mommy, please tell Daddy to do what the man says. I'm all right, but I'm scared, Mommy. I don't want to spend Christmas here. I'm doing just what the man tells me to. Please hurry and do what the man says. I don't want to spend Christmas here. I don't like it and the man says he'll bring me home. So, please hurry."

Ronnie's voice quit abruptly. For an endless length of time—actually a few short seconds—the record revolved in mechanical silence. Cameron lit a cigarette. Smoke reached the Captain's nostrils. Leather squeaked as Connatser moved uneasily on the red divan. A man's voice took up where the child's voice had stopped:

> *"Your son's been kidnapped, but he hasn't been harmed. It's to prove that that I'm letting him talk to you. You'll be better off if you keep the police out of this as well as the F.B.I. Press me too hard and you'll never hear his voice again, let alone see him. If you follow our instructions to the letter you'll have him back very shortly. In case you don't think that's your son who was speaking, I'm going to offer you further proof. Ask him any two questions you want—questions that only he can answer. Put it in a Personal in the* New York Times *of Tuesday December the seventeenth. Sign it 'E.C.' You'll be answered by Ronnie on the next record we send to you. That's all for now. You'll never see me. Just call me: Junior."*

"Is that all?" The Captain sat up straight in his chair, his face grim.

"End of Record One," Cameron told him.

Maclain swiftly adjusted the disc to play the last few lines a second time.

Faintly, but clearly, through the man's last few words had come the sound of chimes pealing the opening bars of "Silent Night." Then a singer had begun:

> "Silent Night,
> Holy Night,
> All is—"

The song had ended with the click of the mike as the man said "Junior."

"The musical interlude," Cameron said glumly, "is the

first song on Side One of Bing Crosby's Decca Recording DL-8128, entitled 'Merry Christmas.' Sales to date about two million. On the last report from our bunion-ridden Agents in Miami, they have found some two hundred radio, record, and music shops, super-markets, drive-ins, and various other publicity-minded places of business, including second-hand-car lots that have P.A. systems working overtime. They have been deafening the public for a week or more to let them know the time of year. No. 1 on the Hit Parade is Bing's little dose of Christmas Cheer." He viciously snubbed out his cigarette.

"We don't think Ronnie's in Miami, anyhow. This Jules Rosine—who is trying hard to make us believe that that's his name by calling himself Junior from the initials J.R.—just doesn't strike me as the type, Captain, who would mail a letter or anything from a city where he has that boy. As a matter of fact, he jumps around the country like a twelve legged flea. The second record is from Kansas City and the third one is from Cleveland."

The Captain sat pinching his upper lip and saying nothing.

Cameron put the second envelope on his desk. "Here's the one where Ronnie answers his mother's questions. Mailed Wednesday, December the eighteenth. Air mail from K.C."

There was a tremor in the Captain's sensitive fingers as he removed the first record and put the second on.

"Mommy the man says that you and Daddy can hear me if I talk in here, but I don't see how you can hear me if I can't see you. He said I was to tell you what picture Ted Schuyler and I were going to see with Mrs. Murchison, and what I call my electric engine that pulls the train, and if I didn't tell you I wouldn't get back home. I thought you knew that Ted and I were going to see 'Snow White and the Seven Dwarfs'—except Daddy wanted me to come to the plant to meet him and I drank the Pepsi-Cola the chauffeur got me and got so sleepy. And you know my engine is called the Camel because it has a

hump-back in its middle. I know you told me not to repeat things, but the man said unless I told you that and unless Daddy did just what he says, I won't get home for Christmas. I don't want to stay here. There's nobody to play with and I want to come home."

The man's voice took it up from there:

"That answers the questions you had in the Times and proves beyond doubt that your son's alive. Nobody is trying to torture you. You'll see when we write again that we're not after money. It's possible that we have even more of that than you. The next will tell you what we want. We know what you want, but don't think we're fooling. Stay away from the police and the F.B.I. and do exactly what I tell you or your precious son is going to die. Cheerio! Junior."

"Junior seems to have split himself in two," the Captain said as he took off the record. "The *man* has become *we*. Do you think it's merely a cover-up, Arnold, or is there really someone else involved besides the man?"

"Anywhere from two to two million. They're after something more precious than money." He put the third record on the desk. "Listen to this one and you'll see."

Agent Hank Weeks said, "I'm betting there's a woman. Purely because they've kept Ronnie harping on *the man*."

The Captain nursed his chin for a moment. "I'm inclined to agree." He put the final record on.

"Do you mind if I have another brandy?" Alan Connatser's voice was tight and dry.

"Drink it all," the Captain said. "Ronnie isn't my son, but nevertheless these records are really getting me."

Connatser poured his drink and returned to his seat. "They're somehow worse than ransom notes to Evelyn and me. They're sadistic. Mean. I find myself wanting to answer Ronnie. Scream at him: 'Tell me where you are!'—as though he were hiding away in some ghostly world of his own. It's unbearable."

"I'd merely sound inane if I tried to express my sympathy." A sharp cold fury was setting the Captain's skin to tingling, turning him into a ruthless inhuman machine. His mind was being honed to a razor edge on a whetstone of revenge and implacability. "This is the one from Cleveland?"

"Mailed air mail yesterday. Thursday the nineteenth. It arrived in New York this morning at seven. We have a tag out for them at the Post Office. They notified us right away."

The Captain flipped the lever to LISTEN and started the disc to play.

"Mommy did you hear what I told you about the picture show? The Seven Dwarfs? And my engine, the Camel, on the electric train? I wish that you and Daddy would come for me, or answer me if you heard me, like the man said. He says he's telling Daddy exactly what to do right now, and if Daddy does it I'll come back home. Mommy tell him to hurry, please. Hurry and do it because I miss you so much and I want to see the Macy's parade and get my presents."

More unbearable silence then until the man cut in:

"At six-o'-clock, P.M.—eighteen hours Service Time— you and your pilot, Steven Donegan, will take off from the air strip at your plant on Long Island, flying your Cessna Twin. You will file no flight plan with anyone. At your regular cruising speed of two-hundred-and-ten miles per hour, flying at eight thousand feet, you will follow the regular plane route from New York to Philadelphia. From Philadelphia to Baltimore. From Baltimore to Washington. From Washington to Richmond. From Richmond to Wilmington, North Carolina. From Wilmington to Charleston, South Carolina. From Charleston to Savannah, Georgia. From Savannah to Jacksonville, Florida.

From Jacksonville to Daytona. From Daytona to Vero Beach, and from Vero Beach to Miami.

Be on the alert. Somewhere between two of the places named you will be contacted by radio. When contact is made, if you broadcast an alarm your son will be killed. Remember we'll be tuned in on you, too. We want the complete plans of the SF-800T Missile. Those plans consist of forty-four sheets of blueprints that were delivered to you by the Navy a month ago. You are the only one living who has immediate access to them all. Those forty-four blueprints are the price of your son. Particularly the details of the cone.

Once they are received they will be checked immediately by engineers just as competent as you. If they are not approved, or any attempt at trickery is discovered, your boy will die. The clearer those specifications are, the quicker you get your son. Remember, it's his life that's at stake.

Put the plans in a large portmanteau—not a dispatch-case—and weight the portmanteau with a couple of sash-weights. Paint the portmanteau with phosphorescent paint and be ready to drop it on a moment's notice. You will be contacted by the words: 'Cessna come down!' and will immediately start descending to a thousand feet still holding your course. Watch the ground. One minute before the drop you will be contacted again. Answer: Roger, Junior! and look for a red flasher that will turn on on top of a car. When you spot it say: Condition red! and drop portmanteau as close as possible to the flasher. You will be directed if you have to make a second try. Follow the straightest compass course between points and there will be no trouble. Another record will tell you where to pick up your boy. If weather reports are generally bad don't attempt to start. That's your hard luck and you'll have to make another try. Happy landings! Junior."

"Sounds like something from out of the wild blue yonder," Maclain said as he stopped the record. "A modern

Chekov nightmare manufactured in Moscow. What are the chances of pulling off such a scheme?"

"My pilot, Steve, says there's a damn good chance," Connatser told him. "I'm a pilot, myself, with some missions behind me, and I'm afraid I agree. Junior knows that we'll break our necks to drop that luminous suitcase on his head, if possible. He also knows that the SF-800T is an ace we have in the hole. So I'm supposed to stake the life of my son against the safety of my country."

The Captain gnawed at his clipped mustache. "At least the Soviets have one weakness that will never change: We know that it's impossible to fathom their way of thinking—but they fully believe that they know the thinking of every other country in the world. Now, it's the life of a child against the lives of untold millions. Tomorrow night! That's not much time to make up forty-four sheets of phony blueprints. What does the F.B.I. think, Arnold? What are you going to do?"

"Mr. Connatser is going to drop the plans as ordered," Cameron said promptly. "You're right about Soviet thinking. We've learned a lot since the days of Klaus Fuchs and Harry Gold. Naval Intelligence draws up two sets of plans, today —when the design is for anything as vital as the SF-800T. The second set is slightly different. To discover the bugs in it might take a corps of scientists a half a year. That's the set we're feeding to Junior tomorrow night."

"Leaving three people only on the hot seat: Ronnie, my wife, and me!" Connatser's voice was low and deadly. "They're not going to keep Ronnie alive for six months. So they may find some bugs in a couple of days, and kill him then. Then there's always the chance when they get the plans that they'll consider it safer to murder him anyhow."

"So we better get busy with what we have, Mr. Connatser: Three records, the sound of a kidnapper's voice, and a snatch of song from a P.A. speaker." Maclain shook his head. "It's not very much, but somehow among us we've got to put it together. Before those plans are examined at all, we've got to find your boy. There is no other alternative."

"Knowing you as well as I do," Arnold Cameron said, "I have a vague uneasy feeling that you may be on to something that we've managed to overlook. God only knows, I hope so."

"I have some questions." There were lines creased on Maclain's forehead and his mobile face was set in a look of concentration as though his mind were far away. "Why did this man pick Audograph records?"

"We have fifteen Audographs in our office at the plant," Connatser explained. "I also have one for dictation at home."

"Do you think he was an ex-employee, Arnold?"

"That's a possibility that we're checking. We're getting a rundown on everyone who has worked at Connatser Products since the war. It's a big job, but it's a top-security plant so it shouldn't be impossible. But it is going to take plenty of time."

"Of which we have none," Connatser grunted. "Personally, I think it more likely that Junior called in as a salesman and saw the machines. Employees in our place are too closely checked for comfort."

"How would he know you had one home?"

"Maybe he didn't, but he knew I could always get one and take it home, since he's addressing his records to Evelyn there."

"Okay," Maclain said shortly. "I'm going to start just as though I knew what I was talking about: the same voices made all those records—Ronnie's and Junior's. Let's take it for granted that it's the same man who picked up Ronnie, and drove you to work under the name of Jules Rosine. Would you know him again, Mr. Connatser, if you saw him?"

Connatser gave it a little thought. "I doubt it. He wore a chauffeur's livery. He was dark, I believe, seemed personable enough, slightly built—that is, he didn't impress me as being particularly big and strong. I didn't see him standing up. From the few words he spoke, I'd say he had a French accent. On the drive to Long Island, after dropping Ronnie at school in the morning, I was reading the paper and busy with some figures in the back seat of the car. Since I was occupied, I didn't give him too much thought really."

"He is French, according to Leon Gerard," Hank Weeks stated positively. "He spoke fluent French to Leon when he held him up in his room and forced him to phone the housekeeper."

"So his speech on the records, while marking him an educated man, has words in it that are British as a dish of bubble-and-squeak," Maclain declared. "'Phosphorescent paint'—'portmanteau'—'dispatch-case.' We'd say briefcase, or luminous suitcase. But his accent isn't really British—just the words he uses. Let's mark him as a French Canadian—Quebec, or Montreal. Do you agree?"

"I think I'll buy that Canadian angle right now," Weeks said. "Since Igor Gouzenko skipped the Russian Embassy in Ottawa, in 1946, and turned up Klaus Fuchs, they've had troubles aplenty with certain Reds in Canada."

"What would you guess his age to be?" the Captain asked.

"Between thirty and forty at a guess." Connatser sounded a little unsure.

"Well, later if nothing happens, it might pay you to run back through the Year Books of Graduates in Engineering at McGill—University of Toronto, too. A picture just might jog your memory enough to spot him. There's another point I'd like to get clear: Ronnie certainly wasn't kidnapped in your own car—that is I don't think they'd chance driving him very far."

"Just across the Queensboro Bridge," Cameron said. "The police found Mr. Connatser's Imperial parked under the approach to the bridge on the Long Island side at 6:20. Ronnie was going to a picture show with another boy, Ted Schuyler, at four. You heard that."

Maclain nodded. "I'm interested as to how this Rosine got him to come along without a fuss, and then transferred him to another car. That's not easy in New York City between three and four in the afternoon."

"You know as much as we do, Captain. From what Ronnie says on the records, the kidnapper gave him a line that Mr. Connatser wanted Ronnie to meet him at the plant. He bought Ronnie a bottle of Pepsi-Cola on the way. The police found the bottle still in the car and analyzed what was left. It showed Ronnie must have drunk three or four grains of Seconal. That would have put him out cold in fifteen minutes to half-an-hour, and he would have stayed out for eight to ten hours, maybe longer, according to the Medical Examiner. Of course they could have given him more on the trip if they were driving far."

Maclain took a box of paper-clips from the middle desk drawer and slowly began to chain them together.

"That's what I was trying to figure—how long would they drive Ronnie and how far. Let's say four hundred miles —ten hours driving. That would put them where they were going about four in the early morning. I think Junior lives there and owns a house most likely. It's not easy to rent a place to hide a child. It must be fairly large—the town, I mean, or the city. Far too dangerous to take him to a small town—"

"What about an isolated farm?" Agent Weeks broke in on the Captain's audible reverie.

"Not close enough to a Post Office and an airport." The Captain put his clips back in the drawer and closed it with a snap of certainty. "Let's consider these records: It's obvious that nobody is flying around the country with a kidnapped boy. So the boy's in one place—probably guarded by Junior's wife or paramour. Women are better with children, anyhow. Now, listen to this." He found the Miami record and put it on, keeping his hand held up for silence until it was through.

"That record was made by Ronnie and the man on the machine, and at the same time. The machine may be old, or defective, for there's a murmuring drone in the background that records itself all the way through. Junior didn't notice it, so it must be a noise that he's used to. He noticed the start of 'Silent Night' quick enough and shut off the machine."

"The record was mailed from Miami, Captain," Cameron reminded him.

"That's my point, Arnold—nearness to an airport. The woman's mailing records to him. I believe that record was made Saturday evening, giving Ronnie time to come around and get instructions as to what he should say. Then Junior took it with him as soon as it was finished and caught a flight to Miami. In his suitcase he was carrying another Audograph machine. He mailed the record from Miami on Sunday. That would check as to time—ample time for him to stop off and make arrangements for the pick-up with some Deputy Sheriff, or town constable confederate, at any point along the way."

"You're right there," Cameron said glumly. "Deputy Sheriffs and Constables are a dime a dozen, and a police car is made to order—two way telephone, flasher and all. We can't police every point between here and Miami."

"So again the best bet is to find the woman and the boy," Maclain said. "She'll talk, I believe, if Junior has told her anything. We can be sure if he'd made arrangements in Miami the record wouldn't have been mailed from there, any more than if Ronnie was there. Anyhow, we know that after the record was mailed, he hopped the first flight for Kansas City."

"Typical Commie technique, that hopping about," Hank Weeks remarked. "The Boss, in his book 'Masters of Deceit' says they call it 'dry cleaning'—driving three hundred miles to cover thirty so no one will know where you've been or where you are."

"Go on, Captain!" Cameron sounded impatient. "You've got this Commie Canuck with his Audograph in K.C. now. Where do we go from there—outside of Cleveland?"

Without replying, Maclain put on the second record and played it to the end. "I know that Ronnie made this record on the same machine that recorded record No. 1. All the time that Ronnie is speaking you can hear that noise that runs through the first one. As soon as Junior starts to speak, the noise is gone. We must assume that the woman mailed this record to Junior in K.C., and he filled his part in on the Audograph he has with him. The *New York Times* is available in most cities the same, or the following day. The woman could have seen the personal and told Ronnie what to say, or Junior could have seen it and could have called her long-distance."

"Still more dry cleaning," Cameron said, "to help us Special Agents earn our pay, and put us through a wringer like we're going through today. Let's hear No. 3."

The Cleveland record just served to clinch the Captain's beliefs more firmly. A background noise when Ronnie was speaking, while Junior's words were clear.

"Could that noise come from a car or a plane?" Connatser asked. "I've used an Audograph in both, but I haven't been conscious of anything like that in the playbacks. Still, I might have overlooked it just like Junior has."

"It just won't hold water." The Captain's agile fingers beat a tattoo on the desk top. "I don't believe that Ronnie and his captor made that first record while driving in a car. There's that 'Silent Night' music, for one thing. Can you picture a man with a kidnapped boy in his car dictating a record and telling the boy what to say? Then a stop in front of a music store where there's a blaring P.A.?"

Hank Weeks said, "Hell no! Nor can I picture the kid being flown around to make records in a plane."

Maclain stood up abruptly. "Let's get what we can from the horse's mouth—the Sound Engineer at Gray Audograph. Let him hear these and see what he has to say."

In less than an hour they were in the Gray Audograph offices at 521 Fifth Ave., talking to Carl Schantz, the company's Chief Sound Engineer. Schantz, a stocky, phlegmatic, brilliant German, listened to Cameron, then played the three records through without comment.

Finished, he sat down in his desk chair and stared from one to another of his visitors through his gold-rimmed glasses. "The boy's voice and the man's—all of record one

—was dictated to the same machine. The man's voice on records two and three was dictated to another machine. I'd say that both machines were old. Probably our Model Three, but there's nothing the matter with either of them. I'm certain of that."

"How do you know that?" Cameron asked. "The differences in the machines, I mean."

Schantz gave a slow smile. "You know from your work in the F.B.I. that there's a difference in every typewriter. Well, there's a difference in the needles of every dictating machine. They cut grooves of different depths on the records. The difference in those grooves is infinitesimal, but it shows up on a tape made by the electric-micrometer on our testing machine—the one I just played those on." He handed the S.A.C. a wide piece of ruled paper marked in purple ink with three wavy parallel lines. "Look for yourself."

All of the line made by record one, and the two lines made by Ronnie's voice on two and three were noticeably similar. There was a difference when Junior started to speak on the Kansas City and Cleveland records, but it still could be seen with the naked eye that those two lines were similar to each other.

"Does this mean that if we find those two machines and bring them in you can identify them for us?" Cameron's voice was eager.

"You bring them in. We'll give it a try!"

"What about that noise in the background?"

Schantz shrugged his heavy shoulders. "I'm afraid I can't help you there. Frankly, I don't know."

"Could it come from a nearby power plant or high-tension lines, something like that?" the Captain asked him.

Schantz shook his head. "We have Audographs running in offices with air-conditioners, calculators, and IBM sorting machines, sometimes right in the same room, and there's nothing but voice on the dictated record. Now and then, if you're not careful, you can get a loose connection in the six-hole receptacle where the mike plugs in. That will cause a nasty roar—but you can't dictate to the machine." He thought a moment. "The nearest thing to that noise I've heard was on a record dictated in an auto running at high speed with the windows open. The machine didn't pick up the motor, but it picked up the sound of the wind rushing by. That sound you have is steady like that, but deeper. It's almost like the lad was speaking through some distant hurricane." He sighed. "I'm really sorry I can't help you more."

"About those few lines of 'Silent Night'—have you any ideas there?" the Captain asked as Schantz was showing them out.

"I thought of a radio in another room, but it's too muffled. It's probably from outside the house from a juiced-up P.A. system. If that's it, the place is right next door, or at the most right across the street. Anyhow, it must be very near."

All afternoon, the Captain sat in his penthouse office listening to the records that Cameron had left with him. He had played them back through the Audograph speaker; listened to them with headphones on and finally using a jackplug, hopped them up to deafening volume on his hi-fi machine.

That background sound was all enveloping. The longer he listened to it, the more it took possession of him, until he almost believed what Schantz had said about a distant hurricane.

He thought of the ocean. It could keep people awake the first night, and in a day or two the noise would be gone. But the ocean wouldn't record like that unless it might be a wind-lashed sea.

Could they have the boy on a ship at sea? In a seven day storm? And mailing records air-mail to Junior in Kansas City? It showed how feeble the mind could get if you worked it on and on!

He kept coming back to that power plant. Why, when Schantz had said it wouldn't record? Could Schantz be wrong? Or could he, Maclain, whose ears had replaced his eyes, be clutching at straws and building into roaring volume some tiny wisp of sound? Was that noise, that should be a thousand jet planes busy ripping the skies, merely the hum of a washing machine, or an electric dryer? It had to be more.

Power! Overwhelming power! It had to be. With the life of a six-year-old boy at stake, he didn't dare to be wrong.

He'd stick to his own obsessions, too: They'd taken the boy, maybe dressed as a girl, on a single trip of ten hours. Four hundred miles at least. Then why not into Canada? If Junior was a Canadian, his car could have Canadian tags. It would be easy to cross the International Bridge in the middle of the night with a sleeping little girl accompanied by her father and mother . . .

The Captain jumped from the red divan, shut off the Audograph, and took his Braille map of New York State from a flat cabinet drawer. Moving faster than the eye could follow, he traced a line from New York City to Buffalo. Just three hundred and seventy-five miles!

Five minutes later he had Arnold Cameron on the phone. "I've got a fix, Arnold. Two points of sound, like when you're hunting down a hidden radio. Crosby singing 'Silent Night'—and the noise of the biggest power plant in the whole world. Now it's up to you to get that boy!" For a minute more he stammered on.

"Don't tell us how to run our business," Cameron cut in. "Get off the line so I can phone the Border Patrol of the Royal Canadian Mounted Police. It should be twice as easy to get a boy, since they're the chaps who always get their man!"

Just outside of the city limits, running at right angles to the river between Stanley Ave. and the Parkway, is a short street with eight neat houses on it. Five on one side and three on the other. On the side with the three houses and not quite forming a corner with the Parkway stands the Maple Leaf Tavern, boasting ten spotless bedrooms on the second floor, and downstairs a very good restaurant and a bar.

At seven o'clock, on Friday, Dec. 20th, Mr. Burns, who had owned and run the Maple Leaf for forty years, left his wife to superintend the cooking of dinner in the kitchen. He came into the bar to start his pick-up with Bing Crosby's "Merry Christmas" record. The first few chimes introducing "Silent Night" had scarcely pealed forth from the loud speaker over the Maple Leaf's front door, when Det. Sgt. McMurtrie, of the Ontario Provincial Police walked into the bar.

He and Burns were old friends. McMurtrie, tall and cadaverous with sad black eyes, was a startling contrast to the sandy-haired Burns, a Scot grown fat with good living through the years.

They shook hands. McMurtrie ordered an ale and sat down at a table in the empty bar. Burns joined him a moment later carrying two bottles and glasses.

"I'll have an ale wi' ye, Mac."

"On me, if ye like. Looks to me, Matey, like you've driven all your trade away wi' that racket over the front door."

"A racket ye call it! Don't be blasphemous, Mac. 'Tis one of God's songs, and there's others to come. I've been playing it every night now, except Sundays, for the past ten nights. 'Tis weather that's driven the trade away and not my offering passers-by a bit of warmth and Christmas cheer."

"Hmph!" McMurtrie swallowed some ale, his Adam's apple moving up and down. "And would ye have a permit, Burns, to play that thing? Seems to me the good folks on this street would be kicking with you disturbing their TV and their sleep."

"'Tis you who know perfectly well I have a permit, McMurtrie. Even though I'm outside of the city line, who but you has poked his long nose in here every chance he gets, checking every license and permit. And as for the folks on this street kicking, they're all good customers and friends of mine and glad of a little music."

"All?" Det. McMurtrie narrowed his bushy brows. "Now

there was one I recalled that you turned in for making sub-versive talk here during the war. What was his name?"

"Zwicker," Burns said. "Francois Zwicker." Burns held up his glass of sparkling ale and looked at the bubbles against the light. "He owns the house right across the street. Number 3. God be praised, a year ago he lost his job at the Electric, where he was engineer, and moved away. The house stood vacant for a spell; then was rented for three months in the summer, to be vacant again until just this last Saturday."

"Rented?"

"No, he and his missus are back, but it won't be long, mark me. He'll hold a job nowhere with his anarchistic tongue. I've forbid him my place. His missus is no prize, either. Louise is her name, a Frenchie like him. Quebec or Three Rivers. She's there by herself right now. He's off again, hunting another job, I'll say. Not that he'll keep it long."

A party of four came in. Burns finished his ale and got up to greet them. "The ale's on me, Mac. Drop in again, and a Merry Christmas to ye!"

Outside, the detective got in a big black car where four men were waiting for him. "Let's go and get the search war-rant," he said. "Zwicker's the name. The house is No. 3." The car moved off.

An hour later to the accompaniment of Bing's voice sing-ing "I'll Be Home for Christmas," McMurtrie rang the door-bell of No. 3. The door was opened finally by a white-faced woman with burning black eyes and raven hair.

"Provincial Police, Mrs. Zwicker," McMurtrie said. "There are four men posted about the house, and we have a search warrant. Let me in, please. We've come to get the boy."

At 6:00 P.M., on Saturday, Dec. 21st, Alan Connatser's Cessna Twin took off from the air strip at Connatser Prod-ucts, on Long Island. With Steven Donegan, and Connatser, at the twin controls, it headed south as ordered. Instead of a phosphorescent-painted portmanteau, it was carrying Special Agent Hank Weeks, member of the F.B.I.

Ronnie, safely home with his mother, had made it in time for Macy's Christmas Parade.

Contact by radio was made at 8:20, and almost instantly a red flasher was turned-on on the ground in a large open area some twenty miles north of New Bern, North Carolina. As the Cessna headed for a point directly over the flasher, Hank Weeks spoke into the microphone:

"Zwicker, hear this now! This is a Special Agent of the F.B.I. speaking to you from the Cessna. Your wife has been arrested and we have the boy. She gave us the name of Walter Vollmer, the County Official who is with you now in that Patrol Car. You were followed and we know exactly where you are—in between Vanceboro and Blount Creek. You are hopelessly trapped, for cars are posted all along U.S. 17 and along State Road 33, as well as the country road you came in on. They have heard this and are closing in right now. That's all! There's no use your trying to escape."

The Cessna began to climb. "There's just one thing that gripes me, Hank," Connatser said disgruntledly. "Think of all the trouble you'd have saved if you'd done what Steve and I wanted to—loaded that portmanteau with just one little ol' bomb!"

Way up north in the Maple Leaf Tavern, Mr. Burns turned over the "Merry Christmas" record for the third time and started "Silent Night" again. On guard in the empty house across the street, in the event that the plans went wrong and Zwicker returned to his home, two members of the Ontario Provincial Police were engaged in a game of Rummy.

"It would be a silent night if Burns would shut that blasted thing off," one said to the other, slapping a card on the table.

"Aye," said the other, "still as the dead, if you're asking me!"

They went on playing unaware of the noise that filled every room, every cranny and every house and every street for miles around. They had lived in the midst of its deep reverberation far too long to hear it—the stunning boom of the Horseshoe Falls of Niagara, dumping its endless deafening millions of gallons down a drop of a hundred and fifty-eight feet just a half block away.

"What makes you think the murderer is a dance
instructor?"

ITEM

The members of the "Silver Slipper" Club continued their revels into Christmas morning.... No regard to season is paid in police procedure. Christmas morning in the police is the same as any other morning. Therefore arrangements were made for inspecting the "Silver Slipper" on Christmas morning. The police were satisfied to take the names and addresses of those present together with bottled samples.

A London Newspaper, Dec. 27, 1927

Fanny Stevenson did not care much for Dr. Jekyll and Mr. Hyde. She considered it a reworking of "Markheim," an earlier story she liked better. She eventually changed her mind, but the lady had a point.

But then, her husband was always a perplexing writer. He alternated good novels with weak ones throughout his career. He wrote knowingly and feelingly about the special world of children while turning out "shilling shockers" about demonic possession and murder at the same time. He once wrote a piece denouncing adultery while carrying on an affair with a married woman. Some of his sunniest pieces were written in the throes of tuberculosis. He was a complex character, though his writing does not always reflect it.

Stevenson's mysteries are two-dimensional. Good struggles against evil. There are no gradations between. It is a child's view of life, an unsophisticated one, because Stevenson clung tightly to childhood all his life. What redeems his outmoded view of life is his sweeping romantic style. He knew how to catch up his reader in words and carry him wherever he pleased.

In "Markheim," he transports us to the twisted inner world of the holiday shopper. Interestingly, the first rustlings of consumer advocacy may be found here. Caveat vendor!

Markheim

By Robert Louis Stevenson

"Yes," said the dealer, "our windfalls are of various kinds. Some customers are ignorant, and then I touch a dividend on my superior knowledge. Some are dishonest," and here he held up the candle, so that the light fell strongly on his visitor, "and in that case," he continued, "I profit by my virtue."

Markheim had but just entered from the daylight streets, and his eyes had not yet grown familiar with the mingled shine and darkness in the shop. At these pointed words, and before the near presence of the flame, he blinked painfully and looked aside.

The dealer chuckled. "You come to me on Christmas Day," he resumed, "when you know that I am alone in my house, put up my shutters, and make a point of refusing business. Well, you will have to pay for that; you will have to pay for my loss of time, when I should be balancing my books; you will have to pay, besides, for a kind of manner that I remark in you today very strongly. I am the essence of discretion, and ask no awkward questions; but when a customer cannot look me in the eye, he has to pay for it."

The dealer once more chuckled; and then, changing to his usual business voice, though still with a note of irony, "You can give, as usual, a clear account of how you came into the possession of the object?" he continued. "Still your uncle's cabinet? A remarkable collector, sir!"

And the little pale, round-shouldered dealer stood almost on tip-toe, looking over the top of his gold spectacles, and nodding his head with every mark of disbelief. Markheim returned his gaze with one of infinite pity, and a touch of horror.

"This time," said he, "you are in error. I have not come to sell, but to buy. I have no curios to dispose of; my uncle's cabinet is bare to the wainscot; even were it still intact, I have done well on the Stock Exchange, and should more likely add to it than otherwise, and my errand to-day is simplicity itself. I seek a Christmas present for a lady," he continued, waxing more fluent as he struck into the speech he had prepared; "and certainly I owe you every excuse for thus disturbing you upon so small a matter. But the thing was neglected yesterday; I must produce my little compliment at dinner; and, as you very well know, a rich marriage is not a thing to be neglected."

There followed a pause, during which the dealer seemed to weigh this statement incredulously. The ticking of many clocks among the curious lumber of the shop, and the faint rushing of the cabs in a near thoroughfare, filled up the interval of silence.

"Well, sir," said the dealer, "be it so. You are an old customer after all; and if, as you say, you have the chance of a good marriage, far be it from me to be an obstacle. Here is a nice thing for a lady now," he went on, "this hand glass— fifteenth century, warranted; comes from a good collection, too; but I reserve the name, in the interests of my customer, who was just like yourself, my dear sir, the nephew and sole heir of a remarkable collector."

The dealer, while he thus ran on in his dry and biting voice, had stopped to take the object from its place; and, as he had done so, a shock had passed through Markheim, a start both of hand and foot, a sudden leap of many tumultuous passions to the face. It passed as swiftly as it came, and left no trace beyond a certain trembling of the hand that now received the glass.

"A glass," he said hoarsely, and then paused, and repeated it more clearly. "A glass? For Christmas? Surely not?"

"And why not?" cried the dealer. "Why not a glass?"

Markheim was looking upon him with an indefinable expression. "You ask me why not?" he said. "Why, look here —look in it—look at yourself! Do you like to see it? No! nor—nor any man."

The little man had jumped back when Markheim had so suddenly confronted him with the mirror; but now, perceiving there was nothing worse on hand, he chuckled. "Your future lady, sir, must be pretty hard-favoured," said he.

"I ask you," said Markheim, "for a Christmas present, and you give me this—this damned reminder of years, and sins and follies—this hand-conscience? Did you mean it? Had you a thought in your mind? Tell me. It will be better for you if you do. Come, tell me about yourself. I hazard a guess now, that you are in secret a very charitable man?"

The dealer looked closely at his companion. It was very odd, Markheim did not appear to be laughing; there was something in his face like an eager sparkle of hope, but nothing of mirth.

"What are you driving at?" the dealer asked.

"Not charitable?" returned the other gloomily. "Not charitable; not pious; not scrupulous; unloving, unbeloved; a hand to get money, a safe to keep it. Is that all? Dear God, man, is that all?"

"I will tell you what it is," began the dealer, with some sharpness, and then broke off again into a chuckle. "But I see this is a love match of yours, and you have been drinking the lady's health."

"Ah!" cried Markheim, with a strange curiosity. "Ah, have you been in love? Tell me about that."

"I," cried the dealer. "I in love? I never had the time, nor have I the time to-day for all this nonsense. Will you take the glass?"

"Where is the hurry?" returned Markheim. "It is very pleasant to stand here talking; and life is so short and insecure that I would not hurry away from any pleasure—no, not even from so mild a one as this. We should rather cling, cling to what little we can get, like a man at a cliff's edge. Every second is a cliff, if you think upon it—a cliff a mile high—high enough, if we fall, to dash us out of every feature of humanity. Hence it is best to talk pleasantly. Let us talk of each other: why should we wear this mask? Let us be confidential. Who knows, we might become friends?"

"I have just one word to say to you," said the dealer. "Either make your purchase, or walk out of my shop!"

"True, true," said Markheim. "Enough fooling. To business. Show me something else."

The dealer stooped once more, this time to replace the glass upon the shelf, his thin blond hair falling over his eyes as he did so. Markheim moved a little nearer, with one hand in the pocket of his greatcoat; he drew himself up and filled his lungs; at the same time many different emotions were depicted together on his face—terror, horror, and resolve, fascination and a physical repulsion; and through a haggard lift of his upper lip, his teeth looked out.

"This, perhaps, may suit," observed the dealer: and then, as he began to re-arise, Markheim bounded from behind upon his victim. The long, skewerlike dagger flashed and fell. The dealer struggled like a hen, striking his temple on the shelf, and then tumbled on the floor in a heap.

Time had some score of small voices in that shop, some stately and slow as was becoming to their great age; others garrulous and hurried. All these told out the seconds in an intricate chorus of tickings. Then the passage of a lad's feet, heavily running on the pavement, broke in upon these smaller voices and startled Markheim into the consciousness of his surroundings.

He looked about him awfully. The candle stood on the counter, its flame solemnly wagging in a draught; and by that inconsiderable movement, the whole room was filled with noiseless bustle and kept heaving like a sea: the tall shadows nodding, the gross blots of darkness swelling and dwindling as with respiration, the faces of the portraits and the china gods changing and wavering like images in water. The inner door stood ajar, and peered into that leaguer of shadows with a long slit of daylight like a pointing finger.

From these fear-stricken rovings, Markheim's eyes returned to the body of his victim, where it lay both humped and sprawling, incredibly small and strangely meaner than in life. In these poor, miserly clothes, in that ungainly attitude, the dealer lay like so much sawdust. Markheim had feared to see it, and, lo! it was nothing. And yet, as he gazed, this bundle of old clothes and pool of blood began to find eloquent voices. There it must lie; there was none to work the cunning hinges or direct the miracle of locomotion—there it must lie till it was found. Found! ay, and then? Then would this dead flesh lift up a cry that would ring over England, and fill the world with the echoes of pursuit. Ay, dead or not, this was still the enemy.

"Time was that when the brains were out," he thought; and the first word struck into his mind. Time, now that the deed was accomplished—time, which had closed for the victim, had become instant and momentous for the slayer.

The thought was yet in his mind, when, first one and then another, with every variety of pace and voice—one deep as the bell from a cathedral turret, another ringing on its treble notes the prelude of a waltz—the clocks began to strike the hour of three in the afternoon.

The sudden outbreak of so many tongues in that dumb chamber staggered him. He began to bestir himself, going to and fro with the candle, beleaguered by moving shadows, and startled to the soul by chance reflections. In many rich mirrors, some of home designs, some from Venice or Amsterdam, he saw his face repeated and repeated, as it were an army of spies; his own eyes met and detected him; and the sound of his own steps, lightly as they fell, vexed the surrounding quiet.

And still, as he continued to fill his pockets, his mind accused him with a sickening iteration, of the thousand faults of his design. He should have chosen a more quiet hour; he should have prepared an alibi; he should not have used a knife; he should have been more cautious, and only bound and gagged the dealer, and not killed him; he should have been more bold, and killed the servant also; he should have done all things otherwise—poignant regrets, weary, incessant toiling of the mind to change what was unchangeable, to plan what was now useless, to be the architect of the irrevocable past.

Meanwhile, and behind all this activity, brute terrors, like the scurrying of rats in a deserted attic, filled the more remote chambers of his brain with riot; the hand of the constable would fall heavy on his shoulder, and his nerves would jerk like a hooked fish; or he beheld, in galloping defile, the dock, the prison, the gallows, and the black coffin.

Terror of the people in the street sat down before his mind like a besieging army. It was impossible, he thought, but that some rumour of the struggle must have reached their ears and set on edge their curiosity; and now, in all the neighbouring houses, he divined them sitting motionless and with uplifted ear—solitary people, condemned to spend Christmas dwelling alone on memories of the past, and now startlingly recalled from that tender exercise; happy family parties, struck into silence round the table, the mother still with raised finger: every degree and age and humour, but all, by their own hearths, prying and hearkening and weaving the rope that was to hang him.

Sometimes it seemed to him he could not move too softly; the clink of the tall Bohemian goblets rang out loudly like a bell; and alarmed by the bigness of the ticking, he was tempted to stop the clocks. And then, again, with a swift transition of his terrors, the very silence of the place appeared a source of peril, and a thing to strike and freeze the passer-by; and he would step more boldly, and bustle aloud among the contents of the shop, and imitate, with elaborate bravado, the movements of a busy man at ease in his own house.

But he was now so pulled about by different alarms that, while one portion of his mind was still alert and cunning, another trembled on the brink of lunacy. One hallucination in particular took a strong hold on his credulity. The neighbour hearkening with white face beside his window, the passer-by arrested by a horrible surmise on the pavement— these could at worst suspect, they could not know; through the brick walls and shuttered windows only sounds could penetrate.

But here, within the house, was he alone? He knew he was; he had watched the servant set forth sweet-hearting, in her poor best, "out for the day" written in every ribbon and smile. Yes, he was alone, of course; and yet, in the bulk of empty house above him, he could surely hear a stir of delicate footing—he was surely conscious, inexplicably conscious of some presence. Ay, surely; to every room and corner of the house his imagination followed it; and now it was a faceless thing, and yet had eyes to see with; and again it was a shadow of himself; and yet again behold the image of the dead dealer, reinspired with cunning and hatred.

At times, with a strong effort, he would glance at the open door which still seemed to repel his eyes. The house was tall, the skylight small and dirty, the day blind with fog; and the light that filtered down to the ground story was exceedingly faint, and showed dimly on the threshold of the shop. And yet, in that strip of doubtful brightness, did there not hang wavering a shadow?

Suddenly, from the street outside, a very jovial gentleman began to beat with a staff on the shop-door, accompanying his blows with shouts and railleries in which the dealer was continually called upon by name. Markheim, smitten into ice, glanced at the dead man. But no! he lay quite still; he was fled away far beyond earshot of these blows and shoutings; he was sunk beneath seas of silence; and his name, which would once have caught his notice above the howling of a storm, had become an empty sound. And presently the jovial gentleman desisted from his knocking and departed.

Here was a broad hint to hurry what remained to be done, to get forth from this accusing neighbourhood, to plunge into a bath of London multitudes, and to reach, on the other side of day, that haven of safety and apparent innocence—his bed. One visitor had come; at any moment another might follow and be more obstinate. To have done the deed, and yet not to reap the profit, would be too abhorrent a failure. The money; that was now Markheim's concern; and as a means to that, the keys.

He glanced over his shoulder at the open door, where the shadow was still lingering and shivering; and with no conscious repugnance of the mind, yet with a tremor of the belly, he drew near the body of his victim. The human character had quite departed. Like a suit half-stuffed with bran, the limbs lay scattered, the trunk doubled, on the floor; and yet the thing repelled him. Although so dingy and inconsiderable to the eye, he feared it might have more significance to the touch.

He took the body by the shoulders, and turned it on its back. It was strangely light and supple, and the limbs, as if they had been broken, fell into the oddest postures. The face was robbed of all expression; but it was as pale as wax, and shockingly smeared with blood about one temple. That was, for Markheim, the one displeasing circumstance. It carried him back, upon the instant, to a certain fair-day in a fishers' village: a gray day, a piping wind, a crowd upon the street, the blare of the brasses, the booming of drums, the nasal voice of a ballad singer; and a boy going to and fro, buried over head in the crowd and divided between interest and fear, until, coming out upon the chief place of concourse, he beheld a booth and a great screen with pictures, dismally designed, garishly coloured: Brownrigg with her apprentice; the Mannings with their murdered guest; Weare in the death-grip of Thurtell; and a score besides of famous crimes.

The thing was as clear as an illusion; he was once again

that little boy; he was looking once again, and with the same sense of physical revolt, at these vile pictures; he was still stunned by the thumping of the drums. A bar of that day's music returned upon his memory; and at that, for the first time, a qualm came over him, a breath of nausea, a sudden weakness of the joints, which he must instantly resist and conquer.

He judged it more prudent to confront than to flee from these considerations; looking the more hardily in the dead face, bending his mind to realise the nature and greatness of his crime. So little a while ago that face had moved with every change of sentiment, that pale mouth had spoken, that body had been on fire with governable energies; and now, by his act, that piece of life had been arrested, as the horologist, with interjected finger, arrests the beating of the clock. So he reasoned in vain; he could rise to no more remorseful consciousness; the same heart which had shuddered before the painted effigies of crime, looked on its reality unmoved. At best, he felt a gleam of pity for one who had been endowed in vain with all those faculties that can make the world a garden of enchantment, one who had never lived and who was now dead. But of penitence, no, not a tremor.

With that, shaking himself clear of these considerations, he found the keys and advanced towards the open door of the shop. Outside, it had begun to rain smartly; and the sound of the shower upon the roof had banished silence. Like some dripping cavern, the chambers of the house were haunted by an incessant echoing, which filled the ear and mingled with the ticking of the clocks. And, as Markheim approached the door, he seemed to hear, in answer to his own cautious tread, the steps of another foot withdrawing up the stair. The shadow still palpitated loosely on the threshold. He threw a ton's weight of resolve upon his muscles, and drew back the door.

The faint, foggy daylight glimmered dimly on the bare floor and stairs; on the bright suit of armour posted, halberd in hand, upon the landing; and on the dark wood-carvings, and framed pictures that hung against the yellow panels of the wainscot. So loud was the beating of the rain through all the house that, in Markheim's ears, it began to be distinguished into many different sounds. Footsteps and sighs, the tread of regiments marching in the distance, the chink of money in the counting, and the creaking of doors held stealthily ajar, appeared to mingle with the patter of the drops upon the cupola and the gushing of the water in the pipes.

The sense that he was not alone grew upon him to the verge of madness. On every side he was haunted and begirt by presences. He heard them moving in the upper chambers; from the shop, he heard the dead man getting to his legs; and as he began with a great effort to mount the stairs, feet fled quietly before him and followed stealthily behind. If he were but deaf, he thought, how tranquilly he would possess his soul! And then again, and hearkening with ever fresh attention, he blessed himself for that unresting sense which held the outposts and stood a trusty sentinel upon his life. His head turned continually on his neck; his eyes, which seemed starting from their orbits, scouted on every side, and on every side were half-rewarded as with the tail of something nameless vanishing. The four-and-twenty steps to the first floor were four-and-twenty agonies.

On that first story, the doors stood ajar, three of them like three ambushes, shaking his nerves like the throats of cannon. He could never again, he felt, be sufficiently immured and fortified from men's observing eyes; he longed to be home, girt in by walls, buried among bedclothes, and invisible to all but God. And at that thought he wondered a little, recollecting tales of other murderers and the fear they were said to entertain of heavenly avengers. It was not so, at least, with him. He feared the laws of nature, lest, in their callous and immutable procedure, they should preserve some damning evidence of his crime. He feared tenfold more, with a slavish, superstitious terror, some scission in the continuity of man's experience, some wilful illegality of nature.

He played a game of skill, depending on the rules, calculating consequence from cause; and what if nature, as the defeated tyrant overthrew the chessboard, should break the mould of their succession?

The like had befallen Napoleon (so writers said) when the winter changed the time of its appearance. The like might befall Markheim: the solid walls might become transparent and reveal his doings like those of bees in a glass hive; the stout planks might yield under his foot like quicksands and detain him in their clutch; ay, and there were soberer accidents that might destroy him: if, for instance, the house should fall and imprison him beside the body of his victim; or the house next door should fly on fire, and the firemen invade him from all sides. These things he feared; and, in a sense, these things might be called the hands of God reached forth against sin. But about God Himself he was at ease; his act was doubtless exceptional, but so were his excuses, which God knew; it was there, and not among men, that he felt sure of justice.

When he had got safe into the drawing-room, and shut the door behind him, he was aware of a respite from alarms. The room was quite dismantled, uncarpeted besides, and strewn with packing cases and incongruous furniture; several great pier-glasses, in which he beheld himself at various angles, like an actor on a stage; many pictures, framed and unframed, standing with their faces to the wall, a fine Sheraton sideboard, a cabinet of marquetry, and a great old bed, with tapestry hangings. The windows opened to the floors; but by great good fortune the lower part of the shutters had been closed, and this concealed him from the neighbours. Here, then, Markheim drew in a packing case before the cabinet, and began to search among the keys.

It was a long business, for there were many; and it was irksome, besides; for after all there might be nothing in the cabinet, and time was on the wing. But the closeness of the occupation sobered him. With the tail of his eye he saw the door—even glanced at it from time to time directly, like a

besieged commander pleased to verify the good estate of his
defences. But in truth he was at peace. The rain falling in the
street sounded natural and pleasant. Presently, on the other
side, the notes of a piano were wakened to the music of a hymn,
and the voices of many children took up the air and words. How
stately, how comfortable was the melody! How fresh the
youthful voices!

Markheim gave ear to it smilingly, as he sorted out the
keys; and his mind was thronged with answerable ideas and
images; church-going children and the pealing of the high
organ; children afield, bathers by the brookside, ramblers on
the brambly common, kite-flyers in the windy and cloud-na-
vigated sky; and then, at another cadence of the hymn, back
again to church, and the somnolence of summer Sundays,
and the high genteel voice of the parson (which he smiled a
little to recall) and the painted Jacobean tombs, and the dim
lettering of the Ten Commandments in the chancel.

And as he sat thus, at once busy and absent, he was startled to his feet. A flash of ice, a flash of fire, a bursting gush
of blood, went over him, and then he stood transfixed and
thrilling. A step mounted the stair slowly and steadily and
presently a hand was laid upon the knob, and the lock
clicked, and the door opened.

Fear held Markheim in a vice. What to expect he knew
not, whether the dead man walking, or the official ministers
of human justice, or some chance witness blindly stumbling
in to consign him to the gallows. But when a face thrust into
the aperture, glanced round the room, looked at him, nodded
and smiled as if in friendly recognition, and then withdrew
again, and the door closed behind it, his fear broke loose
from his control in a hoarse cry. At the sound of this the
visitant returned.

"Did you call me?" he asked pleasantly, and with that he
entered the room and closed the door behind him.

Markheim stood and gazed at him with all his eyes. Perhaps there was a film upon his sight, but the outlines of the
newcomer seemed to change and waver like those of the

idols in the wavering candlelight of the shop; and at times he thought he knew him; and at times he thought he bore a likeness to himself; and always, like a lump of living terror, there lay in his bosom the conviction that this thing was not of the earth and not of God.

And yet the creature had a strange air of the commonplace, as he stood looking on Markheim with a smile; and when he added: "You are looking for the money, I believe?" it was in the tones of everyday politeness.

Markheim made no answer.

"I should warn you," resumed the other, "that the maid has left her sweetheart earlier than usual and will soon be here. If Mr. Markheim be found in this house, I need not describe to him the consequences."

"You know me?" cried the murderer.

The visitor smiled. "You have long been a favourite of mine," he said; "and I have long observed and often sought to help you."

"What are you?" cried Markheim; "the devil?"

"What I may be," returned the other, "cannot affect the service I propose to render you."

"It can," cried Markheim; "it does! Be helped by you? No, never; not by you! You do not know me yet; thank God, you do not know me!"

"I know you," replied the visitant, with a sort of kind severity or rather firmness. "I know you to the soul."

"Know me!" cried Markheim. "Who can do so? My life is but a travesty and slander on myself. I have lived to belie my nature. All men do, all men are better than this disguise that grows about and stifles them. You see each dragged away by life, like one whom bravos have seized and muffled in a cloak. If they had their own control—if you could see their faces, they would be altogether different, they would shine out for heroes and saints! I am worse than most; myself is more overlaid; my excuse is known to men and God. But, had I the time, I could disclose myself."

"To me?" inquired the visitant.

"To you before all," returned the murderer. "I supposed you were intelligent. I thought—since you exist—you could prove a reader of the heart. And yet you would propose to judge me by my acts! I was born and I have lived in a land of giants; giants have dragged me by the wrists since I was born out of my mother—the giants of circumstance. And you would judge me by my acts! But can you not look within? Can you not see within me the clear writing of conscience, never blurred by any willful sophistry, although too often disregarded? Can you not read me for a thing that surely must be common as humanity—the unwilling sinner?"

"All this is very feelingly expressed," was the reply, "but it regards me not. These points of consistency are beyond my province, and I care not in the least by what compulsion you may have been dragged away, so as you are but carried in the right direction. But time flies; the servant delays, looking in the faces of the crowd and at the pictures on the hoardings, but still she keeps moving nearer; and remember, it is as if the gallows itself was striding towards you through the Christmas streets! Shall I help you; I, who know all? Shall I tell you where to find the money?"

"For what price?" asked Markheim.

"I offer you the service for a Christmas gift," returned the other.

Markheim could not refrain from smiling with a kind of bitter triumph. "No," said he, "I will take nothing at your hands; if I were dying of thirst, and it was your hand that put the pitcher to my lips, I should find the courage to refuse. It may be credulous, but I will do nothing to commit myself to evil."

"I have no objection to a deathbed repentance," observed the visitant.

"Because you disbelieve their efficacy!'" Markheim cried.

"I do not say so," returned the other; "but I look on these things from a different side, and when the life is done my interest falls. The man has lived to serve me, to spread black looks under colour of religion, or to sow tares in the wheat-field, as you do, in a course of weak compliance with desire. Now that he draws so near to his deliverence, he can add but one act of service—to repent, to die smiling, and thus to build up in confidence and hope the more timorous of my surviving followers. I am not so hard a master. Try me. Accept my help. Please yourself in life as you have done hitherto; please yourself more amply, spread your elbows at the board; and when the night begins to fall and the curtains to be drawn, I tell you, for your greater comfort, that you will find it even easy to compound your quarrel with your conscience, and to make a truckling peace with God. I came but now from such a deathbed, and the room was full of sincere mourners, listening to the man's last words; and when I looked into that face, which had been set as a flint against mercy, I found it smiling with hope."

"And do you, then, suppose me such a creature?" asked Markheim. "Do you think I have no more generous aspirations than to sin, and sin, and sin, and, at the last, sneak into heaven? My heart rises at the thought. Is this, then, your experience of mankind? Or is it because you find me with red hands that you presume such baseness? And is this crime of murder indeed so impious as to dry up the very springs of good?"

"Murder is to me no special category," replied the other. "All sins are murder, even as all life is war. I behold your race, like starving mariners on a raft, plucking crusts out of the hands of famine and feeding on each other's lives. I follow sins beyond the moment of their acting; I find in all that the last consequence is death; and to my eyes, the pretty maid who thwarts her mother with such taking graces on a question of a ball, drips no less visibly with human gore than such a murderer as yourself. Do I say that I follow sins? I follow virtues also; they differ not by the thickness of a nail, they are both scythes for the reaping angel of Death. Evil, for which I live, consists not in action but in character. The bad man is dear to me; not the bad act, whose fruits, if we could follow them far enough down the hurtling cataract of the ages, might yet be found more blessed than those of the rarest virtues. And it is not because you have killed a dealer, but because you are Markheim, that I offer to forward your escape."

"I will lay my heart open to you," answered Markheim. "This crime on which you find me is my last. On my way to it I have learned many lessons; itself is a lesson, a momentous lesson. Hitherto I have been driven with revolt to what I would not; I was a bond-slave to poverty, driven and scourged. There are robust virtues that can stand in these temptations; mine are not so: I had a thirst of pleasure. But to-day, and out of this deed, I pluck both warning and riches —both the power and a fresh resolve to be myself. I become in all things a free actor in the world; I begin to see myself all changed, hands the agents of good, this heart at peace. Something comes over me out of the past; something of what I have dreamed on Sabbath evenings to the sound of the church organ, of what I forecast when I shed tears over noble books, or talked, an innocent child, with my mother. There lies my life; I have wandered a few years, but now I see once more my city of destination."

"You are to use this money on the Stock Exchange, I think?" remarked the visitor; "and there, if I mistake not, you have already lost some thousands?"

"Ah," said Markheim, "but this time I have a sure thing."

"This time, again, you will lose," replied the visitor quietly.

"Ah, but I keep back the half!" cried Markheim.

"That also you will lose," said the other.

The sweat started down Markheim's brow. "Well, then, what matter?" he exclaimed. "Say it be lost, say I am plunged again in poverty, shall one part of me, and that the worst, continue until the end to override the better? Evil and good run strong in me, haling me both ways. I do not love the one thing, I love all. I can conceive great deeds, renunciations, martyrdoms; and though I be fallen to such a crime as murder, pity is no stranger to my thoughts. I pity the poor; who knows their trials better than myself? I pity and help them; I prize love, I love honest laughter; there is no good thing nor true thing on earth but I love it from my heart. And are my vices only to direct my life, and my virtues without effect, like some passive lumber of the mind? Not so; good, also, is a spring of acts."

But the visitant raised his finger. "For six-and-thirty years that you have been in this world," said he, "through many changes of fortune and varieties of humour, I have watched you steadily fall. Fifteen years ago you would have started at a theft. Three years back you would have blanched at the name of murder. Is there any crime, is there any cruelty or meanness, from which you still recoil?—five years from now I shall detect you in the fact! Downward, downward, lies your way; nor can anything but death avail to stop you."

"It is true," Markheim said huskily, "I have in some degree complied with evil. But it is so with all; the very saints, in the mere exercise of living, grow less dainty, and take on the tone of their surroundings."

"I will propound to you one simple question," said the other; "and as you answer, I shall read to you your moral horoscope. You have grown in many things more lax; possibly you do right to be so; and at any account, it is the same with all men. But granting that, are you in any one particular, however trifling, more difficult to please with your own conduct, or do you go in all things with a looser rein?"

"In any one?" repeated Markheim, with an anguish of consideration. "No," he added, with despair, "in none! I have gone down in all."

"Then," said the visitor, "content yourself with what you are, for you will never change; and the words of your part on this stage are irrevocably written down."

Markheim stood for a long while silent, and indeed it was the visitor who first broke the silence. "That being so," he said, "shall I show you the money?"

"And grace?" cried Markheim.

"Have you not tried it?" returned the other. "Two or three years ago did I not see you on the platform of revival meetings, and was not your voice the loudest in the hymn?"

"It is true," said Markheim; "and I see clearly what remains for me by way of duty. I thank you for these lessons from my soul; my eyes are opened, and I behold myself at last for what I am."

At this moment, the sharp note of the door-bell rang through the house; and the visitant, as though this were some concerted signal for which he had been waiting, changed at once in his demeanour.

"The maid!" he cried. "She has returned, as I forewarned you, and there is now before you one more difficult passage. Her master, you must say, is ill; you must let her in, with an assured but rather serious countenance—no smiles, no overacting, and I promise you success! Once the girl within, and the door closed, the same dexterity that has already rid you of the dealer will relieve you of this last danger in your path. Thenceforward you have the whole evening—the whole night, if needful—to ransack the treasures of the house and to make good your safety. This is help that comes to you with the mask of danger. Up!" he cried; "up, friend; your life hangs trembling in the scales: up, and act!"

Markheim steadily regarded his counsellor. "If I be condemned to evil acts," he said, "there is still one door of freedom open—I can cease from action. If my life be an ill thing, I can lay it down. Though I be, as you say truly, at the beck of every small temptation, I can yet, by one decisive gesture, place myself beyond the reach of all. My love of good is damned to barrenness; it may, and let it be! But I have still my hatred of evil; and from that, to your galling disappointment, you shall see that I can draw both energy and courage."

The features of the visitor began to undergo a wonderful and lovely change: they brightened and softened with a tender triumph, and, even as they brightened, faded and dislimned. But Markheim did not pause to watch or understand the transformation. He opened the door and went downstairs very slowly, thinking to himself. His past went soberly before him; he beheld it as it was, ugly and strenuous like a dream, random as chance-medley—a scene of defeat. Life, as he thus reviewed it, tempted him no longer; but on the farther side he perceived a quiet haven for his bark.

He paused in the passage, and looked into the shop, where the candle still burned by the dead body. It was strangely silent. Thoughts of the dealer swarmed into his mind, as he stood gazing. And then the bell once more broke out into impatient clamour.

He confronted the maid upon the threshold with something like a smile.

"You had better go for the police," said he. "I have killed your master."

If Christmas Day on Monday be,
A great winter that year you'll see,
And full of winds, both loud and shrill;
But, in summer, truth to tell,
High winds shall there be and strong,
Full of tempests lasting long,
While battles they shall multiply,
And great plenty of beasts shall die....

—*Traditional*

Once upon a time, reading was one of man's principal sources of fun. This was sometime after the discovery of sex and before the invention of television. Damon Runyon was one of the principal reasons reading became fun.

His methods were deceptively simple. He took big city life with all its inherent frustrations, and made it seem warm and humorous. He transformed O. Henry's *Four Million* into a collection of guys and dolls who were either putting gin into a bathtub or carrying it around on their hip.

Respectable types, who would have blanched if they ran into the real Nathan Detroit or Dancing Dan in a dark alley, found them great fun when encountered in the safety of their favorite armchair. Runyon's stories were hugely popular in their day, creating a style that was much imitated.

Today, unfortunately, Runyon's art is out of fashion in an age that considers sentimentality a bigger literary crime than illiteracy. Happily there are still many Runyon Revolutionists around. If reading again becomes one of man's principal sources of fun, a Runyon renaissance is guaranteed.

Dancing Dan's Christmas

by Damon Runyon

Now ONE TIME it comes on Christmas, and in fact it is the evening before Christmas, and I am in Good Time Charley Bernstein's little speakeasy in West Forty-seventh Street, wishing Charley a Merry Christmas and having a few hot Tom and Jerrys with him.

This hot Tom and Jerry is an old time drink that is once used by one and all in this country to celebrate Christmas with, and in fact it is once so popular that many people think Christmas is invented only to furnish an excuse for hot Tom and Jerry, although of course this is by no means true.

But anybody will tell you that there is nothing that brings out the true holiday spirit like hot Tom and Jerry, and I hear that since Tom and Jerry goes out of style in the United States, the holiday spirit is never quite the same.

Well, as Good Time Charley and I are expressing our holiday sentiments to each other over our hot Tom and Jerry, and I am trying to think up the poem about the night before Christmas and all through the house, which I know will interest Charley no little, all of a sudden there is a big knock at the front door, and when Charley opens the door, who comes in carrying a large package under one arm but a guy by the name of Dancing Dan.

This Dancing Dan is a good-looking young guy, who always seems well-dressed, and he is called by the name of Dancing Dan because he is a great hand for dancing around and about with dolls in night clubs, and other spots where there is any dancing. In fact, Dan never seems to be doing anything else, although I hear rumors that when he is not dancing he is carrying on in a most illegal manner at one thing and another. But of course you can always hear rumors in this town about anybody, and personally I am rather fond of Dancing Dan as he always seems to be getting a great belt out of life.

Anybody in town will tell you that Dancing Dan is a guy with no Barnaby whatever in him, and in fact he has about as much gizzard as anybody around, although I wish to say I always question his judgment in dancing so much with Miss Muriel O'Neill, who works in the Half Moon night club. And the reason I question his judgment in this respect is because everybody knows that Miss Muriel O'Neill is a doll who is very well thought of by Heine Schmitz, and Heine Schmitz is not such a guy as will take kindly to anybody dancing more than once and a half with a doll that he thinks well of.

Well, anyway, as Dancing Dan comes in, he weighs up the joint in one quick peek, and then he tosses the package he is carrying into a corner where it goes plunk, as if there is something very heavy in it, and then he steps up to the bar alongside of Charley and me and wishes to know what we are drinking.

Naturally we start boosting hot Tom and Jerry to Dancing Dan, and he says he will take a crack at it with us, and after one crack, Dancing Dan says he will have another crack, and Merry Christmas to us with it, and the first thing anybody knows it is a couple of hours later and we still are still having cracks at the hot Tom and Jerry with Dancing Dan, and Dan says he never drinks anything so soothing in his life. In fact, Dancing Dan says he will recommend Tom and Jerry to everybody he knows, only he does not know anybody good enough for Tom and Jerry, except maybe Miss

Muriel O'Neill, and she does not drink anything with drugstore rye in it.

Well, several times while we are drinking this Tom and Jerry, customers come to the door of Good Time Charley's little speakeasy and knock, but by now Charley is commencing to be afraid they will wish Tom and Jerry, too, and he does not feel we will have enough for ourselves, so he hangs out a sign which says "Closed on Account of Christmas," and the only one he will let in is a guy by the name of Ooky, who is nothing but an old rumdum, and who is going around all week dressed like Santa Claus and carrying a sign advertising Moe Lewinsky's clothing joint around in Sixth Avenue.

This Ooky is still wearing his Santa Claus outfit when Charley lets him in, and the reason Charley permits such a character as Ooky in his joint is because Ooky does the porter work for Charley when he is not Santa Claus for Moe Lewinsky, such as sweeping out, and washing the glasses, and one thing and another.

Well, it is about nine-thirty when Ooky comes in, and his puppies are aching, and he is all petered out generally from walking up and down and here and there with his sign, for any time a guy is Santa Claus for Moe Lewinsky he must earn his dough. In fact, Ooky is so fatigued, and his puppies hurt him so much that Dancing Dan and Good Time Charley and I all feel very sorry for him, and invite him to have a few mugs of hot Tom and Jerry with us, and wish him plenty of Merry Christmas.

But old Ooky is not accustomed to Tom and Jerry and after about the fifth mug he folds up in a chair, and goes right to sleep on us. He is wearing a pretty good Santa Claus make-up, what with a nice red suit trimmed with white cotton, and a wig, and false nose, and long white whiskers, and a big sack stuffed with excelsior on his back, and if I do not know Santa Claus is not apt to be such a guy as will snore loud enough to rattle the windows, I will think Ooky is Santa Claus sure enough.

Well, we forget Ooky and let him sleep, and go on with

out hot Tom and Jerry, and in the meantime we try to think up a few songs appropriate to Christmas, and Dancing Dan finally renders My Dad's Dinner Pail in a nice baritone and very loud, while I do first rate Will You Love Me in December As You Do in May?

About midnight Dancing Dan wishes to see how he looks as Santa Claus.

So Good Time Charley and I help Dancing Dan pull off Ooky's outfit and put it on Dan, and this is easy as Ooky only has this Santa Claus outfit on over his ordinary clothes, and he does not even wake up when we are undressing him of the Santa Claus uniform.

Well, I wish to say I see many a Santa Claus in my time, but I never see a better looking Santa Claus than Dancing Dan, especially after he gets the wig and white whiskers fixed just right, and we put a sofa pillow that Good Time Charley happens to have around the joint for the cat to sleep on down his pants to give Dancing Dan a nice fat stomach such as Santa Claus is bound to have.

"Well," Charley finally says, "it is a great pity we do not know where there are some stockings hung up somewhere, because then," he says, "you can go around and stuff things in these stockings, as I always hear this is the main idea of a Santa Claus. But," Charley says, "I do not suppose anybody in this section has any stockings hung up, or if they have," he says, "the chances are they are so full of holes they will not hold anything. Anyway," Charley says, "even if there are any stockings hung up we do not have anything to stuff in them, although personally," he says, "I will gladly donate a few pints of Scotch."

Well, I am pointing out that we have no reindeer and that a Santa Claus is bound to look like a terrible sap if he goes around without any reindeer, but Charley's remarks seem to give Dancing Dan an idea, for all of a sudden he speaks as follows:

"Why," Dancing Dan says, "I know where a stocking is hung up. It is hung up at Miss Muriel O'Neill's flat over here in West Forty-ninth Street. This stocking is hung up by nobody but a party by the name of Gammer O'Neill, who is Miss Muriel O'Neill's grandmamma," Dancing Dan says. "Gammer O'Neill is going on ninety-odd," he says, "and Miss Muriel O'Neill tells me she cannot hold out much longer, what with one thing and another, including being a little childish in spots.

"Now," Dancing Dan says, "I remember Miss Muriel O'Neill is telling me just the other night how Gammer O'Neill hangs up her stocking on Christmas Eve all her life, and," he says, "I judge from what Miss Muriel O'Neill says that the old doll always believes Santa Claus will come along some Christmas and fill the stocking full of beautiful gifts. But," Dancing Dan says, "Miss Muriel O'Neill tells me Santa Claus never does this, although Miss Muriel O'Neill personally always takes a few gifts home and pops them into the stocking to make Gammer O'Neill feel better.

"But, of course," Dancing Dan says, "these gifts are nothing much because Miss Muriel O'Neill is very poor, and proud, and also good, and will not take a dime off of anybody and I can lick the guy who says she will.

"Now," Dancing Dan goes on, "it seems that while Gammer O'Neill is very happy to get whatever she finds in her stocking on Christmas morning, she does not understand why Santa Claus is not more liberal, and," he says, "Miss Muriel O'Neill is saying to me that she only wishes she can give Gammer O'Neill one real big Christmas before the old doll puts her checks back in the rack.

"So," Dancing Dan states, "here is a job for us. Miss Muriel O'Neill and her grandmamma live all alone in this flat over in West Forty-ninth Street, and," he says, "at such an hour as this Miss Muriel O'Neill is bound to be working, and the chances are Gammer O'Neill is sound asleep, and we will just hop over there and Santa Claus will fill up her stocking with beautiful gifts."

Well, I say, I do not see where we are going to get any beautiful gifts at this time of night, what with all the stores being closed, unless we dash into an all-night drug store and buy a few bottles of perfume and a bum toilet set as guys always do when they forget about their ever-loving wives until after store hours on Christmas Eve, but Dancing Dan says never mind about this, but let us have a few more Tom and Jerrys first.

So we have a few more Tom and Jerrys and then Dancing Dan picks up the package he heaves into the corner, and dumps most of the excelsior out of Ooky's Santa Claus sack, and puts the bundle in, and Good Time Charley turns out all the lights, but one, and leaves a bottle of Scotch on the table in front of Ooky for a Christmas gift, and away we go.

Personally, I regret very much leaving the hot Tom and Jerry, but then I am also very enthusiastic about going along to help Dancing Dan play Santa Claus, while Good Time Charley is practically overjoyed, as it is the first time in his life Charley is ever mixed up in so much holiday spirit.

As we go up Broadway, headed for Forty-ninth Street, Charley and I see many citizens we know and give them a large hello, and wish them Merry Christmas, and some of these citizens shake hands with Santa Claus, not knowing he is nobody but Dancing Dan, although later I understand there is some gossip among these citizens because they claim a Santa Claus with such a breath on him as our Santa Claus has is a little out of line.

And once we are somewhat embarrassed when a lot of little kids going home with their parents from a late Christmas party somewhere gather about Santa Claus with shouts of childish glee, and some of them wish to climb up Santa Claus' legs. Naturally, Santa Claus gets a little peevish, and calls them a few names, and one of the parents comes up and wishes to know what is the idea of Santa Claus using such language, and Santa Claus takes a punch at the parent, all of which is no doubt astonishing to the little kids who have an idea of Santa Claus as a very kindly old guy.

Well, finally we arrive in front of the place where Dancing Dan says Miss Muriel O'Neill and her grandmamma live, and it is nothing but a tenement house not far back of Madison Square Garden, and furthermore it is a walk-up, and at

this time there are no lights burning in the joint except a gas
jet in the main hall, and by the light of this jet we look at the
names on the letter boxes, such as you always find in the
hall of these joints, and we see that Miss Muriel O'Neill and
her grandmamma live on the fifth floor.

This is the top floor, and personally I do not like the idea
of walking up five flights of stairs, and I am willing to let
Dancing Dan and Good Time Charley go, but Dancing Dan
insists we must all go, and finally I agree with him because
Charley is commencing to argue that the right way for us to
do is to get on the roof and let Santa Claus go down a
chimney, and is making so much noise that I am afraid he
will wake somebody up.

So up the stairs we climb and finally we come to a door
on the top floor that has a little card in a slot that says
O'Neill, so we know we reach our destination. Dancing Dan
first tries the knob, and right away the door opens, and we
are in a little two- or three-room flat, with not much furniture in it, and what furniture there is, is very poor. One
single gas jet is burning near a bed in a room just off the one
the door opens into, and by this light we see a very old doll
is sleeping on the bed, so we judge this is nobody but Gammer O'Neill.

On her face is a large smile, as if she is dreaming of
something very pleasant. On a chair at the head of the bed is
hung a long black stocking, and it seems to be such a stocking as is often patched and mended, so I can see that what
Miss Muriel O'Neill tells Dancing Dan about her grandmamma hanging up her stocking is really true, although up
to this time I have my doubts.

Finally Dancing Dan unslings the sack on his back, and
takes out his package, and unties this package, and all of a
sudden out pops a raft of big diamond bracelets, and diamond rings, and diamond brooches, and diamond necklaces,
and I do not know what else in the way of diamonds, and
Dancing Dan and I begin stuffing these diamonds into the
stocking and Good Time Charley pitches in and helps us.

There are enough diamonds to fill the stocking to the

muzzle, and it is no small stocking, at that, and I judge that Gammer O'Neill has a pretty fair set of bunting sticks when she is young. In fact, there are so many diamonds that we have enough left over to make a nice little pile on the chair after we fill the stocking plumb up, leaving a nice diamond-studded vanity case sticking out the top where we figure it will hit Gammer O'Neill's eye when she wakes up.

And it is not until I get out in the fresh air again that all of a sudden I remember seeing large headlines in the afternoon papers about a five-hundred-G's stickup in the afternoon of one of the biggest diamond merchants in Maiden Lane while he is sitting in his office, and I also recall once hearing rumors that Dancing Dan is one of the best lone-hand git-'em-up guys in the world.

Naturally, I commence to wonder if I am in the proper company when I am with Dancing Dan, even if he is Santa Claus. So I leave him on the next corner arguing with Good Time Charley about whether they ought to go and find some more presents somewhere, and look for other stockings to stuff, and I hasten on home and go to bed.

The next day I find I have such a noggin that I do not care to stir around, and in fact I do not stir around much for a couple of weeks.

Then one night I drop around to Good Time Charley's little speakeasy, and ask Charley what is doing.

"Well," Charley says, "many things are doing, and personally," he says, "I'm greatly surprised I do not see you at Gammer O'Neill's wake. You know Gammer O'Neill leaves this wicked old world a couple of days after Christmas," Good Time Charley says, "and," he says, "Miss Muriel O'Neill states that Doc Moggs claims it is at least a day after she is entitled to go, but she is sustained," Charley says, "by great happiness in finding her stocking filled with beautiful gifts on Christmas morning.

"According to Miss Muriel O'Neill," Charley says, "Gammer O'Neill dies practically convinced that there is a Santa Claus, although of course," he says, "Miss Muriel O'Neill does not tell her the real owner of the gifts, an all-right guy by the name of Shapiro leaves the gifts with her after Miss Muriel O'Neill notifies him of finding of same.

"It seems," Charley says, "this Shapiro is a tender-hearted guy, who is willing to help keep Gammer O'Neill with us a little longer when Doc Moggs says leaving the gifts with her will do it.

"So," Charley says, "everything is quite all right, as the coppers cannot figure anything except that maybe the rascal who takes the gifts from Shapiro gets conscience-stricken, and leaves them the first place he can, and Miss Muriel O'Neill receives a ten-G's reward for finding the gifts and returning them. And," Charley says, "I hear Dancing Dan is in San Francisco and is figuring on reforming and becoming a dancing teacher, so he can marry Miss Muriel O'Neill, and of course," he says, "we all hope and trust she never learns any details of Dancing Dan's career."

Well, it is Christmas Eve a year later that I run into a guy by the name of Shotgun Sam, who is mobbed up with Heine Schmitz in Harlem, and who is a very, very obnoxious character indeed.

"Well, well, well," Shotgun says, "the last time I see you is another Christmas Eve like this, and you are coming out of Good Time Charley's joint, and," he says, "you certainly have your pots on."

"Well, Shotgun," I says, "I am sorry you get such a wrong impression of me, but the truth is," I say, "on the occasion you speak of, I am suffering from a dizzy feeling in my head."

"It is all right with me," Shotgun says. "I have a tip this guy Dancing Dan is in Good Time Charley's the night I see you, and Mockie Morgan, and Gunner Jack and me are casing the joint, because," he says, "Heine Schmitz is all sored up at Dan over some doll, although of course," Shotgun says, "it is all right now, as Heine has another doll.

"Anyway," he says, "we never get to see Dancing Dan. We watch the joint from six-thirty in the evening until daylight Christmas morning, and nobody goes in all night but old Ooky the Santa Claus guy in his Santa Claus makeup, and," Shotgun says, "nobody comes out except you and Good Time Charley and Ooky.

"Well," Shotgun says, "it is a great break for Dancing Dan he never goes in or comes out of Good Time Charley's, at that, because," he says, "we are waiting for him on the second-floor front of the building across the way with some nice little sawed-offs, and are under orders from Heine not to miss."

"Well, Shotgun," I say, "Merry Christmas."

"Well, all right," Shotgun says, "Merry Christmas."

THE MURDER FOR CHRISTMAS GUIDE TO GIFT GIVING

Obviously there should be a standard value for a certain type of Christmas present. One may give what one will to one's own family or particular friends; that is all right. But in a Christmas house-party there is a pleasant interchange of parcels, of which the string and the brown paper and the kindly thought are the really important ingredients, and the gift inside is nothing more than an excuse for these things. It is embarrassing for you if Jones has apologised for his brown paper with a hundred cigars and you have only excused yourself with twenty-five cigarettes; perhaps still more embarrassing if it is you who have lost so heavily on the exchange. An understanding that the contents were to be worth five shillings exactly would avoid this embarrassment.

And now... I am reminded of the ingenuity of a friend of mine, William by name, who arrived at a large country house for Christmas without any present in his bag. He had expected neither to give nor to receive anything, but to his horror he discovered on the 24th that everybody was preparing a Christmas present for him, and that it was taken for granted that he would require a little privacy and brown paper on Christmas Eve for the purpose of addressing his own offerings to others. He had wild thoughts of telegraphing to London for something to be sent down, and spoke to other members of the house-party in order to discover what sorts of presents would be suitable.

"What are you giving our host?" he asked one of them.

"Mary and I are giving him a book," said John, referring to his wife.

William then approached the youngest son of the house, and discovered that he and his next brother Dick were sharing in this, that, and the other. When he had heard this, William retired to his room and thought profoundly.

He was the first down to breakfast on Christmas morning. All the places at the table were piled high with presents. He looked at John's place. The top parcel said, "To John and Mary from Charles." William took out his fountain-pen and added a couple of words to the inscription. It then read, "To John and Mary from Charles and William," and in William's opinion looked just as effective as before. He moved on to the next place. "To Angela from Father," said the top parcel. "And William," wrote William. At his hostess' place he hesitated for a moment. The first present there was for "Darling Mother, from her loving children." It did not seem that an "and William" was quite suitable. But his hostess was not to be deprived of William's kindly thought; twenty seconds later the handkerchiefs "from John and Mary and William" expressed all the nice things which he was feeling for her. He passed on to the next place....

It is of course impossible to thank every donor of a joint gift; one simply thanks the first person whose eye one happens to catch. Sometimes William's eye was caught, sometimes not. But he was spared all embarrassment; and I can recommend his solution of the problem with perfect confidence to those who may be in a similar predicament next Christmas.

A.A. Milne

Television, that villified form of entertainment, has been largely responsible for the renewed interest in Dorothy L. Sayers and her creation Lord Peter Wimsey. A BBC series starring Ian Carmichael brought this faintly absurd detective to life with such success as to establish him anew among the great detectives of literature. For a whole new generation, Wimsey became not only an important historical figure, but again a very vital one.

Sayers, like Wimsey, was a faintly absurd character. She was an Oxford-trained classical scholar who worked in an advertising agency and wrote detective stories to make ends meet. By 1942, she had become so successful as a writer that she decided to drop the Wimsey series. Five years later she announced that she would give up detective fiction entirely and devote herself to the kind of things she always had wanted to write. From then on she wrote only classical studies and religious plays.

It was later disclosed that she had secretly given birth to a son in 1924. Two years later she married a man described as a "bar-fly and ne'er-do-well," and farmed the son out to be raised by a cousin.

It can be inferred from this that Dorothy L. Sayers was a woman who did exactly as she pleased most of her life. Fortunately it pleased her to give us Lord Peter and his amusing adventures. And that pleases us very much.

The Necklace of Pearls

by Dorothy L. Sayers

SIR SEPTIMUS SHALE was accustomed to assert his authority once in the year and once only. He allowed his young and fashionable wife to fill his house with diagrammatic furniture made of steel; to collect advanced artists and antigrammatical poets; to believe in cocktails and relativity and to dress as extravagantly as she pleased; but he did insist on an old-fashioned Christmas. He was a simple-hearted man, who really liked plum-pudding and cracker mottoes, and he could not get it out of his head that other people, "at bottom," enjoyed these things also. At Christmas, therefore, he firmly retired to his country house in Essex, called in the servants to hang holly and mistletoe upon the cubist electric fittings; loaded the steel sideboard with delicacies from Fortnum & Mason; hung up stockings at the heads of the polished walnut bedsteads; and even, on this occasion only, had the electric radiators removed from the modernist grates and installed wood fires and a Yule log. He then gathered his family and friends about him, filled them with as much Dickensian good fare as he could persuade them to swallow, and, after their Christmas dinner, set them down to play "Charades" and "Clumps" and "Animal, Vegetable, and Mineral" in the drawing-room, concluding these diversions by "Hide-and-Seek" in the dark all over the house. Because Sir Septimus was a very rich man, his guests fell in with this invariable programme, and if they were bored, they did not tell him so.

Another charming and traditional custom which he followed was that of presenting to his daughter Margharita a pearl on each successive birthday—this anniversary happening to coincide with Christmas Eve. The pearls now numbered twenty, and the collection was beginning to enjoy a certain celebrity, and had been photographed in the Society papers. Though not sensationally large—each one being about the size of a marrow-fat pea—the pearls were of very great value. They were of exquisite colour and perfect shape and matched to a hair's-weight. On this particular Christmas Eve, the presentation of the twenty-first pearl had been the occasion of a very special ceremony. There was a dance and there were speeches. On the Christmas night, following, the more restricted family party took place, with the turkey and the Victorian games. There were eleven guests, in addition to Sir Septimus and Lady Shale and their daughter, nearly all related or connected to them in some way: John Shale, a brother, with his wife and their son and daughter Henry and Betty; Betty's fiancé, Oswald Truegood, a young man with parliamentary ambitions; George Comphrey, a cousin of Lady Shale's, aged about thirty and known as a man about town; Lavinia Prescott, asked on George's account; Joyce Trivett, asked on Henry Shale's account; Richard and Beryl Dennison, distant relations of Lady Shale, who lived a gay and expensive life in town on nobody precisely knew what resources; and Lord Peter Wimsey, asked, in a touching spirit of unreasonable hope, on Margharita's account. There were also, of course, William Norgate, secretary to Sir Septimus, and Miss Tomkins, secretary to Lady Shale, who had to be there because, without their calm efficiency, the Christmas arrangements could not have been carried through.

Dinner was over—a seemingly endless succession of soup, fish, turkey, roast beef, plum-pudding, mince-pies, crystallized fruit, nuts, and five kinds of wine, presided over by Sir Septimus, all smiles, by Lady Shale, all mocking deprecation, and by Margharita, pretty and bored, with the necklace of twenty-one pearls gleaming softly on her slender throat. Gorged and dyspeptic and longing only for the horizontal position, the company had been shepherded into the drawing-room and set to play "Musical Chairs" (Miss Tomkins at the piano), "Hunt the Slipper" (slipper provided by Miss Tomkins), and "Dumb Crambo" (costumes by Miss Tomkins and Mr. William Norgate). The back drawing-room (for Sir Septimus clung to these old-fashioned names) provided an admirable dressing-room, being screened by folding doors from the large drawing-room in which the audience sat on aluminum chairs, scrabbling uneasy toes on a floor of black glass under the tremendous illumination of electricity reflected from a brass ceiling.

It was William Norgate who, after taking the temperature of the meeting, suggested to Lady Shale that they should play at something less athletic. Lady Shale agreed and, as usual suggested bridge. Sir Septimus, as usual, blew the suggestion aside.

"Bridge? Nonsense! Nonsense! Play bridge every day of your lives. This is Christmas time. Something we can all play together. How about 'Animal, Vegetable, and Mineral'?"

This intellectual pastime was a favourite with Sir Septimus; he was rather good at putting pregnant questions. After a brief discussion, it became evident that this game was an inevitable part of the programme. The party settled down to it, Sir Septimus undertaking to "go out" first and set the thing going.

Presently they had guessed among other things Miss Tomkins's mother's photograph, a gramophone record of "I want to be happy" (much scientific research into the exact composition of records, settled by William Norgate out of the *Encyclopaedia Britannica*), the smallest stickleback in the stream at the bottom of the garden, the new planet Pluto, the scarf worn by Mrs. Dennison (very confusing, because it was not silk, which would be animal, or artificial silk, which would be vegetable, but made of spun glass—mineral, a very clever choice of subject), and had failed to guess the Prime Minister's wireless speech—which was voted not fair, since nobody could decide whether it was animal by nature or a kind of gas. It was decided that they should do one more word and then go on to "Hide-and-Seek." Oswald Truegood had retired into the back room and shut the door behind him while the party discussed the next subject of examination, when suddenly Sir Septimus broke in on the argument by calling to his daughter:

"Hullo, Margy! What have you done with your necklace?"

"I took it off, Dad, because I thought it might get broken in 'Dumb Crambo.' It's over here on this table. No, it isn't. Did you take it, Mother?"

"No, I didn't. If I'd seen it, I should have. You are a careless child."

"I believe you've got it yourself, Dad. You're teasing."

Sir Septimus denied the accusation with some energy. Everybody got up and began to hunt about. There were not many places in that bare and polished room where a necklace could be hidden. After ten minutes' fruitless investigation, Richard Dennison, who had been seated next to the table where the pearls had been placed, began to look rather uncomfortable.

"Awkward, you know," he remarked to Wimsey.

At this moment, Oswald Truegood put his head through the folding-doors and asked whether they hadn't settled on something by now, because he was getting the fidgets.

This directed the attention of the searchers to the inner room. Margharita must have been mistaken. She had taken it in there, and it had got mixed up with the dressing-up clothes somehow. The room was ransacked. Everything was lifted up and shaken. The thing began to look serious. After half an hour of desperate energy it became apparent that the pearls were nowhere to be found.

"They must be somewhere in these two rooms, you

know," said Wimsey. "The back drawing-room has no door and nobody could have gone out of the front drawing-room without being seen. Unless the windows—"

No. The windows were all guarded on the outside by heavy shutters which it needed two footmen to take down and replace. The pearls had not gone out that way. In fact, the mere suggestion that they had left the drawing-room at all was disagreeable. Because—because—

It was William Norgate, efficient as ever, who coldly and boldly, faced the issue.

"I think, Sir Septimus, it would be a relief to the minds of everybody present if we could all be searched."

Sir Septimus was horrified, but the guests, having found a leader, backed up Norgate. The door was locked, and the search was conducted—the ladies in the inner room and the men in the outer.

Nothing resulted from it except some very interesting information about the belongings habitually carried about by the average man and woman. It was natural that Lord Peter Wimsey should possess a pair of forceps, a pocket lens, and a small folding foot-rule—was he not a Sherlock Holmes in high life? But that Oswald Truegood should have two liver-pills in a screw of paper and Henry Shale a pocket edition of *The Odes of Horace* was unexpected. Why did John Shale distend the pockets of his dress-suit with a stump of red sealing-wax, an ugly little mascot, and a five-shilling piece? George Comphrey had a pair of folding scissors, and three wrapped lumps of sugar, of the sort served in restaurants and dining-cars—evidence of a not uncommon form of klepto-mania; but that the tidy and exact Norgate should burden himself with a reel of white cotton, three separate lengths of string, and twelve safety-pins on a card seemed really re-markable till one remembered that he had superintended all the Christmas decorations. Richard Dennison, amid some confusion and laughter, was found to cherish a lady's garter, a powder-compact, and half a potato; the last named, he said, was a prophylactic against rheumatism (to which he was subject), while the other objects belonged to his wife. On the ladies' side, the more striking exhibits were a little book on palmistry, three invisible hairpins, and a baby's photograph (Miss Tomkins); a Chinese trick cigarette-case with a secret compartment (Beryl Dennison); a *very* private letter and an outfit for mending stocking-ladders (Lavinia Prescott); and a pair of eyebrow tweezers and a small packet of white powder, said to be for headaches (Betty Shale). An agitating moment followed the production from Joyce Trivett's handbag of a small string of pearls—but it was promptly remembered that these had come out of one of the crackers at dinner-time, and they were, in fact, synthetic. In short, the search was unproductive of anything beyond a general shamefacedness and the discomfort always produced by undressing and re-dressing in a hurry at the wrong time of day.

It was then that somebody, very grudgingly and haltingly, mentioned the horrid word "Police." Sir Septimus, naturally, was appalled by the idea. It was disgusting. He would not allow it. The pearls must be somewhere. They must search the rooms again. Could not Lord Peter Wimsey, with his experience of—er—mysterious happenings, do something to assist them?

"Eh?" said his lordship. "Oh, by Jove, yes—by all means, certainly. That is to say, provided nobody supposes —eh, what? I mean to say, you don't know that I'm not a suspicious character, do you, what?"

Lady Shale interposed with authority.

"We don't think *anybody* ought to be suspected," she said, "but, if we did, we'd know it couldn't be you. You know *far* too much about crimes to want to commit one."

"All right," said Wimsey. "But after the way the place has been gone over—" He shrugged his shoulders.

"Yes, I'm afraid you won't be able to find any footprints," said Margharita. "But we may have overlooked something."

Wimsey nodded.

"I'll try. Do you all mind sitting down on your chairs in

the outer room and staying there. All except one of you—I'd better have a witness to anything I do or find. Sir Septimus —you'd be the best person, I think."

He shepherded them to their places and began a slow circuit of the two rooms, exploring every surface, gazing up to the polished brazen ceiling, and crawling on hands and knees in the approved fashion across the black and shining desert of the floors. Sir Septimus followed, staring when Wimsey stared, bending with his hands upon his knees when Wimsey crawled, and puffing at intervals with astonishment and chagrin. Their progress rather resembled that of a man taking out a very inquisitive puppy for a very leisurely constitutional. Fortunately, Lady Shale's taste in furnishing made investigation easier; there were scarcely any nooks or corners where anything could be concealed.

They reached the inner drawing-room, and here the dressing-up clothes were again minutely examined, but without result. Finally, Wimsey lay down flat on his stomach to squint under a steel cabinet which was one of the very few pieces of furniture which possessed short legs. Something about it seemed to catch his attention. He rolled up his sleeve and plunged his arm into the cavity, kicked convulsively in the effort to reach farther than was humanly possible, pulled out from his pocket and extended his folding foot-rule, fished with it under the cabinet, and eventually succeeded in extracting what he sought.

It was a very minute object—in fact, a pin. Not an ordinary pin, but one resembling those used by entomologists to impale extremely small moths on the setting-board. It was about three-quarters of an inch in length, as fine as a very fine needle, with a sharp point and a particularly small head.

"Bless my soul!" said Sir Septimus. "What's that?"

"Does anybody here happen to collect moths or beetles or anything?" asked Wimsey, squatting on his haunches and examining the pin.

"I'm pretty sure they don't," replied Sir Septimus. "I'll ask them."

"Don't do that." Wimsey bent his head and stared at the

floor, from which his own face stared meditatively back at him.

"I see," said Wimsey presently. "That's how it was done. All right, Sir Septimus. I know where the pearls are, but I don't know who took them. Perhaps it would be as well— for everybody's satisfaction—just to find out. In the meantime they are perfectly safe. Don't tell anyone that we've found this pin or that we've discovered anything. Send all these people to bed. Lock the drawing-room door and keep the key, and we'll get our man—or woman—by breakfast-time."

"God bless my soul," said Sir Septimus, very much puzzled.

Lord Peter Wimsey kept careful watch that night upon the drawing-room door. Nobody, however, came near it. Either the thief suspected a trap or he felt confident that any time would do to recover the pearls. Wimsey, however, did not feel that he was wasting his time. He was making a list of people who had been left alone in the back drawing-room during the playing of "Animal, Vegetable, and Mineral." The list ran as follows:

Sir Septimus Shale
Lavinia Prescott
William Norgate
Joyce Trivett and Henry Shale (together, because they had
    claimed to be incapable of guessing anything unaided)
Mrs. Dennison
Betty Shale
George Comphrey
Richard Dennison
Miss Tomkins
Oswald Truegood

He also made out a list of the persons to whom pearls might be useful or desirable. Unfortunately, this list agreed in almost all respects with the first (always excepting Sir Septimus) and so was not very helpful. The two secretaries had both come well recommended, but that was exactly what they would have done had they come with ulterior designs; the Dennisons were notorious livers from hand to mouth; Betty Shale carried mysterious white powders in her handbag, and was known to be in with a rather rapid set in town; Henry was a harmless dilettante, but Joyce Trivett could twist him round her little finger and was what Jane Austen liked to call "expensive and dissipated"; Comphrey speculated; Oswald Truegood was rather frequently present at Epsom and Newmarket—the search for motives was only too fatally easy.

When the second housemaid and the under-footman appeared in the passage with household implements, Wimsey abandoned his vigil, but he was down early to breakfast. Sir Septimus with his wife and daughter were down before him, and a certain air of tension made itself felt. Wimsey, standing on the hearth before the fire, made conversation about the weather and politics.

The party assembled gradually, but, as though by common consent, nothing was said about pearls until after breakfast, when Oswald Truegood took the bull by the horns.

"Well now!" said he. "How's the detective getting along? Got your man, Wimsey?"

"Not yet," said Wimsey easily.

Sir Septimus, looking at Wimsey as though for his cue, cleared his throat and dashed into speech.

"All very tiresome," he said, "all very unpleasant. Hr'rm. Nothing for it but the police, I'm afraid. Just at Christmas, too. Hr'rm. Spoilt the party. Can't stand seeing all this stuff about the place." He waved his hand towards the festoons of evergreens and coloured paper that adorned the walls. "Take it all down, eh, what? No heart in it. Hr'rm. Burn the lot."

"What a pity, when we worked so hard over it," said Joyce.

"Oh, leave it, Uncle," said Henry Shale. "You're bothering too much about the pearls. They're sure to turn up."

"Shall I ring for James?" suggested William Norgate.

"No," interrupted Comphrey, "let's do it ourselves. It'll give us something to do and take our minds off our troubles."

"That's right," said Sir Septimus. "Start right away. Hate the sight of it."

He savagely hauled a great branch of holly down from the mantelpiece and flung it, crackling, into the fire.

"That's the stuff," said Richard Dennison. "Make a good old blaze!" He leapt up from the table and snatched the mistletoe from the chandelier. "Here goes! One more kiss for somebody before it's too late."

"Isn't it unlucky to take it down before the New Year?" suggested Miss Tomkins.

"Unlucky be hanged. We'll have it all down. Off the stairs and out of the drawing-room too. Somebody go and collect it."

"Isn't the drawing-room locked?" asked Oswald.

"No. Lord Peter says the pearls aren't there, wherever else they are, so it's unlocked. That's right, isn't it, Wimsey?"

"Quite right. The pearls were taken out of these rooms. I can't tell yet how, but I'm positive of it. In fact, I'll pledge my reputation that wherever they are, they're not up there."

"Oh, well," said Comphrey, "in that case, have at it! Come along, Lavinia—you and Dennison do the drawing-room and I'll do the back room. We'll have a race."

"But if the police are coming in," said Dennison, "oughtn't everything to be left just as it is?"

"Damn the police!" shouted Sir Septimus. "They don't want evergreens."

Oswald and Margharita were already pulling the holly and ivy from the staircase, amid peals of laughter. The party dispersed. Wimsey went quietly upstairs and into the drawing-room, where the work of demolition was taking place at a great rate, George having bet the other two ten shillings to a tanner that they would not finish their part of the job before he finished his.

"You mustn't help," said Lavinia, laughing to Wimsey. "It wouldn't be fair."

Wimsey said nothing, but waited till the room was clear. Then he followed them down again to the hall, spluttering, suggestive of Guy Fawkes' night. He whispered to Sir Septimus, who went forward and touched George Comphrey on the shoulder.

"Lord Peter wants to say something to you, my boy," he said.

Comphrey started and went with him a little reluctantly, as it seemed. He was not looking very well.

"Mr. Comphrey," said Wimsey, "I fancy these are some of your property." He held out the palm of his hand, in which rested twenty-two fine, small-headed pins.

"Ingenious," said Wimsey, "but something less ingenious would have served his turn better. It was very unlucky, Sir Septimus, that you should have mentioned the pearls when you did. Of course, he hoped that the loss wouldn't be discovered till we'd chucked guessing games and taken to 'Hide-and-Seek.' The pearls might have been anywhere in the house, we shouldn't have locked the drawing-room door, and he could have recovered them at his leisure. He had had this possibility in mind when he came here, obviously, and that was why he brought the pins, and Miss Shale's taking off the necklace to play 'Dumb Crambo' gave him his opportunity.

"He had spent Christmas here before, and knew perfectly well that 'Animal, Vegetable, and Mineral' would form part of the entertainment. He had only to gather up the necklace from the table when it came to his turn to retire, and he knew he could count on at least five minutes by himself while we were all arguing about the choice of a word. He had only to snip the pearls from the string with his pocket-scissors, burn the string in the grate, fasten the pearls to the mistletoe with the fine pins. The mistletoe was hung on the chandelier, pretty high—it's a lofty room—but he could easily reach it by standing on the glass table, which wouldn't show footmarks, and it was almost certain that nobody would think of examining the mistletoe for extra berries. I shouldn't have thought of it myself if I hadn't found that pin which he had dropped. That gave me the idea that the pearls had been separated and the rest was easy. I took the pearls off the mistletoe last night—the clasp was there, too, pinned among the holly-leaves. Here they are. Comphrey must have got a nasty shock this morning. I knew he was our man when he suggested that the guests should tackle the decorations themselves and that he should do the back drawing-room—but I wish I had seen his face when he came to the mistletoe and found the pearls gone."

"And you worked it all out when you found the pin?" said Sir Septimus.

"Yes; I knew then where the pearls had gone to."

"But you never even looked at the mistletoe."

"I saw it reflected in the black glass floor, and it struck me then how much mistletoe berries looked like pearls."

"You'll be sorry you did this, Agnes!"

Plum pudding is one of the best known, but least sampled of Christmas dishes. It is very difficult to prepare properly, as it takes much time and patience. It was never made with plums ('plum' probably coming from a word meaning plump). Instead it is made from porridge, meat, raisins, currants, rum, brandy, flour, sugar, butter, eggs and a variety of spices. Several objects like a button or a ring would be mixed in with the pudding, which would have a special significance to the finder. A poorly prepared pudding could be a great ordeal for the diner....

The legacy of O. Henry is the American short story. Eight years after his death, the American Society of Arts and Sciences founded an award in his name that is given to the best American efforts in that form each year. English professors have coined the term "O. Henry twist" to describe the sudden ironic turn of events that often concluded his stories. He drew on every aspect of American life, from Manhattan to the frontier—places he had known first-hand.

Perhaps the most arresting fact about O. Henry is that almost all his stories, thirteen volumes in all, were written in the last six years of his life. When he died, he left enough unpublished material to fill four additional collections.

Porter was a newspaper reporter and raconteur who spent much of his life travelling. He even served some time in jail on a charge of embezzlement. By the time he got around to setting his stories down on paper, he had probably told them many times over. Although he could be ironic and fatalistic about situations, he was never bitter. His stories had a folksy, humanistic touch that made him a durable storyteller, one of America's best loved.

"A Chaparral Christmas Gift" comes from the collection Whirligigs published in the last year of his life. It is a thoughtful story, well told, about the West Porter knew in his younger days. American crime fiction owes much to the style *and susbstance of O. Henry. His influence can be traced through succeeding generations of writers as diverse as Damon Runyon and Dashiel Hammett, to works on which the ink is yet undried.*

A Chaparral Christmas Gift

by O. Henry

THE ORIGINAL CAUSE of the trouble was about twenty years in growing. At the end of that time it was worth it.

Had you lived anywhere within fifty miles of Sundown Ranch you would have heard of it. It possessed a quantity of jet-black hair, a pair of extremely frank, deep-brown eyes and a laugh that rippled across the prairie like the sound of a hidden brook. The name of it was Rosita McMullen; and she was the daughter of old man McMullen of the Sundown Sheep Ranch.

There came riding on red roan steeds—or, to be more explicit, on a paint and a flea-bitten sorrel—two wooers. One was Madison Lane, and the other was the Frio Kid. But at that time they did not call him the Frio Kid, for he had not earned the honours of special nomenclature. His name was simply Johnny McRoy.

It must not be supposed that these two were the sum of the agreeable Rosita's admirers. The bronchos of a dozen others champed their bits at the long hitching rack of the Sundown Ranch. Many were the sheeps'-eyes that were cast in those savannas that did not belong to the flocks of Dan McMullen. But of all the cavaliers, Madison Lane and Johnny McRoy galloped far ahead, wherefore they are to be chronicled.

Madison Lane, a young cattleman from the Nueces country, won the race. He and Rosita were married one Christmas day. Armed, hilarious, vociferous, magnanimous, the cowmen and the sheepmen, laying aside their hereditary hatred, joined forces to celebrate the occasion.

Sundown Ranch was sonorous with the cracking of jokes and six-shooters, the shine of buckles and bright eyes, the outspoken congratulations of the herders of kine.

But while the wedding feast was at its liveliest there descended upon it Johnny McRoy, bitten by jealousy, like one possessed.

"I'll give you a Christmas present," he yelled, shrilly, at the door, with his .45 in his hand. Even then he had some reputation as an offhand shot.

His first bullet cut a neat underbit in Madison Lane's right ear. The barrel of his gun moved an inch. The next shot would have been the bride's had not Carson, a sheepman, possessed a mind with triggers somewhat well oiled and in repair. The guns of the wedding party had been hung, in their belts, upon nails in the wall when they sat at table, as a concession to good taste. But Carson, with great promptness, hurled his plate of roast venison and frijoles at McRoy, spoiling his aim. The second bullet, then, only shattered the white petals of a Spanish dagger flower suspended two feet above Rosita's head.

The guests spurned their chairs and jumped for their weapons. It was considered an improper act to shoot the bride and groom at a wedding. In about six seconds there were twenty or so bullets due to be whizzing in the direction of Mr. McRoy.

"I'll shoot better next time," yelled Johnny; "and there'll be a next time." He backed rapidly out the door.

Carson, the sheepman, spurred on to attempt further exploits by the success of his plate-throwing, was first to reach the door. McRoy's bullet from the darkness laid him low.

The cattlemen then swept out upon him, calling for vengeance, for, while the slaughter of a sheepman has not always lacked condonement, it was a decided misdemeanour in this instance. Carson was innocent; he was no accomplice at the matrimonial proceedings; nor had any one heard him quote the line "Christmas comes but once a year" to the guests.

But the sortie failed in its vengeance. McRoy was on his horse and away, shouting back curses and threats as he galloped into the concealing chaparral.

That night was the birthnight of the Frio Kid. He became the "bad man" of that portion of the State. The rejection of his suit by Miss McMullen turned him to a dangerous man. When officers went after him for the shooting of Carson, he killed two of them, and entered upon the life of an outlaw. He became a marvellous shot with either hand. He would turn up in towns and settlements, raise a quarrel at the slightest opportunity, pick off his man and laugh at the officers of the law. He was so cool, so deadly, so rapid, so inhumanly blood-thirsty that none but faint attempts were ever made to capture him. When he was at last shot and killed by a little one-armed Mexican who was nearly dead himself from fright, the Frio Kid had the deaths of eighteen men on his head. About half of these were killed in fair duels depending upon the quickness of the draw. The other half were men whom he assassinated from absolute wantonness and cruelty.

Many tales are told along the border of his impudent courage and daring. But he was not one of the breed of desperadoes who have seasons of generosity and even of softness. They say he never had mercy on the object of his anger. Yet at this and every Christmastide it is well to give each one credit, if it can be done, for whatever speck of good he may have possessed. If the Frio Kid ever did a kindly act or felt a throb of generosity in his heart it was once at such a time and season, and this is the way it happened.

One who has been crossed in love should never breathe the odour from the blossoms of the ratama tree. It stirs the memory to a dangerous degree.

One December in the Frio country there was a ratama tree in full bloom, for the winter had been as warm as springtime. That way rode the Frio Kid and his satellite and co-murderer, Mexican Frank. The kid reined in his mustang, and sat in his saddle, thoughtful and grim, with dangerously narrowing eyes. The rich, sweet scent touched him somewhere beneath his ice and iron.

"I don't know what I've been thinking about, Mex," he remarked in his usual mild drawl, "to have forgot all about a Christmas present I got to give. I'm going to ride over to-morrow night and shoot Madison Lane in his own house. He got my girl—Rosita would have had me if he hadn't cut into the game. I wonder why I happened to overlook it up to now?"

"Ah, shucks, Kid," said Mexican, "don't talk foolishness. You know you can't get within a mile of Mad Lane's house to-morrow night. I see old man Allen day before yesterday, and he says Mad is going to have Christmas doings at his house. You remember how you shot up the festivities when Mad was married, and about the threats you made? Don't you suppose Mad Lane'll kind of keep his eye open for a certain Mr. Kid? You plumb make me tired, Kid, with such remarks."

"I'm going," repeated the Frio Kid, without heat, "to go to Madison Lane's Christmas doings, and kill him. I ought to have done it a long time ago. Why, Mex, just two weeks ago I dreamed me and Rosita was married instead of her and him; and we was living in a house, and I could see her smiling at me, and—oh! h——l, Mex, he got her; and I'll get him—yes, sir, on Christmas Eve he got her, and then's when I'll get him."

"There's other ways of committing suicide," advised Mexican. "Why don't you go and surrender to the sheriff?"

"I'll get him," said the Kid.

Christmas Eve fell as balmy as April. Perhaps there was a hint of far-away frostiness in the air, but it tingled like seltzer, perfumed faintly with late prairie blossoms and the mesquite grass.

When night came the five or six rooms of the ranch-house were brightly lit. In one room was a Christmas tree, for the Lanes had a boy of three, and a dozen or more guests were expected from the nearer ranches.

At nightfall Madison Lane called aside Jim Belcher and three other cowboys employed on his ranch.

"Now, boys," said Lane, "keep your eyes open. Walk around the house and watch the road well. All of you know the 'Frio Kid,' as they call him now, and if you see him, open fire on him without asking any questions. I'm not afraid of his coming around, but Rosita is. She's been afraid he'd come in on us every Christmas since we were married."

The guests had arrived in buckboards and on horseback, and were making themselves comfortable inside.

The evening went along pleasantly. The guests enjoyed and praised Rosita's excellent supper, and afterward the men scattered in groups about the rooms or on the broad "gallery," smoking and chatting.

The Christmas tree, of course, delighted the youngsters, and above all were they pleased when Santa Claus himself in magnificent white beard and furs appeared and began to distribute the toys.

"It's my papa," announced Billy Sampson, aged six. "I've seen him wear 'em before."

Berkly, a sheepman, an old friend of Lane, stopped Rosita as she was passing by him on the gallery, where he was sitting smoking.

"Well, Mrs. Lane," said he, "I suppose by this Christmas you've gotten over being afraid of that fellow McRoy, haven't you? Madison and I have talked about it, you know."

"Very nearly," said Rosita, smiling, "but I am still nervous sometimes. I shall never forget that awful time when he came so near to killing us."

"He's the most cold-hearted villain in the world," said Berkly. "The citizens all along the border ought to turn out and hunt him down like a wolf."

"He has committed awful crimes," said Rosita, "but—I—

don't—know. I think there is a spot of good somewhere in everybody. He was not always bad—that I know."

Rosita turned into the hallway between the rooms. Santa Claus, in muffling whiskers and furs, was just coming through.

"I heard what you said through the window, Mrs. Lane," he said. "I was just going down in my pocket for a Christmas present for your husband. But I've left one for you, instead. It's in the room to your right."

"Oh, thank you, kind Santa Claus," said Rosita, brightly.

Rosita went into the room, while Santa Claus stepped into the cooler air of the yard.

She found no one in the room but Madison.

"Where is my present that Santa said he left for me in here?" she asked.

"Haven't seen anything in the way of a present," said her husband, laughing, "unless he could have meant me."

The next day Gabriel Radd, the foreman of the X O Ranch, dropped into the post-office at Loma Alta.

"Well, the Frio Kid's got his dose of lead at last," he remarked to the postmaster.

"That so? How'd it happen?"

"One of old Sanchez's Mexican sheep herders did it!— think of it! the Frio Kid killed by a sheep herder! The Greaser saw him riding along past his camp about twelve o'clock last night, and was so skeered that he up with a Winchester and let him have it. Funniest part of it was that the Kid was dressed all up with white Angora-skin whiskers and a regular Santy Claus rig-out from head to foot. Think of the Frio Kid playing Santy!"

"Your tomato surprise, sir."

"Where did we go wrong, Mother?
Where did we go wrong?"

In 1944 Lillian de la Torre, the wife of an English professor, introduced the noted eighteenth century lexicographer and literary arbiter Dr. Samuel Johnson to the world in the surprising role of detective. She decided that Johnson, perhaps the most imposing personality of his time, had many of the keen intellectual qualities necessary to a great detective. Conveniently, he also has a built-in Watson in the person of his biographer James Boswell.

A collection of Dr. Johnson stories appeared in 1946 under the title Dr. Sam: Johnson, Detector. It met with considerable success among the critics, including the New York Times's revered Anthony Boucher who called it "perhaps the most attractive book of detective shorts ever published."

A second collection was assembled in 1960, bringing the total number of stories close to thirty; a third collection has been scheduled. In each case de la Torre was able to present style and period flavor without compromising accessibility.

"The Stolen Christmas Box" is one of the earliest in the series and features an intriguing problem of interlocking puzzles.

The Stolen
Christmas Box

by Lillian de la Torre

THE DISAPPEARANCE OF little Fanny Plumbe's Christmas box was but a prelude to a greater and more daring theft; and was itself heralded by certain uneasy signs and tokens. Of these was the strange cypher message which Mrs. Thrale intercepted; while I myself was never easy in my mind after seeing the old sailorman with the very particular wooden leg.

Dr. Sam: Johnson and I passed him on Streatham common as we approached the estate of the Thrales, there to spend our Christmas. He sat on a stone hard by the gates in the unseasonable sunshine, and whittled. He wore the neckerchief and loose pantaloons of a sea-faring man. He had a wind-beaten, heavy, lowering face, and a burly, stooped frame. His stump stuck out straight before him, the pantaloon drooping from it. That on which he whittled was his own wooden leg.

'Twas a very particular wooden leg. The cradle that accommodated his stump was high-pooped and arabesqued about like a man-of-war's bow with carvings, upon the embellishment of which he was at the moment engaged. Into the butt was screwed a cylindrical post of about half the bigness of my wrist, turned in a lathe and wickedly shod with iron.

As the carriage passed him at an easy pace, I stared down upon him. He extended his greasy flapped hat, and my venerable companion dropped into it a gratuity.

We found the Thrale household pernitious dumpish, for all it was nigh onto Christmas. The tall, silent brew-master Thrale greeted us with his usual cold courtesy, his diminutive rattle of a wife with her usual peacock screeches of delight. Of the party also were Thrale's grenadier of a sister, a strapping virago born to support the robes of a Lady Mayoress, and well on her way to that honour on the coat-tails of her husband, Alderman Plumbe. Plumbe topped his brother-in-law in height and doubled him in girth. His features were knobby and his temper cholerick. He scowled upon his children, Master Ralph, a lubber of fourteen, and Miss Fanny, a year older.

Master Ralph was rapidly shooting to his parents' height, but unable to keep pace in solidity. He continually closed his short upper lip over his long upper teeth, which as continually protruded again. He bowed and grinned and twisted his wrists in our honour.

Miss Fanny executed her duty curtsey with downcast eyes. Her person was tall and agreeably rounded, and sensibility played in red and white upon her cheek, playing the while,. I own it, on the sensitive strings of my heart. Indeed, I could have been a knight-errant for Miss Fanny, had not I found below-stairs the veriest little witch of a serving-wench, pretty Sally, she who . . . but I digress.

Among the company circulated learned Dr. Thomas, the schoolmaster, assiduously pouring oil, as became a clergyman, on waters that were soon revealed to be troubled. Miss Fanny was in a fit of the sullens ('twas of a lover dismissed, I gathered so much), and Mrs. Plumbe was clean out of humour, and the Alderman alternately coaxing and shouting.

In an ill moment the latter conceived the idea of bribing Miss out of her pouts, and accordingly he fetches out the young lady's Christmas box, four days too soon, and bestows it upon her then and there; a step which he was bitterly to regret before the week was out.

"O Lud!" screamed Mrs. Thrale. "O Lud, 'tis a very Canopus!"

" 'Tis indeed," said Dr. Sam: Johnson, "a star of the first magnitude."

'Twas a handsome jewel, though to my eyes scarce suitable for so young a lady—an intaglio artfully cut, and set with a diamond needlessly great, whether for the brooch or for the childish bosom 'twas designed to adorn.

"Sure," screeched Mrs. Thrale in her usual reckless taste, "such a size it is, it cannot be the right gem. Say, is't not paste?"

"Paste!" cried the Alderman, purpling to his wattles. "I assure you, ma'am, 'tis a gem of the first water, such that any goldsmith in the city will give you £200 for."

Ralph Plumbe sucked a front tooth; his prominent eyes goggled. Pretty Sally, the serving-maid, passing with the tea tray, stared with open mouth. Little Dr. Thomas joined his fingertips, and seemed to ejaculate a pious word to himself. The Alderman pinned the gem in his daughter's bosom, a task in which I longed to assist him. She bestowed upon him a radiant smile, like sun through clouds.

Her fickle heart was bought. She yielded to him with a pretty grace, those love-letters for which she had previously contested, and the footman carried them over the way that very afternoon to poor jilted Jack Rice, while Miss Fanny preened it with her jewel like a peacock.

'Twas a day or two later that I made one in a stroll about the Streatham grounds. Dr. Johnson and Mrs. Thrale beguiled our perambulation in discourse with learned Dr. Thomas about Welsh antiquities. Master Ralph Plumbe, ennuied by the disquisition, threw stones alternately at rocks and at Belle, the black-and-tawny spaniel bitch.

Coming by the kitchen garden, we marked curvesome Sally, in her blue gown and trim apron, skimming along under the wall. She passed us under full sail, with the slightest of running curtseys. Mrs. Thrale caught her sleeve.

"Pray, whither away so fast?"

"Only to the kitchen, ma'am."

Our sharp little hostess pounced.

"What have you in your hand?"

"Nothing, ma'am."

Mrs. Thrale, for all she is small, has a strong man's hand. She forced open the girl's plump fingers and extracted a folded billet.

"So, miss. You carry *billets doux*."

"No, ma'am. I found it, if you please, ma'am," cried the girl earnestly.

"Ho ho," cried hobbledehoy Master Ralph, " 'tis one of Fan's, I'll wager."

"We shall see," said Mrs. Thrale curtly, and unfolded the billet.

I craned my neck. 'Twas the oddest missive (save one) that I have ever seen. 'Twas all writ in an alphabet of but two letters:

```
aababbabbaaaabaaba ababbabbabbaaaabaaba
abbaa'abbabbaabaaabaabaaab baabaaabaa
aabbbaaaaaababaababaaabaa ababa'aabaaaaaabaabb
abbabbaabbabaaa ababa'aaaaabaabbabbaaaabaa
abaaabaaaaabaa baabaaabaa
aabbaaaaabaaaaaabbaabaa aabbbaaaaabaaaabbaaaabaa
aaaaaabaaaababaababaaabaa aababaaaabaaaaaabaaabbaabaaba
```

Learned Dr. Thomas scanned the strange lines.

" 'Tis some unknown, primordial tongue, I make no doubt."

" 'Tis the talk of sheep!" I cried. "Baabaaabaa!"

"No, sir; 'tis cypher," said Dr. Sam: Johnson.

"Good lack," screeched Mrs. Thrale, " 'tis a French plot, I'll be bound, against our peace."

"No, ma'am," I hazarded, half in earnest, " 'tis some imprisoned damsel, takes this means to beg release."

"Pfoh," said Mrs. Thrale, "ever the ruling passion, eh, Mr. Boswell?"

"To what end," demanded Dr. Johnson, "do we stand disputing here, when we might be reading the straight of the message?"

"My husband has the new book of cyphers," cried Mrs. Thrale, "I will fetch it at once."

She sailed off, pretty Sally forgotten; who put her finger to her eye and stood stock-still in the path, until, perceiving how eagerly I followed where Dr. Johnson and the cypher led, she flounced off with dry eyes.

Dr. Johnson made for the drawing-room, and we streamed after him. Seating himself by the window, he peered at the strange paper. Dr. Thomas, Ralph Plumbe, and I peered with him, and Fanny came from the mirror, where we had surprized her preening, to peer too.

As Dr. Johnson smoothed the billet, I threw up my hands.

"What can be done with this!" I exclaimed. "We are to find out the 24 letters of the alphabet, and in this whole message we find but two symbols."

"What man can encypher, man can decypher," replied Dr. Johnson sententiously, "more especially when the encypherer is one of the inmates of Streatham, and the decypherer is Sam: Johnson. But see where our hostess comes."

She came empty-handed. The new book of cyphers was not to be found.

"Then," said Dr. Johnson, "we must make do with what we have in our heads. Let us examine this billet and see what it has to say to us."

We hung over his shoulder, Mrs. Thrale, Dr. Thomas, the Plumbe children, and I. Ralph sucked air through his teeth in excitement, little Fanny's pretty bosom lifted fast.

"Now, ma'am," began Dr. Johnson, addressing Mrs. Thrale, not ill-pleased to display his learning, "you must know, that cyphers have engaged the attention of the learned since the remotest antiquity. I need but name Polybius, Julius Africanus, Philo Mechanicus, Theodorus Bibliander, Johannes Walchius, and our own English Aristotle, Francis Bacon—"

"Oh, good lack, sir," cried little Fanny with a wriggle, "what does the paper say?"

"In good time, miss," replied the philosopher with a frown. "We have here 330 characters, all either *a* or *b*; writ in 16 groups on a page from a pocket book, with a fair-mended quill. 'Tis notable, that the writer wrote his letters in clusters of five, never more, never less; you may see between every group the little nodule of ink where the pen rested. Let us mark the divisions."

With his pen he did so. I watched the lines march:

```
aabab/abbab/baaaa/baaba ababb/abbab baaaa baaba
abbaa'/abbab/baaba/aabaa/baaab baaba aabaa
aabbb/aaaaa/ababa/ababa/aabaa . . .
```

"We now perceive," said Dr. Johnson as his pen flicked, "that we have to do, not with a correspondence of letter for letter, but for groups of letters. We have before us, in short, Mr. Boswell, the famous bi-literal cypher of the learned Francis Bacon; as set forth, I make no doubt, in Thrale's missing book of cyphers."

Mrs. Thrale clapped her hands.

"Now we shall understand it. Mark me, 'tis a plot of the French against us."

"Alas," said Dr. Johnson, "I do not carry the key in my head; but I shall make shift to reconstruct it. 'Tis many years since I was a corrector of the press; but the printer's case still remains in my mind to set me right on the frequencies of the letters in English."

"Depend upon it," muttered Mrs. Thrale stubbornly, " 'tis in French."

"You will find," he went on calmly, "*e* occurs the oftenest; next *o*, then *a* and *i*. To find out one consonant from another, remember also their frequency, first *d, h, n, r, s, t;* then the others, in what order I forget; but with these we may make shift."

By this calculation the learned philosopher determined the combination *aabaa* to represent *e;* when a strange fact transpired. Of the sixteen groups, representing perhaps the sixteen words of the message, nine ended with that combination! Dr. Johnson considered this in conjunction with the little marks like apostrophes, and glowered at Mrs. Thrale.

"Can it be French after all?"

In fine, it was; for proceeding partly by trial and errour, and partly by his memory of the cypher's system, the learned philosopher made shift to reconstruct the key, and soon the message began to emerge:

"Fort mort n'otes te—"

"'Tis poetick!" screeched Mrs. Thrale. "*Strong death snatch thee not away!* Alack, this is a *billet doux* after all, a *lettre d'amour* to some enamoured fair!"

"Oh, ay?" commented the philosopher drily, penning the message:

"Fort mort n'otes te halle l'eau oui l'aune ire te garde haine aille firent salle lit."

"'Tis little enough poetick," I muttered, translating the strange hodge-podge:

"Strong death snatch thee not away—market—the water, yes—the alder—anger—keep thee hatred—let him go—they made room—bed."

"O lud, here's a waspish message," cried Fanny.

"Yet what's this of a market, water, and an alder tree?"

"There's an alder tree," cried Ralph with a toothy inspiration, "by the kitchen pump!"

Infected by his excitement, we all ran thither. There was the water, sure enough, in the old pump by the kitchen garden, and drooping its branches over it, not an alder, but a hoary old willow, whose hollow trunk knew the domesticities of generations of owls. There was nothing of any note in the vicinity.

This strange adventure made us none the easier; the less, as we encountered, at his ease on the bench by the kitchen door, the one-legged sailorman. He pulled his forelock surlily, but did not stir. His very particular wooden leg was strapped in its place, and the iron-shod stump was sunk deep in the mud of the door-yard. Belle snapped at it, and had a kick in the ribs for her pains.

The adventure of the cypher much disquieted the Alderman, who incontinently decreed that Miss Fanny's brilliant must be made secure in Thrale's strong-box. Now was repeated the contest of pouts against Papa; Miss Fanny moped, and would not be pleased. At last by treaty the difficulty was accommodated. Let the Alderman make the gem secure today, and Miss Fanny might wear it in honour of the twelve days of Christmas, to begin at dusk on Christmas Eve precisely.

Christmas Eve came all too slowly, but it came at last. We were all in holiday guise, I in my bloom-coloured breeches, Dr. Thomas in a large new grizzle wig, Ralph in peach-colour brocade with silk stockings on his skinny shanks. Even Dr. Sam: Johnson honoured the occasion in his attire, with his snuff-colour coat and brass buttons, and a freshly powdered wig provided by the care of Mr. Thrale.

The ladies coruscated. Mrs. Alderman Plumbe billowed in flame-colour sattin. Mrs. Thrale had a handsome gown in the classick stile, with great sleeves, and gems in her hair. Miss Fanny wore a silken gown, of the tender shade appropriately called maiden's blush; 'twas cut low and her brooch gleamed at her bosom. Even Belle the spaniel was adorned with a great riband tied on with care by the white hand of Miss Fanny.

'Twas Thrale's care to uphold the old customs, and play the 'squire; while at the same time he had a maccaroni's contempt for the lower orders. 'Twas decreed, therefore, that we should have our Christmas games in the library on the lower floor, while the servants might have their merrymaking in the servant's hall, and the strolling rusticks had perforce to receive their Christmas gratuities withoutside.

We supped upon Christmas furmety, a dish of wheat cakes seethed in milk with rich spices. I relished it well, and did equal justice to the noble minced pyes served up with it.

Supper done, we trooped to the library. Impeded by an armful of green stuff, Dr. Johnson came last, edging his way to the door. On the threshold, as he sought to manœuvre the

unmanageable branches through, the crookedest one fairly
lifted his fresh-powdered Christmas wig from his head, and
as he clutched at it with a start, precipitated it in a cloud of
white onto the floor. I relieved him of his awkward burden,
and good-humouredly he recovered his head-covering and
clapped it back in its place, all awry.

In the library all was bustle. It was my part to wreathe the
mantel with green. Pretty Miss Fanny lighted the Christmas
candles, looking the prettier in their glow, her sparkling eyes
rivalling the brilliant at her breast. Thrale ignited the mighty
"Yule clog."

Dr. Johnson was in great expansion of soul, saluting his
hostess gallantly under the mistletoe bough, and expatiating
on the old Christmas games of his boyhood.

"Do but be patient, Dr. Johnson, we'll shew you them
all," cried Thrale with unwonted vivacity. He was busied
over a huge bowl. In it heated wine mingled its fumes with
orange peel and spices, while whole roasted apples by the
fire were ready to be set abob in it. 'Twas the old-time *wassail bowl;* though Dr. Johnson persisted in referring to its
contents, in his Lichfield accent, as *poonch.*

"Here we come a-wassailing among the leaves so green,
   Here we come a-wandering, so fair to be seen . . ."

The notes of the song crept up on us gradually, coming
from the direction of the common, till by the time the second
verse began, the singers stood in the gravel path before the
library windows; which we within threw up, the better to
hear their song:

"We are not daily beggars, that beg from door to door,
   But we are your neighbours' children, whom you have seen before . . ."

Past all doubt, so they were. The servants had crowded to
the door-step in the mild night, and merry greetings were
interchanged as they found friends among the waits. A light
snow was drifting down. The rusticks were fancifully

adorned with ribands, and wore greens stuck in their hats;
they carried lanthorns on poles, and sang to the somewhat
dubious accompaniment of an ancient serpent and a small kit
fiddle. In the ring of listening faces I spied the surly visage
of the one-legged sailor. Belle the spaniel spied her enemy
too. She escaped from the arms of Miss Fanny, eluded the
groom at the house-door, and dashed out into the mud to
snap at his heel. She came back with a satisfied swagger, the
more as she had succeeded in untying her riband and befoul-
ing it in the mud. Miss Fanny admonished her, and restored
the adornment.

> "Now here's to the maid in the lily-white smock
> Who slipped to the door and pulled back the lock,
> Who slipped to the door and pulled back the pin
> For to let these merry wassailers walk in."

There was no suiting the action to the word. Thrale passed
the cup out at window, keeping the lower orders still withoutside. The waits wiped their mouths on their sleeves, and
sang themselves off:

> "Wassail, wassail all over the town,
> Our bread it is white and our ale it is brown,
> Our bowl it is made of the green maple tree—
> In our wassailing bowl we'll drink unto thee!"

Next the mummers came marching. Like the waits, they
had been recruited from the lads about Streatham. Though
every man was disguised in fantastick habiliments, among
them the canine instinct of Belle unerringly found out her
friends. His own mother would not have known the *Doctor*,
he presenting to the world but a high-bridged nose and a
forest of whiskers; but Belle licked his hand, the while he
acknowledged the attention by scratching her ear and making her riband straight. She fawned upon *St. George* (by
which, " 'Tis the butcher's boy!" discovered Mrs. Thrale)
and put muddy foot-marks on the breeches of the *Old Man*,

before her attentions were repelled. She came back with her tongue out and her riband, once again, a-trail. Miss Fanny, defeated, neglected to restore it. She crowded with the rest of the company in the window as the link-boys lifted their torches, and upon the snowy sward the rusticks of Streatham played the famous mumming play of *St. George and the Dragon*.

"Pray, sir, take notice," said the pleased Dr. Johnson, "is not this a relique of great antiquity, the hieratic proceedings of yonder sorcerous *Doctor* with his magick pill? Pray, my man—" out at window to the *Doctor*, "how do you understand these doings?"

"Nor I don't, sir," replied the player huskily, and carried on his part to a chorus of laughter from within.

"And God bless this good company," concluded *St. George* piously. He caught the heavy purse that Thrale threw him, weighed it, and added in his own voice, "God bless ye, sir."

The guests added their largesse. Plumbe hurled a piece of gold; Dr. Johnson and I scattered silver; even withered little Dr. Thomas must needs add his half crown. 'Twas scarce worth the trouble he went to, first to fumble in his capacious pocket for the destined coin, then to wrap it in a leaf from his pocket book, finally to aim it precisely into the hands of *St. George*. His heart was better than his marksmanship; his shot went wide, and a scramble ensued.

"God bless all here," chorused the rusticks, and made off with their torches as we within closed windows and clustered about the fire. Then the bowl was set ablaze, and we adventured our fingers at snapdragon, catching at the burning raisins with merry cries.

"Fan, my love," said the Alderman suddenly, "where is thy Christmas box?"

Everybody looked at the flushed girl, standing with a burned finger-tip between her pink lips like a baby.

"The man," she half-whispered, "the man, Papa, he looked at it so, while the mummers played, I was affrighted and slipped it into a place of safety."

She indicated an exquisite little French enamel vase.

" 'Tis here, Papa."

The Alderman snatched the vase and turned it up. 'Twas empty. Miss Fanny's Christmas box was gone.

The Alderman turned purple.

"The servants—" he roared.

"Pray, Mr. Plumbe, calm yourself," said Dr. Johnson, "we must look for Miss Fanny's diamond within this room."

He pointed, first to the snow now lightly veiling the ground beneath the window, then to the splotch of powder on the threshold. In neither was there any mark of boot or shoe.

But, though the cholerick Alderman turned out the chamber, and though every one present submitted to the most thorough of searches, though Plumbe even sifted out the ashes of the Yule clog, little Fanny's Christmas box was not to be found.

"This is worse than Jack Rice a thousand times," sniggered her brother in my ear.

It was so. Poor pretty Fanny was in disgrace.

" 'Tis a mean thief," cried Dr. Johnson in noble indignation, "that robs a child, and be sure I'll find him out."

Poor Fanny could only sob.

'Twas enough to mar the merriment of Christmas Day. Little Fanny kept her chamber, being there admonished by good Dr. Thomas. The lout Ralph wandered about idly, teasing Belle until the indignant spaniel nipped him soundly; upon which he retired into the sulks. The Alderman and his lady were not to be seen. The master and mistress of the house were busied doing honour to the day. I was by when they dispensed their Christmas beef upon the door-step; pretty Sally handed the trenchers about, and there in the crowd of rusticks, stolidly champing brawn, I saw the one-legged sailor. He seemed quite at home.

Dr. Johnson roamed restlessly from room to room.

BOSWELL: "Pray, sir, what do you seek so earnestly?"

JOHNSON: "Sir, a French dictionary."

BOSWELL: "To what end?"

JOHNSON: "To read yonder cypher aright; for sure 'tis the key to tell us, whither Fanny's brilliant has flown."

BOSWELL: "Why, sir, the words are plain; 'tis but the interpretation that eludes us."

JOHNSON: "No, sir, the words are *not* plain; the words are somehow to be transposed. Now, sir, could I but find a French dictionary printed in *two* columns, 'twould go hard but we should find, in the *second* column, the words we seek, jig-by-jole with the meaningless words we now have."

Upon this I joined the search; but in twenty-four hours we advanced no further in reading the cypher.

After dinner the next day I came upon Dr. Johnson conning it over by the fire, muttering the words to himself:

"Te halle l'eau oui l'aune ire te garde haine . . ."

I was scarce attending. An idea had occurred to me.

"Yonder hollow willow near the garden—" I began.

"How?" cried Dr. Johnson, starting up.

"The hollow willow near the garden—"

"You have it, Bozzy!" cried my companion in excitement. "Te hollow willown ear te gard en."

So strange was the accent and inflection with which my revered friend repeated my words, that I could only stare.

"Read it!" he cried. "Read it aloud!"

He thrust the decyphered message under my nose. I read it off with my best French accent, acquired in my elegant grand tour.

"Can't you see," cried Dr. Johnson, "when you speak it, the words are English—the hollow willow near the garden! 'Twill be the miscreants' post-office, 'tis clear to me now. See, they had cause to distrust the maid who was go-between."

He pointed to the last words: *aille firent salle lit,* I fear Sally.

"How did you do it, Bozzy?"

"I, sir? Trust me, 'twas the furthest thing from my mind. It had come into my head, perhaps by the alder was meant yonder hollow willow—"

"No, sir," returned Dr. Johnson, "there came into your mind, a *picture* of the hollow willow, because you heard, without knowing that you heard, the words I uttered; and when *you* spoke the words, *I* recognized that you were re-peating mine. But come, sir; let us investigate this thieves' post-office."

He fairly ran out at the door.

Coming suddenly about the corner of the house, we sur-prized the sailorman standing under the wall of the kitchen garden; and I could have sworn that I caught the swirl of a skirt where the wall turned. As we came up, the one-legged man finished knotting something into his neckerchief, and made off with astonishing speed. He stumped his way across the common in the direction of the ale-house on the other side.

"Shall we not catch him up?" I cried.

"In good time," replied my friend. "First we must call for the post."

Accordingly we lingered to sound the hollow tree. Save for some grubs and beetles, and a quantity of feathers, it was empty.

Our fortune was better when we passed under the wall where the one-legged man had stood. There we picked up the second of the strange messages that came under our eyes at Streatham.

'Twas a strip of paper, scarce an inch wide and some twelve inches long. Along both its edges someone had made chicken-tracks with a pen. One end was roughly torn away. Search as we might, the missing fragment was not to be found. At last we repaired to the house.

In the library we encountered Mrs. Thrale, in philosophi-cal discourse with Dr. Thomas. She looked at the strange piece of paper, and gave a screech.

" 'Tis Ogam!"

"Ogam?"

"I know it well, 'tis the antique writing of the Irish," said Dr. Thomas, scanning the page with interest. "You must understand, sir, that the untutored savages of Ireland, knowing nothing of pen and paper, had perforce to contrive some way of incising letters upon wood, stone, horn, and the like. They hit upon a system of scratching lines on the edges of these objects, as perpendicular or oblique, and grouped to represent the various letters. Thus it was said of many a deceased Irish hero, 'They dug the grave and they raised the stone and they carved his name in Ogam.' "

"Why, this is a learned jewel-thief. Pray, Dr. Thomas, translate these triangles and dashes."

"Alack, sir, I cannot do it extempore. I must first have my books."

"*You*, ma'am," says Dr. Johnson to the volatile matron, "*you* are mighty familiar with Ogam, pray read it off for us."

"O Lud, sir, not I, I am none of your antiquarians."

"Why, so. Then I must extract the meaning for myself. 'Twill be no harder than the bi-literal cypher."

But try as he would, the strange marks on the edges of the paper would not yield to the theory of the printer's case. At last he leaned back.

"Let us begin afresh."

"No, sir," I begged, "let us have our tea. I am no Spartan boy, to labour while a fox is gnawing my vitals."

"Spartan!" cried my companion. "You have earned your tea, Mr. Boswell. Do but answer me one question first, we may begin afresh and I think proceed in the right direction. Pray, what shape is this paper?"

"Sir, long and flat."

Dr. Johnson dangled it by one end.

"No, sir, 'tis helical."

Indeed as it dangled it coiled itself into a helix.

"Let us restore it to its proper shape," said Dr. Johnson. "Pray, Mr. Boswell, fetch me the besom."

I looked a question, but my sagacious friend said nothing

further, and I went in search of the pretty housemaid and her besoms. After an interlude of knight-errantry, which taught me somewhat about women, but naught at all about our puzzle, I returned with such brooms as the house afforded.

I found my learned friend surrounded by stocks and staves, thick and thin, long and short. Around them, one after one, he was coiling the strange paper as a friseur curls hair about his finger. The results left him but ill satisfied.

"Could I but recall it to mind," he muttered, "there is a thing missing, that is germane to this puzzle; but now 'tis gone from my memory."

"Why, sir," said I, "we are to question the one-legged sailorman."

"Well remembered, Mr. Boswell." He stuffed the coiled paper into his capacious pocket. "Come, let us be off."

I bade farewell to my tea as I followed him. We found the publick room of the Three Crowns nigh empty, its only occupants being the idling tapster, and two men drinking in the ingle; but one of them was the man we sought. His companion was a likely-looking youth with a high-bridged nose, who pledged him in nappy ale.

"Good day, friend," Dr. Johnson accosted the maimed sailor.

The fresh-faced youth rose quietly, pulled a respectful forelock, and made off. Dr. Johnson looked at the sailorman's tankard, now empty, and signed to the tapster.

Not that the sailorman's tongue wanted loosening. Previous potations had already done the business. He was all too ready to spin his yarn.

"Nine sea fights I come through," he cried, "and lost my peg in the end, *mort dieu,* in Quiberon Bay."

He dealt his wooden member a mighty thump with the again emptied tankard. My worthy friend, ever ready to relieve the lot of the unfortunate, once more signed to the tapster. As the can was filling, he animadverted upon the wretchedness of a sea-life.

"I marvel, that any man will be a sailor, who has contrivance enough to get himself into a gaol; for being in a ship is being in gaol with the chance of being drowned."

"Ah," said the peg-legged sailor mournfully, and buried his nose in his pot.

My friend pressed upon him a gratuity in recognition of his perils passed. The sailorman accepted of it with protestations of gratitude.

"'Tis nothing, sir," replied my kindly friend. "Do you but gratify my whim, I'll call myself overpaid."

"How, whim?" says the sailorman.

"I've a whim," says Johnson, "to borrow your wooden leg for a matter of half an hour."

I stared with open mouth, but the sailorman shewed no flicker of surprize. He unstrapped the contrivance immediately and put it in my friend's hand.

"Pray, Bozzy," said Dr. Johnson, "see that our worthy friend here lacks for nothing until I come again."

Before I could put a question he had withdrawn, the unstrapped peg in his hand. I was left to the company of the tapster and the loquacious sailorman. He insisted upon telling me how he had made his peg himself, and how it had often been admired for its artistry.

"Here's this young fellow now," he rattled on, gesturing vaguely across the common, "he thinks it a rarity, and but this morning he had it of me for an hour at a time."

This statement but doubled my puzzlement. What in the world could a two-legged man want with a peg-leg? Surely my learned friend was not intending to personate the one-legged sailorman? Had the high-nosed youth done so? I tried to recall the glimpse I had had of the one-legged beggar by the kitchen garden.

When Dr. Johnson returned, he returned in his own guise. We left the sailorman, by this time snorting with vinous stertorousness in the corner of the ingle, and walked across the common back to the house.

"Pray, sir, what success? Did you find the diamond?"

"Find the diamond? No, sir, I did not find the diamond;

but I know where it is, and I know how to lay the thief by the heels."

He dug from his pocket the strange strip of paper. Between the lines of Ogam he had penned the message:

"£140 tonight 12 a clock yᵉ oak nighest yᵉ 3 crowns"

"What shall this signify?"

"Nay, Bozzy, 'tis plain. But here comes our friend Dr. Thomas. Pray, not a word more."

I was seething with curiosity as we supped at the Thrales' sumptuous table. The talk turned, willy-nilly, to the strange way in which the Christmas gem had been spirited from the library. Dr. Johnson admitted himself baffled. He was in a depression from which he could not be wooed even by the blandishments of the spaniel Belle, who, spurred by hunger, begged eagerly for scraps; until a new larceny, committed against himself, restored him to good humour.

It must be said that Dr. Sam Johnson is scarce a dainty feeder. He is a valiant trencherman, and stows away vast quantities of his favourite comestables.

"Ma'am," says he on this occasion, unbuttoning the middle button of his capacious vest and picking a capon wing in his fingers, "ma'am, where the dinner is ill gotten, the family is somehow grossly wrong; there is poverty, ma'am, or there is stupidity; for a man seldom thinks more earnestly of anything than of his dinner, and if he cannot get that well done, he should be suspected of inaccuracy in other things."

"Oh," says Mrs. Thrale, not knowing how to take this, but willing to turn it against him, "did you never, then, sir, huff your wife about your meat?"

"Why, yes," replied he, taking a second wing in his fingers, "but then she huffed me worse, for she said one day as I was going to say grace: 'Nay, hold,' says she, 'and do not make a farce of thanking GOD for a dinner which you will presently protest to be uneatable.' "

At this there was a general laugh; under cover of which Belle the spaniel, tempted beyond endurance, reared boldly up, snatched the capon wing from the philosopher's fingers, and ran out of door with it.

"Fie, Belle," cried out Mrs. Thrale, "you used to be upon honour!"

"Ay," replied the Doctor with his great Olympian laugh, "but here has been a *bad influence* lately!"

Not another word would he say, but devoted himself to a mighty veal pye with plums and sugar.

Yet when we rose from the table, he sought out the guilty Belle and plied her with dainties.

"'Tis a worthy canine, Bozzy," cried he to me, "for she has told me, not only *how* Miss Fanny's diamond was spirited from the library, but by *whose* contrivance. Between the good Belle, and yonder strange paper of Ogam, I now know *where* the conspirators shall meet, and *when,* and *who* they are, and *what* their object is; to prevent which, I shall make one at the rendezvous. Do you but join me, you shall see all made plain."

I was eager to do so. Muffled in greatcoats, we crossed the common and took up our station under the great oak a stone's cast from the Three Crowns. As the wind rattled the dry branches over our heads, I was minded of other vigils we had shared and other miscreants we had laid by the heels.

The darkness was profound. Across the common we saw window after window darken in the Thrale house as the occupants blew out their candles. Then I became aware of motion in the darkness, and towards us, stealing along the path, came a muffled shape, utterly without noise, flitting along like a creature of the night. For a moment we stood rigid, not breathing; then Dr. Johnson stepped forward and collared the advancing figure. It gave a startled squeak, and was silent. Dr. Johnson pulled the hat from the brow. In the starlight I stared at the face thus revealed.

'Twas Dr. Thomas! I beheld with horror his awful confusion at being detected.

"Alas, Dr. Johnson, 'tis I alone am guilty! But pray, how have you smoaked me?"

"Ogam," says Dr. Johnson, looking sourly upon the clergyman. "Trust me, you knew that was no Ogam. Ogam is incised on *both* edges of a right angle, not scribbled on paper."

"That is so, sir. You have been too sharp for me. I will confess all. 'Tis my fatal passion for Welsh antiquities. I have pawned the very vestments of my office to procure them. I took Miss Fanny's gem, I confess it, and flung it from the window wrapped in a leaf from my pocket book."

"I see it!" I exclaimed. "'Twas thrown at hazard, and the one-legged sailor carried it thence hid in the hollow of his wooden leg."

"Nothing of the kind," said Dr. Johnson. "The role of the sailor and his wooden leg was quite other. But say, how much had you for the gem?"

"Two hundred pounds," replied the fallen clergyman. "Two hundred pounds! The price of my honour! Alas," he cried in a transport of remorse, falling on his knees and holding up his hands to Heaven, "had I, when I stood at those crossroads, gone another way, had I but heeded the voice within me which cried, *Turn aside, turn aside, lest thou fall into the hands of thine enemy,* had I but gone swiftly upon the strait way, then in truth we might at the grave's end have met together in the hereafter. . . ."

Dr. Johnson heard this piteous avowal unmoved, but not so I. 'Twas a solemn sight to see the unfortunate man wring his hands and cry out with anguish, turning up his eyes to Heaven. Suddenly, however, his gaze fixed eagerly upon the darkened inn. In the same instant Dr. Johnson whirled, and ran, swiftly for all his bulk, to where a light coach was just getting in motion. I heard the harness jingle, and then the startled snort of a horse as my fearless friend seized the near animal by the bit and forced it to a halt.

"So," he cried angrily, "you'll meet them hereafter at *Gravesend!* Never a whit. Come down, sir! Come down, miss!"

For a moment there was only the jingle of harness as the nervous horses pranced. Then a figure stepped to earth, a tall young man muffled to his high-bridged nose in a heavy cape, and lifted down after him the cloaked figure of—

Miss Fanny Plumbe!

"Pray, Dr. Johnson," she said statelily, "why do you hinder us? What have we done?"

"You have diddled your father, and all of us," replied my companion sternly, "sending Bacon's cypher to Jack Rice here with those letters you gave up so meekly—once you had the diamond that you might turn into journey-money."

The chit's composure was wonderful.

"Why, sir," she owned with a smile, "you gave me a turn when you decyphered my last message by the hand of Sally; whom indeed, Mr. Boswell—" turning to me—"I no longer dared trust when she became so great with you. But confess, Dr. Johnson, my French held you off, after all, until I was able to convey a new cypher to Jack by the hand of the sailorman."

"And Dr. Thomas was your accomplice in making away with the gem?" I cried in uncontrollable curiosity.

"Be not so gullible, Bozzy," cried my companion impatiently, "trust me, Dr. Thomas knew never a word of the matter until Miss here opened her mind to him in their close conference on Christmas Day. 'Twas the hussy herself that conveyed her diamond to her lover, that he might turn it into money for their elopement."

"Nay, how? For she never left the room."

"But *Belle* did—and carried with her the diamond, affixed to her riband by the hand of Miss Fanny. Out flies the dog to greet her friend the neighbour lad in his mummer's disguise; who apprised of the scheam, caresses his canine friend and removes the brilliant in the same operation."

"That is so, sir," said Jack Rice.

"Surely," said Miss Fanny, "surely I did no wrong, to convey my jewel to the man I mean to wed."

"That's as may be," said my friend, unrelenting, "but now, miss, do you accompany us back to the house, for there'll be no elopement this night."

"Pray, sir," said Dr. Thomas earnestly, "be mollified. The lad is a good lad, and will have a competence when once he turns twenty-one; and I have engaged to make one in their flight and bless their union, which the surly Alderman opposes out of mere ill nature."

"To this I cannot be a party," began my authoritarian friend. The little clergyman was fumbling in his pocket. He brought forth, not a weapon, but a prayer-book.

"Do you, John, take this woman . . ." he began suddenly.

"Hold, hold!" cried Johnson.

"I do," cried the lad in a ringing voice.

"And do you, Fanny . . ."

Jack Rice pulled a seal-ring from his finger.

"I do."

"Then I pronounce you man and wife."

The ring hung loose on the girl's slim finger, but it stayed on.

"You are witnesses, Dr. Johnson, Mr. Boswell," cried the little clergyman. "Will not you salute the bride?"

Dr. Johnson lifted his great shoulders in concession.

"I wish you joy, my dear."

As the coach with its strangely-assorted trio of honeymooners receded in the distance:

"Pray, Dr. Johnson," said I, "resolve me one thing. If the strange message was not Ogam, what was it?"

JOHNSON: "Simple English."

BOSWELL: "How can this be?"

JOHNSON: "The triangles and scratches along the edges of yonder paper were halved lines of writing, and had only to be laid together to be read off."

BOSWELL: "Yet how are the top and bottom of a single strip of paper to be laid together?"

JOHNSON: "The Spartans, of whom you yourself reminded me, did it by means of a staff or *scytale*, around which the strip is wound, edge to edge, both for writing and for reading."

BOSWELL: "Hence your search for a staff or broomstick."

JOHNSON: "Yes, sir. Now it went in my mind, yonder one-legged man had a strange wooden leg, which did not taper as they usually do, but was straight up and down like a post. Was he perhaps both the emissary and the key? At the cost of a half-crown I had it of him—carried it out of his sight that he might not babble of my proceedings—and read the communication with ease."

BOSWELL: "This is most notable, sir. I will make sure to record it this very night."

JOHNSON: "Pray, Mr. Boswell, spare me that; for though the play-acting clergyman with his two hundred pounds and his Welsh antiquities failed to deceive me, yet 'tis cold truth that under my nose a green boy has conspired with a school-girl to steal first a diamond and then the lass herself; so let's hear no more on't."

In his obituaries, he was called "the American Arthur Conan Doyle." Certainly no writer deserves the title more. Rex Stout and his detective Nero Wolfe command a following second only to the Sherlockian horde. The Wolfe Pack, organized December 2, 1978, meets once a year at its annual Black Orchids Banquet to honor Stout and present awards for excellence in mystery writing. Wolfe has recently been portrayed in a television series. Stout has been the subject of an award-winning biography. The Wolfe books are still reprinted, and Stout's vigorous brownstone style brings the legendary figure (a seventh of a ton) to life with a mystique that only Doyle has equalled. In fact, it was once rumored that Wolfe was the illegitimate son of Sherlock Holmes.

"Christmas Party" is one of the best of the Wolfe stories. It captures its hero in an uncharacteristic pose, aided and abetted by his amanuensis Archie Goodwin. It also finds murder at that most barbaric of all holiday institutions, the office Christmas party. Wolfe's physical and intellectual largesse permeate every scene, and Stout regales his reader with his special talent for making this unique corner of New York City come alive.

Wolfe stews, Archie engages, orchids bloom and a good time will be had by all.

Christmas Party

By Rex Stout

"I'M SORRY, SIR," I said. I tried to sound sorry. "But I told you two days ago, Monday, that I had a date for Friday afternoon, and you said all right. So I'll drive you to Long Island Saturday or Sunday."

Nero Wolfe shook his head. "That won't do. Mr. Thompson's ship docks Friday morning, and he will be at Mr. Hewitt's place only until Saturday noon, when he leaves for New Orleans. As you know, he is the best hybridizer in England, and I am grateful to Mr. Hewitt for inviting me to spend a few hours with him. As I remember, the drive takes about an hour and a half, so we should leave at twelve-thirty."

I decided to count ten, and swiveled my chair, facing my desk, so as to have privacy for it. As usual when we have no important case going, we had been getting on each other's nerves for a week, and I admit I was a little touchy, but his taking it for granted like that was a little too much. When I had finished the count I turned my head, to where he was perched on his throne behind his desk, and darned if he hadn't gone back to his book, making it plain that he regarded it as settled. That was much too much. I swiveled my chair to confront him.

"I really am sorry," I said, not trying to sound sorry, "but I have to keep that date Friday afternoon. It's a Christmas party at the office of Kurt Bottweill—you remember him, we did a job for him a few months ago, the stolen tapestries. You may not remember a member of his staff named Margot Dickey, but I do. I have been seeing her some, and I promised her I'd go to the party. We never have a Christmas office party here. As for going to Long Island, your idea that a car is a death trap if I'm not driving it is unsound. You can take a taxi, or hire a Baxter man, or get Saul Panzer to drive you."

Wolfe had lowered his book. "I hope to get some useful information from Mr. Thompson, and you will take notes."

"Not if I'm not there. Hewitt's secretary knows orchid terms as well as I do. So do you."

I admit those last three words were a bit strong, but he shouldn't have gone back to his book. His lips tightened. "Archie. How many times in the past year have I asked you to drive me somewhere?"

"If you call it asking, maybe eighteen or twenty."

"Not excessive, surely. If my feeling that you alone are to be trusted at the wheel of a car is an aberration, I have it. We will leave for Mr. Hewitt's place Friday at twelve-thirty."

So there we were. I took a breath, but I didn't need to count ten again. If he was to be taught a lesson, and he certainly needed one, luckily I had in my possession a document that would make it good. Reaching to my inside breast pocket, I took out a folded sheet of paper.

"I didn't intend," I told him, "to spring this on you until tomorrow, or maybe even later, but I guess it will have to be now. Just as well, I suppose."

I left my chair, unfolded the paper, and handed it to him. He put his book down to take it, gave it a look, shot a glance at me, looked at the paper again, and let it drop on his desk.

He snorted. "Pfui. What flummery is this?"

"No flummery. As you see, it's a marriage license for Archie Goodwin and Margot Dickey. It cost me two bucks. I could be mushy about it, but I won't. I will only say that if I am hooked at last, it took an expert. She intends to spread the tidings at the Christmas office party, and of course I have to be there. When you announce you have caught a fish it helps to have the fish present in person. Frankly, I would prefer to drive you to Long Island, but it can't be done."

The effect was all I could have asked. He gazed at me through narrowed eyes long enough to count eleven, then picked up the document and gazed at it. He flicked it from him to the edge of the desk as if it were crawling with germs, and focused on me again.

"You are deranged," he said evenly and distinctly. "Sit down."

I nodded. "I suppose," I agreed, remaining upright, "it's a form of madness, but so what if I've got it? Like what Margot was reading to me the other night—some poet, I think it was some Greek—'O love, resistless in thy might, thou triumphest even—'"

"Shut up and sit down!"

"Yes, sir." I didn't move. "But we're not rushing it. We haven't set the date, and there'll be plenty of time to decide on adjustments. You may not want me here any more, but that's up to you. As far as I'm concerned, I would like to stay. My long association with you has had its flaws, but I would hate to end it. The pay is okay, especially if I get a raise the first of the year, which is a week from Monday. I have grown to regard this old brownstone as my home, although you own it and although there are two creaky boards in the floor of my room. I appreciate working for the greatest private detective in the free world, no matter how eccentric he is. I appreciate being able to go up to the plant rooms whenever I feel like it and look at ten thousand orchids, especially the odontoglossums. I fully appreciate—"

"Sit down!"

"I'm too worked up to sit. I fully appreciate Fritz's cooking. I like the billiard table in the basement. I like West Thirty-fifth Street. I like the one-way glass panel in

the front door. I like this rug I'm standing on. I like your
favorite color, yellow. I have told Margot all this, and
more, including the fact that you are allergic to women.
We have discussed it, and we think it may be worth trying, say for a month, when we get back from the honey-
moon. My room could be our bedroom, and the other
room on that floor could be our living room. There are
plenty of closets. We could eat with you, as I have been,
or we could eat up there, as you prefer. If the trial works
out, new furniture or redecorating would be up to us. She
will keep her job with Kurt Bottweill, so she wouldn't be
here during the day, and since he's an interior decorator
we would get things wholesale. Of course we merely suggest this for your consideration. It's your house."

I picked up my marriage license, folded it, and returned it
to my pocket.

His eyes had stayed narrow and his lips tight. "I don't
believe it," he growled. "What about Miss Rowan?"

"We won't drag Miss Rowan into this," I said stiffly.

"What about the thousands of others you dally with?"

"Not thousands. Not even a thousand. I'll have to look up
'dally.' They'll get theirs, as Margot has got hers. As you
see, I'm deranged only up to a point. I realize—"

"Sit down."

"No, sir. I know this will have to be discussed, but right
now you're stirred up and it would be better to wait for a day
or two, or maybe more. By Saturday the idea of a woman in
the house may have you boiling even worse than you are
now, or it may have cooled you down to a simmer. If the
former, no discussion will be needed. If the latter, you may
decide it's worth a try. I hope you do."

I turned and walked out.

In the hall I hesitated. I could have gone up to my room
and phoned from there, but in his present state it was quite
possible he would listen in from the desk, and the call I
wanted to make was personal. So I got my hat and coat from
the rack, let myself out, descended the stoop steps, walked

to the drugstore on Ninth Avenue, found the booth unoccupied, and dialed a number. In a moment a musical little voice—more a chirp than a voice—was in my ear.

"Kurt Bottweill's studio, good morning."

"This is Archie Goodwin, Cherry. May I speak to Margot?"

"Why, certainly. Just a moment."

It was a fairly long moment. Then another voice. "Archie, darling!"

"Yes, my own. I've got it."

"I knew you could!"

"Sure, I can do anything. Not only that, you said up to a hundred bucks, and I thought I would have to part with twenty at least, but it only took five. And not only that, but it's on me, because I've already had my money's worth of fun out of it, and more. I'll tell you about it when I see you. Shall I send it up by messenger?"

"No, I don't think—I'd better come and get it. Where are you?"

"In a phone booth. I'd just as soon not go back to the office right now because Mr. Wolfe wants to be alone to boil, so how about the Tulip Bar at the Churchill in twenty minutes? I feel like buying you a drink."

"I feel like buying *you* a drink!"

She should, since I was treating her to a marriage license.

II

When, at three o'clock Friday afternoon, I wriggled out of the taxi at the curb in front of the four-story building in the East Sixties, it was snowing. If it kept up, New York might have an off-white Christmas.

During the two days that had passed since I got my money's worth from the marriage license, the atmosphere around Wolfe's place had not been very seasonable. If we had had a case going, frequent and sustained communication would have been unavoidable, but without one there was nothing that absolutely had to be said, and we said it. Our handling of that trying period showed our true natures. At table, for instance, I was polite and reserved, and spoke, when speaking seemed necessary, in low and cultured tones. When Wolfe spoke he either snapped or barked. Neither of us mentioned the state of bliss I was headed for, or the adjustments that would have to be made, or my Friday date with my fiancée, or his trip to Long Island. But he arranged it somehow, for precisely at twelve-thirty on Friday a black limousine drew up in front of the house, and Wolfe, with the brim of his old black hat turned down and the collar of his new gray overcoat turned up for the snow, descended the stoop, stood massively, the mountain of him, on the bottom step until the uniformed chauffeur had opened the door, and crossed the sidewalk and climbed in. I watched it from above, from a window of my room.

I admit I was relieved and felt better. He had unquestionably needed a lesson and I didn't regret giving him one, but if he had passed up a chance for an orchid powwow with the best hybridizer in England I would never have heard the last of it. I went down to the kitchen and ate lunch with Fritz, who was so upset by the atmosphere that he forgot to put the lemon juice in the soufflé. I wanted to console him by telling him that everything would be rosy by Christmas, only three days off, but of course that wouldn't do.

I had a notion to toss a coin to decide whether I would have a look at the new exhibit of dinosaurs at the Natural History Museum or go to the Bottweill party, but I was curious to know how Margot was making out with the license, and also how the other Bottweill personnel were making out with each other. It was surprising that they were still making out at all. Cherry Quon's position in the setup was apparently minor, since she functioned chiefly as a receptionist and phone-answerer, but I had seen her black eyes dart daggers at Margot Dickey, who should have been clear out of her reach. I had gathered that it was Margot who was mainly relied upon to wrangle prospective customers into the corral, that Bottweill himself put them under the spell, and that Alfred Kiernan's part was to make sure that before the spell wore off an order got signed on the dotted line.

Of course that wasn't all. The order had to be filled, and that was handled, under Bottweill's supervision, by Emil Hatch in the workshop. Also funds were required to buy the ingredients, and they were furnished by a specimen named Mrs. Perry Porter Jerome. Margot had told me that Mrs. Jerome would be at the party and would bring her son Leo, whom I had never met. According to Margot, Leo, who had no connection with the Bottweill business or any other business, devoted his time to two important activities: getting enough cash from his mother to keep going as a junior play-boy, and stopping the flow of cash to Bottweill, or at least slowing it down.

It was quite a tangle, an interesting exhibit of bipeds alive and kicking, and, deciding it promised more entertainment than the dead dinosaurs, I took a taxi to the East Sixties.

The ground floor of the four-story building, formerly a de luxe double-width residence, was now a beauty shop. The second floor was a real-estate office. The third floor was Kurt Bottweill's workshop, and on top was his studio. From the vestibule I took the do-it-yourself elevator to the top, opened the door, and stepped out into the glossy gold-leaf elegance I had first seen some months back, when Bottweill had hired Wolfe to find out who had swiped some tapestries. On that first visit I had decided that the only big difference between chrome modern and Bottweill gold-leaf modern was the color, and I still thought so. Not even skin deep; just a two-hundred-thousandth of an inch deep. But on the panels and racks and furniture frames it gave the big skylighted studio quite a tone, and the rugs and drapes and pictures, all modern, joined in. It would have been a fine den for a blind millionaire.

"Archie!" a voice called. "Come and help us sample!"

It was Margot Dickey. In a far corner was a gold-leaf bar, some eight feet long, and she was at it on a gold-leaf stool. Cherry Quon and Alfred Kiernan were with her, also on stools, and behind the bar was Santa Claus, pouring from a champagne bottle. It was certainly a modern touch to have Santa Claus tend bar, but there was nothing modern about his costume. He was strictly traditional, cut, color, size, mask, and all, except that the hand grasping the champagne bottle wore a white glove. I assumed, crossing to them over the thick rugs, that that was a touch of Bottweill elegance, and didn't learn until later how wrong I was.

They gave me the season's greetings, and Santa Claus poured a glass of bubbles for me. No gold leaf on the glass. I was glad I had come. To drink champagne with a blonde at one elbow and a brunette at the other gives a man a sense of well-being, and those two were fine specimens—the tall, slender Margot relaxed, all curves, on the stool, and little slant-eyed black-eyed Cherry Quon, who came only up to my collar when standing, sitting with her spine as straight as a plumb line, yet not stiff. I thought Cherry worthy of notice not only as a statuette, though she was highly decorative, but as a possible source of new light on human relations. Margot had told me that her father was half Chinese and half Indian —not American Indian—and her mother was Dutch.

I said that apparently I had come too early, but Alfred Kiernan said no, the others were around and would be in shortly. He added that it was a pleasant surprise to see me, as it was just a little family gathering and he hadn't known others had been invited. Kiernan, whose title was business manager, had not liked a certain step I had taken when I was hunting the tapestries, and he still didn't, but an Irishman at a Christmas party likes everybody. My impression was that he really was pleased, so I was too. Margot said she had invited me, and Kiernan patted her on the arm and said that if she hadn't he would. About my age and fully as handsome, he was the kind who can pat the arm of a queen or a president's wife without making eyebrows go up.

He said we needed another sample and turned to the bartender. "Mr. Claus, we'll try the Veuve Clicquot." To us: "Just like Kurt to provide different brands. No monotony for Kurt." To the bartender: "May I call you by your first name, Santy?"

"Certainly, sir," Santa Claus told him from behind the mask in a thin falsetto that didn't match his size. As he stooped and came up with a bottle a door at the left opened and two men entered. One of them, Emil Hatch, I had met before. When briefing Wolfe on the tapestries and telling us about his staff, Bottweill had called Margot Dickey his contact woman, Cherry Quon his handy girl, and Emil Hatch his pet wizard, and when I met Hatch I found that he both looked the part and acted it. He wasn't much taller than Cherry Quon and skinny, and something had either pushed his left shoulder down or his right shoulder up, making him lop-sided, and he had a sour face, a sour voice, and a sour taste.

When the stranger was named to me as Leo Jerome, that placed him. I was acquainted with his mother, Mrs. Perry Porter Jerome. She was a widow and an angel—that is, Kurt Bottweill's angel. During the investigation she had talked as if the tapestries belonged to her, but that might have only been her manners, of which she had plenty. I could have made guesses about her personal relations with Bottweill, but hadn't bothered. I have enough to do to handle my own personal relations without wasting my brain power on other people's. As for her son Leo, he must have got his physique from his father—tall, bony, big-eared and long-armed. He was probably approaching thirty, below Kiernan but above Margot and Cherry.

When he shoved in between Cherry and me, giving me his back, and Emil Hatch had something to tell Kiernan, sour no doubt, I touched Margot's elbow and she slid off the stool and let herself be steered across to a divan which had been covered with designs by Euclid in six or seven colors. We stood looking down at it.

"Mighty pretty," I said, "but nothing like as pretty as you. If only that license were real! I can get a real one for two dollars. What do you say?"

"*You!*" she said scornfully. "You wouldn't marry Miss Universe if she came on her knees with a billion dollars."

"I dare her to try it. Did it work?"

"Perfect. Simply perfect."

"Then you're ditching me?"

"Yes, Archie darling. But I'll be a sister to you."

"I've got a sister. I want the license back for a souvenir, and anyway I don't want it kicking around. I could be hooked for forgery. You can mail it to me, once my own."

"No, I can't. He tore it up."

"The hell he did. Where are the pieces?"

"Gone. He put them in his wastebasket. Will you come to the wedding?"

"What wastebasket where?"

"The gold one by his desk in his office. Last evening after dinner. Will you come to the wedding?"

"I will not. My heart is bleeding. So will Mr. Wolfe's— and by the way, I'd better get out of here. I'm not going to stand around and sulk."

"You won't have to. He won't know I've told you, and anyway, you wouldn't be expected—Here he comes!"

She darted off to the bar and I headed that way. Through the door on the left appeared Mrs. Perry Porter Jerome, all of her, plump and plushy, with folds of mink trying to keep up as she breezed in. As she approached, those on stools left them and got onto their feet, but that courtesy could have been as much for her companion as for her. She was the angel, but Kurt Bottweill was the boss. He stopped five paces short of the bar, extended his arms as far as they would go, and sang out, "Merry Christmas, all my blessings! Merry merry merry!"

I still hadn't labeled him. My first impression, months ago, had been that he was one of them, but that had been wrong. He was a man all right, but the question was what kind. About average in height, round but not pudgy, maybe

forty-two or -three, his fine black hair slicked back so that
he looked balder than he was, he was nothing great to look
at, but he had something, not only for women but for men
too. Wolfe had once invited him to stay for dinner, and they
had talked about the scrolls from the Dead Sea. I had seen
him twice at baseball games. His label would have to wait.

As I joined them at the bar, where Santa Claus was pouring Mumms Cordon Rouge, Bottweill squinted at me a moment and then grinned. "Goodwin! You here? Good! Edith,
your pet sleuth!"

Mrs. Perry Porter Jerome, reaching for a glass, stopped
her hand to look at me. "Who asked you?" she demanded,
then went on, with no room for a reply, "Cherry, I suppose.
Cherry *is* a blessing. Leo, quit tugging at me. Very well,
take it. It's warm in here." She let her son pull her coat off,
then reached for a glass. By the time Leo got back from
depositing the mink on the divan we all had glasses, and
when he had his we raised them, and our eyes went to Bottweill.

His eyes flashed around. "There are times," he said,
"when love takes over. There are times—"

"Wait a minute," Alfred Kiernan cut in. "You enjoy it too.
You don't like this stuff."

"I can stand a sip, Al."

"But you won't enjoy it. Wait." Kiernan put his glass on
the bar and marched to the door on the left and on out. In
five seconds he was back, with a bottle in his hand, and as
he rejoined us and asked Santa Claus for a glass I saw the
Pernod label. He pulled the cork, which had been pulled
before, filled the glass halfway, and held it out to Bottweill.
"There," he said. "That will make it unanimous."

"Thanks, Al." Bottweill took it. "My secret public vice."
He raised the glass. "I repeat, there are times when love
takes over. (Santa Claus, where is yours? but I suppose you
can't drink through that mask.) There are times when all the
little demons disappear down their ratholes, and ugliness itself takes on the shape of beauty; when the darkest corner is
touched by light; when the coldest heart feels the glow of

warmth; when the trumpet call of good will and good cheer
drowns out all the Babel of mean little noises. This is such a
time. Merry Christmas! Merry merry merry!"

I was ready to touch glasses, but both the angel and the
boss steered theirs to their lips, so I and the others followed
suit. I thought Bottweill's eloquence deserved more than a
sip, so I took a healthy gulp, and from the corner of my eye
I saw that he was doing likewise with the Pernod. As I lowered the glass my eyes went to Mrs. Jerome, as she spoke.

"That was lovely," she declared. "Simply lovely. I must
write it down and have it printed. That part about the trumpet call—*Kurt!* What is it? *Kurt!*"

He had dropped the glass and was clutching his throat
with both hands. As I moved he turned loose of his throat,
thrust his arms out, and let out a yell. I think he yelled
"Merry!" but I wasn't really listening. Others started for
him too, but my reflexes were better trained for emergencies
than any of theirs, so I got him first. As I got my arms
around him he started choking and gurgling, and a spasm
went over him from head to foot that nearly loosened my
grip. They were making noises, but no screams, and someone was clawing at my arm. As I was telling them to get
back and give me room, he was suddenly a dead weight, and
I almost went down with him and might have if Kiernan
hadn't grabbed his arm.

I called, "Get a doctor!" and Cherry ran to a table where
there was a gold-leaf phone. Kiernan and I let Bottweill
down on the rug. He was out, breathing fast and hard, but as
I was straightening his head his breathing slowed down and
foam showed on his lips. Mrs. Jerome was commanding us,
"Do something, do something!"

There was nothing to do and I knew it. While I was holding onto him I had got a whiff of his breath, and now, kneeling, I leaned over to get my nose an inch from his, and I
knew that smell, and it takes a big dose to hit that quick and
hard. Kiernan was loosening Bottweill's tie and collar.
Cherry Quon called to us that she had tried a doctor and

couldn't get him and was trying another. Margot was squatting at Bottweill's feet, taking his shoes off, and I could have told her she might as well let him die with his boots on but didn't. I had two fingers on his wrist and my other hand inside his shirt, and could feel him going.

When I could feel nothing I abandoned the chest and wrist, took his hand, which was a fist, straightened the middle finger, and pressed its nail with my thumbtip until it was white. When I removed my thumb the nail stayed white. Dropping the hand, I yanked a little cluster of fibers from the rug, told Kiernan not to move, placed the fibers against Bottweill's nostrils, fastened my eyes on them, and held my breath for thirty seconds. The fibers didn't move.

I stood up and spoke. "His heart has stopped and he's not breathing. If a doctor came within three minutes and washed out his stomach with chemicals he wouldn't have with him, there might be one chance in a thousand. As it is—"

"Can't you *do* something?" Mrs. Jerome squawked.

"Not for him, no. I'm not an officer of the law, but I'm a licensed detective, and I'm supposed to know how to act in these circumstances, and I'll get it if I don't follow the rules. Of course—"

"*Do something!*" Mrs. Jerome squawked.

Kiernan's voice came from behind me. "He's dead."

I didn't turn to ask what test he had used. "Of course," I told them, "his drink was poisoned. Until the police come no one will touch anything, especially the bottle of Pernod, and no one will leave this room. You will—"

I stopped dead. Then I demanded, "Where is Santa Claus?"

Their heads turned to look at the bar. No bartender. On the chance that it had been too much for him, I pushed between Leo Jerome and Emil Hatch to step to the end of the bar, but he wasn't on the floor either.

I wheeled. "Did anyone see him go?"

They hadn't. Hatch said, "He didn't take the elevator. I'm sure he didn't. He must have—" He started off.

I blocked him. "You stay here. I'll take a look. Kiernan, phone the police. Spring seven-three-one-hundred."

I made for the door on the left and passed through, pulling it shut as I went, and was in Bottweill's office, which I had seen before. It was one-fourth the size of the studio, and much more subdued, but was by no means squalid. I crossed to the far end, saw through the glass panel that Bottweill's private elevator wasn't there, and pressed the button. A clank and a whirr came from inside the shaft, and it was coming. When it was up and had jolted to a stop I opened the door, and there on the floor was Santa Claus, but only the outside of him. He had molted. Jacket, breeches, mask, wig . . . I didn't check to see if it was all there, because I had another errand and not much time for it.

Propping the elevator door open with a chair, I went and circled around Bottweill's big gold-leaf desk to his gold-leaf wastebasket. It was one-third full. Bending, I started to paw, decided that was inefficient, picked it up and dumped it, and began tossing things back in one by one. Some of the items were torn pieces of paper, but none of them came from a marriage license. When I had finished I stayed down a moment, squatting, wondering if I had hurried too much and possibly missed it, and I might have gone through it again if I hadn't heard a faint noise from the studio that sounded like the elevator door opening. I went to the door to the studio and opened it, and as I crossed the sill two uniformed cops were deciding whether to give their first glance to the dead or the living.

III

Three hours later we were seated, more or less in a group, and my old friend and foe, Sergeant Purley Stebbins of Homicide, stood surveying us, his square jaw jutting and his big burly frame erect.

He spoke. "Mr. Kiernan and Mr. Hatch will be taken to the District Attorney's office for further questioning. The rest of you can go for the present, but you will keep yourselves available at the addresses you have given. Before you go I want to ask you again, here together, about the man who was here as Santa Claus. You have all claimed you know nothing about him. Do you still claim that?"

It was twenty minutes to seven. Some two dozen city employees—medical examiner, photographer, fingerprinters, meat-basket bearers, the whole kaboodle—had finished the on-the-scene routine, including private interviews with the eyewitnesses. I had made the highest score, having had sessions with Stebbins, a precinct man, and Inspector Cramer, who had departed around five o'clock to organize the hunt for Santa Claus.

"I'm not objecting," Kiernan told Stebbins, "to going to the District Attorney's office. I'm not objecting to anything. But we've told you all we can, I know I have. It seems to me your job is to find him."

"Do you mean to say," Mrs. Jerome demanded, "that no one knows anything at all about him?"

"So they say," Purley told her. "No one even knew there was going to be a Santa Claus, so they say. He was brought to this room by Bottweill, about a quarter to three, from his office. The idea is that Bottweill himself had arranged for him, and he came up in the private elevator and put on the costume in Bottweill's office. You may as well know there is some corroboration of that. We have found out where the costume came from—Burleson's on Forty-sixth Street. Bottweill phoned them yesterday afternoon and ordered it sent here; marked personal. Miss Quon admits receiving the package and taking it to Bottweill in his office."

For a cop, you never just state a fact, or report it or declare it or say it. You admit it.

"We are also," Purley admitted, "covering agencies which might have supplied a man to act Santa Claus, but that's a big order. If Bottweill got a man through an agency there's no telling what he got. If it was a man with a record, when he saw trouble coming he beat it. With everybody's attention on Bottweill, he sneaked out, got his clothes, whatever he had taken off, in Bottweill's office, and went down in the elevator he had come up in. He shed the costume on the way down and after he was down, and left it in the elevator. If that was it, if he was just a man Bottweill hired, he wouldn't have had any reason to kill him—and besides, he wouldn't have known that Bottweill's only drink was Pernod, and he wouldn't have known where the poison was."

"Also," Emil Hatch said, surer than ever, "if he was just hired for the job he was a damn fool to sneak out. He might have known he'd be found. So he wasn't just hired. He was someone who knew Bottweill, and knew about the Pernod and the poison, and had some good reason for wanting to kill him. You're wasting your time on the agencies."

Stebbins lifted his heavy broad shoulders and dropped them. "We waste most of our time, Mr. Hatch. Maybe he was too scared to think. I just want you to understand that if we find him and that's how Bottweill got him, it's going to be hard to believe that he put poison in that bottle, but somebody did. I want you to understand that so you'll understand why you are all to be available at the addresses you have given. Don't make any mistake about that."

"Do you mean," Mrs. Jerome demanded, "that we are under suspicion? That *I* and *my son* are under suspicion?"

Purley opened his mouth and shut it again. With that kind he always had trouble with his impulses. He wanted to say, "You're goddam right you are." He did say, "I mean we're going to find that Santa Claus, and when we do we'll see. If we can't see him for it we'll have to look further, and we'll expect all of you to help us. I'm taking it for granted you'll all want to help. Don't you want to, Mrs. Jerome?"

"I would help if I could, but I know nothing about it. I only know that my very dear friend is dead, and I don't intend to be abused and threatened. What about the poison?"

"You know about it. You have been questioned about it."

"I know I have, but what about it?"

"It must have been apparent from the questions. The medical examiner thinks it was cyanide and expects the autopsy to verify it. Emil Hatch uses potassium cyanide in his work with metals and plating, and there is a large jar of it on a cupboard shelf in the workshop one floor below, and there is a stair from Bottweill's office to the workroom. Anyone who knew that, and who also knew that Bottweill kept a case of Pernod in a cabinet in his office, and an open bottle of it in a drawer of his desk, couldn't have asked for a better setup. Four of you have admitted knowing both of those things. Three of you—Mrs. Jerome, Leo Jerome, and Archie Goodwin—admit they knew about the Pernod but deny they knew about the potassium cyanide. That will—"

"That's not true! She did know about it!"

Mrs. Perry Porter Jerome's hand shot out across her son's knees and slapped Cherry Quon's cheek or mouth or both. Her son grabbed her arm. Alfred Kiernan sprang to his feet, and for a second I thought he was going to sock Mrs. Jerome, and he did too, and possibly would have if Margot Dickey hadn't jerked at his coattail. Cherry put her hand to her face but, except for that, didn't move.

"Sit down," Stebbins told Kiernan. "Take it easy. Miss Quon, you say that Mrs. Jerome knew about the potassium cyanide?"

"Of course she did." Cherry's chirp was pitched lower that normal, but it was still a chirp. "In the workshop one day I heard Mr. Hatch telling her how he used it and how careful he had to be."

"Mr. Hatch? Do you verify—"

"Nonsense," Mrs. Jerome snapped. "What if he did? Perhaps he did. I had forgotten all about it. I told you I won't tolerate this abuse!"

Purley eyed her. "Look here, Mrs. Jerome. When we find that Santa Claus, if it was someone who knew Bottweill and had a motive, that may settle it. If not, it won't help anyone to talk about abuse, and that includes you. So far as I know

now, only one of you has told us a lie. You. That's on the record. I'm telling you, and all of you, lies only make it harder for you, but sometimes they make it easier for us. I'll leave it at that for now. Mr. Kiernan and Mr. Hatch, these men"—he aimed a thumb over his shoulder at two dicks standing back of him—"will take you downtown. The rest of you can go, but remember what I said. Goodwin, I want to see you."

He had already seen me, but I wouldn't make a point of it. Kiernan, however, had a point to make, and made it: he had to leave last so he could lock up. It was so arranged. The three women, Leo Jerome, and Stebbins and I took the elevator down, leaving the two dicks with Kiernan and Hatch. Down the sidewalk, as they headed in different directions, I could see no sign of tails taking after them. It was still snowing, a fine prospect for Christmas and the street cleaners. There were two police cars at the curb, and Purley went to one and opened the door and motioned to me to get in.

I objected: "If I'm invited downtown too I'm willing to oblige, but I'm going to eat first. I damn near starved to death there once."

"You're not wanted downtown, not right now. Get in out of the snow."

I did so, and slid across under the wheel to make room for him. He needs room. He joined me and pulled the door shut.

"If we're going to sit here," I suggested, "we might as well be rolling. Don't bother to cross town, just drop me at Thirty-fifth."

He objected. "I don't like to drive and talk. Or listen. What were you doing there today?"

"I've told you. Having fun. Three kinds of champagne. Miss Dickey invited me."

"I'm giving you another chance. You were the only outsider there. Why? You're nothing special to Miss Dickey. She was going to marry Bottweill. Why?"

"Ask her."

"We have asked her. She says there was no particular reason, she knew Bottweill liked you, and they've regarded you as one of them since you found some tapestries for them. She stuttered around about it. What I say, any time I find you anywhere near a murder, I want to know. I'm giving you another chance."

So she hadn't mentioned the marriage license. Good for her. I would rather have eaten all the snow that had fallen since noon than explain that damn license to Sergeant Stebbins or Inspector Cramer. That was why I had gone through the wastebasket. "Thanks for the chance," I told him, "but I can't use it. I've told you everything I saw and heard there today." That put me in a class with Mrs. Jerome, since I had left out my little talk with Margot. "I've told you all I know about those people. Lay off and go find your murderer."

"I know you, Goodwin."

"Yeah, you've even called me Archie. I treasure that memory."

"I know you." His head was turned on his bull neck, and our eyes were meeting. "Do you expect me to believe that guy got out of that room and away without you knowing it?"

"Nuts. I was kneeling on the floor, watching a man die, and they were around us. Anyway, you're just talking to hear yourself. You don't think I was accessory to the murder or to the murderer's escape."

"I didn't say I did. Even if he was wearing gloves—and what for if not to leave no prints?—I don't say he was the murderer. But if you knew who he was and didn't want him involved in it and let him get away, and if you let us wear out our ankles looking for him, what about that?"

"That would be bad. If I asked my advice I would be against it."

"Goddamn it," he barked, "do you know who he is?"

"No."

"Did you or Wolfe have anything to do with getting him there?"

"No."

"All right, pile out. They'll be wanting you downtown."

"I hope not tonight. I'm tired." I opened the door. "You have my address." I stepped out into the snow, and he started the engine and rolled off.

It should have been a good hour for an empty taxi, but in a Christmas-season snowstorm it took me ten minutes to find one. When it pulled up in front of the old brownstone on West Thirty-fifth Street it was eight minutes to eight.

As usual in my absence, the chain-bolt was on, and I had to ring for Fritz to let me in. I asked him if Wolfe was back, and he said yes, he was at dinner. As I put my hat on the shelf and my coat on a hanger I asked if there was any left for me, and he said plenty, and moved aside for me to precede him down the hall to the door of the dining room. Fritz has fine manners.

Wolfe, in his oversized chair at the end of the table, told me good evening, not snapping or barking. I returned it, got seated at my place, picked up my napkin, and apologized for being late. Fritz came, from the kitchen, with a warm plate, a platter of braised boned ducklings, and a dish of potatoes baked with mushrooms and cheese. I took enough. Wolfe asked if it was still snowing and I said yes. After a good mouthful had been disposed of, I spoke.

"As you know, I approve of your rule not to discuss business during a meal, but I've got something on my chest and it's not business. It's personal."

He grunted. "The death of Mr. Bottweill was reported on the radio at seven o'clock. You were there."

"Yeah. I was there. I was kneeling by him while he died." I replenished my mouth. Damn the radio. I hadn't intended to mention the murder until I had dealt with the main issue from my standpoint. When there was room enough for my tongue to work I went on. "I'll report on that in full if you want it, but I doubt if there's a job in it. Mrs. Perry Porter Jerome is the only suspect with enough jack to pay your fee, and she has already notified Purley Stebbins that she won't be abused. Besides, when they find Santa Claus that may settle it. What I want to report on happened before Bottweill died. That marriage license I showed you is for the birds. Miss Dickey has called it off. I am out two bucks. She told me she had decided to marry Bottweill."

He was sopping a crust in the sauce on his plate. "Indeed," he said.

"Yes, sir. It was a jolt, but I would have recovered, in time. Then ten minutes later Bottweill was dead. Where does that leave me? Sitting around up there through the routine, I considered it. Perhaps I could get her back now, but no thank you. That license has been destroyed. I get another one, another two bucks, and then she tells me she has decided to marry Joe Doakes. I'm going to forget her. I'm going to blot her out."

I resumed on the duckling. Wolfe was busy chewing. When he could he said, "For me, of course, this is satisfactory."

"I know it is. Do you want to hear about Bottweill?"

"After dinner."

"Okay. How did you make out with Thompson?"

But that didn't appeal to him as a dinner topic either. In fact, nothing did. Usually he likes table talk, about anything from refrigerators to Republicans, but apparently the trip to Long Island and back, with all its dangers, had tired him out. It suited me all right, since I had had a noisy afternoon too and could stand a little silence. When we had both done well with the duckling and potatoes and salad and baked pears and cheese and coffee, he pushed back his chair.

"There's a book," he said, "that I want to look at. It's up in your room—*Here and Now*, by Herbert Block. Will you bring it down, please?"

Though it meant climbing two flights with a full stomach, I was glad to oblige, out of appreciation for his calm acceptance of my announcement of my shattered hopes. He could have been very vocal. So I mounted the stairs cheerfully, went to my room, and crossed to the shelves where I keep a few books. There were only a couple of dozen of them, and

I knew where each one was, but *Here and Now* wasn't there. Where it should have been was a gap. I looked around, saw a book on the dresser, and stepped to it. It was *Here and Now,* and lying on top of it was a pair of white cotton gloves.

I gawked.

IV

I would like to say that I caught on immediately, the second I spotted them, but I didn't. I had picked them up and looked them over, and put one of them on and taken it off again, before I fully realized that there was only one possible explanation. Having realized it, instantly there was a traffic jam inside my skull, horns blowing, brakes squealing, head-on collisions. To deal with it I went to a chair and sat. It took me maybe a minute to reach my first clear conclusion.

He had taken this method of telling me he was Santa Claus, instead of just telling me, because he wanted me to think it over on my own before we talked it over together.

Why did he want me to think it over on my own? That took a little longer, but with the traffic under control I found my way through to the only acceptable answer. He had decided to give up his trip to see Thompson, and instead to arrange with Bottweill to attend the Christmas party disguised as Santa Claus, because the idea of a woman living in his house—or of the only alternative, my leaving—had made him absolutely desperate, and he had to see for himself. He had to see Margot and me together, and to talk with her if possible. If he found out that the marriage license was a hoax he would have me by the tail; he could tell me he would be delighted to welcome my bride and watch me wriggle out. If he found that I really meant it he would know what he was up against and go on from there. The point was this, that he had shown what he really thought of me. He had shown that rather than lose me he would do something that he wouldn't have done for any fee anybody could name. He would rather have gone without beer for a week than admit it, but now he was a fugitive from justice in a murder case and needed me. So he had to let me know, but he wanted it understood that that aspect of the matter was not to be mentioned. The assumption would be that he had gone to Bottweill's instead of Long Island because he loved to dress up like Santa Claus and tend bar.

A cell in my brain tried to get the right of way for the question, considering this development, how big a raise should I get after New Year's? but I waved it to the curb.

I thought over other aspects. He had worn the gloves so I couldn't recognize his hands. Where did he get them? What time had he got to Bottweill's and who had seen him? Did Fritz know where he was going? How had he got back home? But after a little of that I realized that he hadn't sent me up to my room to ask myself questions he could answer, so I went back to considering whether there was anything else he wanted me to think over alone. Deciding there wasn't, after chewing it thoroughly, I got *Here and Now* and the gloves from the dresser, went to the stairs and descended, and entered the office.

From behind his desk, he glared at me as I crossed over.

"Here it is," I said, and handed him the book. "And much obliged for the gloves." I held them up, one in each hand, dangling them from thumb and fingertip.

"It is no occasion for clowning," he growled.

"It sure isn't." I dropped the gloves on my desk, whirled my chair, and sat. "Where do we start? Do you want to know what happened after you left?"

"The details can wait. First where we stand. Was Mr. Cramer there?"

"Yes. Certainly."

"Did he get anywhere?"

"No. He probably won't until he finds Santa Claus. Until they find Santa Claus they won't dig very hard at the others.

The longer it takes to find him the surer they'll be he's it. Three things about him: nobody knows who he was, he beat it, and he wore gloves. A thousand men are looking for him. You were right to wear the gloves, I would have recognized your hands, but where did you get them?"

"At a store on Ninth Avenue. Confound it, I didn't know a man was going to be murdered!"

"I know you didn't. May I ask some questions?"

He scowled. I took it for yes. "When did you phone Bottweill to arrange it?"

"At two-thirty yesterday afternoon. You had gone to the bank."

"Have you any reason to think he told anyone about it?"

"No. He said he wouldn't."

"I know he got the costume, so that's okay. When you left here today at twelve-thirty did you go straight to Bottweill's?"

"No. I left at that hour because you and Fritz expected me to. I stopped to buy the gloves, and met him at Rusterman's, and we had lunch. From there we took a cab to his place, arriving shortly after two o'clock, and took his private elevator up to his office. Immediately upon entering his office, he got a bottle of Pernod from a drawer of his desk, said he always had a little after lunch, and invited me to join him. I declined. He poured a liberal portion in a glass, about two ounces, drank it in two gulps, and returned the bottle to the drawer."

"My God." I whistled. "The cops would like to know *that.*"

"No doubt. The costume was there in a box. There is a dressing room at the rear of his office, with a bathroom—"

"I know. I've used it."

"I took the costume there and put it on. He had ordered the largest size, but it was a squeeze and it took a while. I was in there half an hour or more. When I re-entered the office it was empty, but soon Bottweill came, up the stairs from the workshop, and helped me with the mask and wig.

They had barely been adjusted when Emil Hatch and Mrs. Jerome and her son appeared, also coming up the stairs from the workshop. I left, going to the studio, and found Miss Quon and Miss Dickey and Mr. Kiernan there."

"And before long I was there. Then no one saw you unmasked. When did you put the gloves on?"

"The last thing. Just before I entered the studio."

"Then you may have left prints. I know, you didn't know there was going to be a murder. You left your clothes in the dressing room? Are you sure you got everything when you left?"

"Yes. I am not a complete ass."

I let that by. "Why didn't you leave the gloves in the elevator with the costume?"

"Because they hadn't come with it, and I thought it better to take them."

"That private elevator is at the rear of the hall downstairs. Did anyone see you leaving it or passing through the hall?"

"No. The hall was empty."

"How did you get home? Taxi?"

"No. Fritz didn't expect me until six or later. I walked to the public library, spent some two hours there, and then took a cab."

I pursed my lips and shook my head to indicate sympathy. That was his longest and hardest tramp since Montenegro. Over a mile. Fighting his way through the blizzard, in terror of the law on his tail. But all the return I got for my look of sympathy was a scowl, so I let loose. I laughed. I put my head back and let it come. I had wanted to ever since I had learned he was Santa Claus, but had been too busy thinking. It was bottled up in me, and I let it out, good. I was about to taper off to a cackle when he exploded.

"Confound it," he bellowed, "marry and be damned!"

That was dangerous. That attitude could easily get us onto the aspect he had sent me up to my room to think over alone, and if we got started on that anything could happen. It called for tact.

"I beg your pardon," I said. "Something caught in my throat. Do you want to describe the situation, or do you want me to?"

"I would like to hear you try," he said grimly.

"Yes, sir. I suspect that the only thing to do is to phone Inspector Cramer right now and invite him to come and have a chat, and when he comes open the bag. That will—"

"No. I will not do that."

"Then, next best, I go to him and spill it there. Of course—"

"No." He meant every word of it.

"Okay, I'll describe it. They'll mark time on the others until they find Santa Claus. They've got to find him. If he left any prints they'll compare them with every file they've got, and sooner or later they'll get to yours. They'll cover all the stores for sales of white cotton gloves to men. They'll trace Bottweill's movements and learn that he lunched with you at Rusterman's, and you left together, and they'll trace you to Bottweill's place. Of course your going there won't prove you were Santa Claus, you might talk your way out of that, and it will account for your prints if they find some, but what about the gloves? They'll trace that sale if you give them time, and with a description of the buyer they'll find Santa Claus. You're sunk."

I had never seen his face blacker.

"If you sit tight till they find him," I argued, "it will be quite a nuisance. Cramer has been itching for years to lock you up, and any judge would commit you as a material witness who had run out. Whereas if you call Cramer now, and I mean now, and invite him to come and have some beer, while it will still be a nuisance, it will be bearable. Of course he'll want to know why you went there and played Santa Claus, but you can tell him anything you please. Tell him you bet me a hundred bucks, or what the hell, make it a grand, that you could be a in a room with me for ten minutes and I wouldn't recognize you. I'll be glad to cooperate."

I leaned forward. "Another thing. If you wait till they find you, you won't dare tell them that Bottweill took a drink from that bottle shortly after two o'clock and it didn't hurt him. If you told about that after they dug you up, they could book you for withholding evidence, and they probably would, and make it stick. If you get Cramer here now and tell him he'll appreciate it, though naturally he won't say so. He's probably at his office. Shall I ring him?"

"No. I will not confess that performance to Mr. Cramer. I will not unfold the morning paper to a disclosure of that outlandish masquerade."

"Then you're going to sit and read *Here and Now* until they come with a warrant?"

"No. That would be fatuous." He took in air through his mouth, as far down as it would go, and let it out through his nose. "I'm going to find the murderer and present him to Mr. Cramer. There's nothing else."

"Oh. You are."

"Yes."

"You might have said so and saved my breath, instead of letting me spout."

"I wanted to see if your appraisal of the situation agreed with mine. It does."

"That's fine. Then you also know that we may have two weeks and we may have two minutes. At this very second some expert may be phoning Homicide to say that he has found fingerprints that match on the card of Wolfe, Nero—"

The phone rang, and I jerked around as if someone had stuck a needle in me. Maybe we wouldn't have even two minutes. My hand wasn't trembling as I lifted the receiver, I hope. Wolfe seldom lifts his until I have found out who it is, but that time he did.

"Nero Wolfe's office, Archie Goodwin speaking."

"This is the District Attorney's office, Mr. Goodwin. Regarding the murder of Kurt Bottweill. We would like you to be here at ten o'clock tomorrow morning."

"All right. Sure."

"At ten o'clock sharp, please."

"I'll be there."

We hung up. Wolfe sighed. I sighed.

"Well," I said, "I've already told them six times that I know absolutely nothing about Santa Claus, so they may not ask me again. If they do, it will be interesting to compare my voice when I'm lying with when I'm telling the truth."

He grunted. "Now. I want a complete report of what happened there after I left, but first I want background. In your intimate association with Miss Dickey you must have learned things about those people. What?"

"Not much." I cleared my throat. "I guess I'll have to explain something. My association with Miss Dickey was not intimate." I stopped. It wasn't easy.

"Choose your own adjective. I meant no innuendo."

"It's not a question of adjectives. Miss Dickey is a good dancer, exceptionally good, and for the past couple of months I have been taking her here and there, some six or eight times altogether. Monday evening at the Flamingo Club she asked me to do her a favor. She said Bottweill was giving her a runaround, that he had been going to marry her for a year but kept stalling, and she wanted to do something. She said Cherry Quon was making a play for him, and she didn't intend to let Cherry take the rail. She asked me to get a marriage-license blank and fill it out for her and me and give it to her. She would show it to Bottweill and tell him now or never. It struck me as a good deed with no risk involved, and, as I say, she is a good dancer. Tuesday afternoon I got a blank, no matter how, and that evening, up in my room, I filled it in, including a fancy signature."

Wolfe made a noise.

"That's all," I said, "except that I want to make it clear that I had no intention of showing it to you. I did that on the spur of the moment when you picked up your book. Your memory is as good as mine. Also, to close it up, no doubt you noticed that today just before Bottweill and Mrs. Jerome joined the party Margot and I stepped aside for a little chat. She told me the license did the trick. Her words were, 'Per-

fect, simply perfect.' She said that last evening, in his office, he tore the license up and put the pieces in his
wastebasket. That's okay, the cops didn't find them. I
looked before they came, and the pieces weren't there."

His mouth was working, but he didn't open it. He didn't
dare. He would have liked to tear into me, to tell me that my
insufferable flummery had got him into this awful mess, but
if he did so he would be dragging in the aspect he didn't
want mentioned. He saw that in time, and saw that I saw it.
His mouth worked, but that was all. Finally he spoke.

"Then you are not on intimate terms with Miss Dickey."

"No, sir."

"Even so, she must have spoken of that establishment and
those people."

"Some, yes."

"And one of them killed Bottweill. The poison was put in
the bottle between two-ten, when I saw him take a drink,
and three-thirty when Kiernan went and got the bottle. No
one came up in the private elevator during the half-hour or
more I was in the dressing room. I was getting into that
costume and gave no heed to footsteps or other sounds in the
office, but the elevator shaft adjoins the dressing room, and I
would have heard it. It is a strong probability that the opportunity was even narrower, that the poison was put in the
bottle while I was in the dressing room, since three of them
were in the office with Bottweill when I left. It must be
assumed that one of those three, or one of the three in the
studio, had grasped an earlier opportunity. What about
them?"

"Not much. Mostly from Monday evening, when Margot
was talking about Bottweill. So it's all hearsay, from her.
Mrs. Jerome has put half a million in the business—probably you should divide that by two at least—and thinks she
owns him. Or thought. She was jealous of Margot and
Cherry. As for Leo, if his mother was dishing out the dough
he expected to inherit to a guy who was trying to corner the
world's supply of gold leaf, and possibly might also marry

290 MURDER FOR CHRISTMAS

him, and if he knew about the jar of poison in the workshop, he might have been tempted. Kiernan, I don't know, but from a remark Margot made and from the way he looked at Cherry this afternoon, I suspect he would like to mix some Irish with her Chinese and Indian and Dutch, and if he thought Bottweill had him stymied he might have been tempted too. So much for hearsay."

"Mr. Hatch?"

"Nothing on him from Margot, but, dealing with him during the tapestry job, I wouldn't have been surprised if he had wiped out the whole bunch on general principles. His heart pumps acid instead of blood. He's a creative artist, he told me so. He practically told me that he was responsible for the success of that enterprise but got no credit. He didn't tell me that he regarded Bottweill as a phony and a fourflusher, but he did. You may remember that I told you he had a persecution complex and you told me to stop using other people's jargon."

"That's four of them. Miss Dickey?"

I raised my brows. "I got her a license to marry, not to kill. If she was lying when she said it worked, she's almost as good a liar as she is a dancer. Maybe she is. If it didn't work she might have been tempted too."

"And Miss Quon?"

"She's half Oriental. I'm not up on Orientals, but I understand they slant their eyes to keep you guessing. That's what makes them inscrutable. If I had to be poisoned by one of that bunch I would want it to be her. Except for what Margot told me—"

The doorbell rang. That was worse than the phone. If they had hit on Santa Claus's trail and it led to Nero Wolfe, Cramer was much more apt to come than to call. Wolfe and I exchanged glances. Looking at my wristwatch and seeing 10:08, I arose, went to the hall and flipped the switch for the stoop light, and took a look through the one-way glass panel of the front door. I have good eyes, but the figure was muffled in a heavy coat with a hood, so I stepped halfway to the door to make sure. Then I returned to the office and told Wolfe, "Cherry Quon. Alone."

He frowned. "I wanted—" He cut it off. "Very well. Bring her in."

V

As I have said, Cherry was highly decorative, and she went fine with the red leather chair at the end of Wolfe's desk. It would have held three of her. She had let me take her coat in the hall and still had on the neat little woolen number she had worn at the party. It wasn't exactly yellow, but there was yellow in it. I would have called it off-gold, and it and the red chair and the tea tint of her smooth little carved face would have made a very nice kodachrome.

She sat on the edge, her spine straight and her hands together in her lap. "I was afraid to telephone," she said, "because you might tell me not to come. So I just came. Will you forgive me?"

Wolfe grunted. No commitment. She smiled at him, a friendly smile, or so I thought. After all, she was half Oriental.

"I must get myself together," she chirped. "I'm nervous because it's so exciting to be here." She turned her head. "There's the glove, and the bookshelves, and the safe, and the couch, and of course Archie Goodwin. And you. You behind your desk in your enormous chair! Oh, I know this place! I have read about you so much—everything there is, I think. It's exciting to be here, actually here in this chair, and see you. Of course I saw you this afternoon, but that wasn't the same thing, you could have been anybody in that silly Santa Claus costume. I wanted to pull your whiskers."

She laughed, a friendly little tinkle like a bell.

I think I looked bewildered. That was my idea, after it had got through my ears to the switchboard inside and been routed. I was too busy handling my face to look at Wolfe, but he was probably even busier, since she was looking straight at him. I moved my eyes to him when he spoke.

"If I understand you, Miss Quon, I'm at a loss. If you think you saw me this afternoon in a Santa Claus costume, you're mistaken."

"Oh, I'm sorry!" she exclaimed. "Then you haven't told them?"

"My dear madam." His voice sharpened. "If you must talk in riddles, talk to Mr. Goodwin. He enjoys them."

"But I *am* sorry, Mr. Wolfe. I should have explained first how I know. This morning at breakfast Kurt told me you had phoned him and arranged to appear at the party as Santa Claus, and this afternoon I asked him if you had come and he said you had and you were putting on the costume. That's how I know. But you haven't told the police? Then it's a good thing I haven't told them either, isn't it?"

"This is interesting," Wolfe said coldly. "What do you expect to accomplish by this fantastic folderol?"

She shook her pretty little head. "You, with so much sense. You must see that it's no use. If I tell them, even if they don't like to believe me they will investigate. I know they can't investigate as well as you can, but surely they will find something."

He shut his eyes, tightened his lips, and leaned back in his chair. I kept mine opened, on her. She weighed about a hundred and two. I could carry her under one arm with my other hand clamped on her mouth. Putting her in the spare room upstairs wouldn't do, since she could open a window and scream, but there was a cubbyhole in the basement, next to Fritz's room, with an old couch in it. Or, as an alternative, I could get a gun from my desk drawer and shoot her. Probably no one knew she had come here.

Wolfe opened his eyes and straightened up. "Very well. It is still fantastic, but I concede that you could create an unpleasant situation by taking that yarn to the police. I don't suppose you came here merely to tell me that you intend to. What do you intend?"

"I think we understand each other," she chirped.

"I understand only that you want something. What?"

"You are so direct," she complained. "So very abrupt, that I must have said something wrong. But I do want something. You see, since the police think it was the man who acted Santa Claus and ran away, they may not get on the right track until it's too late. You wouldn't want that, would you?"

No reply.

"I wouldn't want it," she said, and her hands on her lap curled into little fists. "I wouldn't want whoever killed Kurt to get away, no matter who it was, but you see, I know who killed him. I have told the police, but they won't listen until they find Santa Claus, or if they listen they think I'm just a jealous cat, and besides, I'm an Oriental and their ideas of Orientals are very primitive. I was going to make them listen by telling them who Santa Claus was, but I know how they feel about you from what I've read, and I was afraid they would try to prove it was you who killed Kurt, and of course it could have been you, and you did run away, and they still wouldn't listen to me when I told them who did kill him."

She stopped for breath. Wolfe inquired, "Who did?"

She nodded. "I'll tell you. Margot Dickey and Kurt were having an affair. A few months ago Kurt began on me, and it was hard for me because I—I—" she frowned for a word, and found one. "I had a feeling for him. I had a strong feeling. But you see, I am a virgin, and I wouldn't give in to him. I don't know what I would have done if I hadn't known he was having an affair with Margot, but I did know, and I told him the first man I slept with would be my husband. He said he was willing to give up Margot, but even if he did he couldn't marry me on account of Mrs. Jerome, because she would stop backing him with her money. I don't know what he was to Mrs. Jerome, but I know what she was to him."

Her hands opened and closed again to be fists. "That went on and on, but Kurt had a feeling for me too. Last night late, it was after midnight, he phoned me that he had broken with

Margot for good and he wanted to marry me. He wanted to come and see me, but I told him I was in bed and we would see each other in the morning. He said that would be at the studio with other people there, so finally I said I would go to his apartment for breakfast, and I did, this morning. But I am still a virgin, Mr. Wolfe."

He was focused on her with half-closed eyes. "That is your privilege, madam."

"Oh," she said. "Is it a privilege? It was there, at breakfast, that he told me about you, your arranging to be Santa Claus. When I got to the studio I was surprised to see Margot there, and how friendly she was. That was part of her plan, to be friendly and cheerful with everyone. She has told the police that Kurt was going to marry her, that they decided last night to get married next week. Christmas week. I am a Christian."

Wolfe stirred in his chair. "Have we reached the point? Did Miss Dickey kill Mr. Bottweill?"

"Yes. Of course she did."

"Have you told the police that?"

"Yes. I didn't tell them all I have told you, but enough."

"With evidence?"

"No. I have no evidence."

"Then you're vulnerable to an action for slander."

She opened her fists and turned her palms up. "Does that matter? When I know I'm right? When I *know* it? But she was so clever, the way she did it, that there can't be any evidence. Everybody there today knew about the poison, and they all had a chance to put it in the bottle. They can never prove she did it. They can't even prove she is lying when she says Kurt was going to marry her, because he is dead. She acted today the way she would have acted if that had been true. But it has got to be proved somehow. There has got to be evidence to prove it."

"And you want me to get it?"

She let that pass. "What I was thinking, Mr. Wolfe, you are vulnerable too. There will always be the danger that the police will find out who Santa Claus was, and if they find it was you and you didn't tell them—"

"I haven't conceded that," Wolfe snapped.

"Then we'll just say there will always be the danger that I'll tell them what Kurt told me, and you did concede that that would be unpleasant. So it would be better if the evidence proved who killed Kurt and also proved who Santa Claus was. Wouldn't it?"

"Go on."

"So I thought how easy it would be for you to get the evidence. You have men who do things for you, who would do anything for you, and one of them can say that you asked him to go there and be Santa Claus, and he did. Of course it couldn't be Mr. Goodwin, since he was at the party, and it would have to be a man they couldn't prove was somewhere else. He can say that while he was in the dressing room putting on the costume he heard someone in the office and peeked out to see who it was, and he saw Margot Dickey get the bottle from the desk drawer and put something in it and put the bottle back in the drawer, and go out. That must have been when she did it, because Kurt always took a drink of Pernod when he came back from lunch."

Wolfe was rubbing his lip with a fingertip. "I see," he muttered.

She wasn't through. "He can say," she went on, "that he ran away because he was frightened and wanted to tell you about it first. I don't think they would do anything to him if he went to them tomorrow morning and told them all about it, would they? Just like me. I don't think they would do anything to me if I went to them tomorrow morning and told them I had remembered that Kurt told me that you were going to be Santa Claus, and this afternoon he told me you were in the dressing room putting on the costume. That would be the same kind of thing, wouldn't it?"

Her little carved mouth thinned and widened with a smile. "That's what I want," she chirped. "Did I say it so you understand it?"

"You did indeed," Wolfe assured her. "You put it admirably."

"Would it be better, instead of him going to tell them, for you to have Inspector Cramer come here, and you tell him? You could have the man here. You see, I know how you do things, from all I have read."

"That might be better," he allowed. His tone was dry but not hostile. I could see a muscle twitching beneath his right ear, but she couldn't. "I suppose, Miss Quon, it is futile to advance the possibility that one of the others killed him, and if so it would be a pity—"

"Excuse me. I interrupt." The chirp was still a chirp, but it had hard steel in it. "I know she killed him."

"I don't. And even if I bow to your conviction, before I could undertake the stratagem you propose I would have to make sure there are no facts that would scuttle it. It won't take me long. You'll hear from me tomorrow. I'll want—"

She interrupted again. "I can't wait longer than tomorrow morning to tell them what Kurt told me."

"Pfui. You can and will. The moment you disclose that, you no longer have a whip to dangle at me. You will hear from me tomorrow. Now I want to think. Archie?"

I left my chair. She looked up at me and back at Wolfe. For some seconds she sat, considering, inscrutable of course, then stood up.

"It was very exciting to be here," she said, the steel gone, "to see you here. You must forgive me for not phoning. I hope it will be early tomorrow." She turned and headed for the door, and I followed.

After I had helped her on with her hooded coat, and let her out, and watched her picking her way down the seven steps, I shut the door, put the chain-bolt on, returned to the office, and told Wolfe, "It has stopped snowing. Who do you think will be best for it, Saul or Fred or Orrie or Bill?"

"Sit down," he growled. "You see through women. Well?"

"Not that one. I pass. I wouldn't bet a dime on her one way or the other. Would you?"

"No. She is probably a liar and possibly a murderer. Sit down. I must have everything that happened there today after I left. Every word and gesture."

I sat and gave it to him. Including the question period, it took an hour and thirty-five minutes. It was after one o'clock when he pushed his chair back, levered his bulk upright, told me good night, and went up to bed.

VI

At half past two the following afternoon, Saturday, I sat in a room in a building on Leonard Street, the room where I had once swiped an assistant district attorney's lunch. There would be no need for me to repeat the performance, since I had just come back from Ost's restaurant, where I had put away a plateful of pig's knuckles and sauerkraut.

As far as I knew, there had not only been no steps to frame Margot for murder; there had been no steps at all. Since Wolfe is up in the plant rooms every morning from nine to eleven, and since he breakfasts from a tray up in his room, and since I was expected downtown at ten o'clock, I had buzzed him on the house phone a little before nine to ask for instructions and had been told that he had none. Downtown Assistant DA Farrell, after letting me wait in the anteroom for an hour, had spent two hours with me, together with a stenographer and a dick who had been on the scene Friday afternoon, going back and forth and zigzag, not only over what I had already reported, but also over my previous association with the Bottweill personnel. He only asked me once if I knew anything about Santa Claus, so I only had to lie once, if you don't count my omitting any mention of the marriage license. When he called a recess and told me to come back at two-thirty, on my way to Ost's for the pig's knuckles I phoned Wolfe to tell him I didn't know when I would be home, and again he had no instructions. I said I doubted if Cherry Quon would wait until after New Year's to spill the beans, and he said he did too and hung up.

When I was ushered back into Farrell's office at two-thirty he was alone—no stenographer and no dick. He asked me if I had had a good lunch, and even waited for me to answer, handed me some typewritten sheets, and leaned back in his chair.

"Read it over," he said, "and see if you want to sign it."

His tone seemed to imply that I might not, so I went over it carefully, five full pages. Finding no editorial revisions to object to, I pulled my chair forward to a corner of his desk, put the statement on the desk top, and got my pen from my pocket.

"Wait a minute," Farrell said. "You're not a bad guy even if you are cocky, and why not give you a break? That says specifically that you have reported everything you did there yesterday afternoon."

"Yeah, I've read it. So?"

"So who put your fingerprints on some of the pieces of paper in Bottweill's wastebasket?"

"I'll be damned," I said. "I forgot to put gloves on."

"All right, you're cocky. I already know that." His eyes were pinning me. "You must have gone through that wastebasket, every item, when you went to Bottweill's office ostensibly to look for Santa Claus, and you hadn't just forgotten it. You don't forget things. So you have deliberately left it out. I want to know why, and I want to know what you took from that wastebasket and what you did with it."

I grinned at him. "I am also damned because I thought I knew how thorough they are and apparently I didn't. I wouldn't have supposed they went so far as to dust the contents of a wastebasket when there was nothing to connect them, but I see I was wrong, and I hate to be wrong." I shrugged. "Well, we learn something new every day." I screwed the statement around to position, signed it at the bottom of the last page, slid it across to him, and folded the carbon copy and put it in my pocket.

"I'll write it in if you insist," I told him, "but I doubt if it's worth the trouble. Santa Claus had run, Kiernan was calling the police, and I guess I was a little rattled. I must have looked around for something that might give me a line on Santa Claus, and my eye lit on the wastebasket, and I went through it. I haven't mentioned it because it wasn't very bright, and I like people to think I'm bright, especially cops. There's your why. As for what I took, the answer is nothing. I dumped the wastebasket, put everything back in, and took nothing. Do you want me to write that in?"

"No. I want to discuss it. I know you *are* bright. And you weren't rattled. You don't rattle. I want to know the real reason you went through the wastebasket, what you were after, whether you got it, and what you did with it."

It cost me more than an hour, twenty minutes of which were spent in the office of the District Attorney himself, with Farrell and another assistant present. At one point it looked as if they were going to hold me as a material witness, but that takes a warrant, the Christmas weekend had started, and there was nothing to show that I had monkeyed with anything that could be evidence, so finally they shooed me out, after I had handwritten an insert in my statement. It was too bad keeping such important public servants sitting there while I copied the insert on my carbon, but I like to do things right.

By the time I got home it was ten minutes past four, and of course Wolfe wasn't in the office, since his afternoon session up in the plant rooms is from four to six. There was no note on my desk from him, so apparently there were still no instructions, but there was information on it. My desk ashtray, which is mostly for decoration since I seldom smoke—a gift, not to Wolfe but to me, from a former client —is a jade bowl six inches across. It was there in its place, and in it were stubs from Pharaoh cigarettes.

Saul Panzer smokes Pharoahs, Egyptians. I suppose a few other people do too, but the chance that one of them had been sitting at my desk while I was gone was too slim to bother with. And not only had Saul been there, but Wolfe wanted me to know it, since one of the eight million things he will not tolerate in the office is ashtrays with remains. He will actually walk clear to the bathroom himself to empty one.

So steps were being taken, after all. What steps? Saul, a free lance and the best operative anywhere around, asks and gets sixty bucks a day, and is worth twice that. Wolfe had not called him in for any routine errand, and of course the idea that he had undertaken to sell him on doubling for Santa Claus never entered my head. Framing someone for murder, even a woman who might be guilty, was not in his bag of tricks. I got at the house phone and buzzed the plant rooms, and after a wait had Wolfe's voice in my ear.

"Yes, Fritz?"

"Not Fritz. Me. I'm back. Nothing urgent to report. They found my prints on stuff in the wastebasket, but I escaped without loss of blood. Is it all right for me to empty my ashtray?"

"Yes. Please do so."

"Then what do I do?"

"I'll tell you at six o'clock. Possibly earlier."

He hung up. I went to the safe and looked in the cash drawer to see if Saul had been supplied with generous funds, but the cash was as I had last seen it and there was no entry in the book. I emptied the ashtray. I went to the kitchen, where I found Fritz pouring a mixture into a bowl of pork tenderloin, and said I hoped Saul had enjoyed his lunch, and Fritz said he hadn't stayed for lunch. So steps must have been begun right after I left in the morning. I went back to the office, read over the carbon copy of my statement before filing it, and passed the time by thinking up eight different steps that Saul might have been assigned, but none of them struck me as promising. A little after five the phone rang and I answered. It was Saul. He said he was glad to know I was back home safe, and I said I was too.

"Just a message for Mr. Wolfe," he said. "Tell him everything is set, no snags."

"That's all?"

"Right. I'll be seeing you."

I cradled the receiver, sat a moment to consider whether to go up to the plant rooms or use the house phone, decided the latter would do, and pulled it to me and pushed the button. When Wolfe's voice came it was peevish; he hates to be disturbed up there.

"Yes?"

"Saul called and said to tell you everything is set, no snags. Congratulations. Am I in the way?"

"Oddly enough, no. Have chairs in place for visitors; ten should be enough. Four or five will come shortly after six o'clock; I hope not more. Others will come later."

"Refreshments?"

"Liquids, of course. Nothing else."

"Anything else for me?"

"No."

He was gone. Before going to the front room for chairs, and to the kitchen for supplies, I took time out to ask myself whether I had the slightest notion what kind of charade he was cooking up this time. I hadn't.

VII

It was four. They all arrived between six-fifteen and six-twenty—first Mrs. Perry Porter Jerome and her son Leo, then Cherry Quon, and last Emil Hatch. Mrs. Jerome copped the red leather chair, but I moved her, mink and all, to one of the yellow ones when Cherry came. I was willing to concede that Cherry might be headed for a very different kind of chair, wired for power, but even so I thought she rated that background and Mrs. Jerome didn't. By six-thirty, when I left them to cross the hall to the dining room, not a word had passed among them.

In the dining room Wolfe had just finished a bottle of beer. "Okay," I told him, "it's six-thirty-one. Only four. Kiernan and Margot Dickey haven't shown."

"Satisfactory." He arose. "Have they demanded information?"

"Two of them have, Hatch and Mrs. Jerome. I told them it will come from you, as instructed. That was easy, since I have none."

He headed for the office, and I followed. Though they didn't know, except Cherry, that he had poured champagne for them the day before, introductions weren't necessary because they had all met him during the tapestry hunt. After circling around Cherry in the red leather chair, he stood behind his desk to ask them how they did, then sat.

"I don't thank you for coming," he said, "because you came in your own interest, not mine. I sent—"

"I came," Hatch cut in, sourer than ever, "to find out what you're up to."

"You will," Wolfe assured him. "I sent each of you an identical message, saying that Mr. Goodwin has certain information which he feels he must give the police not later than tonight, but I have persuaded him to let me discuss it with you first. Before I—"

"I didn't know others would be here," Mrs. Jerome blurted, glaring at Cherry.

"Neither did I," Hatch said, glaring at Mrs. Jerome.

Wolfe ignored it. "The message I sent Miss Quon was somewhat different, but that need not concern you. Before I tell you what Mr. Goodwin's information is, I need a few facts from you. For instance, I understand that any of you— including Miss Dickey and Mr. Kiernan, who will probably join us later—could have found an opportunity to put the poison in the bottle. Do any of you challenge that?"

Cherry, Mrs. Jerome, and Leo all spoke at once. Hatch merely looked sour.

Wolfe showed them a palm. "If you please. I point no finger of accusation at any of you. I merely say that none of you, including Miss Dickey and Mr. Kiernan, can prove that you had no opportunity. Can you?"

"Nuts." Leo Jerome was disgusted. "It was that guy playing Santa Claus. Of course it was. I was with Bottweill and my mother all the time, first in the workshop and then in his office. I can prove *that*."

"But Bottweill is dead," Wolfe reminded him, "and your mother is your mother. Did you go up to the office a little before them, or did your mother go up a little before you and Bottweill did? Is there acceptable proof that you didn't? The others have the same problem. Miss Quon?"

There was no danger of Cherry's spoiling it. Wolfe had told me what he had told her on the phone: that he had made a plan which he thought she would find satisfactory, and if she came at a quarter past six she would see it work. She had kept her eyes fixed on him ever since he entered. Now she chirped, "If you mean I can't prove I wasn't in the office alone yesterday, no, I can't."

"Mr. Hatch?"

"I didn't come here to prove anything. I told you what I came for. What information has Goodwin got?"

"We'll get to that. A few more facts first. Mrs. Jerome, when did you learn that Bottweill had decided to marry Miss Quon?"

Leo shouted, "No!" but his mother was too busy staring at Wolfe to hear him. "What?" she croaked. Then she found her voice. "Kurt marry *her?* That little strumpet?"

Cherry didn't move a muscle, her eyes still on Wolfe.

"This is wonderful!" Leo said. "This is marvelous!"

"Not so damn wonderful," Emil Hatch declared. "I get the idea, Wolfe. Goodwin hasn't got any information, and neither have you. Why you wanted to get us together and start us clawing at each other, I don't see that, I don't know why you're interested, but maybe I'll find out if I give you a hand. This crowd has produced as fine a collection of venom as you could find. Maybe we all put poison in the bottle and that's why it was such a big dose. If it's true that Kurt had decided to marry Cherry, and Al Kiernan knew it, that would have done it. Al would have killed a hundred Kurts if it would get him Cherry. If Mrs. Jerome knew it, I would think she would have gone for Cherry instead of Kurt, but maybe she figured there would soon be another one and she might as well settle it for good. As for Leo, I think he rather liked Kurt, but what can you expect? Kurt was milking mamma of the pile Leo hoped to get some day, and I suspect that the pile is not all it's supposed to be. Actually—"

He stopped, and I left my chair. Leo was on his way up, obviously with the intention of plugging the creative artist. I moved to head him off, and at the same instant I gave him a shove and his mother jerked at his coattail. That not only halted him but nearly upset him, and with my other hand I steered him back onto his chair and then stood beside him.

Hatch inquired, "Shall I go on?"

"By all means," Wolfe said.

"Actually, though, Cherry would seem to be the most likely. She has the best brain of the lot and by far the strongest will. But I understand that while she says Kurt was going to marry her, Margot claims that he was going to marry *her*. Of course that complicates it, and anyway Margot would be my second choice. Margot has more than her share of the kind of pride that is only skin deep and therefore can't stand a scratch. If Kurt did decide to marry Cherry and told Margot so, he was even a bigger imbecile than I thought he was. Which brings us to me. I am in a class by myself. I despise all of them. If I had decided to take to poison I would have put it in the champagne as well as the Pernod, and I would have drunk vodka, which I prefer—and by the way, on that table is a bottle with the Korbeloff vodka label. I haven't had a taste of Korbeloff for fifteen years. Is it real?"

"It is. Archie?"

Serving liquid refreshments to a group of invited guests can be a pleasant chore, but it wasn't that time. When I asked Mrs. Jerome to name it she only glowered at me, but by the time I had filled Cherry's order for scotch and soda, and supplied Hatch with a liberal dose of Korbeloff, no dilution, and Leo had said he would take bourbon and water, his mother muttered that she would have that too. As I was pouring the bourbon I wondered where we would go from there. It looked as if the time had come for Wolfe to pass on the information which I felt I must give the police without delay, which made it difficult because I didn't have any. That had been fine for a bait to get them there, but what now? I suppose Wolfe would have held them somehow, but he didn't have to. He had rung for beer, and Fritz had brought it and was putting the tray on his desk when the doorbell rang. I handed Leo his bourbon and water and went to the hall. Out on the stoop, with his big round face nearly touching the glass, was Inspector Cramer of Homicide.

Wolfe had told me enough, before the company came, to give me a general idea of the program, so the sight of Cramer, just Cramer, was a letdown. But as I went down the hall other figures appeared, none of them strangers, and that looked better. In fact it looked fine. I swung the door wide and in they came—Cramer, then Saul Panzer, then Margot Dickey, then Alfred Kiernan, and, bringing up the rear, Sergeant Purley Stebbins. By the time I had the door closed and bolted they had their coats off, including Cramer, and it was also fine to see that he expected to stay a while. Ordinarily, once in, he marches down the hall and into the office without ceremony, but that time he waved the others ahead, including me, and he and Stebbins came last, herding us in. Crossing the sill, I stepped aside for the pleasure of seeing his face when his eyes lit on those already there and the empty chairs waiting. Undoubtedly he had expected to find Wolfe alone, reading a book. He came in two paces, glared around, fastened the glare on Wolfe, and barked, "What's all this?"

"I was expecting you," Wolfe said politely. "Miss Quon, if you don't mind moving, Mr. Cramer likes that chair. Good evening, Miss Dickey. Mr. Kiernan, Mr. Stebbins. If you will all be seated—"

"Panzer!" Cramer barked. Saul, who had started for a chair in the rear, stopped and turned.

"I'm running this," Cramer declared. "Panzer, you're

under arrest and you'll stay with Stebbins and keep your mouth shut. I don't want—"

"No," Wolfe said sharply. "If he's under arrest take him out of here. You are not running this, not in my house. If you have warrants for anyone present, or have taken them by lawful police power, take them and leave these premises. Would you bulldoze me, Mr. Cramer? You should know better."

That was the point, Cramer did know him. There was the stage, all set. There were Mrs. Jerome and Leo and Cherry and Emil Hatch, and the empty chairs, and above all, there was the fact that he had been expected. He wouldn't have taken Wolfe's word for that; he wouldn't have taken Wolfe's word for anything; but whenever he appeared on our stoop *not* expected I always left the chain-bolt on until he had stated his business and I had reported to Wolfe. And if he had been expected there was no telling what Wolfe had ready to spring. So Cramer gave up the bark and merely growled, "I want to talk with you."

"Certainly." Wolfe indicated the red leather chair, which Cherry had vacated. "Be seated."

"Not here. Alone."

Wolfe shook his head. "It would be a waste of time. This way is better and quicker. You know quite well, sir, it was a mistake to barge in here and roar at me that you are running my house. Either go, with whomever you can lawfully take, or sit down while I tell you who killed Kurt Bottweill." Wolfe wiggled a finger. "Your chair."

Cramer's round red face had been redder than normal from the outside cold, and now was redder still. He glanced around, compressed his lips until he didn't have any, and went to the red leather chair and sat.

VIII

Wolfe sent his eyes around as I circled to my desk. Saul had got to a chair in the rear after all, but Stebbins had too and was at his elbow. Margot had passed in front of the Jeromes and Emil Hatch to get to the chair at the end nearest me, and Cherry and Al Kiernan were at the other end, a little back of the others. Hatch had finished his Korbeloff and put the glass on the floor, but Cherry and the Jeromes were hanging on to their tall ones.

Wolfe's eyes came to rest on Cramer and he spoke. "I must confess that I stretched it a little. I can't tell you, at the moment, who killed Bottweill; I have only a supposition; but soon I can, and will. First some facts for you. I assume you know that for the past two months Mr. Goodwin has been seeing something of Miss Dickey. He says she dances well."

"Yeah." Cramer's voice came over sandpaper of the roughest grit. "You can save that for later. I want to know if you sent Panzer to meet—"

Wolfe cut him off. "You will. I'm headed for that. But you may prefer this firsthand. Archie, if you please. What Miss Dickey asked you to do last Monday evening, and what happened."

I cleared my throat. "We were dancing at the Flamingo Club. She said Bottweill had been telling her for a year that he would marry her next week, but next week never came, and she was going to have a showdown with him. She asked me to get a blank marriage license and fill it out for her and me and give it to her, and she would show it to Bottweill and tell him now or never. I got the blank on Tuesday, and filled it in, and Wednesday I gave it to her."

I stopped. Wolfe prompted me. "And yesterday afternoon?"

"She told me that the license trick had worked perfectly. That was about a minute before Bottweill entered the studio.

I said in my statement to the District Attorney that she told me Bottweill was going to marry her, but I didn't mention the license. It was immaterial."

"Did she tell you what happened to the license?"

So we were emptying the bag. I nodded. "She said Bottweill had torn it up and put the pieces in the wastebasket by the desk in his office. The night before. Thursday evening."

"And what did you do when you went to the office after Bottweill had died?"

"I dumped the wastebasket and put the stuff back in it, piece by piece. No part of the license was there."

"You made sure of that?"

"Yes."

Wolfe left me and asked Cramer, "Any questions?"

"No. He lied in his statement. I'll attend to that later. What I want—"

Margot Dickey blurted, "Then Cherry took it!" She craned her neck to see across the others. "You took it, you slut!"

"I did not." The steel was in Cherry's chirp again. Her eyes didn't leave Wolfe, and she told him, "I'm not going to wait any longer—"

"Miss Quon!" he snapped. "I'm doing this." He returned to Cramer. "Now another fact. Yesterday I had a luncheon appointment with Mr. Bottweill at Rusterman's restaurant. He had once dined at my table and wished to reciprocate. Shortly before I left to keep the appointment he phoned to ask me to do him a favor. He said he was extremely busy and might be a few minutes late, and he needed a pair of white cotton gloves, medium size, for a man, and would I stop at some shop on the way and get them. It struck me as a peculiar request, but he was a peculiar man. Since Mr. Goodwin had chores to do, and I will not ride in taxicabs if there is any alternative, I had engaged a car at Baxter's, and the chauffeur recommended a shop on Eighth Avenue between Thirty-ninth and Fortieth Streets. We stopped there and I bought the gloves."

Cramer's eyes were such narrow slits that none of the blue-gray showed. He wasn't buying any part of it, which was unjustified, since some of it was true.

Wolfe went on. "At the lunch table I gave the gloves to Mr. Bottweill, and he explained, somewhat vaguely, what he wanted them for. I gathered that he had taken pity on some vagabond he had seen on a park bench, and had hired him to serve refreshments at his office party, costumed as Santa Claus, and he had decided that the only way to make his hands presentable was to have him wear gloves. You shake your head, Mr. Cramer?"

"You're damn right I do. You would have reported that. No reason on earth not to. Go ahead and finish."

"I'll finish this first. I didn't report it because I thought you would find the murderer without it. It was practically certain that the vagabond had merely skeddaddled out of fright, since he couldn't possibly have known of the jar of poison in the workshop, not to mention other considerations. And as you know, I have a strong aversion to involvement in matters where I have no concern or interest. You can of course check this—with the staff at Rusterman's, my presence there with Mr. Bottweill, and with the chauffeur, my conferring with him about the gloves and our stopping at the shop to buy them."

"You're reporting it now."

"I am indeed." Wolfe was unruffled. "Because I understood from Mr. Goodwin that you were extending and intensifying your search for the man who was there as Santa Claus, and with your army and your resources it probably wouldn't take you long when the holiday had ended to learn where the gloves were bought and get a description of the man who bought them. My physique is not unique, but it is—uncommon, and the only question was how long it would take you to get to me, and then I would be under inquisition. Obviously I had to report the episode to you and suffer your rebuke for not reporting it earlier, but I wanted to make it as tolerable as possible. I had one big advantage: I knew that the man who acted as Santa Claus was almost certainly not the murderer, and I decided to use it. I needed first to have a talk with one of those people, and I did so, with Miss Quon, who came here last evening."

"Why Miss Quon?"

Wolfe turned a hand over. "When I have finished you can decide whether such details are important. With her I discussed her associates at that place and their relationships, and I became satisfied that Bottweill had in fact decided to marry her. That was all. You can also decide later whether it is worth while to ask her to corroborate that, and I have no doubt she will."

He was looking at Cherry, of course, for any sign of danger. She had started to blurt it out once, and might again. But, meeting his gaze, she didn't move a muscle.

Wolfe returned to Cramer. "This morning I acted. Mr. Goodwin was absent, at the District Attorney's office, so I called in Mr. Panzer. After spending an hour with me here he went to do some errands. The first one was to learn whether Bottweill's wastebasket had been emptied since his conversation with Miss Dickey in his office Thursday evening. As you know, Mr. Panzer is highly competent. Through Miss Quon he got the name and address of the cleaning woman, found her and talked with her, and was told that the wastebasket had been emptied at about six o'clock Thursday afternoon and not since then. Meanwhile I—"

"Cherry took it—the pieces," Margot said.

Wolfe ignored her. "Meanwhile I was phoning everyone concerned—Mrs. Jerome and her son, Miss Dickey, Miss Quon, Mr. Hatch, and Mr. Kiernan—and inviting them to come here for a conference at six-fifteen. I told them that Mr. Goodwin had information which he intended to give the police, which was not true, and that I thought it best to discuss it first with them."

"I told you so," Hatch muttered.

Wolfe ignored him too. "Mr. Panzer's second errand, or

series of errands, was the delivery of some messages. He had written them in longhand, at my dictation here this morning, on plain sheets of paper, and had addressed plain envelopes. They were identical and ran as follows:

"When I was there yesterday putting on my costume I saw you through a crack in the door and I saw what you did. Do you want me to tell the cops? Be at Grand Central information booth upper level at 6:30 today. I'll come up to you and say 'Saint Nick.'"

"By god," Cramer said, "you admit it."

Wolfe nodded. "I proclaim it. The messages were signed 'Santa Claus.' Mr. Panzer accompanied the messenger who took them to the persons I have named, and made sure they were delivered. They were not so much shots at random as they may appear. If one of those people had killed Bottweill it was likely that the poison had been put in the bottle while the vagabond was donning the Santa Claus costume; Miss Quon had told me, as no doubt she has told you, that Bottweill invariably took a drink of Pernod when he returned from lunch; and, since the appearance of Santa Claus at the party had been a surprise to all of them, and none of them knew who he was, it was highly probable that the murderer would believe he had been observed and would be irresistibly impelled to meet the writer of the message. So it was a reasonable assumption that one of the shots would reach its target. The question was, which one?"

Wolfe stopped to pour beer. He did pour it, but I suspected that what he really stopped for was to offer an opening for comment or protest. No one had any, not even Cramer. They all just sat and gazed at him. I was thinking that he had neatly skipped one detail: that the message from Santa Claus had not gone to Cherry Quon. She knew too much about him.

Wolfe put the bottle down and turned to go on to Cramer. "There was the possibility, of course, that more than one of them would go to you with the message, but even if you decided, because it had been sent to more than one, that it was some hoax, you would want to know who perpetrated it, and you would send one of them to the rendezvous under surveillance. Any one or more, excepting the murderer, might go to you, or none might; and surely only the murderer would go to the rendezvous without first consulting you. So if one of those six people were guilty, and if it had been possible for Santa Claus to observe him, disclosure seemed next to certain. Saul, you may now report. What happened? You were in the vicinity of the information booth shortly before six-thirty?"

Necks were twisted for a view of Saul Panzer. He nodded. "Yes, sir. At six-twenty. Within three minutes I had recognized three Homicide men scattered around in different spots. I don't know if they recognized me or not. At six twenty-eight I saw Alfred Kiernan walk up near the booth and stand there, about ten feet away from it. I was just about to go and speak to him when I saw Margot Dickey coming up from the Forty-second Street side. She approached to within thirty feet of the booth and stood looking around. Following your instructions in case more than one of them appeared and Miss Dickey was one of them, I went to her and said, 'Saint Nick.' She said, 'Who are you and what do you want?' I said, 'Excuse me, I'll be right back,' and went over to Alfred Kiernan and said to him, 'Saint Nick.' As soon as I said that he raised a hand to his ear, and then here they came, the three I had recognized and two more, and then Inspector Cramer and Sergeant Stebbins. I was afraid Miss Dickey would run, and she did start to, but they had seen me speak to her, and two of them stopped her and had her."

Saul halted because of an interruption. Purley Stebbins, seated next to him, got up and stepped over to Margot Dickey and stood there behind her chair. To me it seemed unnecessary, since I was sitting not much more than arm's length from her and might have been trusted to grab her if she tried to start anything, but Purley is never very considerate of other people's feelings, especially mine.

Saul resumed, "Naturally it was Miss Dickey I was interested in, since they had moved in on a signal from Kiernan. But they had her, so that was okay. They took us to a room back of the parcel room and started in on me, and I followed your instructions. I told them I would answer no questions, would say nothing whatever, except in the presence of Nero Wolfe, because I was acting under your orders. When they saw I meant it they took us out to two police cars and brought us here. Anything else?"

"No," Wolfe told him. "Satisfactory." He turned to Cramer. "I assume Mr. Panzer is correct in concluding that Mr. Kiernan gave your men a signal. So Mr. Kiernan had gone to you with the message?"

"Yes." Cramer had taken a cigar from his pocket and was squeezing it in his hand. He does that sometimes when he would like to squeeze Wolfe's throat instead. "So had three of the others—Mrs. Jerome, her son, and Hatch."

"But Miss Dickey hadn't?"

"No. Neither had Miss Quon."

"Miss Quon was probably reluctant, understandably. She told me last evening that the police's ideas of Orientals are very primitive. As for Miss Dickey, I may say that I am not surprised. For a reason that does not concern you, I am even a little gratified. I have told you that she told Mr. Goodwin that Bottweill had torn up the marriage license and put the pieces in his wastebasket, and they weren't there when Mr. Goodwin looked for them, and the wastebasket hadn't been emptied since early Thursday evening. It was difficult to conceive a reason for anyone to fish around in the wastebasket to remove those pieces, so presumably Miss Dickey lied; and if she lied about the license, the rest of what she told Mr. Goodwin was under suspicion."

Wolfe upturned a palm. "Why would she tell him that Bottweill was going to marry her if it wasn't true? Surely a stupid thing to do, since he would inevitably learn the truth.

But it wasn't so stupid if she knew that Bottweill would soon die; indeed it was far from stupid if she had already put the poison in the bottle; it would purge her of motive, or at least help. It was a fair surmise that at their meeting in his office Thursday evening Bottweill had told her, not that he would marry her, but that he had decided to marry Miss Quon, and she decided to kill him and proceeded to do so. And it must be admitted that she would probably never have been exposed but for the complications injected by Santa Claus and my resulting intervention. Have you any comment, Miss Dickey?"

Cramer left his chair, commanding her, "Don't answer! I'm running this now," but she spoke.

"Cherry took those pieces from the wastebasket! She did it! She killed him!" She started up, but Purley had her arm and Cramer told her, moving for her, "She didn't go there to meet a blackmailer, and you did. Look in her bag, Purley. I'll watch her."

IX

Cherry Quon was back in the red leather chair. The others had gone, and she and Wolfe and I were alone. They hadn't put cuffs on Margot Dickey, but Purley had kept hold of her arm as they crossed the threshold, with Cramer right behind. Saul Panzer, no longer in custody, had gone along by request. Mrs. Jerome and Leo had been the first to leave. Kiernan had asked Cherry if he could take her home, but Wolfe had said no, he wanted to speak with her privately, and Kiernan and Hatch had left together, which showed a fine Christmas spirit, since Hatch had made no exceptions when he said he despised all of them.

Cherry was on the edge of the chair, spine straight, hands together in her lap. "You didn't do it the way I said," she chirped, without steel.

"No," Wolfe agreed, "but I did it." He was curt. "You ignored one complication, the possibility that you had killed Bottweill yourself. I didn't, I assure you. I couldn't very well send you one of the notes from Santa Claus, under the circumstances; but if those notes had flushed no prey, if none of them had gone to the rendezvous without first notifying the police, I would have assumed that you were guilty and would have proceeded to expose you. How, I don't know; I let that wait on the event; and now that Miss Dickey has taken the bait and betrayed herself it doesn't matter."

Her eyes had widened. "You really thought I might have killed Kurt?"

"Certainly. A woman capable of trying to blackmail me to manufacture evidence of murder would be capable of anything. And, speaking of evidence, while there can be no certainty about a jury's decision when a personable young woman is on trial for murder, now that Miss Dickey is manifestly guilty you may be sure that Mr. Cramer will dig up all he can get, and there should be enough. That brings me to the point I wanted to speak about. In the quest for evidence you will all be questioned, exhaustively and repeatedly. It will—"

"We wouldn't," Cherry put in, "if you had done it the way I said. That would have been proof."

"I preferred my way." Wolfe, having a point to make, was controlling himself. "It will be an ordeal for you. They will question you at length about your talk with Bottweill yesterday morning at breakfast, wanting to know all that he said about his meeting with Miss Dickey in his office Thursday evening, and under the pressure of inquisition you might inadvertently let something slip regarding what he told you about Santa Claus. If you do they will certainly follow it up. I strongly advise you to avoid making such a slip. Even if they believe you, the identity of Santa Claus is no longer important, since they have the murderer, and if they come to me with such a tale I'll have no great difficulty dealing with it."

He turned a hand over. "And in the end they probably won't believe you. They'll think you invented it for some cunning and obscure purpose—as you say, you are an Oriental—and all you would get for it would be more questions. They might even suspect that you were somehow involved in the murder itself. They are quite capable of unreasonable suspicions. So I suggest these considerations as much on your behalf as on mine. I think you will be wise to forget about Santa Claus."

She was eying him, straight and steady. "I like to be wise," she said.

"I'm sure you do, Miss Quon."

"I still think you should have done it my way, but it's done now. Is that all?"

He nodded. "That's all."

She looked at me, and it took a second for me to realize that she was smiling at me. I thought it wouldn't hurt to smile back, and did. She left the chair and came to me, extending a hand, and I arose and took it. She looked up at me.

"I would like to shake hands with Mr. Wolfe, but I know he doesn't like to shake hands. You know, Mr. Goodwin, it must be a very great pleasure to work for a man as clever as Mr. Wolfe. So extremely clever. It has been very exciting to be here. Now I say good-by."

She turned and went.

Boxing Day
Bonus

D.B. Wyndham Lewis is a name almost unknown on this side of the Atlantic. Yet he was for years one of England's most celebrated wits and satirists.

He came from a prominent Welsh family and was headed for a career in Law when he decided to try writing. His first book was a successful biography of Francois Villon, the famous French rogue and poet.

"Ring Out, Wild Bells" shows his patients-taking-over-the-lunatic-asylum view of life. Here he takes aim at the English country house school of crime fiction and hits it right between the eyes.

Later in life he characterized himself as "a man who deplores the decline of culture, manners and civilization which has been going on since the Thirteenth Century, and at an accelerated pace since the Eighteenth." However Wyndham Lewis's writing leads one to believe that, if he thought civilization had been raped over the past seven centuries, he was one of those who was secretly enjoying it.

His famous collection is Welcome to All This (1930). He and another Englishman, Charles Bennett, collaborated on an original story about ordinary people caught in an assassination plot which they later adapted for Alfred Hitchcock's celebrated film The Man Who Knew Too Much (1934, remade 1956).

Ring Out, Wild Bells

by D. B. Wyndham Lewis

NOTHING COULD BE more festive than the breakfast-room at Merryweather Hall this noontide of 29th December. On the hearth a huge crackling fire bade defiance to the rain which lashed the tall french windows. The panelled walls were gay with holly and mistletoe and paper decorations of every hue. On the long sideboard were displayed eggs in conjunction with ham, bacon, and sausages, also boiled and scrambled; kedgeree, devilled kidneys, chops, grilled herrings, sole, and haddock, cold turkey, cold goose, cold grouse, cold game pie, cold ham, cold beef, brawn, potted shrimps, a huge Stilton, fruit of every kind, rolls, toast, tea, and coffee, all simmering on silver heaters or tempting the healthy appetite from huge crested salvers. Brooding over all this with an evil leer, the butler, Mr. Banks, looked up to see a youngish guest with drawn and yellow face, shuddering violently.

"Breakfast, sir?" asked Banks, rubbing his hands.

The guest, a Mr. Reginald Parable, nodded and held out his palm. Banks shook into it two tablets from a small bottle.

"They're all in the library," said Banks, pouring half a tumbler of water. "Cor, what they look like—well," said Banks, chuckling, "it's just too bad."

Mr. Parable finished breakfast in one swallow and went along to the library. In every arm-chair, and lying against each other on every settee, eyes closed, faces worn with misery, each wearing a paper cap from a cracker, lay Squire Merryweather's guests. The squire believed in a real old-fashioned Christmas, and for five days now his guests had tottered, stiff with eating, from table to chair, only to be roused by the jovial squire with a festive roar ten minutes later.

The countryside was under water; and as nobody could go out from morning to night, Squire Merryweather could, and did, devise every kind of merrie old-time entertainment for his raving guests.

Thunderous distant chuckles as Mr. Parable wavered into the only unoccupied corner of a huge leather settee announced that the squire had been consulting his secret store of books of merriment once more. And even as Mr. Parable hastily turned to feign epilepsy in his corner, Squire Merryweather bustled in.

"Morning," said a weak voice, that of Lord Lymph.

"Wake all these people up," said the squire.

When everybody was awake the squire said: "Colonel Rollick has five daughters, Gertrude, Mabel, Pamela, Edith, and Hilda. Mabel is half the age that Gertrude and Edith were when Hilda and Mabel were respectively twice and one-and-a-half times as old as Pamela will be on 8th May 1940. Wait a minute—that's right, 8th May. Every time the colonel takes his five daughters to town for the day it costs him three pounds fifteen and eight-pence-halfpenny in railway fares, first return. One Christmas night Colonel Rollick says to his guests: 'Let's play rectangles.' 'I don't know how it's played,' says old Mrs. Cheeryton, who happens to be present. 'Why,' says the colonel, 'like this: we get the Ague-Browns to drop in, and form ourselves into four units, the square on the hypotenuse of which is equal to the sum of the squares on the—'"

At this point a lovely, lazy, deep-voiced blonde, Mrs. Wallaby-Threep, roused herself sufficiently to produce a dainty pearl-handled revolver from her corsage and fire at Squire Merryweather twice, missing him each time.

"Eh? Who spoke?" asked the squire abruptly, without raising his eyes from *Ye Merrie Christmasse Puzzle-Booke*.

"Tiny Tim," replied Mrs. Wallaby-Threep, taking one more shot. This time, however, she missed as before.

"You probably took too much of a pull on the trigger," murmured the rector with a deprecating smile. The squire was patron of the living and he felt a duty towards his guests.

"I'll get him yet," said Mrs. Wallaby-Threep.

"Charades!" shouted Squire Merryweather suddenly, waving a sprig of holly in his right hand.

"Again?" said a querulous Old Etonian voice. It was that of Mr. Egbert Frankleigh, the famous gentleman-novelist, who wanted to tell more stories. Since Christmas Eve there had been five story-telling sessions, each guest supplying some tale of romance, adventure, mystery, or plain boredom. After every story the squire had applauded loudly and called for wassail, frumenty, old English dances, and merrymaking—even after two very peculiar stories about obsessional neuroses told by two sombre young Oxford men, Mr. Ebbing and Mr. Crafter, both of whom took hashish with Avocado pears, wore black suède shoes, and practised Mithraism.

"Charades!" roared Squire Merryweather, tucking his book under his arm and rubbing his hands with a roar of laughter. "Hurrah! Come along, everybody. Jump to it, boys and girls! This is going to be fun! Two of you, quick!"

A choking snore from poor old Lady Emily Wainscot, who was quite worn out (she died the following week, greatly regretted), was the only reply. Fourteen pairs of lack-luster-ringed-with-blue eyes stared at him in haggard silence.

"Eh? What?" asked the squire, more bewildered than hurt.

"You said *charades,* sir?" said Mr. Ebbing. "We shall be delighted to assist!"

Booming like a happy bull, the squire flung an arm round

each of the two young men and danced them out of the room.

"Me for the hay," said Mrs. Wallaby-Threep, snuggling into a cushion and closing her eyes. The rest of the company were not slow to follow suit. Very soon all were asleep, and snoring yelps and groans filled the library of Merryweather Hall.

It was bright, sunshiny daylight when the banging of the gong by the second footman roused the squire's guests from nearly twenty-four hours of deep, refreshing sleep. The sardonic Banks stood before them. He seemed angry, and addressed himself to Lord Lymph.

"I just found the squire's body in a wardrobe trunk, my lord."

"In a *trunk*, Banks?"

"That's all right," said Lady Ura Treate, yawning. "It's an old Oxford trick. Body in a trunk. All these neurotics do it. Where *are* those two sweet chaps, Banks?"

"They've hopped it, my lady."

"Well, that's all right, Banks," said Freddie Slouche. "Body in trunk. Country-house mystery. Quite normal."

As he spoke, the guests, chattering happily, were already streaming out to order the packing and see to their cars. In a few moments only Banks and Mr. Parable were left in the room. Banks seemed aggrieved.

"It's all pretty dam fine, Mr. Whoosis, but who gets it in the neck when the cops get down? Who'll be under suspicion as per usual? Who always is? The butler! Me!"

"Just an occupational risk," said Mr. Parable, politely.

"It would be if I wasn't a bit smart," said Banks.

Mr. Parable nodded and hurried out as the servants began looting the hall.

MERRY CHRISTMAS!

MORE MYSTERIOUS PLEASURES

HAROLD ADAMS
The Carl Wilcox mystery series

MURDER	#501	$3.95
PAINT THE TOWN RED	#601	$3.95
THE MISSING MOON	#602	$3.95
THE NAKED LIAR	#420	$3.95
THE FOURTH WIDOW	#502	$3.50
THE BARBED WIRE NOOSE	#603	$3.95

TED ALLBEURY

THE SEEDS OF TREASON	#604	$3.95

ERIC AMBLER

HERE LIES: AN AUTOBIOGRAPHY	#701	$8.95

ROBERT BARNARD

A TALENT TO DECEIVE: AN APPRECIATION OF AGATHA CHRISTIE	#702	$8.95

EARL DERR BIGGERS
The Charlie Chan mystery series

THE HOUSE WITHOUT A KEY	#421	$3.95
THE CHINESE PARROT	#503	$3.95
BEHIND THAT CURTAIN	#504	$3.95
THE BLACK CAMEL	#505	$3.95
CHARLIE CHAN CARRIES ON	#506	$3.95
KEEPER OF THE KEYS	#605	$3.95

JAMES M. CAIN

THE ENCHANTED ISLE	#415	$3.95
CLOUD NINE	#507	$3.95

ROBERT CAMPBELL

IN LA-LA LAND WE TRUST	#508	$3.95

CHRIS WILTZ
The Neal Rafferty mystery series
A DIAMOND BEFORE YOU DIE   #645 $3.95

CORNELL WOOLRICH/LAWRENCE BLOCK
INTO THE NIGHT   #646 $3.95

██